# The Heartless Alpha

## Magic Shifter Series, Volume 1

S.V. Smith

Published by S.V. Smith, 2023.

# COPYRIGHTS

# Table of Contents

# CHAPTER 1

"Hurry up, Slave! Goddess, you have nothing to work with anyway! Did you even bathe?!"

I rolled my eyes for what felt like the millionth time. Why our Luna decided her spoiled, stuck-up daughter, who also hated my guts, would be the perfect person to help me get ready for my wedding was beyond me. Although 'helping' was far reached. So far, she had pulled me out of bed by my hair, handled me into my creaky chair in front of my sorry excuse for a vanity, and screamed at me to get ready. Since then, she had done nothing but dick around on her phone and occasionally insult me.

"Yes, Evelyn." I clipped out. She snorted in response and went back to her phone.

I was nearly ready. My thick red hair was pulled up into a French twist, my veil tucked into it nicely. I had no makeup to speak of, so I had no choice but to go natural. It didn't bother me much; my skin was flawless in terms of acne. I would have liked something to try and conceal how sallow my cheeks were and the bags under my eyes though. I was extremely pale, due to a lack of food and nutrition, which made me look sickly. My full lips were dry and peeling slightly. I hadn't had a drink in over twenty-four hours, and how I wish I could say it was from nerves. Sadly, it wasn't. I had a straight, proud nose so I guess that was a plus. The only feature I really loved was my eyes. They were unbelievably green, like emeralds but... more. They almost shone with the depth of their color.

My gaze swept down to my dress. It was gorgeous. The only thing I had ever received from the Alpha in the thirteen years I'd been in this pack.

Alpha Theo and his Luna, Tina of the Snow Moon Pack had "adopted" me when I was five years old. I have no recollection of my life or family from before. Many times, I had tried to remember, but it was black, fuzzy. Eventually, I stopped trying. My first memory was thirteen years ago, entering Snow Moons borders and staggering around until I came across the packhouse.

Foolishly, I'd raided the kitchen as I had been starving, and the Luna had caught me red-handed. Terrified and alone, she had taken me in. Though I quickly found out she was not a Luna of mercy as I was made to clean, cook and serve the pack with harsh punishments if I strayed or argued or talked back.

Her daughter, Evelyn, was the same age as me, and just as cruel as her parents. Her main source of enjoyment was to torment me.

Once, when we were ten, I spilled a glass of orange juice on the floor. Evelyn had walked right up to me and dumped the remaining glass over her head, immediately screaming for her parents, claiming I had thrown a glass at her, and then dumped the juice on her when I missed. None of her friends had backed me up, and I'd spent three days in a cell in the basement with no food or water and merciless beatings from the Alpha and Luna both. I had no idea how I survived, and at the time, I wasn't overly happy that I did.

Over the years, however, I'd simply learned to stay away from everyone as much as possible. When that wasn't possible, I just kept my eyes down and my mouth shut. The punishments happened less and less, but when they did happen, they were extreme. If Evelyn had a bad day at school, she would take it out on me. Sometimes her friends would join in, leaving me in whatever state when they were done. More often than not, I'd wished for death. Until I got my wolf, Aya.

It was thanks to her that I found my voice again; My will to fight back somewhat. She was strong, snarky, and my only friend. She was the only reason I'd managed to keep my sanity. I smiled to myself, remembering the night she finally came forward.

### ***FLASHBACK***

*I was in the last room of the main floor, just finishing the mopping. Suddenly a voice had me screaming and dropping the mop, splashing water everywhere.*

*"Hey!"*

*"Who...who's there?" I asked nervously. I spun in a slow circle, looking for a sign of another person.*

*Laughter. "No need to be so jumpy. I won't hurt you, Lily."*

*I realized the voice was in my head. " You're my wolf!"*

*"Bingo!"*

*"Is that your name? Bingo?" I asked. Odd.*

*"What? No silly girl. My name is Aya, and it is so nice to finally be here with you."*

*"It's really nice to meet you too! I thought... I mean... I figured..." I trailed off helplessly.*

*"That you didn't have a wolf? I know."*

*"You do?"*

*She sighed. "I've always been here, Lily. I know those assholes told you that you 'couldn't possibly have a wolf' and all the other bullshit they've put you through. I'm so sorry. I'm sorry I wasn't here to help you. But I'm here now, and you'll always have me to watch your back. Fuck this pack, and fuck them for the Hell they've put you through!"*

*I laughed, full of joy. I had a wolf! This was the best day of my life!*

*"Oh, Lily?"*

*"Yes, Aya?" I answered.*

*"Happy Birthday."*

*I grinned so much, that I didn't even mind I had to re-mop the floor.*

### ***END FLASHBACK***

That was last month, my eighteenth birthday. I hadn't shifted yet, as wolves shift for the first time on the full moon after their eighteenth birthday. I couldn't wait to see what Aya looked like.

My reminiscing was interrupted by Evelyn's high-pitched voice.

"What the fuck are you smiling about?"

Aya snarled in my head. I shook my head but declined to answer. Evelyn narrowed her eyes at me and stood up, moving towards me. She stood behind me with her hands on her hips, cocking her head to the side.

"You know, Slave, I think you could use a little color in your cheeks." She smiled wickedly.

I immediately sprang up and tried to dash to the door, but she was quick. Grabbing my arm, she spun me around and landed a vicious blow to my left cheek. While I was still stunned, she repeated the action to my right cheek.

Tears sprang to my eyes to accompany the stinging on my face. Aya roared in my head, momentarily deafening me while Evelyn laughed. I didn't even hear the insult she threw at me. Holding my cheeks, I turned swiftly for the door, exiting the room with Evelyn hot on my heels.

"You'll be back, you know." She said. "I know you think this marriage is your ticket out of here, but it's not. As soon as your groom realizes whom my parents are marrying him off to, he'll throw you out faster than you can blink. I'll be surprised if he even goes through with the ceremony!" She hissed. Stepping in front of me, she grabbed my throat roughly.

"You will always be nothing but a slave! A nobody, just worthless!"

Evelyn released me, shoving me back a few feet. Without another glance, she marched down the hall and out of sight around the corner. I leaned against the wall, taking deep breaths.

*"She's wrong. Don't listen to her, Lily."* My wolf tried to soothe me.

"She's right, though. I've always been a slave. Who could possibly want me? Look at me!"

*"I am. You're stronger than you realize. You've been through so, so much, and you're still here. Still standing. Even if this guy throws you out, we won't come back here."*

I blinked. "You'd go rogue?"

*"I told you I'd always be here with you. Even if we have to be a rogue."*

Tears welled up again, but this time from happiness.

"Wow. Thank you. I love you, Aya."

*"I love you too, Lily. Now, let's go get married!"* She cheered with mock enthusiasm. I laughed quietly.

Straightening my dress and my hair, I began walking down the hallway. With each step, nerves began to pool in my stomach.

See, the craziest thing about my situation was that I didn't know whom I was marrying. This whole thing was arranged without my knowledge, at least, up until last week.

I'd been a server at the yearly Alphas Meeting, which was at Snow Moon this year. The next day, Alpha Theo and Luna Tina dragged me into the Alphas' office and told me I was getting married. They never said to whom, and they never gave me the option to say no. All they said was they were getting more for my hand in marriage than I was worth, and they were glad to be finally getting rid of me. I couldn't say I was unhappy about the prospect of leaving this pack, but I was scared of marrying an unknown man. I couldn't fathom why anyone would want me to be honest.

I assumed it was someone from an ally pack who wanted a slave. The more I thought about this, the more I believed it true. After all, Alpha Theo could pick any random girl to replace me.

Lost in my fears, I finally reached the grand double doors to the hall where the ceremony was taking place. Voices buzzed from inside. I felt like vomiting, but also something... else.

My head began to swim, and I was suddenly too hot. My heart rate was picking up quickly, and I felt lightheaded.

Was I about to pass out minutes before my wedding?

# CHAPTER 2

**LILYS POV**

As I took deep breaths as being coached by my wolf, Alpha Theo snuck up beside me. I had been so focused on my breathing I hadn't even heard him. He grabbed my arm roughly, pulling me to his side.

I flinched.

"Stop fidgeting!" He hissed.

"What are you *doing*?" I asked.

I felt so out of sorts, I didn't even stop to consider my words or the disrespectful tone in which I said them.

Alpha Theo narrowed his eyes at me. The hand at his side twitched like he wanted to strike me.

"Since you have no father here, it is my...duty to walk you down the aisle and give you away. Don't misinterpret this though, I take absolutely no pleasure in touching you."

Uhm, what? Why did it sound like he was insinuating something?

"You mean, you take no pleasure in touching me when it's not violent." I deadpanned.

Aya, who had been pacing in my head, stopped in her tracks. I could feel the shock coming from her. I was shocked too. I'd never spoken to the Alpha like that before, with such confidence. Where the hell had that come from?

The Alpha seemed more shocked than either of us, however. His face was comical. At least it was until his eyes turned black and a low growl came through his teeth.

Shit.

Before Alpha Theo could hit me, or worse, kill me on the spot, the doors in front of us began to open.

He released his hold on my arm instantly and I winced as the blood flow began again. He linked his arm with mine instead, turning me towards the hall.

6

I had no maid of honor, no bridesmaids. Not that anyone would have agreed if I had asked.

As we entered the hall, I was hit in the face with the most amazing scent. It was a mix of lavender and chocolate, with a hint of an almost musky, woodsy smell. It almost knocked me off my feet. It filled the hall and I found myself looking around, searching for the source. Aya was practically jumping in my head, wanting to come out.

*"Mate! MATE!"* She screamed.

What?!

*"Where?"* I asked.

I saw him then. My eyes zeroed in on the most amazingly breathtaking man I'd ever witnessed.

He was taller than Alpha Theo, at least 6'7, a giant, and all muscle. His tuxedo strained against his muscles in a way that had my mouth watering. I could see the hint of a tattoo peeking out front under the shirt collar on his neck. I was less than five feet away now, close enough to see his hair had a slight wave to it, and it was pitch black. My fingers itched to run through it. He had a chiseled jaw, with a five o'clock shadow. Full lips under a straight, long nose, and his eyes. They gazed into mine and held me captive. They were a warm honey gold with flecks of brown.

I had forgotten where I was, the reason, the time, the place.

*"This is our mate?"* I asked Aya.

I couldn't quite believe someone so undeniably perfect was my mate.

*"Yes!"* I could feel her connecting with our mate's wolf. She was purring with joy and happiness.

A loud throat clearing sounded next to me, and I unwillingly cast my gaze away from my mate in annoyance.

Alpha Theo was glaring at me, his arm still linked with mine. It was only then that I'd realized we'd come to a stop. The entire hall was buzzing with hushed whispers, everyone staring at me. I blushed slightly and looked down.

"Alpha Theo." His voice was deep, husky. It sent a shiver down my spine. "I'll take her from here."

My head shot up.

Wait... I was marrying *him?* My mate?

*"Who did you think? He's the only one up here other than the old guy!"* Snarked Aya.

Truthfully, I hadn't even noticed anyone else, but she was right. Only the Elder who was blessing the marriage stood at the altar with my mate.

I glanced around him.

Didn't he have groomsmen? Friends? Family?

"What are you waiting for?! Go!" hissed Alpha Theo. He released my arm with a not-too-subtle shove.

A growl erupted from my mate's chest at the action, and I peeked up in time to see Alpha Theo's face go pale. He bowed his head in apology and went to take his seat next to his Luna.

I spotted Evelyn seated next to her mother, but I didn't understand her expression. Truthfully, the second I realized whom I was marrying, I could only imagine how jealous Evelyn would be. I mean, this man was a God! But she looked.... smug. She had a wicked little smile on her face, laughter in her eyes. Her expression had anxiety pooling in my stomach.

"Ahem!"

I jerked my attention back to the man in front of me. He was glaring at me now, annoyance clear on his face.

"I'd like to get started, if you're willing to pay attention now?" He grumbled.

Without waiting for an answer, he signaled to the Elder to begin the ceremony.

"Ladies and gentlemen, it is my honor to be here at Snow Moon today to bless the union of these two Children of the Moon Goddess. Shall we?"

He looked at my mate. He nodded once.

The Elder looked at me with a soft smile, which I returned.

"Do you Lily..." He stumbled for a second and I blushed a deep red.

Traditionally, he would use my full name, but since I had no memory of my past, I didn't know my last name. Or even if I had a middle name. Out of the corner of my eye, I saw my mate raise his eyebrows in confusion.

The Elder cleared his throat and started again. "Do you, Lily of the Snow Moon Pack, accept this marriage and my Blessing of it?"

"I do." I replied quietly.

"And do you acknowledge and accept that henceforth, you will no longer be a member of the Snow Moon Pack?"

"Yes." I replied a little more eagerly.

"Then as an Elder of the Werewolf Sitting Council, I hereby strip you of any ties to the Snow Moon Pack. Alpha Theo?" The Elder gestured to my Alpha who stood up.

"I accept." He said.

I felt a tear in my chest, and I gasped. Everyone in the hall except the Elder and my groom gasped and clutched their chests along with me. Losing a pack member was painful for everyone, but I took the pain with a smile, knowing I was officially no longer a member of this horrid pack. I felt an intense wave of freedom not to be tied to them anymore.

When everyone was quiet again, the Elder turned to my mate.

"Do you, Alpha Demitri Varlos accept Lily, former member of the Snow Moon Pack, as your wife and mate, and therefore Luna of the Blood Moon Pack?"

My breathing hitched to a stop.

*"Alpha? Varlos? As in, the cold-blooded killer Alpha Varlos?"* I asked Aya.

*"I guess so. But his wolf..."*

*"I don't care about his wolf Aya! I can't accept this! He's a MURDERER!"*

I was shaking as the reality of my situation started to sink in. They were marrying me off to the cruelest, most vicious Alpha on this side of the world! And to make matters worse, he was my mate. What kind of sick sense of humor did the Moon Goddess have? I hadn't suffered enough, she thought she'd toss me to the merciless Alpha?

"I do."

I felt the mate bond intensify. I ground my teeth together, and kept my eyes downcast, avoiding eye contact with Alpha Varlos.

"Lily, former member of the Snow Moon Pack, do you accept Alpha Demitri Varlos of the Blood Moon Pack to be your husband and your mate, thereby accepting your title as his Luna?"

"I..."

I didn't. I didn't want to go with him. These were my options then? Stay here and be a slave and get beat, go with the murdering Alpha who, or go rogue and have nobody. Tears welled in my eyes at my situation.

*"Please don't reject him."* Aya whimpered.

*"Aya... we can't accept him. He's-"*

*"I know!"* She cut me off. *"But you need to remember that you wouldn't be the only one losing a mate!"* She snapped.

Closing my eyes, I sighed quietly.

When I opened them, I looked into the Alphas eyes. He was staring at me with such anger, I actually took a step back.

*"Please?"* Whispered Aya.

"Lily?" The Elder stepped forward.

I heard a snicker I'd know anywhere behind me. Now I know why Evelyn was so smug earlier.

Taking a deep breath, I looked away from Alpha Varlos and down at my shoes.

"I do." I whispered.

The mate bond intensified again with my words. I blinked away unshed tears as I sealed my fate. The Elder stepped back, giving me a short look of something close to sympathy.

"It is my great joy to pronounce you man and wife. You may kiss-"

"That won't be necessary." Alpha Varlos cut across him. He turned to me. "Come."

Dragging my feet, I turned to follow my new husband.

# CHAPTER 3

LILYS POV

Alpha Demitri Varlos strode down the platform, stopping briefly to shake my former Alpha's hand. They exchanged no words, but it felt disrespectful to me, like a "good doing business with you" vibe. I wondered for the first time how much he had offered for me; It couldn't have been very much as I was nothing but a lowly slave for the pack. More than likely, they were probably just glad to be rid of me.

Keeping my eyes down and my feet shuffling forward, I felt bad for whomever they replaced me with in the future.

A deep sigh interrupted my thoughts, and I glanced up to see my mate's annoyed face.

"Can you move any faster? I'd like to get home sometime today if that's okay with you." He snapped.

"Sorry." I mumbled.

He rolled his eyes. "Your things are packed and already loaded in the car. Let's go."

He reached for my arm, and I instinctively flinched back. It wasn't entirely his fault; I'd been beaten since the age of five, and fast movements tended to cause me to react like that. Whether he knew of how I was treated here or not though, he stopped reaching for me and dropped his hand to his side.

"Can I... Should I change first?" I asked him.

"Why?"

I blinked at him. "Am I supposed to show up to your pack in a wedding dress?"

"Why does it matter?"

It didn't really. I was stalling, not wanting to be in a close, personal space like a car with him.

"Look, I've come and got what I needed here. Now I'm going home. If you're not in the car in two minutes, you can walk to Blood Moon." With that, he turned and walked away from me.

*"Wow. He's a real charmer."*

*"I know he's a bit rough around the edges. But his wolf is really nice."*

*"That's supposed to make me feel better?"*

*"Yes."*

My turn to roll my eyes.

Dutifully, I followed my husband out of the packhouse to a waiting black SUV. He was already seated in the driver\'s seat, tapping his fingers impatiently on the steering wheel.

I climbed in somewhat awkwardly thanks to the skirt of my dress and shut my door. Glancing in the backseat, I saw a single suitcase. That would be my things, as sad as that was. Clicking my seatbelt into place, I stared out the windshield. We weren't moving. Two minutes passed. Then three. And five minutes later, we still were parked in the drive of the packhouse. I broke the silence.

"Aren't we leaving?" I asked him. After all, he'd been the one to rush me.

"Yes. As soon as these idiots get the rest of your stuff."

I looked at him quizzically. "What?"

He jabbed a thumb over his shoulder, indicating my suitcase. I actually laughed.

"That is the rest of my stuff."

Now it was his turn to look confused.

"That is all you have?"

"Yes."

"Where are the rest of your clothes?"

"They're in there. I don't have much." I replied quietly.

"Much? You don't have *anything*." He barked.

I shrugged again. He continued to look at me with an indecipherable expression before his expression hardened again.

"Whatever." He grumbled.

Finally, he started the car and put it in the drive.

Leaning back in my seat, I started out at the houses passing us by, giving way to more and more trees until we left Snow Moon behind completely.

Turning onto the highway, I let out a breath I didn't know I'd been holding.

*"I can't believe it..."*

*"I know. We're actually out of Snow Moon. We don't ever have to go back Lily! We're free!"* Aya whooped in my head.

Free. Somehow this didn't feel like freedom. I'd gone from being a slave to a Luna in less than a day to a man who might actually kill me as he'd done so many others. Even as a slave, I'd heard all the stories of Alpha Demitri Varlos. He was feared near and far for his ability to kill. He'd wiped out entire packs. He had no mercy, no heart. He was actually known as The Heartless Alpha. And here I was, sitting in a car with him, accompanying him to his pack as his Luna and wife.

It felt surreal.

Should I speak to him; try to make conversation?

I floundered around in my head, searching for something to ask him that didn't involve his kill streak or how many people he had decapitated.

Hours passed. It was dark outside now, the trees a dark blur as we sped past.

Suddenly, it popped into my head, and out of my mouth before I could stop it.

"Why didn't you kiss me?" I blurted out.

Alpha Varlos glanced at me and then back to the road. Silence.

"Alpha?" I tried again. Nothing.

I'd been so caught up in the shock before, I hadn't even minded that he didn't kiss me. But now, as my reality began to really set in, it seemed important to know why.

Was I that repulsive? Why did this matter so much to me anyway? He was a cold-blooded murderer; I shouldn't even be thinking about kissing him. Stupid mate bond.

However, it seemed my mouth was not connected to my brain as I whispered, "I'm your mate..."

"Enough!" He snapped loudly.

I flinched away from him, hurt.

Stupid, stupid mate bond.

I didn't speak a single word for the rest of the trip. My gaze traveled between the window and my shoes, I refused to look at him. An hour ago, he'd told me we'd crossed into his land, and I'd simply nodded. Was I being disrespectful? Probably. But he wasn't chatting me up either way, so I didn't care.

"We're here."

He pulled up to a huge ten-foot gate that looked to be made of iron. Two guards were stationed on our side, and two more just beyond. All four men were huge, but nowhere close to their Alpha. The closest guard gave a signal and the gates swung open. Despite my qualms about this situation, I was impressed as we drove further toward the packhouse. Most of the area was covered in trees, but I could spot houses in the dense forestry. Here and there, quaint cottages were dotted around with cute balconies and porch swings, gardens, stone walk paths. I even spotted a few garden gnomes. Not at all what I had been imagining when I learned who my husband-to-be was.

Fifteen minutes later, Alpha Varlos pulled up to what could only be the packhouse.

The driveway was a big semi-circle of stone bricks, with a water fountain stationed in the middle. Cars were parked in a line along the edge, Jeeps and SUVs. Taking a minute to admire the house itself, I was honestly awestruck. The packhouse was ginormous; at least five stories tall and just as wide. Lush flower beds lined the front, giving way to a beautiful green front lawn. Vines crawled up between the windows sprouting little buds. Morning glories, I thought. Lights were on in various windows of the house, casting a yellow glow. It felt.... homey.

"Are you going to sit there and stare all night? I'm tired." Grumbled my mate.

I shook my head, speedily opening my door and stepping out. I hadn't moved much over the course of the long car ride, and my legs were super stiff. I took a second to stretch them while still admiring the house. Upon closer inspection, I noticed the whole place was constructed of deep redwood. I bet it looked even better in the daylight.

"Lily."

It took me a minute for him to catch my attention. Nobody used my name; I'd always been called 'slave' or 'mutt', or other various derogatory terms.

"Yes, I'm coming. Just let me get my stu-"

"Don't bother."

"But-"

"I'll get you some new clothes tomorrow. You can throw that suitcase out, and everything in it."

He began to walk to the house, but stopped when I opened the back door of the SUV. He sighed loudly, clearly irritated. Opening the suitcase, I dug through the 'clothes' that had been packed, (really, they were just rags), until I found my objective. Closing the door, I clutched my necklace and joined him.

"What's that?" He asked.

"It's a necklace."

He raised an eyebrow.

"It's... well... it's the only thing I have that's really mine. I don't remember who gave it to me, but I had it before I came to Snow Moon... so..."

Why was I explaining this?

"Okay." He turned on his heel and I followed him, mentally rolling my eyes. He really was an ass.

He didn't hold the door for me, which I expected. Glancing around as I followed him through the door, I was again awestruck by how big this place was.

Paintings decorated the walls that I'd have to inspect closer later. The floor was carpeted a deep purple, contrasting nicely with the wooden interior. Antique looking furniture was placed vicariously along the walls.

"This way. This floor has the common room, the kitchen, game area, and a room we use for Alpha meetings. It also has the dining room for meals. Second floor belongs to my Gamma and his family. Third floor is for my Beta and his family. The fourth floor is for us, and the fifth floor is the library."

That was the most he'd said to me since we'd met. Wait... us?

*"Us?"* I squeaked.

# CHAPTER 4

**LILYS POV**

He stopped on the stairs and looked down at me. As if he wasn't tall enough, this was even more intimidating.

"Yes, *us*. You are my wife, and Luna of this pack."

"Uh..."

"Don't worry. You have your own room."

Huh?

Before I could ask, he trotted up the stairs, me scrambling to keep up. I was feeling lightheaded and gasping for breath by the time we reached our floor. Years of being starved for long periods of time will do that to you, I guess. I shuffled down the hall, nearly running into the back of him when he stopped abruptly in front of a door.

"This is your room. My room is across the hall." He pointed to a door adjacent to mine. "Clothes will arrive tomorrow for you."

Without another word, he opened his door and stepped inside, closing it on my shocked face. Numbly, I opened my own door and stepped inside. I don't know why I expected it to be small; old habits, I guess. It was huge. The floor was plush, soft grey carpet. A king-size bed was set against the wall, begging for a good night's sleep. Across from the bed was an old-fashioned fireplace, already lit and filling the room with warmth and a soft glow; a neatly stacked pile of wood was placed to its side. White curtains were drawn across glass doors that looked to open to a balcony. I assumed the door to my right was a bathroom, and the double wooden doors led to a closet. Again, not what I had imagined.

*"But then we didn't imagine we'd have our own room, did we?"* Aya grumbled.

*"No. But it's better than sleeping with him, right?"*

*"Maybe. But what was the point of all this if we're not going to be together?"*

I didn't have an answer to that. It did seem pointless. He acted as if a mate and Luna, let alone a wife, was the last thing he wanted.

*"Maybe it's better this way? He is... him after all."*

*"I need to bond with my mate too Lily. What if he doesn't let us?"* She whimpered.

*"We live here Aya. Sooner or later, we'll meet his wolf."*

*"I guess."*

It wasn't the same thing, I knew. Aya needed to make her own bond with the Alphas wolf. Play together, hunt together. The thought of her not being able to do those things made her extremely sad.

*"He has a name you know."* She said.

*"It feels weird calling him Demitri though. What if he doesn't like it? What if no one else calls him that?"*

*"You're overthinking things."*

*"I don't think so."*

Yawning, I slipped off my shoes and made my way to the bed. A huge grin plastered my face as I lay down. I'd never slept in a real bed before. My sleeping arrangements at Snow Moon consisted of a couple dirty mattresses filled with holes on the floor. Comparatively, this was Heaven. Having nothing else to sleep in, I arranged the skirts of my dress under the covers and fell asleep in minutes.

***

I woke up to someone nudging my shoulder. It couldn't have been Evelyn; she would have just yanked me out of bed. As I became more conscious, memories of the previous day came rushing back and I shot up so fast, whoever was sitting next to me yelped in surprise.

"Sorry! I didn't mean to scare you!"

A girl stood at the edge of the bed, hands raised as if in surrender. She had medium length golden blond hair, a pale flawless complexion, and a body to die for. Her hourglass figure was the stuff of envy. What I noticed most were her eyes though. They were a similar shade to that of my husbands, perhaps a little darker. I blinked at her and noticed she actually did look quite a lot like Dimitri.

"Who are you?" I asked.

She smiled softly at me, extending her hand. "I'm Thara, Dimitris sister. He sent me up here to have a look at you. I didn't mean to wake you so suddenly."

I took her hand and shook once. "Look at me?"

"I'm a doctor at the pack hospital. Dimitri said you looked... a little unhealthy. Do you mind if I examine you?"

"Do I have a choice?"

She laughed. "No, not really. You are the Luna after all, we need you in tip top shape!"

"Uhm... okay, go ahead."

"I'm going to need you to change first. Clothes arrived for you this morning. I put some shorts and t-shirt in the bathroom for you."

"This morning? What time is it now?"

"Just a little after one."

Well shit. I slept well over twelve hours. I couldn't complain though, I felt more rested than I had in years. I sat up and stretched, swinging my legs over the side of the bed and making my way to the bathroom. Shutting the door, I did my business while looking around. There was a stand in shower with what looked like three different heads for the water, and a separate white claw foot tub that I was definitely going to take advantage of later. The counter had one long sink with two faucets, a gigantic mirror and was polished to shine. The floor was black tile, also exceptionally shiny, with floral designed bathmats placed in front of the shower and tub. I stripped out of my dress and threw it in the wicker laundry basket near the door.

Taking a breath, I looked at my reflection in the mirror and gasped. Holy fuck, no wonder Dimitri hadn't wanted to kiss me! Or touch me, or even be around me for that matter. Bright purple and black bruises patched my cheeks where Evelyn had slapped me. My lip was also busted, how had I not noticed that? My hair had fallen out of its twist while I slept and was now a tangled mess. My gaze travelled lower, and I winced. Bruises dotted my skin in varying sizes from my shoulders down my torso, and my legs were no better. I could count my ribs and my collar bone jutted out sickeningly against my pale flesh.

I'd always had a large chest, regardless of my weight, but it looked odd and disfigured in contrast to every other part of me. There was absolutely no muscle on me, I was literally skin and bone. I was hideous. A quiet cry left my lips as I grabbed the clothes Thara had set for me and dressed quickly. Wiping my eyes, I opened the door and strode back into the room. Thara was arranging tools on the bed, a stethoscope, a blood pressure cuff. Something that resembled a little hammer.

"If you could sit on the edge of the bed, I'll take your vitals." She said. I sat dutifully as she wrapped the cuff around my arm and looked at her watch, counting. Her eyebrows furrowed slightly, and she jotted something in a little black notebook. Next, she listened to my breathing and tested my reflexes. Her expression became more and more concerned as she carried on with her exam.

"Luna, can you lie on the bed please?" She asked while writing in her book. I did as she asked and placed my hands on my stomach.

"You can call me Lily." I said. She glanced up and smiled.

"Lily it is." Setting her notebook aside. "I'm going to have to examine your middle... I need you to remove your shirt. It's not invasive, and it won't take long, I promise."

"Uhm... yeah, okay. Sure." I sat up and removed my shirt, lying back again. Tharas eyes widened as she stared at me. A small gasp left her lips before she shook it off and went to work. Poking and prodding with her fingers, she asked me if this and that area were tender, if it was sore. She gave me a hard look when I said no, so I relented a little and was honest. As she scribbled furiously in her little book, she asked me to turn onto my stomach. When I did, the sound of pen against paper stopped abruptly.

"My Goddess..."

I squeezed my eyes shut in shame and embarrassment. I knew what my back looked like. When Alpha Theo was in a particularly violent mood, he would use a silver knife on me. Only ever on my back though, as it was the easiest part of me to cover up. The skin was jagged with scars that would never fully heal. They ranged from below my shoulder blades down to the bottom of my spine all over.

"What... How did you get these?" Asked Thara. She ran her finger over a particularly deep scar.

"Silver." I mumbled.

"Silver what? A blade?"

I nodded mutely.

"Who did this to you? You couldn't have done this yourself. Who?" She demanded.

What was I supposed to say? I couldn't implicate Alpha Theo. I doubted Thara would believe me anyways.

*"Who?"* Thara more harshly.

"A member of Snow Moon." I said.

*"Which* member?"

I shook my head. She let out an exasperated sigh. I sat up and threw my shirt on quickly.

"All right. You don't have to tell me. But I'm telling you now that Dimitri is going to want to know."

"Why? It's not like he cares anyway. Just another thing about me that's repulsive." "What on Earth makes you think that?" She asked wide-eyed.

# CHAPTER 5

**DIMITRIS POV**

"How are we for patrols on the Eastern border?"

I was in my office with my Beta, Ben, and my Gamma, Luke. I needed some sort of distraction this morning. I'd sent Thara to look over Lily, for obvious reasons. The girl was covered head to toe in bruises and cuts. I needed some sort of plan to get her healthy again. A strong Luna made a strong Alpha, and she wasn't strong. At all.

"We have enough for the East, but we could reinforce the South. Rogues have been targeting along there more frequently." Said Ben.

"Alright. Get Ned on it ASAP." Ned was my head warrior, and Ben's twin brother. Both had fought for the Beta title, but Ben won fair and square. Luke came from a long line of Gammas, so he was the obvious choice for the role. Ned was more than happy to take the lead as head warrior and train others into the best damn group of fighters this side of the country.

"Will do Boss."

Before either of them could say anything else, the door slammed opened and Thara marched in, breathing hard with a destructive expression on her face.

"You and you. Out." She pointed to Ben and Luke, who raised their eyebrows at me. I nodded, so they left looking confused. I turned my chair towards Thara.

"Well?" I asked.

"Well?! Dimitri, that girl is covered in marks! And her back..." She gulped. "What the fuck happened at that pack?!"

"Her back? What's wrong with her back?"

"It's mutilated! She wouldn't tell me who did it, only that it was caused by silver. It looks like someone cut her with a blade over and over and over..."

Thara sat heavily in one of the chairs across from my desk, tossing her little black notebook at me. I started flipping through the pages. Goddess.

21

Lily wasn't just unhealthy, she was malnourished, dehydrated, severely underweight. Bruises covering most of her body, signs of physical and mental abuse...

I closed the book.

"What's the treatment?" I asked straight faced.

"Food and water. Lots of it, often. But small meals first, I doubt her stomach can handle a hearty meal. I couldn't understand why her wolf wasn't healing the minor injuries. like the bruises. But she's so weak, so that means her wolf is too. With good care, and rest, her wolf should start to heal her again. But her back... it'll never heal properly." She shuddered.

I nodded slowly. "I'll have the cooks prepare something for her, at least six times a day for now."

"She thinks your repulsed by her." Thara said suddenly.

"What?"

"Exactly what I said. Dimitri, your her mate. And her husband. But, more importantly, her mate. The bond between you two will also help her heal."

I rolled my eyes. "I don't have time to wait hand and foot on her Thara."

She glared at me. "Are you even going to complete the mate bond?"

I shrugged. "Of course. When she's not so fragile."

"Physically? Or mentally?" She demanded.

"Physically, obviously."

"So, what? If she's not ready to complete the bond, you're going to force her?!"

I sighed. "I'm not having this conversation with you again Thara. You know-"

"Oh, I know Dimitri! I know that you don't give a shit about that girl upstairs! I know that you have this ridiculous notion that you didn't even have a mate! But here's what I know; I know that if you force Lily to complete the bond when she doesn't feel ready, she will *never* be the strong Luna you want her to be! She has been abused by someone, or multiple someone's, probably for a very long time-"

"And I will find who is responsible Thara!" I growled.

She took a deep breath. After a brief silence, she turned on her heel and left, slamming the door on her way out. I sighed heavily. I was being a dick, but she didn't understand. She never had! She was right about one thing; at twenty-three years old, I had given up a long time ago thinking I had a mate out there. I'd looked everywhere in this pack, looked at every unmated girl. I went to neighboring packs, and nothing. What are the chances I'd happen to find her at an Alpha meeting that I hadn't even wanted to attend?

Ben had basically dragged me to Snow Moon, the one pack we didn't really associate with because it's Alpha was beyond useless. I hadn't been there since I was a kid, with my father when he was Alpha. Alpha meetings were supposed to be about renewing allies, gaining new ones, and discussing potential threats. I hadn't even considered that I'd meet a girl with haunting green eyes and a wildflower citrusy scent who would turn out to be my mate. As soon as she'd entered the room, Ajax my wolf, had gone absolutely wild. It had taken almost all of my self-control to reign him in and keep him from marking her right there in the middle of the hall.

The same hall I'd married her in a week later. Admittedly, seeing her walk down the aisle in her long white dress, the way the skirts flowed around her as she moved... she looked beautiful. And awful. Red marks that would surely turn to bruises soon had covered her cheeks, and a thin line of blood was running from her busted lip. Already formed bruises had dotted her bare shoulders, and I assumed from that that the volume of her gown was purposefully made to hide the extent of her injuries and the state of her body. Now I know I had been right.

But did I care about her? No. That may sound horrible, but Mates, Lunas especially, were potentially disasters waiting to happen. They served to make one stronger, that was all. When an Alpha lost his Luna, it was well known that he would never be the same. Most killed themselves just to escape the pain. When I had been younger, I'd idolized the idea of finding that one person, my other half, to love and love me back. But over the years, I learned that while a mate made you stronger, they could also be your downfall. This is why I would complete the bond with Lily, but she would never be my mate, the way mates usually worked.

There would be no intimacy, no real love. I didn't have time for love.

"Alpha?"

I raised my head to see Jennine standing in the doorway.

*"Don't you dare."* Ajax growled in my head.

Occasionally, Jennine and I would fuck. There were no feelings between us, she was simply really easy and a good stress relief. And I was pretty stressed right now.

*"Shut up."* I told Ajax and beckoned Jennine forward. She smiled and closed the door. The dress she was wearing left nothing to the imagination, but for some reason I wasn't aroused.

*"I'm not doing this. We're not. We have a mate now."*

*"So? We haven't completed the bond."*

*"I don't care! I'm not going to let you hurt our mate by fucking this whore!"*

"You're so tense baby." Jennine had moved to stand behind me, moving her hands over my shoulders in what she classified as a massage; really, it felt like talons digging into my skin. Her touch made me uncomfortable, edgy in a way it never had before.

"I'm not in the mood for foreplay." I grumbled.

She stepped into the side, swiveling my chair to face her. In one quick motion, she had my pants unzipped and pulled down. Her tits were practically hanging out of her dress as she leant forward. I had the urge to look away.

"That's fine. We can get straight to it. I'm always eager to please my Alpha." She purred. Had her voice always been that nasally? Goddess, it was annoying.

"Sure." I mumbled.

Down went my boxers, and embarrassment coloured my expression. I wasn't hard at all. I mean, *at all.* Jennine raised her eyebrows, clearly not expecting that. I didn't say a thing.

"Are you not excited to see me baby?" She asked.

*"No."* Ajax growled.

I was silent.

"Maybe this will get things going." Standing up, she reached back, and I heard her zipper. The dress fell in a puddle around her feet, and she smiled at me. Of course, she wasn't wearing anything underneath. I looked back at her dispassionately. I should be rock hard right now; she had a great body. But my wolfs adamant unwillingness to betray our mate wouldn't allow me to appreciate it.

*"It's not just me. You don't want to do this anymore than I do."*

Didn't I? I sat there, not saying a word, and Jennine's smile faltered a bit. Little things I hadn't noticed before, right now really bugged me about her. Her eyes were too close together, and a boring dull shade of blue. Her hair was so fake blond, I was surprised it was still intact from all the bleaching. Her lips were thin, and her nose was a little upturned. her body... yes attractive, but just... average too. These little things should be inconsequential, but they weren't. I wasn't shallow per se, but in my head, I saw a pair of bright green eyes and I heard Lily's laugh. Jennine was just an easy lay that had run its course.

Standing up, I fixed my clothes.

"What are you-"

"Sorry, this isn't going to happen. And it's probably best that it doesn't ever again." I said. Her jaw dropped.

"But... Dimitri-"

"Alpha! I am Alpha to you! Now, go." I walked over and opened the door, not even caring that if anyone walked passed, they would see her naked.

She huffed angrily and I rolled my eyes. Grabbing her clothes, she quickly slid into them and walked out. I slammed the door behind her.

*"I hate you."* I told Ajax.

*"You would have hated yourself more."*

If he was right, I didn't acknowledge it.

# CHAPTER 6

**LILYS POV**

It had been one week since I was brought to Blood Moon. A whole week. Seven days, seven fucking days, and Dimitri had not come to see me once; honestly, I was pissed off. Every morning, I would hear him leave his room. And every night, I heard him return. But not once did he check up on me.

I'd been getting six steady meals a day, mostly soups and breads. I was slowly beginning to eat more and more, actually feeling full without the accompanying nausea. That first day, Thara had found me in the bathroom clutching my stomach and being violently sick in the bathroom. She had warned me that eating too much too soon would do more harm than good, and to take it slow. Now I could handle some solid meats along with my meals, which I was more than happy about.

I'd also been sleeping. A lot. Thara's rules were sleep and rest so I, and Aya, could heal properly, and we were. Lately, the connection between my wolf and I had grown. She was much more apparent in my head; in a way I never knew she could be. The constant aching of my body had disappeared, and the bruises were all but gone. I was still too thin, but I had some colour in my cheeks now; I showered daily and felt just *better* than I ever had.

Physically at least. Thara had tried to convince me to see a therapist, but I refused; I didn't want to talk about my past. If I never had to go back to Snow Moon, I was happy. I could move on. Sure, I'd never forget, or forgive, but hashing it out with a stranger didn't seem likely to help. Talking to my mate might, but he was decidedly absent from my life. He was so close yet couldn't be bothered with me. Each day that passed, I grew angrier. What was the point in bringing me here if he was going to act like I didn't exist? For the millionth time, I thought over my conversation with his sister.

**\*\*\*ONE WEEK AGO\*\*\***

*"What on Earth makes you think that?" Thara asked.*

*"Oh, come on. He married me, wouldn't kiss me at the alter, dragged me back here and dumped me in a room by myself." I huffed.*

26

*She blinked. "He didn't kiss you?"*

*"He hasn't touch me at all!"*

*Pinching the bridge of her nose, she sat down on the edge of the bed.*

*"Luna-"*

*"Lily."*

*"Lily. Dimitri is... well... he's a hard one. He's one of the youngest Alphas in the world, he took over early when our father...died. You've heard all the stories about him, I'm sure. The Heartless Alpha." She scoffed. "Believe it or not, there was a time when Dimitri was a happy person. Smiling and laughing."*

*"Really? Did this Dimitri kill that one?" I asked sarcastically. Thara laughed.*

*"Some days it seems like it. I miss the old Dimitri, my happy brother. The one who wasn't cold and stubborn and..."*

*"A killer." I said.*

*Thara gave me a hard look. "Yes. He has killed people. A lot of people. But I can advocate that he has never killed anyone who didn't deserve worse than what he gave them. You shouldn't believe everything you hear. Give him a chance Lily."*

### ***PRESENT***

I sighed. How was I supposed to give him a chance if he never gave me the opportunity? And did I even want to? Maybe not all the stories were true, but even so. He sure as hell hadn't made a good first impression on me, and it wasn't getting any better as the time passed. I wasn't going to beg him for attention, if that's what he wanted. On the other hand, staying in this room was driving me stir crazy. My whole life, I'd been going, going, going, cleaning and cooking and doing work. Now I was holed up in a room in a bed in unfamiliar territory and admittedly, too nervous to leave said room. What is everyone was as unwelcoming as my mate?

*"Thara is nice."* Aya reminded me.

*"True."*

*"Why don't we go exploring?"*

*"Outside?"*

*"YES!"* She yipped.

Getting out of bed, I walked into my closet. It was bigger than my bathroom; the clothes Dimitri had got for me didn't even cover one third of it. Dressing in a pair of faded blue jeans a red tee, I grabbed a pair of hiking boots and threw them on before I left. I glanced at the door across from mine, catching a faint hint of Dimitris scent, allowing myself a second of appreciating it. Only a second, then I was headed off down the hall, down the stairs and out the front door.

*"You didn't have an asthma attack that time!"* Laughed Aya.

*"Not funny. Wait till we have to go back up."*

*"Stop for a rest this time."*

*"Sounds like a plan."*

I wandered aimlessly around the side of the packhouse, not wanting to venture too far yet. I wasn't up for meeting a lot of the pack yet, but I hoped a lot of them were like Thara There were a few people outside; a group of teenage boys near the edge of the forest throwing a football around, an elderly lady tending to the gardens, and a man who looked to be running laps. As I passed the gardener, she looked up and smiled brightly. I returned her smile and stopped to admire her work. A particular flower caught my eye.

"Excuse me Miss, but what kind of flower is that?" I asked pointing.

"Oh, that one is my favourite. It's called a Blue Stargazer Lily."

"It's beautiful." I said.

"It really is."

Standing up, she wiped dirt on her pants before offering me her hand.

"Names Greta. What's your name dear?"

I smiled wider. "Actually, Lily."

Greta laughed loudly. "Well, isn't that a coincidence!"

"Are you the official gardener here?" I asked.

"Oh, no. I actually work in the kitchens. This is just a hobby of mine. Helps out the folks who garden if I tend to them a little here and there."

"That's nice of you."

She shrugged. "Helping others is a privilege I find."

*"I like her."* Chirped Aya.

*"Me too."* I replied.

"I haven't seen you around before Lily. Did you just move to Blood Moon?" Asked Greta.

"Something like that. I... uhm.. I'm actually the Alphas mate."

Her eyes widened. "Oh! So, *you're* our new Luna! Well, welcome to Blood Moon, and my apologies for not using your title!"

"It's fine, really, Greta. You can call me Lily."

Greta beamed at me. "My dear, no offense, but you are awfully skinny. What have we been feeding you? Not enough clearly."

I laughed. "Actually, the food here is fantastic. I was told to take it slow, not too much at a time."

Her eyes dawned with understanding.

"Ahh. Well, I'm on duty tonight for dinner. I'm going to make you something special, don't you worry, it will be plentiful, but not too much!"

"Wow. Thank you, but you don't have to go do extra work just for me."

She waved her hand. "It's no trouble, no trouble at all!"

*"Oh, I can't wait!"* Aya was practically dancing in my head.

"My wolf is very excited. I should go now; it was very nice to meet you. Let me know if you ever want help out here, I love flowers." I said.

"I will. It was so nice to finally meet you too dear."

I waved and continued walking, a small smile on my face. Five minutes out the door and I was already feeling a little more positive towards this pack. Making my way to the end of the house, I stopped to admire the lush forest surrounding it. Aya was going to have so much fun running here when we were able to shift.

*"That's only three days away you know."*

*"I know."* I said.

*"Are you nervous?"*

*"A little maybe. Are you?"*

*"Yeah. Our mate should be with us the first time."*

I frowned.

*"Aya... I don't think we should expect him to be there with us."*

*"It'll be so much worse if he's not though. We need them."* She whimpered.

I sighed. *"I know."*

I knew I had to talk to Dimitri about this. Females really got the shit end of the stick. We had heats, pregnancy, labour, birth. As if that wasn't enough, our first shifts were also really hard on us. There were the lucky girls who found their mates before the first shift, and the males would help them through it. Just having physical contact with their mate was enough to ease the pain and make the process go more smoothly. I'd seen girls go through the first shift without a mate, and it wasn't something I had looked forward to. It seemed, however, that that would be the case for me whether I had a mate or not.

"Hey!"

# CHAPTER 7

An embarrassingly loud scream left my lips as I spun around, my hand clutched to my chest in fright. The man who was running laps earlier stood in front of me, his hands raised in a gesture of apology.

"Sorry, sorry! I didn't mean to scare you! I was just wondering if you were okay?"

"What?" I gasped.

"Well... you looked kind of sad, maybe. And you were standing here all alone. I thought maybe you were lost or something..." He trailed off.

"I was talking to Aya." I blurted out. His eyebrows creased in confusion as he glanced around me. He probably thought I was crazy. "My wolf." I clarified for him.

"Oh..."

"Yeah."

Now he looked embarrassed. He shoved his hand s into his pockets and looked around awkwardly. It was pretty adorable honestly. Up close, he really wasn't as much of a man so much as a boy. Maybe my age or even younger. He certainly had the body of a man, but his face held onto his youth, making him look cute and shy. His hair hung into his eyes, which were a light blue.

"Uh...that's a pretty name. Aya, I mean." He said.

"Thanks."

"I'm Clint." He offered me his hand we shook once. His hand was warm and soft. A warrior, he was not.

"Lily."

"Haven't seen you around before Lily. Did you just move here?"

I shuffled my feet a bit. "Yeah. Last week." I replied.

"Cool." Clint smiled and I hesitantly returned the gesture.

"So uhm... what do you do for fun around here?"

"Usually hang around in the game area, or the common room. When I'm not out training anyways."

"Is that what you were doing?"

"Not really. I was just running out some stress."

"Oh." I paused. "What uh... are you stressed about?" I asked.

"The warrior exams. They're tomorrow. I'm hoping to pass and begin warrior training, give my dad something to brag about." He ran his hands through his hair as he talked.

"Your dad doesn't brag about you?"

"Well, sometimes, but mostly he saves the bragging rights for my older brother." Clint rolled his eyes so heavily I was surprised they didn't get stuck. I didn't really know how to reply to that, but I found myself relaxing as we talked.

"Can I help you get home?" He asked suddenly.

"Huh? Oh, no thanks. I know the way pretty well." I looked pointedly at the packhouse.

"You live here? Wait..." His eyes widened. "Are you the new Luna that arrived last week?"

Why was is so hard for me to admit I was the Luna of this pack? Maybe it was just hard to admit I was mated to the Alpha of this pack.

"Yup, that would be me." I clipped out.

Clint was staring at me like I'd grown a second head. "What?" I asked.

"Nothing. Just...wow. Sorry, I mean..." He stopped to take a breath. "I just... didn't take you for a Luna at first." He mumbled hurriedly. I laughed out loud at his expression. He looked so...frightened!

"It's alright Clint. No need to look like your seconds away from being thrown in a dungeon." I giggled. "I'm not exactly Luna material, I know."

His face softened. "Nah, I don't believe that. Yeah... looking at you now..." He stepped to the right, putting his fingers to his chin as if in deep thought. "Yeah, from this angle, I can totally tell. You're definitely a Luna."

"Stop it." I giggled again.

"It's a pleasure to finally meet Blood Moons new Luna." Clint made an exaggerated bow.

I rolled my eyes. "I'm not technically Luna yet." I said.

Clint glanced at my neck and away again.

"Well, may I escort you back inside Luna Lily?" He offered me his arm, earning him another eye roll.

"I guess so."

Taking his arm, we began the walk back to the front of the packhouse. Suddenly, I had the feeling I was being watched. Looking behind me, I froze in place. Dimitri was standing under a tree not far away, his arms crossed, his expression stone cold. How long had he been there? And how had I not noticed him before? Our gazes locked and shiver ran from my head to the soles of my feet.

"What's wrong?" Clint asked. Following my gaze, he spotted Dimitri and he paled. Immediately, he dropped my arm and stepped away from me.

"Oh, shit." He whispered.

I looked between Clint and Dimitri, making a decision. A really fucking stupid decision. Taking Clints hand, I turned my back on Dimitri, and continued walking, towing Clint behind me.

"Are you crazy? I *like* living Lily!" Clint breathed. I shrugged.

"I'm allowed to have friends, aren't I?" I asked him.

"Well yeah, but-"

"But nothing. You haven't done anything wrong. You were nice enough to come talk to me and offer to show me the way back to the front door. That doesn't mean you're getting a death sentence."

"It might!" He squealed. The look on his face would have been funny, if I didn't believe he was serious. Some mate I had.

We rounded the corner, out of Dimitris sight. Walking up the drive to the door, I said goodbye to Clint and wished him luck on his exams. He was glancing around nervously, as if expecting my mate to come charging out of nowhere and murder him. He took off rather quickly and I let out a sad sigh. Heading into the house, I made my way to the stairs, taking them one slow step at a time. By the time I reached the second floor, I was gasping for breath.

*"Sit down for a minute."* Aya chided me.

I didn't even have it in me to argue. Slumping to the landing between the flights of stairs, I leaned my head against the banister. I sounded like a chain smoker. So attractive. At least this gave me a few minutes to reflect on my dumbass behavior. Maybe Clint was right, and I *was* crazy. It wasn't that I thought Dimitri cared for me in any way he'd been pretty obvious that he didn't. But I had just blatantly disrespected not only my Alpha, but my mate and husband. It would be a miracle if I lived through the night after what I just did. Or maybe he would take his anger out on Clint... that thought had me feeling extremely guilty. What had I just done?

"You look like you're about to throw up."

For the second time today, I screamed at an unknown voice. Except this one offered no apologies, just an amused smirk.

"You want some help? Or maybe a bucket?" He asked.

He stood on the second last stair, leaning against the railing. Brown wavy hair complimented his chocolate eyes and mocha skin. He had a carefree air about him, but there was something else; An aura of authority that surrounded him. As Dimitri was the Alpha, I guessed this was either his Beta or Gamma.

"No, thanks." I declined.

"Suit yourself. Only forty-two more stairs to go to reach your floor. Good luck." He patted me on the back as he went to pass.

"Wait!" He paused to look down at me. "Forty-two?" I asked.

He shrugged. "Give or take a couple steps."

I groaned loudly. "I'll take that help if it's still on the table?"

I heard a snicker, and then I was lifted off the floor and set on my feet. Flourishing his hand dramatically, he gestured for me to go first. We began the horrid climb together, him a step behind me.

"Dimitri needs to install an elevator." I gasped.

"You're only the hundredth person to make that suggestion."

I glanced behind me. "Beta or Gamma?" I asked him.

"Beta. Benjamin, Ben for short. Don't ever call me Benji though."

"Okay...nice to meet you Beta."

"You can call me Ben, Luna."

I stopped short, nearly tripping over a step. Ben caught me by the elbow, helping me right myself.

"You can't honestly be surprised that I know who you are?" He asked.

"No... No, I guess not. You're just the first person to address me as Luna today without me having to tell you who I was. It caught me off guard."

He smirked and we continued up in silence. By the time we reached my floor, I was once again winded and cursing every stair in this house.

"I can make it from here. Thanks, Bet- Ben."

"Anytime Luna." Ben saluted me before turning and trotting down the stairs. Literally, the way he moved reminded me of a horse.

"You can call me Lily!" I called after him.

"Lillith?" He shouted back.

"NO!"

His laughter floated up to me. Shaking my head, I headed down the hallway to my room. Dimitri's scent was faint in the hall. Remembering my conversation with Aya, I debated if I should wait for him or not. We really needed to talk. But then I remembered my stunt with Clint, and I quickly fled into my room instead.

# CHAPTER 8

**DIMITRIS POV**

Today was a shit day. I'd gotten barely any sleep this last week due to stress. Rogues were attacking the borders almost daily now, becoming more and more violent. My men were taking care of them, but more just kept coming. I needed to figure out where the fuck they were coming from, and why there were so many. On top of that bullshit, Jennine hadn't left me alone all fucking week. The bitch was desperate. It seemed no matter where I was, she was right fucking there too. The kitchens, the training grounds, skulking around the packhouse, hanging onto me shamelessly. Staff who worked in the packhouse were starting to talk; it was only a matter of time until rumors made there way to Lily.

*"But they aren't exactly rumors."* Snickered Ajax.

*"They are. Nothing is going on between Jennine and I anymore."*

*"The key word there is 'anymore'. I don't think our mate will care about the differentiation."*

*"Why would she care anyway? You saw her today with that boy."*

*" I thought you didn't care about her? That she was only here to serve one purpose. Why do you care who she talks to?"*

*"Fuck off."*

My hand gripped the rail on the stairs so hard my knuckles turned white. Remembering the way Lily had laughed and giggled with that mutt made me pissed off all over again. I'd been out on a run, blowing off steam, when I heard her scream. Ajax had immediately changed course, heading to our mate. I'd shifted and run to the packhouse, but what I saw made me see red. Lily was talking to another man, a boy rather, laughing and giggling like a schoolgirl. I vaguely recognized him from training, he was supposed to be taking the warrior exams tomorrow.

What really got me was the intense rush of feelings I'd experienced. Wishing it had been *me* that she was laughing for. *Me* that she blushed for. *Me* that was holding her hand. Lily must be really naïve not to have noticed that that boy was flirting with her. And when he had looked at her neck... her unmarked neck... I'd had to hold myself back from killing him on the spot.

So, all in all, a really shitty end to a really shitty week. All I wanted was to go to my room, and sleep. I heard Ben coming down the stairs, laughing to himself. When he saw me, he skipped the last two steps, coming to a stop.

"Hey Boss."

"Hey. What are you doing up here?"

"I helped your Luna up to bed."

He was up against the wall so fast I wasn't even sure how it happened. My fist was pulled back aimed for his face, my other hand fisted in his shirt.

"What did you say?!" I growled.

"Whoa! Chill Dimitri! It was a joke, I was joking!"

I let him go, stepping back. He adjusted his shirt, eyeing me like I'd lost my mind.

"Where is she?" I demanded.

"Upstairs. Truth is, she had trouble getting back upstairs, I found her on the landing on my floor. I offered to make sure she got up here alright. You really do need to invest in an elevator man."

"Why didn't you mind link me?" I snapped at him.

Ben blinked at me several times. "I..."

*"He didn't think you'd care enough to come help Lily. Was he wrong?"* Ajax asked sarcastically.

I ignored him and focused on Ben. "Next time, you link me. Got it?"

Ben nodded, waving as he continued down to his floor. Taking the steps two at a time, I caught Lily's scent and inhaled deeply. It calmed my nerves somewhat. Turning the corner, I saw her, and my breath whooshed out in relief. She was standing in the middle of the hallway looking between my door and hers. A small part of me wished she would knock on my door. A bigger part of me wished she would turn around so I could see her face. Fuck, what was wrong with me? The next second though, she sped into her room and slammed the door. I heard the lock click.

*"Great. Now she's locking herself in."* Grumbled Ajax.

*"I have a key dumbass."* I shot back.

*"Oh yeah? What's the plan Dimitri? Unlock the door, storm in and force our mark on her?"* He scoffed.

A small smile crept onto my face. *"Not quite."*

Marching to my room, I threw open the door and headed straight for my nightstand. The top drawer had all the keys for this floor; I grabbed the one for Lilys and walked out of the room, not even bothering to shut the door behind me. With no hesitation, I unlocked her door and walked in. Her scent hit me like a brick wall. Closing the door softly behind me, I reapplied the lock and looked around. Light peaked out from under the bathroom door and the sound of water running hit my ears. She was in the shower. Images of her washing herself popped into my head and my sweatpants tented almost instantly.

Crossing the room silently, I sat on the edge of the bed waiting. Five minutes later, the water shut off and I could hear her on the other side of the door. If she walked out naked... I don't think I'd be able to hold myself back.

*"This is a really dumb idea."* My wolf whined.

The bathroom door opened and, mercifully, Lily was wrapped in a towel. Her hair was still wet and hung around her shoulders and down her back. She looked so much better than she did when she got here. The bruises were gone, and she even looked like she'd gained a little weight. Her scent wafted in from the bathroom, carried by the lingering steam of the shower. Goddess, she smelled amazing...

It took all of five seconds for Lily to notice me. Those eyes, those fucking eyes of hers widened considerably and she let out a small gasp.

"W-what are you doing in here?!" She demanded.

I decided to play dumb. "I live here."

She looked to the door, and I watched as her throat moved in an audible gulp. Plotting escape? Not likely.

"What are you doing in *here*?"

I got to my feet, watching her every move. "This is my house."

"Okay. So?"

I stepped forward. She stepped back.

"So... since this is my house, I have the right to come and go from any room as I please."

Another step forward. Another step back.

"You couldn't have waited until I was... clothed?"

Step. Step.

"Wolves don't usually have any qualms about being naked in front of each other."

"Well, I do."

One more step and Lilys back hit the wall. I closed the distance between us, placing my hands on either side of her head, trapping her. She really was a tiny little thing. I dwarfed her, having to lean down so our faces were inches apart.

"Around everyone? Or just me?" I asked.

I could hear her heart pick up speed. Her breathing was heavier, but her eyebrows creased in confusion.

"What do you mean?"

"I *mean*, would you have a problem being naked in front of that boy you were talking to earlier? Or do you just have a problem being naked in front of me? Your *mate*."

Her reaction wasn't what I anticipated. She straightened her back and fixed me with a steely glare.

"I have a problem being naked in front of *anyone*. Especially-," She stepped forward, shocking me into taking a step back. "-, people who bring me into their home, and then act as if I don't exist. Especially around people who dump me in a room by myself and don't bother to check up on me. And *especially* around people who buy me but are too repulsed by me to even touch me even though I'm their mate!"

I opened my mouth, but she held up her hand.

"I'm not done." She snapped. "You can't come up here after a week and bitch me out for talking to someone, boy or girl, when you haven't bothered to say one word to me since the day I got here. If you must know, Clint isn't the only one I talked to today. I also met one of the cooks, Greta. Now, if you had seen me talking to *her*, would you be in here right now? No."

Where the hell did this little spitfire come from?

"Furthermore, Alpha, if you were expecting something from me by barging in here while I'm undressed, well you can just forget it. The man who didn't even want to kiss me at my own wedding-"

"You're still on that?" I interrupted her.

Her eyes narrowed. "You're the one who came in here throwing the word mate around. If you really can't understand why that hurt me, then you're a bigger asshole than I thought."

# CHAPTER 9

LILYS POV

The shock I got from seeing Dimitri in my room was nothing compared to the shock of me telling him off. Never in a million years would I have dreamed that I'd be standing in a bedroom alone, in nothing but a towel, giving a big verbal middle finger to the most dangerous Alpha. The idea would have been laughable but here I was, running my big mouth. Maybe you could chalk it up to a week worth of stress, but I think I preferred a lifetimes. It was as if something in me had snapped and all the years of being treated like shit had finally bubbled up and boiled over at the worst possible time. This was not the bear to poke.

Aya had been yelling at me this entire time telling me shut up.

"You're the one who came in here throwing the word mate around. If you really can't understand why that hurt me, then you're a bigger asshole than I thought."

His eyes went flat as he froze at my words.

"What did you say?" He growled.

*"Now you've done it."* Said Aya.

"You think I'm an asshole?" Dimitri asked. "You have no idea, Lily."

"I have a good idea actually."

"Based on what? Rumors? Let me tell you the truth- those stories you've heard aren't anything compared to what really happened. No, what *really* happened was much worse. Tell me, have you heard the one where I killed the Alpha and Luna before burning the pack to the ground?"

My stomach churned. I *had* heard that story.

"Answer me!" Dimitri shouted.

"Y-yes. I heard that." I whispered.

"Do you want to know why I did it?" He continued before I could answer. "That Alpha had beaten his Luna to the point that she couldn't bear children. She had rejected him years before, and he accepted it. Instead of letting her go, he kept her in a room chained with silver, raping her and

41

abusing her. His pack had abandoned him, the whole place was filled with rogues. Rogues who were killing and raping women and children. I killed the 'Alpha' and burnt the pack to the ground, killing all those disgusting creatures with it. As for her... the Luna... she wasn't even here anymore, not really. I brought her *here*, where she could get better. But she didn't. She wouldn't eat, wouldn't talk, she didn't even sleep. She would never be the same again, and she wasn't even really living. So, I ended her life hoping she might find some semblance of peace."

I was stunned into silence. What was I supposed to say to all that? Obviously, he'd had good reasons for what he did. Even killing that Luna, I couldn't blame him. If it were me, I would have done the same thing. Dimitri was looking at me and for the first time, I saw a hint of emotion in his eyes. Regret.

"I'm sorry." I said.

" I don't need your apologies, Lily."

Alright then. An awkward silence fell between us. I was the one to break it.

"The full moon is soon." I said.

Dimitri raised one eyebrow. "I'm aware."

"It'll be my first shift."

"So?"

So? Was he serious?

"So... can you... are you... will you be there with me?"

"Yes."

His quick agreement was another shock.

"Okay." I became very aware that I was still in nothing but a towel. Heat crept up my neck and into my cheeks. "Uhm, can I get dressed now? Alone?"

He rolled his eyes but turned for the door. Exhaling a breath of air, I turned for my closet.

"Lily."

My hand paused on the door. "Yes?" I answered without looking back.

"Make sure your friends know not to cross a line. I might not have so much self-control next time." With that he opened the door and was gone.

I stared at the spot he had vacated for a moment, silently asking the Moon Goddess what she had gotten me into.

***

The next morning, I decided I would have breakfast downstairs for the first time. Getting up and down those treacherous steps was only going to get easier the more I did it. So, once I was dressed, I made my way down and followed my nose and the smell of food through the house. Dimitri must have an eye for art; expensive looking paintings lined the walls all the way to the dining room. I stopped to admire a few on my way, they were beautiful.

"Hey, can I help you get somewhere?"

For once, I didn't scream. It seemed people just liked to sneak up on others around here. I turned to see a young girl standing beside me. She had a hesitant smile on her face, and kind hazel eyes. Freckles dotted across her cheeks and nose, and her long chestnut hair fell down in waves. I returned her smile.

"I'm just on my way to breakfast." I said.

"Oh, me too. I can walk you there if you want?"

"Sure."

She fell into step beside me.

"I'm Lily by the way."

"Nice to meet you, Lily. I'm Hazel."

"Oh, like your eyes."

She giggled. "Exactly actually. I'm the only one in my whole family who doesn't have blue eyes. Apparently, that so was special, my parents had to name me after them."

"It's a really pretty name." I said.

"Thanks. I like your name too."

Hazel pushed open a swinging double door at the end of the hall, and my jaw dropped. The dining room was huge! Long picnic like tables were set in five rows that stretched back to the end of the room. To the right, a huge buffet style breakfast was set up with enough food to feed a small pack. My mouth instantly started watering at the sight of eggs, bacon, hashbrowns, pancakes, french toast, fruit salads, sausages, and everything in between that could be considered breakfast. Grabbing Hazels arm, I dragged her over to the food and started filling a plate.

"Are you really going to eat all of that?" Hazel asked as she eyed my growing plate of food.

"I'm certainly going to try."

I grabbed an orange juice and Hazel led me to the far end of one of the tables. I picked up my fork and dove into the pancakes, moaning loudly at the taste.

"You'd think you'd never eaten before." Laughed Hazel.

"I've never eaten anything *this* good, that's for sure." I replied.

She smiled, and we ate in silence for a while. I felt like I should try to carry a conversation with her, but that would have been difficult considering my mouth was full of food.

"Hey Lily?" Hazel asked after a while.

"Yeah?"

"Uhm... why is everyone staring at you?"

I swallowed a piece of bacon and looked around. I'd been totally focused on my food, that I honestly hadn't noticed the amount of people in here. And sure enough, almost everyone was staring at me, looking away quickly when they caught my eye. Whispers floated around the room that I hadn't been listening to before.

"I guess probably because I'm the new Luna." I told Hazel.

"Oh. Well, that would do it."

I raised my eyebrows. That was less climactic than other reactions when they found out who I was.

Hazel looked up through her lashes at me. "I kind of figured that out to be honest. You're living in the pack house, and I've never seen you before. Also, word got around that we finally had a Luna. I just didn't know your name."

"So... everyone knows?"

She shrugged. "Mostly everyone, yeah. News like that is hard to keep quiet."

Looking around at the sea of faces again, I saw a lot of people were looking at me skeptically. For the first time, I felt self-conscious about who I was, who I was meant to be. Would I even make a good Luna for this pack? Could I be everything they needed me to be? This was Blood Moon. And I had been a slave my whole life. Would I be able to step up and into the role of Luna of such a pack?

I felt a hand cover mine across the table. Meeting Hazels eyes she said, " Hey, stop worrying. I can tell you're going to be a great Luna."

"How do you know?" I whispered.

"I just do. You came from Snow Moon, didn't you?"

I blinked at her. "Yeah. How did you know that?"

"Like I said, news travels fast around here."

Wonderful. How fast would the word travel that I had been a slave?

"Well, if it isn't little whore Hazel!"

Hazel shrank in her seat slightly, bowing her head. Three girls were walking between the tables towards us. Two of them looked to be twins, one with bright red dyed hair, and the other had shorter blond hair with red streaks. The girl in front was platinum blond that was obviously fake if her eyebrows were any indication. She was tall, but that could have been because the four-inch stiletto's she was wearing. Her boobs were practically spilling out of her top, a white mid-drift paired with the shortest skirt I'd ever seen. The girls behind her were dressed similarly. They stopped behind Hazel and Blondie glanced at me.

"Making new friends Hazel? Or just trying to climb the social ladder again?" She sneered. Her voice was really annoying.

Hazel lowered her eyes but didn't say anything.

"Hello?" Blondie bent over and waved her hand in front of Hazels face. "Are you deaf as well as dumb? I asked you a question whore."

Hazel looked close to tears, and I'd heard just about enough. This girl was reminding me more and more of Evelyn.

"She obviously doesn't want to talk to you." I snapped.

All three girls looked at me. Blondie straightened up, flipping her hair over her shoulder.

"I don't believe I asked your opinion. *Luna.*"

# CHAPTER 10

LILYS POV

The way this girl used my title had my back up. Aya snarled in my head, angry at being disrespected. I didn't think I would have this type of reaction, after all, I wasn't technically Luna yet; Dimitri hadn't marked me, and I hadn't been officially made a member of Blood Moon. Even though Dimitri had accepted me at our wedding, we had to exchange blood and oaths, which would be done at my Luna ceremony. Then I would officially be a member, able to mind-link within the pack.

*"Who is this bitch to talk to us like that?"* Growled Aya.

I fixed Blondie with a glare of my own.

"Well, that's too bad because you got it." I snapped at her.

Her blue eyes turned black before fading to blue again.

"Do you know who I am?" She sneered.

"Do I care?"

"You should." A smug smile appeared on her face. "I'm Dimitris girlfriend."

My heart stopped along with my breath. He had a girlfriend? Is that why he wanted nothing to do with me? Aya whimpered in pain at the thought of our mate being intimate with another. However, I wasn't going to let her know her words had upset me.

"Really?" I asked. "That's funny."

"Funny?" She looked confused.

"Yes, funny. You say your Dimitris girlfriend, but I'm his *wife*. As well as his *mate*." Leaning back in my seat, I crossed my arms. "It's funny that you would call Hazel a whore when you claim to be sleeping with a man who is taken. I think that makes you the whore, not to mention a hypocrite."

"Oooohs" and "Damn!" arose from the crowd. I hadn't realized until now that most of the crowd were listening in to our interaction. Hazel laughed, trying to cover it with a cough. Blondie glared at the people around us before turning back to me.

"I never said we were sleeping together."

"So, then you're saying that you're his girlfriend, but he won't touch you? That's just sad."

This time Hazel laughed out loud, along with most of the breakfast crowd.

"No, what's sad is having *you* for our Luna. Look at you! You're a toothpick. And how disgraceful to Blood Moon and our Alpha that we are stuck with a *slave* to lead us. Pathetic!" She spit. Literally, saliva spewed from her mouth. Gross.

"More pathetic than a grown ass woman bullying pack members and disrespecting the ranked members?" I shot back.

Everyone looked to her, waiting for a response. Her mouth opened. Closed.

"That's what I thought." I stood up, gesturing for Hazel to do the same. Together we walked away, leaving Blondie standing behind us. People nodded their heads as a sign of respect to me as we passed them. I nodded back. I saw Clint walking towards us, grinning.

"That was awesome!" He enthused as he fell into step with Hazel and I.

"Thanks."

His scent hit me before I saw him. I locked eyes with Dimitri as we reached the door. His expression was a mix of surprise and amusement. Clint and Hazel bowed their heads in respect to him, but I just glared. Without saying a word, I walked around him, pushing open the doors and leaving. Clint and Hazel followed me.

"Who the hell was that bitch anyways?" I asked them.

"Jennine Parker. She's the diva around here. Also, the pack bicycle."

I gave him a question mark look.

"Bicycle. You know, because everyone's had a ride?" He said.

Hazel laughed. I didn't.

"Does that include Dimitri?"

"That's what I've heard. But that doesn't mean she means anything to him."

"She seems to think otherwise."

"Jennine thinks very highly of herself. She had this idea that our Alpha would make her Luna because he didn't have a mate." Hazel rolled her eyes.

Clint shuddered. "Goddess, Blood Moon would crash and burn with her as Luna."

"She's just jealous that Alpha Dimitri finally found you, and she could never hope to live up to the Luna you're going to be." Hazel smiled.

"And if what happened back there is any indication of the type of Luna you're going to be, I can safely say we're in good hands. You're going to be a badass Luna!" Clint added.

"Don't let her get to you. She's nothing but a bully." Hazel said.

I sighed. "Thanks guys." I smiled at them, and they beamed back.

Clint looked at his watch. "Oh shit! I have to go. The warrior exams start in fifteen minutes!" He waved at us and ran down the hall.

"Good luck!" We called after him.

"Did you have any plans today?" Hazel asked me.

"Not really. I'm supposed to be taking it easy, but I feel great today."

"Want to hang out? We could have a movie marathon or something?"

Excitement bubbled inside me. "Sure!"

"Do you like Disney movies?"

"Uhm... Maybe? I've never really watched any."

"Any?" She looked shocked.

"Well... I didn't have much time to watch TV or movies at my old pack."

A white lie, kind of. It wasn't that I hadn't had time, I simply wasn't allowed. A few times I'd been caught trying when I was a kid and I'd been punished for it.

Hazel grabbed my hand and started pulling me with her. "Well, that changes today. Get ready, because you are in for a long experience."

I groaned inwardly when we reached the stairs, but thankfully she let me rest for a few minutes in between flights. When we got to my room, I remembered.

"Shit. I don't have a TV in here."

Hazel walked to the fireplace. A little switch I hadn't noticed before was on the side of the mantle. When she flicked it up, the wall above the fireplace rotated out and turned, revealing a flat-screen TV.

"I wish I'd known that earlier. I've been bored out of my mind up here!" I said.

She laughed. "The remote should be in the nightstand."

When everything was set up, we settled in at the end of my bed to begin our marathon. I had questions burning on the end of my tongue, but I didn't want to voice them. Hazel seemed really nice, and I wasn't used to having anyone I could call a friend. I really wanted to be able to call her that.

A few hours and two movies later, which I thoroughly enjoyed and would be watching again, a knock sounded on my door.

"Lunch!" said as voice as my door opened.

"Greta!"

"Hello dear! How are you?"

"I'm great, thanks. What's on the menu today?"

"One of my specialties. Potato leek soup, homemade rolls, and a healthy portion of beef stew."

"Ohhhh yum!" I practically drooled.

"I brought enough for you and your friend." She smiled at us.

"Thank you so much." Said Hazel.

"Eat up girls, while it's still hot."

Greta placed the trays on the bed, waving as she left. We dug in and my Goddess... this was even better than breakfast. I stirred my soup around, biting my lip.

"Hazel..."

She looked up at me. "Yeah?"

"I was just... just wondering... I mean, I'm not trying to be rude, or offend you or anything-"

"You're wondering why Jennine likes to pick on me?" She interrupted.

"Kind of, yeah."

Setting her bowl aside, she sighed.

"Never mind. You don't have to tell me."

"No, it's okay. You'll eventually hear the story, and I'd rather you hear it from me."

"Okay."

She looked down, playing with her fingers. "My dad works in the pack hospital. Sometimes I help out there, I'm hoping to get a job there too when I'm older."

"How old are you?" She looked to be around my age.

"Seventeen. Eighteen in a couple of weeks. Anyways, last year we had a really bad attack on the northern border. Rogues. A lot of people were injured, and I was helping my dad in the emergency ward, mostly just cleaning wounds and taking vitals. There was this guy, James. He talked to me the entire time I was cleaning him up, flirting with me. Afterward, he stayed in touch, coming to the hospital when I was there to bring me flowers and stuff. We started dating."

She took a breath, letting it out slowly.

"I... I thought he was my mate. I didn't know, obviously, I don't have my wolf yet. But I really hoped he was. He was sweet and funny and kind. I wanted to wait and see if we were mates before... you know...."

"Yeah."

"He told me he loved me. That if we slept together, it would only make him love me more. Still, I hesitated, and he grew...distant. He started flirting with other girls in front of me. I confronted him, but he said he needed a woman, not a girl. He was so sure we were mates, but if I was going to hold off, he "had to take care of his urges somehow.""

I rolled my eyes heavily. What a dick move.

"I... I finally gave in. He actually brought me to this very room. Told me that I was his princess and deserved the very best. That my first time should be special. It wasn't." She whispered. Taking another deep breath, she continued. "It... didn't last very long. Maybe a couple minutes. And it hurt. A lot. I asked James to be gentle but... he wasn't. When he was done, he congratulated me on 'becoming a woman.' And then he left."

There were tears in Hazels eyes which she desperately tried to blink away. My anger was boiling at the son of a bitch who used her like that.

"The next day.... the next day...."

"Hazel-"

"No, I'm okay. The next day, I went to the training yard to see him. He literally laughed in my face and told me there was no way we could be mates. Rumors started going around about me, that I gave myself to him without a second thought.... that I flung myself at any and every guy in the pack too. James never disputed any of it, he even helped spread some of the stories to his friends. My friends stopped talking to me. It was only after everything that I found out exactly who James was; the packs' lead warrior."

# CHAPTER 11

**LILYS POV**

I gasped. Hazel nodded with sad eyes.

"He hid it very well. I never paid attention to any of the warriors, aside from treating them on occasion. That's why Jennine picks on me. She told everyone that I used James to try and become a higher rank in the pack. A lot of people believed her. They still do."

"Goddess, that's awful! I'm so sorry Hazel." I said.

"Thank you. And Lily, I swear that's not what I'm doing here. I just...I just thought you could use a friend. Goddess knows I could use one. I-"

I held up my hand to stop her and smiled. "Hazel, never once did I get any vibes that you were using me. And I do need a friend. It sucks coming into a new situation and a new home without having anybody. I'm glad you spoke to me today and I'm glad to call you a friend."

"I'm glad to call you a friend too." She smiled.

"And as your friend, I am going to do something for you. Don't ask me what," I said as she opened her mouth, "Just know that I am going to take care of you. And to do that, I need to go see Dimitri."

Hazel looked nervous now. "Oh...okay?"

I patted her hand on the bed. "Don't worry about a thing."

With that, I hopped off the bed and marched to the door, telling Hazel she could stay as long as she liked. Once I was in the hallway, I stopped to listen to see if Dimitri was in his room. Silence. So, his office then. I assumed, anyways. One of these doors must be it. Wandering past each door, I stopped to listen and also see if I caught his scent. Until I came to the door with a plaque on it reading "ALPHA'S OFFICE". Well. That was pretty obvious in hindsight actually. Gathering up my courage, I twisted the knob and opened the door.

Dimitri was sitting behind a large oak desk, papers spread out everywhere and a laptop open to his left. His head snapped up as I walked in and closed the door behind me. Taking a second to glance around, I took in his office as a whole. He had bookshelves stacked behind him with thick books covering every inch. A few pictures hung on the wall, more like the artwork I was admiring earlier. A comfortable looking black sofa was placed against the wall to my right, but my guess was he didn't use it much. It was spotless with no imprints on it at all. The walls were a dark gray and the carpet was black. Very manly.

"Ever heard of knocking?"

My attention was pulled back to my Alpha. He was annoyed, that was obvious. Whatever.

"I have." I replied casually.

"Good. Next time, do so."

"I need to talk to you."

"Yes, I gathered that. What do you want?" He sat back in his chair, and for the first time, I noticed how rugged he looked. His hair was a mess, as if he'd been running his hands through it. His shirt was ruffled, and he had the beginnings of stubble on his face. Actually, he looked hot as hell, not that I was going to point that out. Instead, I took the seat across from him and crossed my legs. I wasn't one for beating around the bush usually, so I decided to get straight to the point.

"Were you aware that your lead warrior was abusing one of your pack members?" I asked bluntly.

His jaw dropped slightly. Clearly that's not what he had expected when I barged in on him.

"What?" He asked.

"Your lead warrior, James. He manipulated a pack member into sleeping with him, and then shunned her, and started spreading rumors about her."

Dimitris jaw set. "You're talking about Hazel."

"Yes." I replied.

"I'm well aware of the rumors. There isn't much that's said in my pack that I don't hear."

"Okay. So what are you going to do about it?"

"Excuse me?"

"You *are* going to do something right?"

"That happened months ago."

"So?"

He stood up from his desk. "So... even if what you're saying is true, there isn't much I *can* do about it. She never came forward with any claims of abuse. And besides that, the matter is done with."

Now my jaw dropped. Was he serious right now?

"Are you kidding me?" I laughed humorlessly. "It's far from being *done with*!" I air quoted him.

"Look." He pinched the bridge of his nose and sighed. "I'm extremely busy. And, yay, you found a friend. But did you ever stop to consider that maybe she wasn't telling you the whole story? Or even part of it? Did you stop to consider that maybe she lied?"

My anger boiled over at his words. I flew to my feet and glared at him.

"Seriously?! She didn't lie! You just want to push the matter aside because you don't want to punish any of your precious warriors! Tell me, if Hazel *had* come to you months ago, would you have done something about it?"

"Of course I-"

"Bull!" I nearly shouted. "You wouldn't have because of who the person in question is, and his rank. It also doesn't help that his buddies backed him up. It would have been his words against hers, which makes her word count for nothing. Especially given *her* rank! Why would you jeopardize your lead warriors reputation over a simple Omega? You wouldn't have. As for the matter being done, it's clearly not. She is still being taunted and bullied to this day! Mostly by *your* girlfriend, I might add!"

His eyes widened at my outburst but narrowed when I mentioned Jennine.

"She is not my girlfriend." He gritted out.

I scoffed. "You should try telling her that sometime."

"So that's the real issue is it? You came here to yell at me because your jealous that I slept with someone before you?"

This man made me want to pull my hair out in frustration.

"I'm not jealous. I don't care who you slept with. I came here for one reason only, and that's because I heavily disagree with what James did to Hazel. Did you stop to consider that he might have done it with other girls as well?"

Throwing his words back at him like that made him stop for a minute. Whatever he was going to say clearly no longer applied, and I seemingly stumped him for a moment. Finally, he spoke again.

"It's not like he raped her. She was willing."

"She wasn't. She told him she wasn't ready, that she wanted to wait to see if they were mates. He manipulated her by flirting with other women in front of her, until she finally gave in. He brought her to *this* floor, to *my* room. She told me he was less than accommodating too, considering it was her first time. She may have been willing, but that doesn't make what he did right." I spat.

"James brought her here?"

I nodded. "While you were away on business."

His face darkened. "I'm going to need to speak to her. I need to hear this from her, not you. If she wants to make a formal complaint, then *she* is the one who has to come forward."

"Fine." I shrugged.

We stood in silence. Awkward silence. I didn't know what to do now and it seemed neither did he. Of course, he chose to break the silence by being an asshole.

"Don't think you can come in here anytime you want to yell at me. I don't tolerate disrespect."

"Right. Not from me anyways. Just from the men in your pack."

The next thing I knew, I was pinned against the wall, his hands on either side my head, his face inches from mine.

"What did you say?" He growled.

Nervousness pooled in my stomach and my hands started to shake. Despite that, I raised my chin defiantly and met his gaze.

"You heard me." I said.

"Listen to me, and listen good. You may be my mate and wife, but that doesn't mean you can disrespect my pack *or* me. Maybe James is an asshole, but he is one of many men in this pack, and not all of them are the same. You will not slander all based on your opinion of one. And until something is proven, it is just your opinion."

"Being your mate makes me Luna of this pack. As Luna, it's my job to care for pack members. I won't stand by if even one is being mistreated."

At my words, something in eyes changed, some emotion came to the surface. He blinked it away before I could decipher what it was.

"Regardless, you will wait until I've investigated the matter. I don't want you speaking of this until I have."

"....Okay."

Dimitri searched my face, looking for any hint that I would go back on my word. His breath fanned my face, his scent overwhelming me. Suddenly, the atmosphere around changed. His gaze went from searching to tracing my features, landing on my lips. I'd be lying if I said his closeness wasn't affecting me too. The mate bond wasn't that strong between us yet, as I hadn't fully shifted. I knew it would be much stronger afterwards. A part of me worried about that, because I still wasn't sure about Dimitri at all. I wasn't ready to be close to him, not yet. Right now it was fairly easy to ignore him and be away from him. But soon, all too soon, the bond would start effecting us both more, making us want to give into our base desires.

Dimitri moved closer and shocked rippled through me. Was he going to kiss me?! Now? After a fight of all times as well? Through the shock though, I couldn't find it in myself to move or push him away. My eyes closed as he came closer still. Another inch...

**\*KNOCK KNOCK KNOCK\***

# CHAPTER 12

## DIMITRIS POV

I nearly growled out loud at the sound of someone knocking on my door. However, a bigger part of me was relieved. What was I thinking?

*"You were thinking that you wanted to be close to our mate."* Ajax said.

*"Shut up. I don't."* I snapped.

I yanked the door open and this time I did growl. As if I needed another headache right now.

"Hello Dimitri." Jennine purred.

"What the hell do you want Jennine?" I snapped.

I hadn't forgotten what she did earlier today. She must really think highly of herself to attack Lily the way she did. To say I had been pissed was putting it mildly. Ajax had been begging me to let him out to teach her, her place. It took a lot for me to keep him in this morning. The only thing that calmed him down was watching Lily handle herself. And she handled herself alright. Not many pack members stood up Jennine and her friends. I'd felt pride for my mate this morning, just like I had a few minutes ago when she said what she had about standing by the pack members.

Jennine stepped into my office like she had an open invitation to do so.

"I thought we'd have some fun." She smiled and fluttered his lashes at me. I almost rolled my eyes.

I felt anger coming from my mate and I glanced in her direction. She was giving Jennine a look so cold, I was surprised she didn't turn to ice under her stare. So much for not being jealous.

"Not in the mood Jennine. Especially with you." I said.

She laughed, the sound grating my eardrums. "Oh come on baby. You know you-"

It was that moment she noticed Lily. Her eyes narrowed into slits and the smile dropped from her face.

"What is she doing here?" Jennine hissed.

*"Let me out! I need to teach this slut a lesson!"* Ajax snarled.

*"Calm down! I'll handle it."*

"She's here because she had something to discuss with me. Furthermore, this *is* our floor. She lives up here too. Not that any of that is your business. However, it's actually good that you're here Jennine." I leaned down so we were eye level. "Care to explain why you attacked my mate this morning?" I asked.

Her eyes went wide and she started to look nervous.

"I...I..."

"Spit it out already."

Planting her feet, she met my eyes.

"She's not good enough Dimitri. Look at her! She's small and useless. She will never be a good Luna for our pack. She will never be good enough for you!"

With one move, I had her pinned against the wall by her throat. Her legs dangled, trying to find grip where there wasn't any. I squeezed, cutting off her air.

"You will *not* speak that way about your Luna. I've let you get away with so much for far too long Jennine. You think you're very high and mighty, but don't forget your place. You *will* respect me and you *will* respect Lily, or there will be consequences. Do I make myself clear?" I growled.

She made a squeaking sound that I took as confirmation and I dropped her. She dropped to the floor, her hand going to her throat.

"Oh, and one more thing. You are *not* my girlfriend. If I hear you telling one more person you are, I will personally throw you in the dungeon myself. You were an easy fuck, that's all." I snarled. Jennine looked at me with tears in her eyes but I couldn't care less. Shakily, she got to her feet and fled; I slammed the door behind her. Good riddance.

A small whimper had me turning my attention to my mate. She stood off to the side now, probably to avoid Jennine's body when I slammed into the wall. The look on her face though sent me into automatic alert mode.

"What is it? What's wrong?" I asked.

She just shook her head, taking a tiny step back.

*"You idiot. You scared her!"* Ajax said.

*"Huh?"*

*"Remember how she arrived here? Obviously she was abused at that pathetic excuse for a pack. And you just went all Big Bad Alpha in front of her."*

*"Oh."*

There was definitely fear in her eyes. She was shaking too. An unfamiliar feeling crept up on me; It took me a second to put a name to it. Regret. I felt regret for scaring my mate? I never felt regret for anything.

*"She needs to toughen up. I'm an Alpha. I'll do what I have to in order to ensure my pack stays in line."*

*"Wow. You really are an asshole Dimitri."*

Ajax retreated to the back of my mind. At the same time, Lily threw the door open and ran from the office. Literally ran. More regret ran through me but I shoved it down. What did she expect from the cruelest Alpha after all? Sitting down at my desk, I went back to my work. However, my mind kept replaying her face. Why did it bother me so much that she openly feared me? Many people feared me. I didn't care. perhaps it would stop her from coming into my office unannounced and yelling at me.

But no matter how I justified my actions, the urge to go and see if Lily was okay wouldn't go away. I drowned myself in paperwork well into the evening. Or I tried to. After reading the same page a dozen times, I finally gave up. Sleep is what I needed. Locking the door behind me, I made my way to my room. Pausing with my hand on the knob, I glanced at Lily's door. Tomorrow night she would shift. And the mate bond would start to become more forceful between us. Ajax had been going on all week about how excited he was to meet his mate, his other half. He couldn't wait for tomorrow night, but me... I wasn't sure about it.

Alpha Theo told had me Lily was an Omega. Weak. It was confusing that I would have a weak mate, given that I was an Alpha. But if she made me stronger, what did I care? I'd intrigued about her past, but he couldn't give me much. Just that they adopted her when she was a kid, and she didn't know where she came from. They assumed she was an orphan and she never mentioned her parents or what pack she was from. She looked weak, but that could be because of her lack of care. She certainly didn't act weak. On the contrary, she was rather sassy.

Shaking my head, I went into my room. The girl occupied far too much of my mind today, resulting in me getting absolutely nothing done. I took off my clothes, save my boxers, and climbed into bed. Sleep came lazily, and I was almost there when images of what having Lily in my bed would be like. Having her under me, or on top of me. I groaned loudly. I'd never get to sleep if she kept invading my mind!

*"It's because she's close to her shift."* Ajax said. *"You could embrace it you know. The bond."*

*"I thought you were ignoring me?"* I grumbled.

*"Just think about it Dimitri. She's our mate. Ours. And I don't want to lose her."*

*"We're not going to lose her."*

*"Really? Did you see her face today?"*

The image flashed in my mind for the ten millionth time.

*"Keep going like this, and you will lose her. And then it won't matter why you chose to bring her here, because she'll be gone."*

# CHAPTER 13

**LILYS POV**

I woke up the next day with my stomach in a pile of knots. For a myriad of reasons: Today was the full moon, I was finally able to shift. That was enough to cause anxiety in itself. Then there was Hazel. She hadn't been happy about what I'd done, but I'd eventually calmed her enough to see the situation rationally. I hoped beyond hope I hadn't lost a friend. Letting out a huge yawn, I flopped back onto my pillow and pulled the covers over my head. I wasn't ready to get up yet... in fact I didn't even want to leave my room until I absolutely had to.

*"I'll do all the work Lily. And our mate will be there to help us through the pain."* Aya said in my head.

I cringed. Dimitri was the last person I wanted to see right now. Or maybe ever again. The way he'd handled Jennine last night in his office... part of me was admittedly super happy that he'd put her in her place. But an equally loud voice was telling me that it was way too easy for him to manhandle her the way he did. He seemed to have no qualms about being violent... a quality that I certainly did not find welcoming in any way. Obviously, I knew he was violent, but to his own pack members? No matter what they did...

*"You're thinking too much into this."* Aya clipped.

*"Am I? I don't think so."* I snorted.

*"Obviously, words don't have much effect on the bitch. I bet he'd told her before to back off and she didn't. Maybe this was the only way to get her to listen?"*

*"It's still wrong Aya. You wouldn't be saying this if it had been me in her place last night."*

For that, she had no response, because she knew I was right.

All night I'd been thinking about Dimitri and my first shift. Trying to find a way to get through it without him, without him knowing. I'd briefly thought about bringing Hazel with me, but I didn't want to put her

60

through that. The first shift was gruesome, I didn't want to freak her out. I'd considered Clint too, but if Dimitri did happen to come around, he'd probably kill him. No, not probably. He would definitely kill him. So that only left one option; To do it by myself.

Dimitri could justify what he did a million different ways, but his behavior, seeing the beast inside, it had truly frightened me. Shift or no shift, I wanted to avoid him. Aya didn't agree with my plans, of course. She was pacing in my head, getting more and more edgy as time ticked by. Eventually, I got up and showered, dressed, did my hair. Distraction methods. Greta brought me lunch, a pork stew with a side of freshly cooked vegetables. It smelled so delicious I almost drooled but my stomach didn't feel like it could handle food.

"Don't worry about it dear." Greta said, seeing my facial expression. "It's normal not to be hungry before your first shift. You're body is preparing."

I stared at her. "How did you know-?"

She gave me a half smile. "I've raised four children, not including their friends who were always at our house. I've seen many, many first shifts. The signs are obvious, if you know what to look for."

I sighed. "I'm sorry Greta."

"For what?"

I waved my hand over the tray the food. "You shouldn't have gone to so much work."

"It was no work at all, or trouble sweety. Tell you what, I'll leave it here in case you get hungry. I have to get back to the kitchens though. Good luck tonight!" And then she gave me a reassuring hug and bustled out the door. I glanced back at the food, my stomach coiling.

*"I hate to waste it, but it might be a good idea to listen to our body. I'd hate even more for that to come back up later."*

*"Agreed."* Aya said.

Sitting on the edge of my bed, I blew out a long breath. My legs were bouncing in an unsteady rhythm. I was getting more and more restless by the hour.

*"Maybe-"*

*"No Aya."*

*"Lily, it's going to be so much worse without him."*

*"I don't care. I've gotten through so much without him. We have. We will get through this too."*

*"You are so stubborn Lily."*

*"And you aren't?"*

*"Can we at least go outside? I don't want to be in here anymore."* She grumbled.

Fresh air sounded really good right now. So did walking. There was only so many times I could pace my room. Aya sighed in relief as I threw my shoes on and opened the door. For a couple seconds, I stood in the doorway, listening for any signs of Dimitri. His scent was faint, a few hours old. He hadn't been up here in a while, probably not since breakfast. Inhaling deeply, I noticed his scent, though old, was stronger now. More defined. It sent a tiny shiver through me and the image of him and I last night before Jennine interrupted flashed into my mind. What would it be like to kiss him? To have his hands on me?

I shook my head, hard. What the hell was I even thinking? I was trying to avoid the man for Goddess sake!

*"Our bond is getting stronger. After we shift tonight, it will almost be complete."*

*"Almost?"* I asked.

*"The bond will be at it's strongest when we've been mated and marked."*

Unfortunately I didn't blanch the way I wanted to. The idea of Dimitri and I mating right now didn't seem so bad. Giving my head another shake, I stepped into the corridor, closing the door behind me.

*"Not going to happen Aya."*

*"It has to eventually."*

I didn't reply. She seemed cheered by the idea of being marked, and I would be too... under different circumstances. Right now, I was focused on getting to my destination-outside- without being seen by him. Keeping my head down, I flew down the stairs and through the front foyer. Once I was finally out, I felt a sense of huge relief. Like getting into a nice hot shower after working out.

*"Let's go to the woods."*

Nodding, I jumped down the stone steps, heading around the back of the house. I nodded politely to people I passed, saying a quick "hi."

At the edge of the trees that lined the property, I glanced back over my shoulder, scanning the house, the workers. Nobody was paying attention to me, so I quietly slipped into the shadows of the forest. It was quiet. Peaceful. The only distinct sounds were the occasional chirping of the birds and crunching of leaves and twigs under my feet. I walked for hours, only paying attention when I noticed the sun beginning it's descent behind the far mountains. I'd been feeling to much better, being out here, but anxiety shot through me as I watched the sun getting lower and lower.

Instinctively, I turned, heading back towards the packhouse. My feet seemed to have a mind of their own as they carried me back the way I'd come. Part of me wondered why I was going back, when the whole point was to find somewhere private to go through this. I didn't really know, so I just kept walking. By the time I stepped through the trees into a small clearing, one I'd passed hours earlier, it was dark with the full moon peaking above the tops of the trees. I stopped to catch my breath, staring at it. So many times before, I'd looked up at the same moon, hearing the screams throughout the pack of those first shifters. It had always put me on edge knowing someday I would go through the same thing. The only thing that made me look forward to it, that made anyone look forward to it, was the joyous howls that followed.

I'd pictured more times than I could count what it would be like to finally be in my wolf form; the feeling of freedom, of strength. Things I did not have for so long in my life, things I craved. Even if I was convinced for a long time that I didn't have a wolf, I dreamed. Hard. I dreamt of shifting and leaving my abusers, my Hell. Of never having to go back. Maybe finding another pack, people who actually cared about me. Who would look after me. Of finding a mate who would love me.

A sole tear ran down my cheek as I stared at the moon. Maybe I'd gotten part of my wish. There were people here who cared about me. Greta, fore sure. And then Hazel, and maybe even Clint. People I could call friends. My heart wobbled with the thought of my other wish, a mate who would love me. I didn't think Dimitri was capable of loving anyone. I sat on the ground, wiping my face. Thoughts swirled in my mind while I sat on the hard ground and stared at the hazy moon.

# CHAPTER 14

**LILYS POV**

I sat, still as stone, until my hands started to itch. I rubbed them absently, but the itch persisted. So much so that it was bordering on painful. The feeling spread through my palms and up my arms, my neck, down my chest and soon through my whole body. It felt like a million bees were trapped under my skin, stinging me over and over.

*"It's starting Lily."* Aya whispered. She was panting in my head. Panic shot through me at her words.

*"Aya... What... How do I..."*

*"You don't have to. I'll do everything, but it's going to suck."*

*"It already does."*

*"This is just the start Lily. It gets much worse from here."*

As soon as she stopped speaking, I felt my wrist bone snap. I screamed. Loud. More screams followed as the bones in my fingers snapped and started reshaping themselves. The itch had now transformed into a burn, slow and fierce, spreading through my veins and muscles and nerves. It felt like someone had shoved me into a fire. More bones broke, in my feet and ankles this time. Every single inch of my body hurt and I slumped to my side, curling into a ball. My shoes felt much too restraining, but I couldn't find the energy or the will to care about removing them.

The burn moved to my head, splitting my skull into pieces. I scrunched my eyes shut, fighting against the pain.

*"Make it stop! Goddess make it stop!"* I pled silently.

*"It will... Lily don't fight..."*

Aya's words hit a wall, the wall I'd spent years building. It was an automatic instinct now to shield myself mentally through pain. It had been the only thing that got me through all my abuse. Just shut your eyes and go to a happy place. My response was built into me. And compared to this, my former packs torture was nothing. I'd take it again, gladly. Anything but this.

*SNAP*

I shrieked so loudly my eardrums popped.

*I wish Dimitri were here.*

It was both a wish and a thought. I had been beyond foolish to think I could do this without the help of my mate. Any doubts or fears I had of him right now were completely and totally insignificant. Was I even a person anymore? By now I felt as though I should resemble a broken glass, shattered across a floor in a million pieces. How was it possible that I could come out of this whole? Endless tears streamed down my face accompanied by broken, gasping sobs.

I don't know if the Moon Goddess took pity on me, or if Aya was just done struggling against me and called his wolf, but suddenly the pain reduced exponentially. The burn that was eating me from the inside went back to a mild itch. Uncomfortable, but bearable. The pain of my bones breaking and reshaping was also, unbelievably, bearable. It still hurt like a bitch, but I could manage it, focus around it. Through that came his scent. Much stronger now, and calling me. Lifting my head slightly, I looked into Dimitris eyes. I could see anger, possibly at my stupidity. However, the dominant emotion on his face right now was worry.

What was more shocking, probably to the both of us, was my reaction to seeing him here with me. His hand was resting lightly on my waist but I knew I needed more. With every ounce of strength I could gather, I flung myself up and into his embrace. His arms wrapped around me as I lay my head against his shoulder, right over his marking spot. His scent was so strong there. It helped so much.

"Don't go." I heard myself whispering.

"I won't. I'm here, I'm staying here with you." Dimitri replied.

A loud groan escaped me as my shoulders hunched in on themselves.

"You're doing great Lily. Just great. It'll be over soon."

But it wasn't. Together we sat on the hard ground, my form going from beast to human and back again, over and over. What was happening? I'd never heard of this happening to anyone else before. Dimitri kept talking, but he was growing tense, rigid. I could feel something was wrong and a horrible thought struck me. What if I couldn't shift? That would be some joke; convinced at not having a wolf, only to get one and then not be able to shift.

"Lily." He rubbed my back. "Listen to me. You have to let go. Let your wolf take control."

I whimpered against him, shaking my head.

"Why not?" He asked.

"I...I'm scared... so scared..." I whispered.

Dimitris hands moved from my back, up my arms and over my shoulders to settle holding my face between his palms. He leaned back far enough to look into my eyes.

"You don't need to be scared. I'm here and you will get through this. We will, together. You just need to let go." He told me.

*"He's....right. Stop...stop fighting....it..."* Aya panted.

But I couldn't. Every fear, every taunt and jab and insult from my past was flooding my mind, reinforcing my wall.

"What is holding you back Lily?" Dimitri demanded.

A fresh sob broke from my chest. "I cant! I will never.... be anything... never...worthy of...my title..." I choked.

*"Yes we are! Let me... let me show you. Special... we're so special Lily."* Aya grunted.

I heard her words but I watched Dimitris face. Worry was replaced by sadness and...regret? In the second it took for his face to change, I was pressed back into his shoulder, his lips at my ear.

"Together Lily. I'll shift with you. Together. Okay?"

The desperation in his voice made my decision. Clenching my teeth, I nodded mutely. Fighting against every instinct I had, I finally let my wolf take control. My body shook as it transformed, and when my hands became paws this time, they stayed that way. My back arched painfully, even with my mate there. My face contorted, teeth growing into long sharp canines. I felt fur sprout from my skin and cover myself.

"Lily?"

I heard Dimitris voice, but it sounded far away. All I knew was the pain was getting worse, his touch wasn't bringing as much comfort anymore. And then-

*"Oof!"*

My pain doubled. Tripled. Exceeded anything I'd ever imagined. My eyes shot open to see my mate lying on the ground some five feet away. Strangely, I was looking down at him. I didn't have much to process it though, because the pain in my body started to gather into one area- My heart. It was like it was sucking all the pain into it and I nearly fainted from the intensity. It felt like hours had gone by, when in reality it was only a few seconds, when the pain suddenly stopped and I crashed to the ground completely and utterly exhausted.

# CHAPTER 15

**DIMITRIS POV**

I rubbed my eyes. Multiple times actually. I couldn't be seeing this right.

Lily lay on the ground a few feet from me, panting heavily in her wolf form and whimpering quietly. I opened my mouth to say something to her, but it closed again of it's accord. Words weren't processing for me right now. My entire being was dominated by shock and disbelief. Even more shocking, Ajax wasn't saying anything either. He was just as shocked as I was, maybe a little more.

After a whole sixty seconds ticked by, she finally lifted her head, shaking it a bit. Her eyes met mine and I gulped. For the first time in my life, I, Dimitri Varlos actually gulped.

*"She's... they're beautiful..."* Ajax whispered to me.

I simply nodded. Lilys wolf was pure white. Strikingly white, not a mark on her. A light glow surrounded her entire being, almost like fireflies were dancing around her. Her eyes were the same majestic green, a startling contrast with her fur. Even her nose was white. I briefly wondered if her tongue was too? A stupid thought, but I was dazed.

What had me pinned to the ground, unmoving, though was not only color, but her *size.* She was huge. Larger than any wolf I'd ever seen, larger than me. That point was only emphasized when she shakily got her to feet, causing me to crane my neck to look up at her. She stood around ten feet tall. It would take three of Ajax piled onto one another to measure up to her.

*"She's a Mother Wolf."* Ajax said.

*"She...she can't be. They don't exist."*

*"Are you dumb or blind?!"*

Definitely dumb. Slowly, I got to my feet, and Lily's eyes widened as if she just realized that I was so far beneath her. Taking a couple steps back, she looked down at herself. Shaking her head back and forth, she suddenly bolted through the trees away from me.

"Wait! Lily!" I called after her.

I shifted quickly, not even caring about my clothes, and took off after her. She wasn't hard to follow, obviously. Ajax was fast, but his speed was outdone by her long legs. She covered more space in one stride then we did in four. I would never catch up to her, so I could only follow and not lose sight of her. Finally, she stopped near the small lake in the woods. I also came to a halt, watching her from a distance. Should I approach her? She was gazing into the water at her reflection. And then she lifted her head and howled. The sound reverberated off the trees and filled the forest. It was so loud, I was certain it reached back to the pack. The soft glow around her became stronger, a shine instead of a glow. The sight of her like this would be forever etched into my memory.

And just like that, her eyes landed on me. There was no fear in me whatsoever as I approached her. Every story I'd ever heard of the Mother Wolf was filled with fear. I had none. Maybe because she was my mate, or maybe because I was an Alpha. Either way, I didn't care. Ajax was desperate to go to his mate, and when we reached her, they touched noses.

*"Best forget about ever mating in wolf form. There's no way."* I snickered.

*"Shut it. I'll manage somehow."* Was his reply.

Lily crouched down and they started to play together. I retreated into the background and let him have his moment. It was a little awkward, given her size, but the way she yipped and jumped around, she looked like a pup. A ginormous pup, but one all the same. I could feel them communicating, so I didn't intrude. Knowing Ajax, it was probably crude anyways. After a while, her body began to tremble and I knew she was going to shift back. Ajax gave me back control and I trotted over to a tree where we kept a stash of clothes in a large trunk. Useful for those who shifted and didn't have clothes with them. I opened it and grabbed a pair of sweat pants for me and a shirt and jeans for Lily. When I came out, she was already in her human form, sitting on the ground with her knees hugged to her chest. I avoided looking at her as I tossed her the clothes.

"Thanks." She muttered. A few seconds later, she tapped me on the shoulder. Sparks erupted where she touched, making my eyes widen.

*"The bond is so much stronger now!"* Ajax said.

*"Yeah, I noticed."* I replied.

Aside from the sparks, I also felt an urge to go to her, touch her, take in her scent. The overwhelming desire to be close to her took me by surprise. I wanted to claim her, hold her. Bury myself inside her.

*"Uh oh... she looks pissed."* Ajax said.

Only then did I really look at her. She did indeed look pissed. But that wasn't why my jaw dropped silently. Lily looked... totally different. Instead of the thin, frail girl, now stood before me was a healthy and curvy woman. My gaze traveled from her face to her toes and back again. She was... stunning.

"What are you staring at?"

My eyes snapped to hers.

"How..."

"I don't know how."

"You're a Mother Wolf." I said.

"Yeah, so I noticed." She looked away, across the water.

"You look..."

Her gaze met mine again, and the anger was back.

"I look? What?" She snapped.

"Uhm... different?"

"Yeah I noticed that too. Apparently being a supernatural wolf has its perks. But don't think it changes anything."

"Excuse me?"

She took a step towards me, almost touching my chest with hers.

"You don't get to have me now just because of who I am. You didn't want me before, so this changes nothing. *Nothing.* You only wanted me around because it made you stronger to have your mate by your side, am I right?"

I flinched a little.

"That's what I thought. I'm not as stupid as you think I am. Why would someone like you-" She gestured up and down my body- "Be with someone like me when I was the way I was? You wouldn't, even if I was your mate. Now that I'm apparently some mythical wolf, you still don't get to have me, mate or not."

"You're... you're going to reject me?" I asked through gritted teeth.

"No. I could never do that Aya. I will stay here, and we will be mates, but in name only."

Was she serious? Of course she was. All I'd done since she got here was ignore her and insult her. I lowered my gaze, ashamed to meet her eyes.

"Don't!" She snapped. "Don't pretend to give a fuck when you don't!" She took a deep breath, "I only have one condition."

"What?" I asked.

"We let our wolves out with each other. Aya loves her mate, and he loves her. Just because we don't, doesn't mean we have to deprive them of each other. So we have to let them be together, be happy."

Anger rose in me. "So you're giving orders now? To me?"

Her eyes flashed. "You're damn right *Alpha*. Are you saying you'll deprive your wolf of his mate? Are you really *that* selfish?" She scoffed.

I clenched my jaw. Whatever happened to her turned her into a real piece of work. The really aggravating thing was even though she was pissing me off, all I could think about was shutting her up with my mouth. Or my dick.

"I'll think about it." I said.

She rolled her eyes heavily. "Typical." She muttered. "I'm going home. I'm exhausted."

I caught her elbow as she passed me. The sparks zipped through my fingertips and spread through my body. I made an immense effort to focus.

"You can't just walk away from me. After all, I had to come looking for you. Imagine what you would have gone through without me being here!"

"Oh, I almost forgot. Thank you for coming to find me, even though it was totally obvious that I ran away *from you*. I didn't ask you to come find me. And I can walk away from you. Just watch."

She ripped her arm from my grasp and walked away through the trees. My fists clenched and I let out a breath. I hated to admit it, but Lily was really sexy while telling me off. I always found her attractive, but now? Damn. This whole mate thing just got a lot more complicated.

# CHAPTER16

Dimitri hadn't followed me back home. I assumed he went for another run after I left. Or maybe he went to find Jennine. I didn't really care. Most of my mind was still reeling from two shocking events; The fact that I was a Mother Wolf, and the out-of body experience I'd had during my shift. I doubt Dimitri was aware of it. Lying on my bed, I closed my eyes and replayed the memory in my head.

*I hit the ground and everything went black. When I opened my eyes, I wasn't in my wolf form. Disappointment flooded through me. I really wasn't able to shift?*

*"Hello Lily."*

*I spun around at the sound of my name and gasped. The most gorgeous woman I'd ever laid eyes on was standing in front of me, a sweet smile on her face. Her hair was long and black with a tinge of blue and a little wave to it. It swayed behind her and caressed her waist in the wind. She had a heart shaped face with well proportioned features and plump red lips. Her body was incredible, even under the white dress she wore. Her eyes were a deep purple, but light and friendly. She was also the palest person I'd ever seen. Her skin could rival snow, but she was flawless.*

*"Who are you?" I asked.*

*Her smile widened. "My name is Celeste. But you may know me as Moon Goddess."*

*My eyes widened. The Moon Goddess?!*

*"Uhm..."*

*"I know, it's a lot to take in. Why don't we have a seat and talk?"*

*I looked around for the first time. We were standing in a meadow with tall grass and wildflowers. The sky was cloudless and peaceful. The meadow went on as far as the eye could see, seemingly with no end. Small hills rose up here and there. It was a beautiful place.*

*"Okay." I sank to the ground and Celeste laughed merrily. With a wave of her hand, a sofa appeared, looking very out of place in the meadow.*

*"Come sit, this is much more comfortable." She patted the cushion next to her. Awkwardly, I got up and joined her.*

*"You must have many questions Lily." Celeste began.*

*I nodded. "Why am I here? Did I...?"*

*"No you did not die. I called you here, but only temporarily."*

*"Why?"*

*She cupped my face in her hands gently and met my gaze. "You are extremely special to me Lily. I have chosen you for as great task. A dangerous one too. I cannot tell you everything, but I can tell you that I believe I have chosen wisely."*

*"Task? What task?"*

*Her hands dropped from my face to grasp mine.*

*"There is danger ahead Lily. A danger that could kill many, many of my children. I won't say they all deserve to live, because some of them do not. Some of them have chosen not to follow me anymore. All they care about now is attaining power and using my name to get what they want, killing mercilessly and without just cause. It needs to end."*

*"Okay. That's sad. But what can I do? I can't even make it up the stairs!" I said.*

*She laughed louder this time.*

*"I will help you with that Lily, don't worry. You will not be burdened by the effects of your past anymore."*

*A thought struck me with her words, and I took my hands from hers.*

*"Speaking of my past? Can I ask why? Why did you let me go through everything I did? Why did you let me suffer? You're suppose to love all your children, but you turned a blind eye to my abuse!" Tears sprung to my eyes while I talked, and by the end I was nearly shouting.*

*Celeste smiled sadly. "I am so sorry Lily. You are wrong though. I never turned away from you. Every mark inflicted on you was a hole in my heart. Would you believe me if I told you it was necessary?"*

*"No. How could that be necessary?" I cried.*

*"I give all my children free will. I could not control your abusers even though I wanted to. If I step in every time, where does it end? It's also not fair. Those who do bad will face their sins when they meet me. That is all I can do."*

*"You're right. It's not fair."*

*"I am sorry."*

*We sat in silence for a while. Celeste was the one to break it.*

*"Your mate is not a bad person." She said.*

*"What?"*

*"Dimitri. Truly, he is not bad. He has a good heart. A good soul. But he is lost right now."*

*"Okay?"*

*"Lily, I need you to not give up on him. He may have only accepted you for the wrong reasons, but with time-"*

*"Wrong reasons? What are you talking about?" I interrupted.*

*"Oh, I thought Ajax would have told Aya by now. Dimitri accepted you to make himself stronger. A Luna makes their Alpha strongest when they are by their side." She said it as if the words didn't cut through me.*

*"What?! Are you joking?! I'm to kill him!" I yelled.*

*Celeste placed her hand on top of mine.*

*"Please do not. I am not saying do not be angry. But you and Dimitri are made for each other. I paired the two of you for a reason. When you are ready, you will find that nobody loves you more."*

*"Right. Is Dimitri even capable of love?" I asked.*

*"He is. As I said, he is lost. Help him find himself. Can you do that for me Lily?"*

*I thought about it. "I'll....try."*

*"That's all I can ask."*

*Celeste's image trembled in front of me. I blinked, sure I was imagining things. But it happened again, and again.*

*"It is time for you to go back Lily. Remember what I've said, and I hope you can forgive me for your past. I love you."*

*She cupped my cheeks once more and pressed her lips lightly to my forehead. My vision went white, then black. And then I was back in the clearing with my mate.*

Opening my eyes, I stared at the ceiling. Celeste wanted me to forgive her. I had. I mean, she was the Moon Goddess. I couldn't hate her even if I tried. Her choices confused the hell out of me, but she was right. She couldn't bring down flames and fire every time someone messed up. I hated to accept it, but I did. However, her other request... was less complicated. I'd promised to try with Dimitri, but the way he looked at me after my shift, as if I was everything he ever wanted? That pissed me off. Where was that look before? I was only good enough for him when I wasn't thin and weak? He was so shallow.

I knew I was different, I just didn't know how much. I was scared to look in the mirror. In fact, I'd been avoiding it. Taking a deep breath, I closed my eyes and got up from the bed. Slowly, and blindly, making my way to the bathroom, I stopped in front of the mirror. Grasping the sink for dear life, I peeked one eye open. Then the other. And then I just stared. Yeah, I should have avoided this a little longer.

"Is... that can't be me."

"Yup. That's you. You're fucking hot!" Aya chuckled in my head.

I was too stunned to answer her. My hair was the same shade of red, but it looked shinier, healthier. My breasts now didn't look so out of proportion with the rest of me, as I had every curve a girl could want. Hips, thighs, boobs and butt. Every part of me was thicker. My face was filled out, no longer skin on bone, and it made my features stand out.

"That's not all. Take off your shirt."

"Huh?"

"Just do it, and turn around."

I did as my wolf asked, in a kind of daze. When I looked over my shoulder into the mirror, I gasped.

My gasp was echoed from the doorway, along with a "Holy *shit!*"

# CHAPTER 17

**LILYS POV**

My head spun to find Thara standing in the doorway gaping at me. I quickly grabbed my shirt from the floor.

"Wait!" Thara gasped. Walking up to me, she grabbed my shoulders and spun me around. Her fingers traced along my back where my scars used to be. All that was left was smooth, new skin.

"How... how is this possible?" Thara whispered.

"You recognize me?" I asked her.

She snorted. "Of course I recognize you! What a silly question. But...how Lily?"

I pulled my shirt back on and faced her. "Uhm... I'm not sure? I mean, I shifted-"

"Shifting wouldn't have healed those scars." She interrupted me.

"Well, maybe not for regular wolves." I replied quietly.

Her eyes narrowed. "What do you mean 'regular wolves'?"

Shuffling my feet, I avoided her piercing gaze.

"Lily?" Hazels voice drifted into the bathroom. A second later, she appeared in the doorway. "Oh. Hello Doctor Varlos."

"Hello Hazel."

"Uhm Lily, could I talk to you for a- Oh my goddess!" She gasped as she finally really saw me. "What the hell happened to you?!"

"I uh, shifted." I said lamely.

Hazel just openly stared at me. I was starting to feel like an attraction at the zoo.

"Okay, okay. Let's just all sit down and talk. I want to know what's up with this-" Thara waved her hand up and down my body-"as well. Come on."

She led us to the bed and we all climbed on, sitting in a circle. The girls looked at me expectantly and I sighed. Then I launched into my story about the nights events, leaving out my visit with Celeste. I don't know why, but that felt private. When I finished, Thara and Hazel looked at each other, then at me, and then back at each other. It seemed neither of them knew exactly what to say.

"Uhm, guys? Can one of you say something? Please?" I asked.

"I'm sorry I'm just...."

"This is just..."

"Wow." They said in unison. I laughed.

"Look, being a Mother Wolf doesn't change who I am. Okay, it may have changed how I look, but I'm still me." I said.

"That's not it Lily. It's just not so easy to actually see it. I mean, we've heard about the Mother Wolf all our lives, as bedtime stories. They don't even exist! Yet, here you are, living proof, and it's honestly amazing!" Thara gushed.

"What did Dimitri say?!" Hazel asked and I flinched.

Thara narrowed her eyes again, this time with a steely look. "What did my idiot brother do?" She asked.

"He didn't *do* anything per se..." I sighed again. "He.... okay maybe I overreacted to his reaction-"

"I doubt that. Tell us." Thara clipped.

"Well, after I shifted back and he saw me like *this*... he looked, well.... I don't know, he had *that* look."

"What look?" Hazel asked.

"You know, the *look*. The look that says "Baby I'll lie down in the dirt so you can walk all over me" kind of look." I said.

"That dumbass." Thara shook her head.

"I don't understand, isn't that good? Don't you want him to look at you like that?" Hazel asked confused.

Thara answered before I could.

"Normally, yes. But my brother has been ignoring Lily since she got here. And then she goes from being well, Lily, to *this* Lily, and all of a sudden he's interested? That's not cool, not cool at all. I'm so going to kick his ass." She growled.

I laughed again, that was something I wanted to see.

"No need Thara, I already told him it wasn't happening."

She clapped her hands. "Good for you girl! Make him work for it! Serves him right."

I smiled, nodding. Inside, I was groaning. Ever since I shifted the bond between Dimitri and I had grown considerably. I'd woken up from an overly intense dream about him, and let's just say it left me in a very edgy mood. All I wanted was to see him, inhale his scent, feel his skin on mine. I was ashamed to admit I was more or less hiding in my room to avoid seeing him. I wasn't entirely sure I could control my hormones or my urges around him.

As if he could hear my thoughts, a knock sounded on my door and Hazel and Thara stopped talking.

"Come in." I called.

Dimitri opened the door, pausing when he saw all of us on the bed. I raised an eyebrow at him.

"Uh, hi." He said.

"Hello Dimitri." Thara said. She gave him a look and he glanced at me. Clearly, he knew I'd ratted him out.

"Can I talk to you a sec?" He asked me. He glanced at his sister and Hazel. "Alone?"

"I guess so." I replied quietly. Thara plopped back onto my pillows and Hazel studied her nails. I glared at them until Thara looked up and nodded her head toward the hall. Rolling my eyes, I got off the bed and followed my mate out the door, closing it behind me.

"This way." Dimitri reached for his door, opening it. I hesitated. "Come on, I don't bite." A hint of a smirk played on his face when he said that, and I gave him a look. I wasn't in the mood to flirt with him. Instead, I straightened my shoulders and walked past him into his room.

His scent hit me and I inhaled deeply. Dimitri's bedroom wasn't what I expected, but then again, nothing about Blood Moon was so far. His walls were a deep grey, almost black. Actually, most of the furnishing was too. This was a very dark room, but it wasn't uncomfortable. It suited Dimitri very well. The colors and his scent mixed very nicely creating a very safe feeling. Looking to my right, the safe feeling turned into something completely different when my gaze landed on his ginormous California king bed. The sound of the door clicking into place snapped me out of my, honestly, embarrassing dirty thoughts. Yet I couldn't seem to take my eyes off the bed.

"Lily?"

It took me a second to realize Dimitri had been talking to me for a while. Shaking my head, I finally averted my gaze and turned to him.

"You wanted to talk?" I asked him.

"Uh, yeah." He ran his hands through his hair, and my heart fluttered. It was a really adorable action.

"Okay. About?"

He walked past me and sat on his bed. My cheeks flushed from my earlier fantasies.

"I talked to James." He said. My eyes flew to his in shock.

"What?"

"I talked to James." He repeated.

I cocked my head to the side. "And?" I asked.

"He denied everything." He deadpanned.

"But...he-"

Dimitri held up his hand and I shut up.

"He denied everything, but I know when someone is bullshitting me. I told him so, and demoted him. James is no longer my head warrior."

My jaw dropped. "Really?"

"Really."

"But I thought you needed to talk to Hazel?"

"I did. She told me everything. So did Celia. And Shelly. And Brittany. And-"

"Wait, wait, wait." I held up my hands in front of me. "There was more than just Hazel?"

"Yeah. A lot more." He blew out a breath, his eyebrows furrowing.

I crossed the room, sitting next to him.

"How? How did you get so many women to-?"

"I didn't. After I talked to James, Celia came to me. She said she overheard us, and decided to finally talk to me. After that, the rest came forward. If I didn't have enough evidence to demote him from Hazel alone, I sure do now."

"That's incredible!" I exclaimed.

Dimitri looked at me like I'd gone crazy.

"I mean, it's not incredible what he's done, obviously. But it is awesome that something is done about it. He won't be able to do it again, will he?"

"No. I'll make sure of it." Dimitri promised.

"Thank you. For listening to me, for doing something. It means a lot, Dimitri."

Without thinking about it, I reached out and placed my hand on his. Sparks shot through my hand and up my arm. Dimitri's eyes darkened and a low growl erupted from his chest. A foreign feeling pooled in my stomach and travelled down between my thighs. My breath started to come faster, and I bit my lip to keep it under control. His eyes dropped to my lips and my heart stuttered. All my thoughts from earlier came flooding back, forcefully. The things I wanted to do to him on this bed- the things I wanted him to do to me. Unconsciously I found myself leaning in, so close that our lips were only an inch apart.

*"Dimitri accepted you to make himself stronger. A Luna makes their Alpha strongest when they are by their side."*

Celeste's words floated through my mind, jolting me out of my daze. I felt as if someone had thrown ice cold water on me. I ripped my hand out of Dimitris and pushed him away. His eyes went wide with shock and confusion, but I was already on my feet, heading to the door.

"Again, thank you for taking care of the James situation. I'll uh, see you around Dimitri." I babbled quickly.

"Lily-"

"Bye."

Slamming his door shut behind me, skipped across to my room. Thara and Hazel looked up as I entered. Judging by the identical looks on their faces, they suspected what had just happened. I shook my head when Thara opened her mouth.

"I don't want to talk about it." I said.

She pursed her lips, but nodded.

"So... movie night?" Hazel asked.

"Yes!" I sighed and gratefully sank onto the bed beside her.

# CHAPTER 18

**\*\*WARNING- THIS CHAPTER CONTAINS SEXUAL ASSAULT! IF YOU DO NOT WISH TO READ IT, PLEASE SKIP AHEAD.\*\***
**LILYS POV**

It had been one week since the 'incident' in Dimitris room. I threw myself into activities in order to avoid thinking about it. Clint had agreed to start training me- I'd never been allowed to train at my old pack, and I was desperate to learn. I'd been keeping company with Greta, Hazel and even Thara at the hospital. I picked up a few tricks on treating wounds with her and decided to add it to my list of interests. Maybe I'd work there officially someday. Goddess knows I'd had more than enough practice cleaning and bandaging my own wounds over the years. Setting broken bones was nothing new to me, something Thara learned about me but did not comment on.

The weekend loomed and all my friends had plans. Plans they had invited me to get in on, and that I'd declined. As much as I was enjoying my new life, (save one person), I was still extremely shy about meeting new people. My little group wanted to attend a club Saturday night, which was way out of my comfort zone. Especially when I learned that most of the pack frequented that particular spot on the weekend to let loose. I knew I wasn't ready for that yet, so come Saturday night, I was holed up in the gym training by myself. I'd completed fifty laps on the track which I was extremely proud of, and was now lifting weights.

*"We've gotten so much stronger."* Said Aya.

*"I know. It's awesome!"* I replied.

*"We would have gotten here eventually, but thank the Moon Goddess for blessing us with this body sooner rather than later."*

*"Agreed."*

Thinking I should move onto the next set of weights, I placed my current ones in the holders and sat up. Sweat dripped from my forehead but it didn't bother me. I liked working out, more than I thought I ever would.

The feeling of being stronger made me proud. Like maybe I could actually step into my role as Luna and be worthy of it someday.

"You look like you could use a water."

An unattractive yelp left me as I jumped to my feet and spun around. An unfamiliar guy was leaning against the weights, arms crossed. He was pretty average looking. Brown hair, blue eyes, lean but muscular build and ripped faded blue jeans with a black t-shirt. His skin was a nice olive colour, but it might have been the only attractive quality about him. The way he was looking at me made me uncomfortable too, like a was a juicy cheeseburger and he was a starved man.

"What are you doing here?" I asked.

The guy laughed and the sound put me on edge. He sounded like one of the villains from the Disney movies Hazel and I had been watching.

"This is the gym, right? Anyone can be here."

I shook my head. "No I mean... I thought everyone was out at the club tonight."

"Most are. I've been there so much, it's become a little boring. I thought I'd try something new tonight." He said.

I looked him up and down quickly. "It doesn't seem like working out is anything new for you."

He smirked. "It's not. But working out on a Saturday night? That is new."

"Oh."

He stared at me with that starved look again and I remembered I was only wearing a pair of black legging and a blue sports bra. I suddenly felt very exposed and crossed my arms in an attempt to show less skin.

"You seem nervous." He stated.

"No." I denied quickly. "I just wasn't expecting anyone to join me. But uhm, you can use the weights if you want. I'm done with them."

"Thanks very much."

I nodded and turned to leave. Halfway to the door I heard him call me.

"Yes?" I turned and looked at him.

"It was nice to meet you Luna."

I blinked. "You know who I am?"

"Oh yes. How could I not know the woman who got me kicked out of my position?"

My heart stopped, and then picked up double time. Holy shit, this was James? No wonder I didn't recognize him from anywhere. I didn't make it habit to seek out scum, so I'd never met him. And Hazel had never given me a description of the guy, other than his personality.

"You look surprised Luna."

His tone was no longer friendly- in fact, it was cold. Aya went into alert mode and I did the same. Instinctively, I turned my body to face him fully, the way Clint had taught me.

"Do I?" I asked.

James nodded. "You didn't think we wouldn't meet eventually?"

"I haven't thought about it really."

"That's too bad." He straightened up and took a few steps in my direction. "Because I've been thinking about you a lot lately."

My feet carried me backwards at his words.

"Why?"

He scoffed. "How could I not be curious about the woman who has our Alpha wrapped around her little finger? I'm not the only one either. Dimitri has been acting different since you showed up."

Ignoring that last part, I replied, "I don't have him wrapped around my finger."

James stopped a few feet from me. His eyes were ice blue and flat.

"Oh really? Then explain something to me. How is that our Alpha never said a word about who I fuck until *you* show up, huh? I've been with tons of women in this pack. Suddenly, we get a Luna, and their all claiming abuse and I get demoted!" He practically yelled.

My reaction to his outburst was totally unexpected. As his words processed, a laugh burst from my chest and out of my mouth.

"Are you serious? Your demotion had nothing to do with *me* James. It was the result of your own stupid, shitty choices. Dimitri never said anything because he didn't know exactly what you were doing, all the disgusting ways you were using and manipulating the women of the pack. Taking them to the packhouse, to the *Alphas* floor, to have sex. Yes, I had a discussion with him about it, but you didn't really think he wouldn't have found out eventually? Even if I had never come into the picture?" I shook my head.

"You stupid bitch, you ruined everything!" James spit.

"No, all I did was help put an end to you abusing women." I shot back.

James laughed humorlessly. A shiver ran down my spine.

*"Can we leave now?"* Aya said.

*"Rule number one- never turn your back on an enemy. And he's definitely our enemy."*

*"Pfft. Like he could take us down."*

*"He could take me down Aya."*

*"True. So let me out."*

*"Not yet."*

"You think you're so brave Luna. So good and strong? Yet, you were stupid enough to make an enemy your first week here. And also stupid enough to come to an empty building, alone, when everyone else is out."

I gulped nervously. I hated to admit it, but he had a point. He took another step and everything Clint had taught me so far washed away, replaced with my old instincts. Turning, I ran for the door, a scream ready in my throat. Suddenly my feet left the ground and I was thrown backwards, landing on my back with a painful gasp.

*"Fuck! Lily, we have to shift!"*

I barely registered Aya's words when James threw himself on top of me, pinning my arms to my sides. Regardless, I struggled against him but even I knew it was a lost fight. He had years of training; I had one week. And if I shifted right under him, I could actually kill him. I didn't want to kill anyone, not even a parasite like James.

"Not so strong now eh?" A sharp sting ran across my cheek and my face whipped to the side as James slapped me.

"Fuck you!" I yelled.

He slapped me again before roughly grabbing my face, forcing me to look at him. His eyes held pure fiery rage. Fear gripped me.

"Be careful what you wish for. Because of you, I haven't gotten laid in a while."

My breathing stopped. Adrenaline kicked in and I bucked my hips in an attempt to throw him off. I twisted and writhed under him, desperately attempting to get my hands free.

"Stop struggling! You can't win."

"Get off of me! Help! HELP!" I screamed. James slammed his hand over my mouth.

"Shut the fuck up!" He hissed. The next second, I sank my teeth into his hand causing him to howl in pain. "Fucking bitch!"

His fist connected with my stomach, winding me. While I gasped for breath, he grabbed a fistful of my hair and yanked. I winced in pain and lust shone in his eyes. He was getting off on this, my pain. Goddess he really was a sick son of a bitch! James leaned down to my ear, his breath fanning my cheek and I shivered in disgust.

"I heard Dimitri hasn't touched you yet. So either you're playing hard to get, or he's simply not interested." He chuckled. "Both are fine with me. I'd hate to have his sloppy seconds anyways."

The hand that wasn't holding my face swept down over my shoulder and down my arm. When he reached my stomach, I whimpered in fear. Panic rushed through me so strongly I began to feel dizzy. James moved his hand higher by inches, prolonging my torture until he was cupping my breast. I choked back vomit and tears at the same time- I would not give him the satisfaction of seeing either.

"Oh yeah, I'm going to enjoy you baby."

Closing my eyes, I went to my happy place. Maybe I would survive what happened next if I stayed there indefinitely.

# CHAPTER 19

**DIMITRIS POV**

I was sitting in my office looking over the new security plan with Ben and Luke. I was oddly on edge this evening, but I chalked it up to just being stressed. I hadn't gone for a run since the night Lily shifted, so that was probably a big factor. The bigger problem was my mate. Well, not her so much, but her attitude towards me. Ever since our talk last week, she'd been conveniently absent. I never saw her at meals- I'd learned from Ben that she was eating in her room again. I didn't see her around the house, and I'd learned from Luke that she'd taken up various activities from training with that Clint boy to working with Thara at the hospital. When she wasn't doing that, she with Hazel. And obviously I didn't see her at night.

It bothered me more than it should that she was obviously ignoring me. The night she shifted, I was so fucking worried when I couldn't find her. How stupid could she be, trying to go through that alone? It took me way too long to find her, and when I did, all I wanted to was to scream at her for being so fucking dumb. But the way she'd clung to me-the way she needed me- over writ all my anger. Then she'd yelled at me and basically told me to fuck off. Okay, yes, she had many good reasons to be angry with me, but really? She could have *died*.

Speaking of, I still don't know how she found out why I brought her here. Nobody knew, not even Ben or Luke. They were under the assumption that with time, I'd warm up to the idea of a mate. I grilled Ajax, but he swore he said nothing to her wolf. Maybe Lily was right and she wasn't as stupid as I originally thought she was. Why else would someone accept there mate only to ignore them and treat them the way I treated her?

*"Sounds like someone is feeling guilty."* Ajax commented smugly.

*"Shut it. I don't feel guilty."*

*"Uh huh. That's why you can't stop thinking about her. Can't stop wanting to see her?"*

*"I said shut it."*

He chuckled but receded to the back of my mind.

"So, I was thinking we put cameras here, here and here." Ben pointed to various spots on the map of our land. "Night vision and heat detection."

"That's dumb. So we'll know when someone is already in our borders?" Luke scoffed. Ben flipped him off.

"I wasn't done. So we put cameras on these spots *and* we put the rest outside the borders at our weak spots. We'll know when someone is coming, and if anybody manages to slip past, we'll know that too."

I rubbed my chin. "I think we should have them here and here too." I pointed.

"I'll have to order more."

"Whatever. I just want us to be secured." I said.

Ben circled the marked spots with a marker and nodded. "Okay, that's done."

"Thank Goddess." Luke mumbled.

I grabbed three glasses from the shelf behind me and a bottle of whiskey. Pouring each of us a drink, I sat down in my chair with a heavy sigh.

"I wish the rogues would get it through their heads- they can't win against us. Why bother even trying?" I grumbled.

"Rogues are generally known for being stupid shits. Who knows what goes on in their heads?" Ben said.

Luke simply stared into his glass, his lips pursed. I knew that look like the back of my hand- he was hiding something. I picked up a paperclip and flicked it at him.

"Something you'd like to share with the group?" I asked, He rolled his eyes and I smirked. I knew him well, and he hated it.

Upending his drink, he swallowed it in one go and blew out a breath. "So... there's something I want to tell you guys."

Ben set his glass down and sat down on the sofa. I propped my feet on my desk and gestured for him to continue.

"Uhm...so.... I uh... I met my mate." Luke mumbled quickly.

"What?!" Ben shouted, jumping to his feet.

"When?" I asked.

"Two weeks ago."

"And you didn't tell us?! What the fuck man!" Ben punched Luke in the arm and scowled at him.

"Well... it... wasn't who I thought it was going to be."

"Who is she?" I asked eagerly. Luke had been waiting so long to meet his mate. Unlike me, he constantly raved about finding the perfect girl and giving her the world. It got on my nerves a lot, but I was genuinely happy that he finally met her.

But Luke didn't look happy at all. In fact, he looked scared shitless. His eyes met mine, and he didn't seem to be able to find the words he wanted. Ben and I waited patiently as he got himself to together enough to tell us.

"It's...uh... well, it's a *he,* not a *she* actually."

I blinked, stunned. His mate was a guy?

"But... you're not gay?" Ben was equally as confused as I was.

Luke blushed a deep red. "I'm not. I'm actually bisexual."

I stared at him, shocked. How did I not know this? I grew up with Luke; spent almost everyday with him. I'd never seen him with any guys, never even seen him look at one that way.

"I'm sorry I didn't tell you. About me, or meeting my mate. I thought... I mean, I didn't know if you'd still want me as your Gamma." He said.

"Why the fuck would you think that?" I asked. Before he could answer I followed up with, "You think I'm some homophobe?"

"No, no! You know, a lot of these other Alphas are real old school, and I don't want you catching flack because you have a Gamma who's mated to a guy."

I scoffed loudly. "Fuck them! I'm proud to have you as my Gamma, no matter who your mate is. and if anyone has anything to say about it, I'll punch them in the jaw. You're one of my best friends Luke. I don't care who you love."

He looked like he was about to cry. "Really?"

"Really. Come here man!" I stood and we hugged. "I'm happy for you. When do we meet him?"

Luke chuckled nervously. "Well, that's the other thing. See, I would have told you guys right away but..."

"But?" Ben asked.

"But... he's a rogue." Luke finished.

"What?!" This time Ben and I yelled together. Luke threw his hands up in front of him quickly.

"I swear, he's not like others! And he's never been apart of the rogues that attacked us! He's different."

"Only because he's your mate." Ben said.

"No! He didn't choose to be a rogue. His pack was destroyed a few years back, and only a few survived. Instead of sticking together, they went their separate ways, and he hasn't found another pack. He wants to meet you Dimitri, wants to join us officially." Luke's eyes were pleading with me, big and wide. He looked like a puppy.

Finally, I gave in. "Fine! Tell him we'll meet him tomorrow. I don't want a him skulking around our borders, he could get attacked. Bring him here tonight, but keep him out of sight for now. Okay?"

"No problem!"

Luke ran out of the office so fast, I almost laughed. I looked at Ben who was shaking his head, a small smile playing on his lips.

"Did you know?" I asked him.

"Nope. When I get the chance, I'm going to grill him about all the guys he's secretly been screwing behind our backs."

"How did we not notice all these years?"

"Right? Though, if you really think about it... he did spend *a lot* of time with Derek."

My eyes widened. Derek was my cousin, and also super gay. He owned it though, and when his my aunt and uncle kicked him out after he came out, my parents took him in. He met his mate a year later and moved to California. Before that though, we all used to spend two weeks every summer at a cabin on the lake. Luke and Derek were always together, practically attached at the hip. I brushed it off as being really good friends and having a lot in common.

"You don't think?"

"Maybe?" Ben said.

"No..."

Together, we burst out laughing at overlooking the obvious all these years. Suddenly, Ajax forced himself to the front of my mind.

*"Somethings wrong."* He said.

*"What are you talking about?"*

*"Aya... Aya and Lily, they're in trouble!"*

My laughter died on my lips and I was on my feet heading to the door within seconds, Ben right on my tail.

"Whoa, hey! What's the matter?" He asked as he tried to keep up with me.

"Ajax says Lily in trouble."

"Shit, okay. Where is she?"

I braked so fast that Ben almost ran into me. "I don't know."

"Okay... She didn't go to the club did she?"

"I don't know."

"Well, who is she with tonight?"

"I don't fucking know!" I yelled. Ben looked at me with worry and a hint of disappointment. I knew what he was thinking- I was a shitty mate.

"Can Ajax find her?" He asked.

I took a deep breath and closed my eyes, letting my wolf come forward and better reach out to his mate.

*"Gym."*

I took off so fast that Ben was left behind. I pushed myself to go faster as I flew down the halls and downstairs. My excelled speed didn't seem fast enough. All I could think about was getting to Lily before anything happened. Before she was hurt.

When I reached the gym doors, I wasted no time in ripping them open and running inside. What I saw had me seeing red. James lay atop my mate, hand on her breast and fisted in her hair.

"Oh yeah, I'm going to enjoy you baby." He hummed down to her.

A ground-shaking roar ripped out of me as I raced to them, throwing his disgusting body into the far wall and away from Lily.

"HOW DARE YOU TOUCH MY MATE?!"

# CHAPTER 20

**DIMITRIS POV**

I was breathing hard, my vision clouded by hate and rage. Ajax push forward forcefully, and I wasn't even trying to hold him back. How dare this scum touch what is mine? When I looked at James, all I saw was my next victim, a disgusting piece of filth that I was going to gut like a fish. Yet I couldn't make myself move from Lily, still on the floor. Part of me wanted to rush James and tear his head off, and an equally large part of me had to stay and protect her. It was a confusing mental battle.

"A-Alpha... I-"

"SHUT UP!" I roared.

*"Warriors to the gym NOW!"* I sent out a mind link.

*"Yes Alpha", "On our way Alpha".*

James and I stared at each other, one with fear the other with murderous intent. The doors opened and closed and I caught Bens scent. Finally, knowing someone I trusted was with me, I moved away from Lily and stalked towards James. Stupidly, he tried to run for the door, but I caught him, slamming him against the wall by the throat.

"You must have a fucking death wish." I hissed.

"What the fuck happened?" Ben asked behind me.

It was at that moment that Lily started crying. It started off as little hiccups but soon turned into broken, raw sobs. Glancing back at her, I saw Ben with a worried expression awkwardly patting her arm. I growled again and he immediately took his hands away from her.

Thara burst through the doors, followed by four warriors. She rushed to Lily while my warriors surrounded me. Slamming James head against the wall for good measure, I gave him up to my men.

"Take him to the dungeon. Put him in the smallest, dirtiest cell you can find and give him two shots of wolfsbane to keep him quiet." I ordered.

"Right away Sir." Two men hoisted James up and flanked by the other two, dragged him out of the room. I turned my attention back to my sister and my mate. Thara was rubbing Lilys back and talking quietly to her while she cried. Ben sat back on his heels and let Thara do her thing.

"He's gone Lily. It's okay now, shh. He's gone." Thara murmured.

"I...I couldn't... do it Thara... I couldn't..." Lily sobbed.

"It's okay sweetie. It's okay."

Thara met my eyes, motioning me forward. Kneeling beside Lily, I took over rubbing her back. Light sparks came through her clothes and into my palm and she started to breath a little easier.

"We'll give you some space." Thara said. Taking Bens arm, she pulled him up.

"Right outside boss." Ben said. I nodded in response.

When the door closed, I scooped my arms under Lily and brought her into my lap. She rested her head against my chest, continuing to cry while I rubbed her back slowly.

"I-I'm sorry... Dimitri... I'm...sorry..." She hiccupped.

"Don't. Don't do that." I said softly. The tone of my voice surprised me. I was never this gentle with anyone. "What happened Lily?"

She scrunched her fists into my shirt. "He... was angry. Because you...demoted him. He said it.. my fault. He tried to... he was going to..." Her words cut off on another sob and it took all my willpower to stay where I was with her and not to go and kill that fucker.

"It's okay. I know. You don't have to say anymore." I told her.

"I tried to shift. I...wanted to. But I couldn't. It would have killed him. I couldn't do it." She cried.

"It's okay Lily. He's gone." I repeated Thara's words.

In that moment, the situation became vivid. Lily had almost been raped. She was scared, and hurting. My hands started to shake as I realized exactly how close she had come to being a victim of the most brutal crime. And I couldn't even deny my fault in it. I hadn't known where she was, if she was with friends or not. I hadn't cared to ask. What would have happened if I hadn't listened to Ajax? If I hadn't gotten to her on time?

"Ow."

I realized I'd unconsciously been squeezing Lily tighter to me. Too tight. Hastily, I let go.

"Sorry."

We sat in silence for a little bit. I didn't know what to say to her, and honestly, the guilt I was feeling was making it hard to talk. She looked calmer now. She was still crying although silently, the tears following their predecessor's paths. The look in her eyes though; I never wanted to see it there again.

"Dimitri."

I turned to see Thara poking her head in the door. She gave me a questioning look and I nodded; Ben came in with her, blanket in hand. He gave it to Thara who proceeded to wrap it around Lily.

"Come on. I'm going to run you a bath and get you some food." She helped Lily to her feet, wrapping her arm around her while leading her to her the door. Lily looked back to me, mumbling, "Thank you." And then they were gone.

Exactly one heartbeat later, Ben's fist connected with my cheek, sending me flying backward.

"What the *fuck*?!"

"What the fuck exactly! What the fuck is the matter with you!" Ben screamed.

"What is wrong with *you*?"

"You didn't know where she was Dimitri! You had no idea! Do you know what would have happened if Ajax hadn't warned you?! Do you even fucking care?"

I stood up angrily. "Of course I do!"

"Do you?! You sure as fuck don't act like it! Why did you even bring her here huh? You're the shittiest excuse for a mate I've ever-"

His head snapped back as I landed a punch. He quickly recovered and tackled me. We rolled around throwing punches and jabs until he pushed me off, wiping blood from his lip.

"Fuck you." I snarled.

"No, fuck *you* Dimitri. I don't know what idea you cooked up when you met her, but *this* isn't how we treat mates. Get your shit together!" He snapped. My eyes widened at his words. Did everyone see through me so easily?

Hitting my shoulder roughly as he passed, I watched him walk out the door. Anger and guilt and regret ran through me as I ran my hands through my hair.

"Fuck!" I yelled.

I had no clue what to do now, and I really didn't want to stop and think about what my Beta said to me. Not yet. Instead, I stripped in the middle of the room and shifted. I needed to run. I needed to get out and decompress for a while. Using my head to push the doors open I jogged down the hall and a startled Omega opened the front door for me. I nodded a thanks as I passed and sprinted towards the woods, disappearing into the trees. I jumped over logs and under branches, feeling the wind rush through my fur and just turned my mind off. I focused on the feeling of the dirt under my paws, the sounds of squirrels and birds and deer in the bush around me. A rabbit jumped into my path, quickly freezing in fear as I passed and then rushing away again. I didn't stop for hours; I couldn't stop. If I did, I'd start to think again and I didn't want to.

*"So we're just running from our problems now?"* Ajax asked. I ignored him. *"That's so Alpha like."*

"Shut up. Shut up, shut up, shut up!"

*"Why? Because you don't want to think about Lily? You don't want to acknowledge that Ben was right and you're a shitty mate?"*

I whimpered.

*"Face it Dimitri. You're becoming exactly like* him."

"I'm not. I...I'm not."

*"You are. But you don't have to. You can change Dimitri. We don't have to end up like him."*

Coming to a stop, I sank to the ground. Memories played in my head, my heart clenching more and more. Then memories of tonight's events joined in. James lying atop my mate. Lily crying. The look in her eyes- broken and lost and haunted. A look I'd been partially responsible for. But I couldn't let her in. Couldn't love her.

Could I?

# CHAPTER 21

**LILYS POV**

My whole body was numb as I sat in the bathtub. The water was hot-too hot in fact, turning my skin red. But I didn't have the energy to call Thara in to let her know. Maybe it was a good thing though- maybe the temperature would aid in burning off his touch. I could feel it, still. His hand on my breast, caressing. His fist in my hair, pulling until it hurt. His excitement rubbing against my lower regions as he prepared to assault me.

The events in the gym replayed in my mind over and over and over again, like a horrible broken record. And the panic I'd felt then was only increasing every time the loop started again.

*"He's gone Lily. He can't get to us again."*

Aya had been repeating that for a while now, but it was like my brain wasn't connected to my body. I knew James was locked away now, but my body was still preparing for the fight. Trying to lock itself down. Slowly, I drew in a long deep breath, holding it for seven seconds. Then I released it just as slowly and attempted to relax my stiff muscles. Without thinking too much, I grabbed my loofa and soap and began to scrub my body. Something clicked as I washed myself, and I began to scrub harder. And harder. Harder until the roughness of the loofa grated against my bare skin, peeling layers off as it went back and forth.

Was there even soap anymore? I didn't care. All I wanted was for every cell of mine he touched to be wiped clean, erased, brand new.

"Hey, foods her- Oh my Goddess! Lily! Stop!"

Thara rushed towards me and yanked the loofa out of my hands, throwing it across the room. Her eyes went wide as she surveyed the damage I'd done.

"Christ Lily. You're bleeding!"

Huh. So I was. Thara looked at my non-caring expression and frowned. Grasping under my arms, she lifted me out of the tub and sat me on the mat. She proceeded to dry me quickly and then tossed me a robe. Shakily, I got to my feet, avoiding her eyes.

"Food is here. Come eat."

"I'm not hungry."

"Too bad. You need to eat something."

"I'm not hungry."

"Lily-"

"I said I'm not eating! Okay?!" I yelled at her.

Thara dropped her head into her hands. "Lily, please don't make this hard. You need to eat."

"No." I grumbled.

"Fine!" She threw her hands up and stormed out of the bathroom. A second later, I heard the bedroom door open and slam shut.

Regret washed through me immediately. Goddess, I was a bitch. Thara had done nothing but help me, and I'd gone and freaked out for no reason. Sighing, I opened my robe and looked at my stomach and chest. The blood was already drying, the wounds already close to being healed. It stung, but oh well. I didn't have the energy to get dressed as I passed my closet on the way to my bed, and a tray with what looked like Greta's beef stew and dinner rolls sat atop it. I sat beside it with a sigh, picking up a roll and picking off tiny pieces.

A light knock sounded on my door. Part of me hoped it was Thara, so I could apologize. But when I called to come in, to my surprise it was Ben. He poked his head around the door and avoided looking at me.

"Are you, uh, decent?" He asked.

"More or less. You can come in."

"Yeah... I'm gonna need that to be *more* and not less before I do. Dimitri-"

"Okay." He didn't need to explain. Ben closed the door while I quickly walked to the closet and located a pair of pajamas, dressing silently. When I was done, I opened the door.

Ben gave me a small smile. "Hey."

"Hey."

"Thought I'd come check on you."

"Thara sent you up here?" I guessed.

"Well...okay, yeah she did."

I opened the door wider. "Come on in."

Ben eyed the tray on my bed. "Not hungry?"

"Not really." I shrugged.

"You need to eat munchkin. You could go into shock, food will help."

I rolled my eyes. "What makes Thara think you can get me to eat when she couldn't?"

He gave me a hard look and I felt his Beta aura. It wasn't anything like Dimitris, but still intimidating. However, I got the message. They weren't going to leave me alone until I ate the damn food, so I'd eat the damn food. I picked up a roll and dipped it in the stew, ripping off a big bite.

"Happy?" I said as I chewed.

Ben nodded. "I'll be happy when you finish it."

He sat on the end of the bed, watching me eat every bite. When I'd finally finished, he smiled.

"Better?"

"I guess so." I replied.

Taking the tray and setting it aside, Ben let out a huge sigh, his eyebrows creased. "I know you don't want to talk about it-"

"I don't." I interrupted.

"But you need to. We can't just pretend that this didn't happy Lily. And James will have to stand trial. I don't know if you know what that means?"

I shook my head.

"It means that when that happens, you will need to stand and give your account of what happened. So you can't just shut it out."

I paled. "But- you were there. You saw it. Why can't you just tell everyone what happened?"

Ben shook his head. "We'll need to know what led to it, what was said. And James will get to have his say too. Though it's not like he can deny it, because we were there for that."

"I don't know if I can do that." I whispered.

"You can. You're stronger than you think munchkin."

"Can you stop calling me that?" I scowled.

"Sorry, would you prefer Lillian instead?"

"Goddess, no!"

Ben laughed and I cracked a small smile. He stood and stretched.

"Get some sleep. You might feel better in the morning." Giving me another smile he headed out.

"Ben?" I called before he shut the door.

"Yeah?"

"Can you tell Thara I'm sorry? Please?"

"I will. And she knows. But I'll tell her all the same, no worries."

"Thanks."

He nodded, and finally left me to rest. I *was* tired; exhausted actually. Turning off the light beside the bed, I curled up on my side, grabbing my pillow and hugging it to my chest. Surprisingly, my mind shut off and pulled me into sleep. Perhaps I dreamed, but maybe I didn't, because the next thing I knew, it was morning and I was wide awake. And Ben was right- I felt different today. I got up and showered, dressed. And all I could think about what that I *was* strong enough to handle the trial. James needed to pay for what he did, and measures needed to be taken to ensure he never did it again. I could do this. I needed to do this.

With a firm handle on my feelings, I went to breakfast. I expected everyone to know about last nights happenings, but nobody blinked at my entrance. It was the same usual morning banter, and Hazel and Clint were sitting at our usual table waving at me. Filling up my plate, I joined them.

"Hey." I said.

"How are you?" Hazel asked. She scrutinized my expression carefully.

"Fine." I replied.

"You sure?" Clint asked.

"Let me guess- Thara told you guys what happened?"

"Yeah." They nodded.

"Did you tell anyone else?"

"No."

"Good. Please don't. And really, I am fine. Okay, I wasn't last night, but I'm fine today. Promise." I gave them a reassuring smile.

They glanced at each other but nodded. We ate in silence for a while until I noticed Thara enter the cafeteria. Telling my friends I'd be right back, I wound through the tables until I reached her.

"Thara?"

She looked at me over her shoulder, giving me her usual smile. There was no hint of anger in her eyes.

"Hey. How are you today?" She asked as she put a stack on pancakes on her plate.

"Good. Uhm, listen, I'm really sor-"

Thara held up her hand. "It's fine. I understand you weren't in a good frame of mind last night, and you vented some of your feelings onto me. If I had a dollar for every time someone did that, I'd be a millionaire."

"Okay, but that doesn't make it right. Just say you forgive me?" I pleaded.

"I forgive you. If it makes you feel better, you are the only person to apologize." She laughed.

"It does, oddly. Thanks." I pulled her into a hug and she chuckled.

"Good morning."

I released Thara, turning to look at her brother. Dimitri stood to the side of us, hands in pockets. My breath caught in my throat when I looked at him- he had bags under his eyes and his hair was a mess. Was he wearing the same clothes as last night too? Did he even sleep?

"Morning big bro. You look like shit." Thara said.

Dimitri scowled in her direction before turning back to me. "Can we talk in my office?"

"Uh, yeah sure."

"See you later Lily." Thara waved.

I followed my mate out of the cafeteria and up the stairs to his office. He gestured for me to go in first, so I went to the sofa and flopped down. Dimitri sat heavily behind his desk, running his hands over his face.

"I really don't want to be the one to tell you this." He groaned.

*Fuck. What now?*

# CHAPTER 22

**LILYS POV**

I sat anxiously as Dimitri gathered his thoughts. Or pretended to. I could tell her he playing for time, not wanting to tell me whatever shitty news he had. Finally, he clasped his hands in front of him on the desk and looked straight into my eyes.

"James is gone. He escaped."

My breathing stopped. Did I hear him right?

"What?" I gasped.

"It looks like he had help..."

He started going into detail, but I didn't hear a word he said. All I could was stare at him with my mouth agape, unblinking and frozen.

"Is this some kind of sick joke?" I asked. Dimitri stopped talking and raised an eyebrow.

"No."

Unbelievably, I laughed. My chest heaved with the effort of expelling the sound and tears came to my eyes. Dimitri looked worried, like I'd lost my mind.

"Are you fucking kidding me?! He was in the dungeon for what? Not even twelve hours? What kind of dungeon do you have where people can just get up and walk out?"

"This has never happened before-"

"That's hard to believe!"

"He killed four of my men-"

"Shocking!" I said sarcastically.

"Look, I'm using everything we have to locate him and bring him back and-"

"For what?! So he can escape again?! It didn't take very long the first time around!" I shouted.

"I have protocols to follow!" He snapped.

"He almost *raped* me! Do you not understand that?!"

*"Yes, I do!"* He yelled. His voice echoed off the surrounding walls, shaking the glass on the windows. "I know what he was going to do, and

I'm grateful I got there before it happened! I never wanted that to happen Lily!" He slammed his hands on his desk, cracking the wood.

Tears sprang to my eyes, but not out of fear at his outburst. These were tears of anger, tears of hatred. Hatred for James. I stood and looked Dimitri in the eye.

"Find him. Because if he finds me first, I won't hesitate this time. I'll kill him." I told him coldly. I watched the colour drain from his face as he took in my words. Without another word, I exited his office and made my way through the packhouse. I had a destination in mind, and I tried not to think too much as I walked there. When I arrived at the dungeons, I didn't hesitate, just walked through the door and up to a man I assumed to be a guard.

"Hi. I'm Lily, and I want to look around the cell that James was in." I said.

The man gave me a sour look. "Nobody goes in without permission from the Alpha. Run along now."

"I don't need permission from the Alpha, because I'm the Luna. I have the same level of clearance he does." I snapped.

His eyes widened as he looked me over. "My apologies Luna. I didn't realize-"

"I don't care. Just show me where I'm going."

Pulling out a ring with at least a dozen keys, he led me to a metal door. He scanned his fingerprint and a ding went off, the door sliding open.

"How the hell did he escape if this place is locked down with that kind of security?" I asked.

"We don't know. We think maybe a guard helped him. Other than us who work here, only the Gamma, Beta and Alpha can open the doors."

My lips squeezed into a thin line as I considered his words. "Are any of the guards missing today?"

"Warriors are checking on that now Luna."

"Good."

We took a left and after opening a second door, descended a flight of stairs. The air was considerably colder down here, and the *smell*. Ugh! I followed the guard as I desperately tried not to gag. We passed a few prisoners as we walked, and the looks they gave me made me want to shrink into the nearest wall. It was obvious most of them were rogues, and a few had the audacity to call out lude comments to me.

"Pipe down! Or you'll not be getting any meals for a week!" Snarled the guard.

We continued on for several minutes more until we came to a dark, dank cell that was basically a hole in the wall with bars. Dimitri had said to put James in the smallest cell, and they weren't kidding.

"This is it."

*"Aya?"*

*"On it."*

I let my wolf come forward, sharpening my senses. It made the smell of the dungeon so much worse, but I'd live. Looking through Aya's eyes, I could see that the cell looked totally normal. Small, dirty, but normal. No bars were bent or broken. I caught a faint whiff of James scent, hours old. I walked a few feet away, but his scent didn't linger. It was secluded to his cell. How was that possible?

"Did you interrogate the other prisoners here?" I asked.

"No point. Not like any of them would tell us the truth."

"Did anyone see this prisoner escape last night?" I called down the corridor. Silence.

*"He's right you know. They won't talk."* Aya said.

"Nobody saw anything? Really? Or are you pissed off that he didn't take you with him?" I called.

I walked to one of the cells and peered inside to see an older woman. Her clothes were torn and she was skin and bone. Her hair was matted and her skin was covered with dirt. Regardless, she met my gaze with cold blue eyes.

Kneeling down, I said, "Or maybe you're not talking because you think he's going to come back for you? Maybe he made you some sort of promise of freedom in exchange for your silence?"

The woman lunged for me through the bars and I quickly jumped back. She spit on the ground in front of me.

"Nobody saw nothing! Nobody promised us nothing! We saw the boy come in, kicking and screaming we did, and just like that, he was gone. Talking to himself 'till he up and vanished in the wind." She growled.

"That's not possible." I said.

"No Oliver 'till three. He was gone before then."

I looked at the guard.

"Oliver was on night duty. He checked on James as midnight, and he was still here. Next check, he was gone." He explained.

I turned back to the woman. "What was James talking about? You said he was talking to himself, what did he say?"

"Nothing important, nope."

"It might be, so tell me."

She started pacing the cell, scratching her arms. "Luna this, Luna that. Mad, mad, mad he was. At Luna. At Alpha. Shouldn't have taken his time, he said, yup." She nodded to herself and cringed. "Olly gave him wolfsbane. Screaming, lots of screaming. Then crying. Luna this, Luna that. Gideon. Alpha would pay." She finished.

"Wait, Gideon? Who is Gideon?" I asked her.

She shrugged. "Don't know, don't care. Next time Olly come down, boy was gone and I had to shit."

Lovely. Trying not to make a face, I stepped towards her cell.

"What's your name?"

She stopped pacing and looked at me, the same cold look from earlier. "Margie."

"Well, thank you Margie. You might have really helped me." I said sincerely.

She blinked at me, but didn't reply. I took that as my cue to leave, and I did as fast I could. The smell was really getting to me; I'd definitely have to change my clothes. On our way up out of the cells, we ran into Ben and another man.

"Hey, what are you doing here?" Ben asked.

"Getting information." I said.

"But... that's my job." He said slowly.

"Well, look at this way. Now you don't have to go down there and deal with the smell."

"Thank Goddess for that." He muttered as he fell into step with me. "Did you find anything?"

I relayed everything Margie had told me, and what I'd found of James cell.

"Hmm. So, she says he just disappeared? Just like that?" Ben asked.

"Apparently."

"Who is Gideon?"

"You're asking me? I don't have any idea Ben. I'm just telling you what she told me." I huffed.

"Okay, okay calm down. I'll look into it."

"And you're sure that nothing in there was touched?" The other man asked me. I shook my head.

"It was still locked."

His brow furrowed and he looked away.

"This is Luke by the way. He's the Gamma." Ben said.

"Oh. Nice to meet you Gamma."

"Just Luke. Sorry, I have to go." He said quickly and then he was running out of sight. Okay.

"Sorry. Seems like he thought of something though. He always does that shit when he has an idea. Probably going to the library." Ben explained. He shook his head before turning to me. "I take it you're feeling better today, since your here playing detective."

"I'm not *playing* anything Ben. It's been less than twenty four hours, and that disgraceful excuse for a wolf somehow escaped and is more than likely plotting someway to hurt me or my mate. I wanted answers, and I wanted them sooner rather later."

Ben held his hands up as if in surrender. "Alright, sorry. You're pissed I know. I heard."

I gave him a questioning look.

"I uh, heard about your 'talk' with Dimitri this morning."

"Oh."

He pursed his lips, clearly debating on whether to continue.

"Just spit it out Ben." I said.

"Alright. You could have given him a break, you know. As soon as he heard what happened, he was the first one here, the first one to question the guards. *And* he went out personally and looked for James himself. He went all night looking for the little shit, he just got back before he went to find you at breakfast. You didn't need to be so hard on him."

His scolding took me off guard. It was the first time I'd heard someone defend Dimitri in such a way, probably ever.

"He didn't tell me that." I said.

"You didn't give him a chance to." Ben sighed. "Look, Dimitri is my best friend. I know he's rough around the edges, and he's an asshole. I know he hasn't treated you right since you've been here, but the guy is... well, he has shit he's working through too. Stuff you don't know about."

"Like what?"

"Not for me to say. He's your mate, not me. He'll tell you when he's ready, but you both need to stop fighting each other. Give him a chance, an honest chance."

I bit my lip. "I don't know Ben."

He groaned loudly. "Goddess, why are you both so stubborn?! You really are perfect for each other."

Punching him in the arm, I said "Shut up."

"Just think about it Lily. Okay? He's not a bad guy. He's just...lost."

That was close to was Celeste had said. It threw my argument off, leaving me stumped for a reply.

"I have other things to think about right now Ben."

"I hate to say this, but it's unlikely we'll find James soon. And it would be a lot easier to do all our jobs without our Luna and Alpha constantly being at each others throats."

"So my love life affects your ability to do your job?"

"Yes! Yes, it does!"

I laughed which earned me a glare. "Go away and let me work. Brat."

"Okay Benji." I snickered.

"*Go!*"

# CHAPTER 23

DIMITRIS POV

Ben had given me all the information Lily got. I was impressed that she'd gotten one of our prisoners to talk so easily. Goddess knew, none of them talked to us, not unless there was some sort of pain infliction involved. More impressive was her ambition to go and find answers for herself. I didn't expect it of her, and I never would have asked her to go to that place. The dungeon was specifically designed to be cruel, depressing. A place people were scared to end up in, motivation to not fuck up badly enough to end up there.

And Lily had gotten some valuable information too. Luke was looking into the possibility of witches being involved, consistently holed up in the library these days. If the rogue was right and James had just vanished, it was a safe bet to say we were on the right track. As it was though, there were no signs of James or any accomplice. All of the guard's whereabouts had been accounted for the night of, and none of the warriors reported anyone crossing our borders. It had been three weeks since the little shit disappeared and it was eating away at me more and more every day. I needed answers, and was coming up empty.

A pack-wide announcement was made announcing James's escape, and I was doing my best to not let panic spread. At first, it had been hard; of course people were frightened. In an attempt to ease minds and worries, I tripled all security detail. I'd also given the warriors double pay for the extra shifts. It was only fair, and my efforts seemed to work. Life seemingly returned to normal around the pack. The exception was Lily; Though she wasn't hiding in her room, I caught her looking over her shoulder a lot. She trained, worked with Thara at the hospital, made time for Greta and Hazel. But she was anxious, nervous.

I'd taken to watching in on her training, not that she knew it. She was getting better, but nowhere near where she could be. I accepted that I needed to know she was able to handle herself. If I had that security, I could sleep easier. So, for the last several days, an idea had taken shape in my mind, one I didn't really think she would go for. But I was going to try nonetheless. That idea is what brought me here, standing off to the side of the training yard, watching her spare with Clint. As I watched them, I had to admit- he was a good fighter. Even I could tell he was taking it easy on Lily, trying not to use his full strength. I'd noticed this a lot, and I also knew that it wasn't helping her.

I cleared my throat loudly, smirking when Clint was distracted and Lily landed a punch to his jaw.

"Oops! I'm sorry!" She exclaimed.

Apologizing? That was another problem.

"Alpha." Clint nodded to me respectfully.

"A word you two?" I asked.

"Sure. What's up?" Lily replied.

She was covered in sweat, little pieces of her hair framing her face. I couldn't help but glance down at her cleavage as she breathed hard from the exertion. My pants were starting to become tight, so I quickly moved my thoughts in a safer direction.

"You two will no longer be training together." I stated.

"What?!"

"Why?"

"You can't stop me from training!" Lily raged.

"You're still going to be training. Just not with him. You'll be training with me from now on."

She blinked at me, her jaw dropping. "Uhm, no."

"Uhm, yes. Starting tomorrow."

"Why? Clint is just as qualified to teach me." She argued.

"He's a good warrior." I turned to him. "I've been watching you two for a while. You go easy on her. You don't give it your best with her, like you do with the men. You're afraid to hurt her. But an enemy isn't. She needs to learn what it's like to fight for her life, and you aren't teaching her that."

"Now wait just a min-"

"No, he's right Lily." Clint interrupted. "I haven't been teaching you properly. I taught you the basics, I got your endurance up. And that's great. But I don't actually want to hurt you. I don't fight you like I do with the other warriors. It's different with you, and I think it's because you're my friend. I don't want to hurt you."

"But Clint-"

"It's fine Lily. We can still do laps and stuff, yeah? But I agree with the Alpha. He has more experience anyways." He glanced sideways at me and I nodded.

"It's settled then. Meet me here tomorrow, same time. See you then."

Lily grabbed my arm, and sparks erupted.

"Clint, can you give us a minute?" She asked.

"Sure. See you." I watched him jog off and then it was just us. She let go of my arm and crossed hers over her chest, effectively pushing her breasts up. She was in a black sports bra and shorts, and the images that ran through my mind looking at her were far from innocent.

"Why does it have to be you? Why can't it be Ben, or Luke?"

"Because I have the most experience."

She scoffed. "I'm sure they have just as much as you."

"Close, yes, but I'm still the best."

"Cocky much?"

I quickly stepped towards her, catching her off guard. In one swift move, I placed my foot behind hers, causing her to lose her balance as she moved. Before she hit the ground, I caught her with one hand around her waist and one wrapped under her neck.

"I'm the fastest. The most lethal. The best. There is a reason I'm the Alpha. So yeah, I have good reason to be cocky." I smirked.

"Not in wolf form." She matched my tone.

I almost smiled. "Maybe not. You have me outmatched there."

"I'll train with you, but on one condition."

I was inches away from her face, and the sparks from our contact were only making me want her more. These were foreign feelings, but if I was going to train with her, I had to learn to control myself.

"What's that?"

"We go for a run tonight."

Ajax whooped in my head. "Deal." I said.

Lily smiled, and my heart throbbed. Did I just make her smile? I gazed at her face, all lit up like I'd just given her the best birthday present. It made me feel... happy? Was that what this was? When was the last time I felt happy?

"Dimitri?"

"Huh?"

"Uh, can you let me go now please?"

Helping her right herself, I took a step back, trying to catch my breath. I wanted to see her smile again.

"So... after dinner? Seven o' clock?"

"Yeah."

She smiled again, and the happiness washed through me.

"See you then."

I watched her walk towards the packhouse, my thoughts in a jumble.

*"Thank you. For saying yes."* Ajax said to me.

*"You miss her, don't you?"* I asked.

*"Of course I do. Aya is my other half, just like Lily is yours."*

*"I'll let you get together more."*

*"Whoa. Wait. You're going to do something nice? Even for me?"*

*"Shut up."*

I didn't want to admit it, but letting our wolves spend time together also allowed us to. And I found I was wanting to spend more time with Lily. As I walked to the packhouse, I tried to bring back the happiness she'd given me a few moments ago. It was unlike me, *wanting* to feel something, and I hadn't realized until now how much I missed feeling happy. Carefree. I had become so use to being angry at everything. Anger was an emotion I could deal with, live with. I'd found out first hand that the things that made one happy could so easily destroy them. Yet, here I was, thinking of different ways to bring Lilys smile back just so I could feel it again.

"What's got you in such a good mood?"

I looked up to see Luke walking towards me.

"What do you mean?"

"You're smiling like an idiot."

I was? Huh.

"Nothing. Just thinking. What's up?" I asked him. He fell into step beside me.

"I think I found something."

"Go on."

"I was digging through our volumes on different spells, specifically transportation spells, and I have an idea on how James escaped. I just don't know the motivation behind it."

"Show me."

I mind linked Ben to meet in my office. Luke ran to the library to get whatever book he'd found. Once we were all assembled, I led us into my office, sitting on the sofa. Lily liked to sit here, though I didn't know why. I'd bought it mostly for decoration, it wasn't even very comfortable. Maybe I'd look into a different one.

"Hey!" Ben snapped his fingers in front of me.

"Don't do that." I scowled.

"Where are you today?" Luke asked.

"Nowhere. Here." They glanced at each other. "Can we get on with it please?"

"Whatever." Luke muttered. He plopped a thick and very dusty book onto my desk, a cloud erupting from the impact. He flipped to a mark page in the back, running his finger over the script as he read. "This says that there are three different types of transportation spells. They all do the same thing, but I guess they're for different levels of witches?"

"Okay." I leaned forward, focusing.

"So, the first one you need to be close to the person your spelling, and whole bunch of ingredients. That's unlikely, since nobody was seen coming or going from the pack. This next one is less complicated, it can be done from a distance, but you need either hair or blood from the person. Possible, but still unlikely."

"And the last one?" Ben asked before I could.

"The last one doesn't need ingredients *and* it can be done from anywhere. *But* it can only be performed by really powerful witches."

"How powerful?" I asked.

"Super powerful. We're talking Clan Elder powerful."

"Shit."

"That's what I thought."

"But what would a Clan Elder want with James? He's a great warrior, but it would make more sense to take one of us, right?" I speculated.

"I thought that too. But then I thought, it *would* make sense to take someone who held a grudge. I'm thinking whoever this is doesn't want you Dimitri, but they want you dead. Everyone else in the dungeon is a rogue. James is a pack member. Who better to give them all the information they want?"

"I think he's right." Ben admitted.

Sadly, I thought so too.

# CHAPTER 24

Luke, Ben and I sat in my office going over every possible reason, theory and hypothesis as to why a Clan Elder would want me dead. The room was now full of books that Luke had carried down from the library, and we each had our own stack to go through, looking for any other vital information. I myself was trying to remember a time where I might have come into contact with a witch, a Clan, anything. I never had. It didn't make sense, not to me anyways. Wolves and witches were enemies, we had been for centuries. According to the book I was reading now the last time the two groups had anything major to do with one another was in the mid eighteenth century, when an uneasy truce had been made; both sides keep to themselves and cease any unnecessary bloodshed.

I was so absorbed that I totally lost track of time, missing dinner. It wasn't until Lily knocked on the office door and Ben let her in that I remembered we had plans.

"If you're busy, we can do this another time." She said as she took in the mess of books and papers lying around.

"No, no. It'll be here when I get back. Let's go." I stood and nodded to my Beta and Gamma.

"Make good choices!" Ben called out after us and I shot him the finger. Lily blushed a deep scarlet before hiding her face.

"So... same place?" She asked quietly.

"Sure."

We walked in silence together, not sure what to say. I had lots I *wanted* to say, but our relationship was unsteady right now. Another fact, I still wasn't sure if I wanted this girl the way a mate should. I was attracted to her, insanely. She was beautiful. Anyone with eyes could see it. It was just too easy to continue with my ways and hold her at a distance.

*"It didn't seem like it this morning."* Ajax snickered.

*"You're not helping, you know."*

*"I am, you just don't know it yet. You want her, you just don't know how to let her in."*

"What makes you such an expert?"

*"Really? My mate loves me. Your mate tolerates you. Just because I'm a beast doesn't mean I don't know how to love. I share things with her, communicate with her. Traits you undoubtedly are lacking in."*

*"So, what do you want me to do? Candle light dinner and star gazing?"* I scoffed. Lily glanced sideways at me but didn't comment.

*"How about asking her a question first dummy. Like, her interests or favourite books or something."*

I pondered his words for a few moments. Maybe I could try...

"Books." I said stupidly.

"What?" Lily gave me a confused look.

"Uh, I mean, you like books?"

She raised an eyebrow but thankfully answered. "Yes..."

"Good. That's uh, good."

"Okay?"

*"Wow."* Ajax was rolling around in my head in complete hysterics.

*"I tried, okay?"*

*"yup. Yup, you did!"*

I growled lightly and Lily came to a stop.

"Ready?" She asked. I looked around; we weren't in the clearing like last time, but still far enough away. I nodded and she walked away behind a tree. Taking the opportunity, I stripped out of my clothes and quickly shifted. Shaking out my fur, I waited for Lily to return. When she did, my breath caught in my throat. I hadn't forgotten what she looked like of course, but it was something else to see it in front of you. She was stunning.

*"Thank you for this."*

I heard a voice in my head that didn't belong to Lily. So this was her wolf?

*"Aya, right?"*

*"Yes."*

*"You don't need to thank me. Ajax wanted to see you too."*

*"Still. Lily is grateful too."*

*"Uh, great. I'm going to give control over to Ajax. Have fun guys."*

I did as I said, and off they went. Mostly I ignored what was going on, letting our wolves have time together more in less in private. Together they played, ran and hunted. Ajax was pouting that he didn't have the biggest kill when they took down a herd of passing deer; After all he was an Alpha. When Aya suggested they hunt something more his speed, such as rabbits, I earned myself a growl for laughing so hard. She was as snarky and had just as much attitude as Lily.

It was after midnight when our wolves decided to give back control, giving each other a fond farewell. The love pouring through the bond between them made me anxious. Also, a bit jealous. I was happy to let Ajax spend time with his mate, though I couldn't spend time with mine the same way. I tried to keep my thoughts to myself because I knew Ajax would blame me for that outcome. Walking to our clothes, we shifted and dressed. Lily was smiling when she emerged from the trees, and I was overcome with emotion.

"That was fun. Thank you so much." She grinned at me.

"Yeah. No problem."

Her smile faltered and I wanted to smack myself. Clearing her throat, her eyes wandered around the forest.

"So I was thinking..."

"Yes?"

"Uhm, we should probably make me an official member soon. Aya can mind link you, when in wolf form, but I can't at all." She studiously ignored my gaze as she talked.

The scene with James flashed in my mind. How different would that have played out if she had been able to mind link someone for help? Even if it wasn't me, someone would have gotten to her.

"That sounds like a good idea. I'll arrange it."

"Okay. Thanks."

I nodded. Silence fell.

"Well... I'll see you tomorrow." I said awkwardly.

"Kay."

"Goodnight Lily."

Her eyes met mine. "Goodnight."

Forcing myself to turn and walk away went against my other instincts. I wanted to walk with her back home, make sure she got there safely. Still, I left her standing behind me, a thoughtful look on her face. It made me wonder *what* she was thinking about, and if it was about me. Was it bad or good? Sneaking a peek over my shoulder, I was disappointed to see her walking away, taking a different route back to the house.

I broke from the tree line, decidedly in a bad mood. Too many thoughts and unfamiliar feelings were washing through me. So it came as no surprise that my mood worsened considerably when I bumped into Jennine. Literally, into the back of her.

"Oh Dimitri! There you are!" She gushed.

"What are you doing out here Jennine?" It was almost one in the morning.

"Oh, you know me. I'm a night owl. I couldn't sleep, so I went for a run." Her eyes sparked with anger.

"Good for you." I attempted to step around her, but she blocked my path.

"Can we talk for a minute?"

"Nope."

I sidestepped but she blocked me again. This bitch was testing my patience.

"Move. Now." I growled.

Placing her hand on her hips, she gave me a cold glare. "I just want to know, for certain, that it's really over between us."

I blinked. Was she for real? I'd slammed her head against a wall and yelled at her. How much more clear could I be on the subject?

"There was nothing *between* us. Like I said before, I needed to get laid, and you were easy. End of story. There was no real relationship Jennine."

"Well, if there was nothing between us then, maybe there can be now." She purred. Her hands moved up my arms and landed on my shoulders. Pressing her body into mine, she batted her fake eyelashes at me; the urge to throw her off, preferably into a tree, was almost overwhelming. As it was, I did remove her hands and gave her a light shove away from me.

"Don't touch me."

"This is ridiculous Dimitri! I know you- you never even wanted a mate! But apparently, that changed just because she's some super wolf?"

My head snapped up. "Were you following us?"

"No. I just happened to come across you and your *mate*. That's why you left me? She might have some powerful wolf Dimitri, but she is not Luna material. She's nothing but a worthless piece of shi-"

*"Enough!"* I snarled. My Alpha voice came out and Jennine's eyes widened in fear. Closing the distance between us, I towered over her. "I told you before, you will not disrespect her like this. Whatever ideas you have about you and I are not up for debate. There is *nothing* between us, there is never *going* to be anything between us. I don't want you, I don't love you. I wouldn't choose you, even if Lily hadn't come into the picture. As for what you classify as 'Luna material', take a good long look in the mirror Jennine, because it's not you. Make me repeat myself again, and you won't like what happens. Do I make myself clear?"

She nodded mutely and I finally stepped around and stormed away. How could one person be so dense?

# CHAPTER 25

**JENNINES POV**

Watching Dimitri walk away from me was infuriating. How could he be so stupid! Lily was clearly manipulating him. And what he said about not loving me... did that mean he loved her? No, no way. It hate to be the mate bond. It was clouding his judgement, making him feel things that weren't really there. He was living in a fantasy world.

I wanted to scream and rage, but I was taught better than that. I *was* better than that. Like mother always told me, 'Hide your true feelings, and play the game smarter than your opponent. You will always win with a poker face.' So that's what I did. The problem was, Dimitri was just as smart as me, maybe smarter. He wasn't Alpha for no reason. But fuck all, he was ruining everything! Everything I'd worked for, everything I'd schemed for.

When we first met, he was seeing some lowlife hippie chick, Giselle. Sure, she wasn't a troll, but she wasn't *me*. And I needed it to be me at his side. So, a few bottles of tequila and some light nudging later, Dimitri had conveniently walked in on her fucking another guy. In his office too, the cherry on top of the cake. As far as I knew, nowadays Giselle hardly showed her face in the pack, always holed up at home. Good riddance. And just like Giselle, I'd gotten rid of a lot of women over the years before he finally noticed me. Each time we saw each other, I gave it my all. I laughed at his jokes, flirted with him, made sure to look my absolute best. When we started sleeping together, I was sure it wouldn't be long before he made me Luna of the pack. I was better, stronger, more qualified than anyone else to lead Blood Moon at his side.

My parents were overjoyed, of course; Me being Luna opened up a whole new world for them. They would no longer be middle class citizens here, no, people would have to start showing our family the respect we deserved. My relationship with Dimitri was the longest he'd ever had. Every pack gathering, my father would drop subtle hint after hint about how our pack needed their Luna. How it would make us stronger, the absolute best.

I truly believed Dimitri was close to making it official with me, to giving me everything I wanted.

Then he went to Snow Moon. He came back different. I greeted him just like usual, but he'd brushed me off. It lasted for several days, and then out of nowhere, he brings his new *wife* and *Luna* home! I was horrified, though not as much as my parents.

"It's not over yet. So he has a mate, so what? He clearly prefers you. Look at her! She's nothing compared to you!" My mother had vented.

"Bring him back Jennine. Wile him, use all the tools at your advantage. We need you to be in her place, and soon. Don't hold back, and don't fuck this up." My father had said.

Groaning, I threw my hands up. It hadn't been such a hard task until now. Who the fuck could have predicted that Lily would turn out to be a Mother Wolf? They weren't even supposed to exist! How glad I was that I'd found out sooner rather later; the original plan was to wait until Lily was made Luna, officially, then challenge her for the Luna position. By law, Dimitri would have no choice but to accept me then. Now, that couldn't happen. I had no chance, none whatsoever, against a Mother Wolf.

Pacing in a circle, my mind turned out idea after idea on how to get rid of the bitch. There had to be some way I could use this to my advantage. I replayed every story I'd ever heard about Lilys wolf, analyzing every aspect, every version. Mother Wolves were supposed to be all powerful, huge, and beautiful.

Suddenly, my feet came to a standstill and a smile started to spread across my face.

*"A tiny village lie on the coast, ripe with cloths of gold and food for trade. It was a prosperous place, filled with child's laughter and music by night. Until one day, the skies grew cloudy. Thunder shook the homes of the happy villagers. Over the hill, beyond the forest lay a Mother Wolf, greedy for riches and thirsty for blood!"* My mothers voice rang in my head with the memory.

*"What did she do mama?"* I'd asked timidly.

*"Dear, she tore through the village and shed innocent blood. The white coat that shone so beautifully was stained in the lives she took that day, her mouth full of the cloth of gold and belly full of the food she stole. Music played no more, and children's voices were silenced forever. This is what happens when the*

*Mother Wolf comes. The wealthiest and kindest are slaughtered out of greed. A Mother Wolf cannot be tamed, and we pray everyday the Moon Goddess does not send one to us."*

Now I knew such stories were told to keep kids from behaving badly. If we acted out, our parents would threaten to send the Mother Wolf on us. They were dangerous, uncontrollable. And it was just the type of fear I needed to get rid of Lily. I'd have to plan it carefully though, no mistakes. I could not afford for this to go wrong- it could cost me everything.

Making sure I was alone, I stripped down and shifted into my wolf, Nia. She was a unique blend of black and white, and strong. She was born to be a Luna, a leader. Gingerly picking up my clothes in my teeth, I took off to the west end of the pack, cutting through yards and skimming through the trees.

*"Connor. You awake?"* I sent out a mind link.

*"Sort of. What do you want?"* Was his groggy reply.

*"I'm on my way over."*

This news perked him up. *"Oh yeah? Doors open. Don't bother getting dressed."*

I rolled my eyes. Connor was handsome, but he was no Dimitri. He was a means to an end, that was all. Still, I used my best flirting tone, *"Of course not."*

When I reached his house, I shifted back, quickly making my way inside. Connors scent was heavy with arousal as I made my way to his room.

"Hey babe."

He was lying on his bed, naked. The sight of his hard cock had me clenching my thighs together. As a warrior, Connor was fit and toned in all the right places. And he knew just what I liked. It was a shame he was naive, it made using him like this too easy.

"Hey."

"Well? Come here. It's been ages since you came over."

I laughed as I crawled on the bed, sitting on his legs. "You can't blame me. It was a little tense last time I came over, remember?" I ran my hand down his abs as I spoke. "Where is Silvia, by the way?"

"At her parents still." He rolled his eyes. "Says she can't forgive me yet."

I pouted. "You want her forgiveness? I thought you enjoyed my company more."

"Well, I kind of need it. You have no idea how annoying this shit is. Every time she cries, I feel it. It distracts me from training."

"Oh, your poor mate." I snickered. "Maybe you should go make it up to her."

"I can think of something I'd like to do more, right here, right now."

"And poor Silvia won't walk in on us again?"

"Babe, I couldn't care less if she did. Maybe she'd see what a real woman does to please her man."

I smirked. "Like this?" I grabbed his dick and started stroking him. His eyes became hooded with lust, his breathing deepening.

"Yeah like that."

Slowly, I bent down and licked his tip. He hissed at the contact before I took him in my mouth. I stroked him while I bobbed my head up and down, rolling my tongue around his sensitive spots.

"Enough." He said. Grabbing my hair, Connor yanked my head up. The next moment, I was on my hands and knees with him behind me. He entered me roughly, grabbing my hips.

"Oh baby." I moaned.

"Best fucking pussy around." He grunted.

It so fucking good, I hated to stop it. But I needed him at my whim if I wanted his cooperation. So I pulled away, much to his disappointment. Pushing him back, I climbed onto his lap and sank onto his dick. His eyes rolled back and a smiled.

"Fuck, you feel so good." He sighed.

"Yeah? How good?"

"Better than anything I've felt."

Leaning down to his ear, I softly bit on the mark left by his mate. Connor tensed, his grip on me tightening.

"Jennine-"

"Don't you wish it was *my* mark there?" I asked softly.

"What?"

"Nothing. Never mind." I ducked my head, pretending to be embarrassed.

"No, look at me. What did you say?"

I peeked at him through my lashes. "It's just... I know she's your mate Connor but... I mean, we could be so happy together, you know?"

He gaped at me, shocked.

"Like I said, never mind." I started moving my hips, grinding against him slowly. I could see the wheels turning in his head, thinking my words through.

"How?" He asked suddenly.

"How what?"

"How would that work? You want me to reject her?"

I feigned surprise. "Would you do that? *Could* you do that?"

He thought about it for a minute. "Yeah I... I think I could. For you."

I smiled widely. "Really?"

He slammed into me, making me gasp. "Yes. I'll do it tomorrow. And I want you here tomorrow night. I want to experience what its like to be with you, without being held back by this stupid bond."

"O-okay."

I couldn't believe how easy my plan had worked. How quickly he agreed to reject his fated me for me. It was only going to get easier from here.

*Watch your back Lily. You have no idea what's in store for you.*

# CHAPTER 26

**LILYS POV**

I was nervous as fuck. Juggling my water bottle between my hands, I waited for Dimitri to join me in the training yard. I'm not proud to admit it, but I took more time this morning picking out an outfit and fixing my hair than I ever did. I'd settled on a high ponytail and a green sports bra and black leggings. I felt way too exposed, but I couldn't train in a t-shirt and jeans, could I? I'd been waiting twenty minutes, glancing in the direction of the packhouse every few seconds. I had no idea what training with Dimitri was going to be like, but I was positive it would be much different than training with Clint.

"Hey."

A loud, echoing scream left my lips and I spun around. Dimitri held up his hands and took a step back.

"Calm down, it's me!"

My hand was placed over my chest, my heart beating rapidly.

"Where the fuck did you come from?!"

He pointed to the forest on the other side of the yard.

"Why?!" I gasped.

"Huh?"

"You were supposed to come from there!" I pointed towards the packhouse.

A look of amusement crossed his face. "I go for a run every morning. It's not a big deal."

"You scared the shit out of me!"

"Sorry." He smirked. "Ready to start?"

My heartbeat picked up double time.

"Uh, sure?"

"You don't sound sure."

I rolled my eyes. "Just start."

"Fine. Fifty laps to start, let's go."

He took off towards the track and I followed. He seemed impressed as we ran, probably because he knew I could barely walk the stairs when I first came here.

"That was good." He said when we finished. I gave him a thumbs up as I chugged my water. Wiping my mouth I asked, "What's next?"

"Sparing."

My jaw dropped. "With you?"

"Yes. What did you think we'd be doing?"

"But... I can't spar with you!"

"Why not?"

I waved my hand up and down his body, giving him a "Duh" look.

"You can't spar with me because I'm...hot?"

My cheeks flushed and I gave him a dirty look. He returned it with an innocent one.

"No jackass. I can't because you're going to kill me. I thought you were going to teach me how to fight, well... not by fighting you!"

"How else are you going to learn?"

"Dimitri, you're at least a hundred and fifty pounds of muscle heavier than I am. I won't be standing after one hit. How am I going to learn anything if I end up in the hospital?" I demanded.

His expression softened. "I would never hurt you like that Lily."

"But you told Clint-"

"I know. I won't go easy on you, but you don't need to be afraid either. I won't hurt you."

I searched his eyes, looking for any hint that he was lying. He seemed sincere though, which eased some of my worry.

"Okay?" He said.

"Okay."

"Come on."

He led me to one of the mats laid out on the yard and ran me through the basics. Most of it I'd already learned, though he did give me some pointers on my stance and positioning. When he took the side opposite me, I gulped. You couldn't even blame me, he was a very intimidating opponent. Taking a fighting stance, I nodded at him. The next thing I knew,

I was on my back on the ground, my breath whooshing out at the impact. What the hell?

"Whoa." I croaked.

"Sorry. You good?"

I took his offered hand, ignoring the sparks. Once my breathing regulated, I groaned.

"Yup. I quit." I sighed.

"Quitting will get you nowhere." Dimitri replied.

"Say that when you have to fight you."

He chuckled, the sound foreign to my ears. Had he ever laughed with me before?

"You just need to focus. You're tense, nervous. You have advantages, you just need to know how to utilize them."

"The only advantage I have is being a huge wolf. Shifting isn't always possible."

"That's not the only thing you have going for you. You're a small human."

He said that like it was a good thing. "How is that an advantage?" I asked.

"There's a warrior here, Karla. She stands around four foot nothing. You know why she's one of my best?"

I shook my head.

"Because nobody can get their hands on her. I've seen that woman duck under grown men's legs."

"Huh. I didn't know you had female warriors."

"I don't have a lot, but the ones I do have more than earned their place in the ranks."

"Can I train with them?" I asked eagerly.

He rubbed his chin, thinking it over. "I'll ask Karla to join us a few times a week. But your main partner is going to be me. Now, get ready."

I groaned again, but got in position. This time, I managed to dodge his first attack, but he had me pinned a minute later. We kept at it until I begged for a water break. Every part of me was sore, and I deeply regretted not taking a firmer stand against this idea of his.

*"You're doing really good."* Aya cheered for me.

*"You're not the one out here."*

*"No, but I think I have an idea that might help. Well, it was Ajax's idea."*

*"Do tell."*

*"Are you forgetting we're a werewolf?"*

I frowned, confused. How could I forget that? It was the only reason I'd been able to make it this long against Dimitri. Finally, what she was saying clicked, and I grinned.

*"Tell Ajax I owe him one."*

"Breaks over!" Dimitri called.

Setting my water down, I joined him on the mat. While he took his position, I focused on my wolf, letting her come forward. My senses sharpened, my muscles tightening. I waited and focused on Dimitri, analyzing his moves. His left foot cocked backward, and my instincts told me he was getting ready to charge. A second later, I twisted out of his way, sending my elbow into his side. I sent a sharp kick to the back of his knee, satisfied when his leg buckled.

He was up in no time, grabbing for my arm. Twisting it behind me, he tried to lock me in a chokehold. I ducked at the last second, aiming a kick to his stomach which he blocked. Using his grasp on my arm, I yanked him towards me, catching him off guard and causing him to lose his grip. Sidestepping, I twisted my body behind his, readying a punch. Just blocking it, he brought my arms to my sides, holding them there. We were both breathing hard, bodies flushed against one another. Dimitri gazed at me with admiration, surprise, and something I couldn't identify.

*"That was excellent Lily!"* Aya yipped.

"Where the hell did that come from?" Dimitri asked at the same time.

I shrugged. "You told me to focus. Aya helped me focus."

"You used your wolf?"

"Is that not allowed?"

His hands slid down my arms, coming to rest lightly behind my back. "No, it's great. It helps a lot actually. Clears the mind, helps you see things more clearly. Great job."

I smiled hugely. When he returned it, my heart burst into sprint. It was the first time he'd smiled at me without any hint of sarcasm or underlying anger. He was gorgeous.

Forcing myself to stop staring at him like an idiot, I asked, "Are we done for today?"

He didn't answer, forcing me to meet his eyes again.

"Dimitri?"

"Yeah. Yeah, we're done for today." He let me go, taking a few steps away.

"Alright. I'm uh, going to shower."

His eyes darkened and returned to normal so quickly, I was almost sure I'd imagined it.

"I'll find Karla, see if she can be here tomorrow."

"Great."

Why did all our conversations end so awkwardly? Giving him a wave, I turned and started walking home. I was all sorts of riled up, and I thought it had a lot to do with the amount of physical contact between Dimitri and I today. The sparks from our bond were very distracting at times. Still, I think I preferred training with him; I learned a lot, not that Clint wasn't a good teacher, but Dimitri was better. At least thanks to Clint, I hadn't started from scratch today. I'd have to thank him for that later.

All in all, I was proud of myself. I focused on that feeling, instead of the way it felt to have his arms around me. I liked it more than I was willing to admit, even to myself. For a second, I was sure he wanted to kiss me. The look in his eyes... would he, if I hadn't said anything? Did I want him to? And, more importantly, was I ready for that?

I looked over my shoulder, only to catch him staring at me intently. I blushed and looked away. Shoving my troubled thoughts aside, I focused on getting inside to a much needed hot shower.

# CHAPTER 27

"What's gotten into you?"

Hazel and I were having lunch at our usual table, but she'd barely eaten anything. Mostly, she was just moving the food around with her fork.

"I don't know. I just don't feel right." She frowned.

"Maybe we should go see Thara?" I suggested.

She shook her head.

"No, I don't feel sick. I just feel... not right."

"Too much cake last night?"

"Maybe."

Yesterday was Hazels birthday, and she finally got her wolf, Lupe. I'd never seen her so happy, and she spent most of the day getting to know her. I'd asked Greta to make her favourite carrot cake, and we'd had a small get together at her parents house. Thara had come along, but Clint had been a no-show. Extra training due to the double shifts put in place by Dimitri. Still, it had been fun, and she seemed fine yesterday.

"Is it hot in here?"

"Not really."

The woodsy scent hit my nose, and I looked up to see Dimitri entering the room. He nodded at a few people while making his way to get his food. Our eyes met, and I quickly looked down.

Our training sessions were becoming more and more difficult. I kept finding myself in compromising positions with him during our spar sessions, which did not help me to focus. This morning had been especially embarrassing. Karla, a cute blond with a wicked sense of humor, was trying to show me how to use Dimitris size against him. In my attempt to take him down, I'd somehow ended up on top of him, his hands grasping my waist. Karla had had to clear her throat three times before we remembered she was there. It didn't help that Karla teased me endlessly about it throughout training. Just thinking about it made my blush deepen.

127

Suddenly, I felt a hand on mine.

"Lily, I think I do need to go. Somethings wrong."

I was instantly on my feet. "Let's go."

Shakily, she stood and I guided her around the table. She was covered in sweat and trembling all over.

"Goddess, I think I'm going to be sick." Hazel moaned.

"Just stay here. I'll get Thara, and bring her back."

We'd made it only three feet before I made her sit down again. I looked around, hoping Thara was in the cafeteria. My eyes caught Dimitris instead; he was looking between me and Hazel, clearly wondering what was going on. I didn't have time to explain it to him though. Reassuring Hazel once more, I rushed through the room and nearly collided with Clint at the doors.

"Oh good you're here. Can you stay with Hazel? I have to go find Thara." I said to him.

He didn't answer me, or even look at me. He was staring behind me, a look of pure wonder on his face.

"Clint?"

"Excuse me." He stepped around me, almost running. My eyes nearly dropped from their sockets when he pulled Hazel up from her seat and kissed her.

The whole room had gone quiet, and then erupted in loud clapping and cheers. It took me a second to realize that Hazel had found her mate-Clint. In hindsight, I should have known; I'd felt the same way before seeing Dimitri. A huge grin broke out on my face as I joined in the clapping. When they broke apart, both had equally big grins on their faces.

"My, what is all the ruckus?" Greta appeared beside me.

I pointed to my friends. "They're mates!"

"Oh my! How wonderful!" She nudged me lightly. "As you kids say nowadays, I totally called that." She laughed and I had to laugh too.

I glanced over at Dimitri. A small pang of jealousy resonated in my chest, but I pushed it aside. I was happy for my friends, even if my mate situation wasn't as easy as theirs.

Hazel and Clint made their way to me, still smiling goofily.

"Congrats guys. I'm so happy for you." I told them.

"Thanks Lily. We're a little surprised, but happy too." Hazel said.

"You two let me know when the wedding is, I'm making the cake." Greta winked and we laughed.

"We wouldn't get anyone else Greta." Said Clint and Hazel blushed adorably.

"I can't believe it! My two best friends are mates!" I exclaimed.

"Congratulations Clint, Hazel." Dimitris voice sounded beside us.

"Thank you Alpha." Clint replied. He tucked Hazel into his side and kissed her head.

"It's not often I actually get to witness my pack members finding their mates. It's really something to see the happiness on both your faces." He glanced at me.

"I had a feeling. I'm glad the Moon Goddess picked this one for me." Clint said and I internally aww'ed.

"Yes. Well, congratulations again." Dimitri offered them a small smile before leaving with his tray of food.

"He's not very good with expressing himself, is he?" Hazel asked as she looked after my mate.

"No, not really." I said.

"I'm sorry I had you worried."

I waved my hand. "You have no idea how relieved I am that it was *this* and not something worse."

They were both shifting awkwardly, and I laughed.

"For Goddess sakes guys, just go! You don't need to hang around here for me. Go do.... whatever it is you want to do with each other."

The look of relief they gave me made me laugh again. Holding hands, they practically ran out of the room. Yeah, I wasn't going to be seeing either of them for as while. Even I knew that newly found mates couldn't keep their hands off each other. It was nothing short of a miracle that I'd managed to keep myself in control this long. But again, my situation was different.

*"And it's not like you haven't fantasized about our mate almost every night."* Aya chimed in.

*"Oh shush."*

Leaving my food behind, I made my way to the stairs. I'd started a new book recently, and since my friends were busy, I might as well try to binge read. Unfortunately, I ran into my least favourite person on the way. I decided to ignore Jennine's existence, but I guess that just couldn't happen.

"You must be so happy for your friends *Luna*." She commented sarcastically. She was sitting on the stairs, clicking away on her phone.

"I am actually. Bye now."

"I guess Hazel gets a higher rank after all."

"Mhmm."

"And this time, she didn't have to lie and whore around for it."

I stopped on the third step, spinning to look down at her. "What is your *problem,* Jennine? Why do you have to be so hateful to everyone?"

"Who said I had a problem?"

"Your bitchy attitude was a major clue."

Jennine stood, taking a step up so we were eye level. I crossed my arms, showing her I wasn't intimidated.

"You have no idea how bitchy I can be." She sneered.

I rolled my eyes. "Am I supposed to be scared of you or something?"

"If you were smart, you would be."

"Wow. Did you get that from some lame villain in a movie?"

"Who's the real villain here? I'm a member of this pack, you're a lowly slave pretending to be a Luna. This pack will crumble with you at Dimitris side."

"Whatever." I turned away, she wasn't worth my time.

"If I were you, I'd watch my back." She said.

Looking over my shoulder at her I said, "Is that a threat?"

Jennine simply smiled, oddly reminding me of a gargoyle, and walked away. That girl had major issues.

# CHAPTER 28

**LILYS POV**

I'd finished my book hours ago and was now currently in the middle of the sequel. I'd never had time to read like this at Snow Moon, it felt great. A light breeze carried through the room from the open balcony doors, the curtains swaying gently. The scent of the forest breezed through the room, only enhancing my relaxation. Totally absorbed in a world full of dragons and adventure, I was rudely shocked out of my euphoria by a piercing, agonized shriek. Throwing my book to the floor, I was out of bed and racing to the double balcony doors. I stepped out and surveyed the area.

A group of people were gathered some distance away, forming a circle. It looked to be mostly men, maybe the warriors? Had there been an attack? Retreating inside, I ran through the house, yanking the door open and jumping down the steps. I had no idea what to do in these situations, but I was Luna; was it not part of my duty to the pack to try and help?

I felt a hand grasp my arm, pulling me to a stop.

"You don't want to go over there." It was Luke.

"Why? What happened? Is someone hurt?"

He nodded.

"Then I need to be there." I yanked my arm away and made my way to the group.

I vaguely recognized some of the warriors; they worked out in the gym a lot with Clint and I. I pushed my way through the tightly packed bodies, coming to stand in front of a scene that confused me. I'd been prepared for blood or a maimed body due to a rogue attack. At the very worst, a corpse. What I did not expect was to see a tiny brunette kneeling before a man, crying her heart and soul out. Was he hurting her? Why hadn't the warriors stepped in? Gazing around at their faces, it seemed nobody had any inclination to step in. Before I could demand that someone explain this to me, the man spoke to the woman on the ground.

"Accept it. I will not change my mind, it's better if you just accept it now."

"P-please....Connor..."

"No! Accept the rejection!" He growled.

My mouth flopped open in shock. He'd rejected her? And he'd done it in public too, as if the act wasn't already humiliating enough? A surge of anger burned through me and I instinctively stepped out of the crowd and towards the poor girl on the ground.

"That's enough!" I said.

"Who the hell are you?" The man, Connor, asked me. I straightened my shoulders and met his eyes.

"Lily. Luna Lily." I answered.

Connor rolled his eyes. "Hate to break it to you Luna, but you don't have the authority to stop a rejection."

"Perhaps not, but I *do* have the authority to tell you to take it elsewhere."

"All she has to do is accept it, and it'll be done." He looked down at his former mate. "But no, you have to make a big scene as usual, right Silvia?" He scoffed.

"Did you not hear me? I said that's enough! You have no right to embarrass this poor girl in front of so many people, your peers and fellow warriors at that. This could have been done privately. So it's you who wanted a show, not her." I spit.

Murmurs erupted in the crowd, a few people nodding in agreement.

Connor simply shrugged. His attitude was pissing me off more and more. I kneeled down beside Silvia, putting my hand on her shoulder. "Honey, you don't need someone like him, mate or not. I'm so sorry he did this to you, this way. I think it's best if you accept his rejection now. You can move on." I told her gently.

"How?" She whimpered.

"With my help. I'm your Luna, I'm here to help you, to care for you. And I will, I promise." It was the first time I'd announced myself as Luna so publicly, but I didn't shy away. It felt weird, still, but this girl needed me right now.

Silvia met my eyes and I nodded reassuringly. Her face was tear stained, but still pretty. Adorable brown eyes framed by long lashes and a light spread of freckles across her pale cheeks. She had an innocent, open face and my heart broke for her, for the fact that she had been mated to such a piece of garbage.

She turned to Connor, not really looking at him. "I, Silvia Thorne, Omega of the Blood Moon Pack, accept your rejection." She whispered.

She clutched her chest at same time Connor did. The aura surrounding them tensed, the air feeling thicker. And then it broke. Silvia released a long breath, wiping her eyes.

"Are you okay?" I asked.

She shook her head.

I helped her stand, then located two men I recognized. "You two. Take her to Dr. Varlos at the hospital. Tell her I sent you, and she's a top priority." They stepped forward and nodded.

"Right away Luna."

The crowd parted, letting them leave. From the corner of my eye, I saw Connor pushing his way through people.

"Not so fast!" I stopped him. "I'm not done with you."

"Excuse me?"

"You think your actions have no consequences?"

"I have the right to reject my mate, just like anyone else. You can't punish me for that."

"Not those actions. Doing it like this." I spread my hands, indicating the curious crowd. "What is your rank?"

"I don't have to answer to you!" He spit.

"Oh, yes you do." Luke came to stand beside me. "She is the Alphas mate, and your Luna. And she asked you a question."

"I'm a warrior." Connor replied grudgingly.

I figured as much. Crossing my arms, I said, "As of this moment, you aren't. I'm demoting you to.... uh...." Shit. I had no practice doing stuff like this. I fumbled around in my head, trying to think of a suitable punishment that went along with the horrible choice he made today. An idea popped into my mind, one I liked very much.

"Actually, I'm not demoting you." Connor raised his eyebrows at me. "From now on, part of your duties will include catering to the other warriors. They want water? You fetch it. They need equipment replaced? You do it." I stepped closer to him, looking him straight in the eye. "If they need someone to wipe the sweat from their brow, you will do it. And *only* you."

"You can't do that!" He raged.

"I can. And I just did."

"I'll never get any training done! I'll lose my position!"

"That's not my problem. You should have thought about that before. And I hope it's just as humiliating for you as this was for your mate. Former mate, I should say."

Connor looked like he was seconds away from having smoke blow out his ears, but I wasn't backing down. A few of the fellow warriors could be heard snickering, earning a glare from him. When he looked back to me, the hate radiating from him was almost palpable.

"You'll regret this." He hissed.

"Did you just threaten your Luna?" Luke demanded.

Completely ignoring the question, he turned and shoved through the crowd.

"Okay, show's over folks. You don't have to go home, but you can't stay here! Move along now." Luke discharged the spectators around us and I finally felt myself relax a little.

When it was just us, I asked, "Was that okay? I'm not officially Luna yet."

"You did great kid! I'm honestly super impressed. You gave him a harsh, but fitting, punishment." Luke clapped me on the shoulder.

"Do you think Dimitri will be mad?"

"Nah, I doubt it."

I narrowed my eyes at him. "You already told him, didn't you?"

Luke laughed lightly. "Caught me."

"What did he say?" I played with my fingers nervously.

"He said it's not the type of punishment he would have thought of, but he's impressed that you did. He said you did a really good job."

Relief washed through me. "Really?"

"Would I lie to you?"

A smile spread over my face. It died soon after as I remembered the other party involved.

"I'm going to check on Silvia; Make sure she's doing alright."

"Sounds like a good plan. I'll see you later. Oh and Lily?"

I looked over my shoulder. "Yeah?"

"I think you did a good job too. I'm proud to call you my Luna." He bowed slightly and I blushed.

"Thanks Luke."

# CHAPTER 29

**DIMITRIS POV**

I'd been patrolling the borders, examining the areas that were lacking in security, when Luke had mind linked me. At first, I wondered why this my problem; people rejected each other every day. It was when he started giving me a play-by-play of what was happening with Lily and the others that I paid attention. She handled it perfectly, and admittedly, skillfully. Myself, I would have simply stuck to demoting Connor-He was only in the ranks because of his father anyway. The man badgered me forever until I finally accepted Connor as a warrior. Generally, he was lazy and unnecessarily smug, not a very valuable asset. Lilys punishment was something I knew he would without a doubt hate.

I was proud of her. Turns out she could be quite wicked, when she wanted to be. I could feel that my Gamma was proud of her too, and I was glad he approved of her so wholeheartedly. Ben too, in fact. It seemed she had a knack for drawing people to her, gaining their respect and love. She was going to make a great Luna for this pack; She already was.

*"She reminds me of your mom."*

*"Oh, man. Gross."*

*"Not like that dummy! The way she puts the pack first. And her kindness. She's a good person at heart, just like your mom was."*

*"Yeah, I can see that."*

*"Speaking of, when are you thinking of holding the ceremony?"*

*"Soon. Probably this week, I've put it off too long."*

*"Other shit has been going on."*

*"Exactly. So, the sooner, the better."*

My phone buzzed in my pocket, alerting me to a text. I glanced at it, thinking. I should get Lily a phone. True, we hardly used them, since mostly everyone preferred to mind-link. I only had one as a way to contact Alphas outside of the pack if I wasn't in the office. Still, I should have thought about getting one for earlier. With that line of thinking, I wondered for the first time if there was anything else she needed. I'd made sure she had the necessities, but didn't girls like to go shopping? Did Lily? Was there things she needed or wanted that I hadn't thought of before? Like make-up or some shit like that?

*"Awwe, look who's starting to care about others!"* Ajax cooed.

*"Do I... should I ask her? Or maybe talk to Thara?"*

*"Hmm... I'd talk to your sister first. She spends more time with her, she might know what Lily needs."*

I checked the time- Thara wouldn't be done work for hours still.

*"Hey, you busy?"* I mind-linked her.

*"I have a minute. What's up?"*

*"Can you meet me later? I want to talk to you about something."*

*"Sure. I should be done by six. Meet at the fountain?"*

*"Sounds good."*

*"See you later bro."*

I spent the next hour surveying the area, taking notes on areas that needed updating. When I was done, I stripped and shifted. There was a stack of paperwork sitting on my desk at home that I wasn't looking forward to, but that was the job. If I did it right, I could cut that stack in half before I had to meet my sister. Shifting at the edge of the trees, I dressed and made my way inside. My enhanced hearing caught snippets of conversations in the packhouse; Mostly snide remarks about Connor and pity for his ex-mate. But a lot of it was praise for Lily. I smiled, carrying that smile all the way to my office.

Going through paperwork didn't even seem as tedious as it normally was today. I signed off on some permits to build new homes, went through a whole pile of submitted complaints. Half an hour before I had to leave, Ben popped in, envelope in hand.

"Whatever it is, just put it with the others." I said.

"I think you'll want to read this one, actually." He set it in front of me. Curiosity got the better of me, but when I opened it, I groaned loudly.

"Already?! Didn't I just attend this stupid thing?"

It was the annual invite to the Alphas Ball. I loathed those functions; Always I would have to contend with she-wolves throwing themselves at me, sometimes literally.

"You have to go. You know that." Ben took the chair opposite me, propping his feet on my desk.

"A whole night of dealing with arrogant Alphas pushing their daughters in my direction, and dealing with bitchy, entitled Lunas. I can't wait." I rolled my eyes.

"Remember Tina?" Ben chuckled.

A shudder ran through me as I vividly recounted the hawklike Luna of the Night Desert Pack. She'd spent a full hour bragging about her daughter, only to introduce me to a girl half my age. As politely as one could manage, I tried to explain I wasn't looking to end up in jail, and she'd thrown wine in my face. The woman was off her rocker.

"Can't you just attend for me this year?"

"It'll be different this time. You have a Luna now."

That brought me up short. Would Lily want to go with me? If she didn't, did that mean I still had to go?

"I know what you're thinking, and the answer is yes." Ben said.

"Damnit all." I groaned again.

*"Hey, where are you?"* Thara mind-linked me. Shit, it was quarter past six.

"I've got to go, I'm meeting Thara. Don't RSVP yet, not until I know of Lily will go with me." I told Ben as I left the office. I caught his look of surprise on the way out, but ignored it.

*"I'm on my way, I was in a meeting with Ben."*

The fountain we met up at was a short walk from the hospital. Patients liked to take walks in the garden surrounding it, or sit and read on one of the benches around it. It was one of our mothers favourite places to go, though I never understood why. Still, it meant something to me for that reason alone, and I often visited when I missed my parents.

When I arrived, Thara was sitting on the bench nearest the rose bushes, still dressed in her work clothes.

"Hey."

"Finally. I'm tired you know."

"Sorry."

I sat next to her, taking in the bags under her eyes and her unwashed hair.

"You look like shit." I commented and she punched my arm.

"Shut it."

"You okay?"

"I just haven't been sleeping well lately. I never do, around this time." She gazed towards the fountain and sadness pierced my heart. The anniversary of our parents' death was coming up, something neither of us liked to think about, but couldn't avoid. Every year we went together to their graves and laid flowers, telling them about our lives. I hadn't had much to say the last few years, or nothing I thought they'd be proud of me for anyways.

"Anyways, you wanted to talk?" She changed the subject, and I was grateful.

"Yeah. Uhm, it's about Lily."

Thara narrowed her eyes at me. "What about her?"

"Well, you two spend time together, and I was thinking today, she probably needs some stuff right? Like girl stuff?"

"Girl stuff?"

"Whatever it is you buy when you go shopping."

She raised an eyebrow at me.

"What?" I asked.

"Are you talking about tampons?"

"What?! No! I meant like underwear or make-up." I defended.

Thara burst into laughter. I didn't get the joke.

"Sorry bro, when you said 'girl stuff'... well, that's girl code for tampons or pads."

"Can you *please* stop saying that?"

She chuckled. "Typical male."

"So, can you take her shopping? And get her a phone too?"

"I would have thought you'd be the one to do that."

"Why would I want to spend all day looking at girls clothes and shit? I thought you loved shopping."

She gave me a look that I didn't understand.

"Dimitri, Lily has never *been* shopping."

I stared at her. "Ever?"

"*Ever.* I couldn't tell you what the girl needs because she doesn't know. She's never owned anything like that before, she was never allowed to go shopping." Thara explained.

I sat back, taking in her words. Truly, I hadn't thought about Lilys life before coming here in the last few weeks. Mostly because she was doing so much better. She never brought it up, and I never asked. The memory of what she looked like before she shifted played in my mind, resurfacing old anger.

"She told you this?" I asked.

Thara nodded. "She's been more open lately. There are things she absolutely refuses to talk about, and she won't give details about anything, but from what I've learned from working with her is that she didn't have much of a life outside of cleaning of cooking. No toys, no vacations, no privileges. I bought her a chocolate bar two weeks ago, and I swear she turned into a five year old eating candy for the first time. After I finally got her to accept it, that is."

A new sadness pinged in my heart, this time for my mate. Hadn't she been at Snow Moon since she was a kid? How could she never have experienced playing with toys, or eating a chocolate bar? How cruel was that pack?

"You promised you'd look into this, when she first came here. Have you?" My sister demanded now. I shook my head and her face fell.

"I'm sorry. I will, I promise. I've had a lot on my mind. And well, I guess I didn't think about it. She's... better."

"She looks better. Mentally, I'm still not sure. There are days I catch her in her own world, looking miserable. I've asked, but like I said, she doesn't talk about it." Looking sideways at me, she continued, "Talking to her mate might be helpful though."

"If she doesn't talk to you, why would she talk to me?"

Thara shrugged. "Maybe she will, or maybe she won't. But you're her mate. You're supposed to be there for her."

"You never know until you try. And lately, it seems like you might want to try."

I gave her a sharp look, and she gave it right back to me.

"I'm not dumb Dimitri. You're much less of the asshole you were before. You're even sort of nice to people now. And twice I've caught you smiling for no reason at meals. So, stop being a pussy, and for once, maybe try to go after the thing that's making you happy."

"You know me too fucking well. It's annoying." I grumbled.

She laughed and mussed my hair. "You're my brother, and I love you. And I love Lily. I want you both to be happy."

Together we sat and looked out at the gardens and fountain, lost in our own thoughts. Something inside me told me that I was getting ready to move on, to let go of my anger at my past. And part of me really hoped I had my mate waiting on the other side of that journey.

# CHAPTER 30

**LUKES POV**

"Let's go guys! What am I doing out here, wasting my time?! Let's go!" I hollered to the group. Two of the ten looked ready to puke, and I could only hope they pulled through.

Nick led another group on the far side of the field, looking worn out and utterly unhappy. Training potential warriors was always a daunting task. They either had it, or they didn't, and judging by the look of Neds' group, most of them didn't have it.

"Gamma, can we take a break? *Please?*" A fairly chunky boy named Greg was standing before me, hands on knees and sweating profusely.

"Finished your laps?"

The look on his face gave me my answer.

"Then no. Get going." I waved him off.

I groaned out loud when, five minutes later, he stopped mid-run and vomited on the track.

"It looks like you're having so much fun out here."

Sparks shot through me as my mates' arms snared around my waist, his chin resting on my shoulder.

"It just got more fun, now that you're here."

Miguel chuckled and kissed my neck. I caught Ned scowling at us, and I shot him the bird. Out of everyone, he was the only one who wasn't at all surprised when my mate turned out to be a guy. I guess it was because he'd walked in on me and Dimitris cousin once, though I swore him to secrecy.

"What are you doing out here?" I asked Miguel.

"I just missed you. And I was a little curious. Your pack trains differently than mine did."

His eyes held a hint of sadness whenever he mentioned his old pack. I knew he missed them a lot, and I was forever grateful that Dimitri had accepted him so easily into Blood Moon. It had been a tense meeting at first, but once Miguel recounted how his pack was all but decimated by rogues, Dimitri and Ben welcomed him with open arms. Dimitri exchanged the traditional oaths and blood that morning, officially making Miguel a Blood Moon member.

"We train hard. But these guys aren't warriors yet." I eyed Greg, sitting on the edge of the track, green faced.

"Are you close to finishing?"

"Almost. Why? You wanted to train together?"

He ran one hand down my spine, making me shiver. "I had a different type of training in mine actually."

This man could get going me in in seconds. I gazed at his face, struck anew by how lucky I was. Shoulder length black hair, beautifully tanned skin that commented his chocolate eyes, and lips to die for. He was a few inches shorter than me, and his body would make a lesser man drool. Miguel was perfect.

"Oh yeah? So that's the real reason you came out here hmm?"

"Possibly."

"I love that you can't get enough of me." I pulled his hair lightly.

"I never will. So maybe you could end your session? I think that ones about to pass out anyway." He pointed to Greg, and I shook my head.

"Alright, we're done for today! Go take a shower!" I called and the resounding sighs of relief filled the air.

"You're leaving?" Ned called.

"Yup. You can stay if you want though."

"We're done!" He shouted to his group, making me laugh.

"Come. I think you need a shower too." Miguel took my hand. The chance at spending time with my mate was too good to pass up. So, I let him lead me back to our room where he proceeded to push me onto the bed.

"I thought I was showering?"

"After our 'training'. I have a feeling we'll both be sweating by the time it's done."

My dick strained against my jeans. The things this man did to me, I swear.

"Let's get started then." Grabbing his hand, I pulled him on top of me, pressing my lips to his. He moaned, yanking my hair to get better access.

We started undressing each other, eager to have skin on skin. He ran his hand down my chest, leaving a trail of tingles. I bit his lower lip, earning a growl.

"Easy there tiger." He said.

"I'm just getting started."

Lying him down, I flipped him onto his stomach and straddled him. I bent down and started leaving soft kisses across his shoulders, over his neck. I looked proudly down at my mark on him, before giving it a soft bite.

"Luke..."

"I can't believe you interrupted me at work." I rubbed my tip against his ass. "I could lose my job."

"Shame. You'd have to spend all your time here with me."

"A tempting offer, actually." I lifted his hips. "You are very tempting."

Grabbing the bottle of lube we kept, I slowly applied it. Thoroughly. I was so hard by this point, it was almost painful. Once I was sure he was ready, I edged into him, inch by inch. His hands tightened on the sheets, a low moan reaching my ears. The sparks from our bond only enhanced the feeling of being inside him, and I loved every second. Keeping a firm grip on his waist, I started to move in and out. The feeling was incredible.

"Goddess Luke!"

Miguel adjusted to all fours, a position I was more than happy to accommodate. Reaching around, I started stroking him while I pumped my hips. Guttural moans sounded from both of us, echoing off the walls. It was a good thing all the rooms in the packhouse were soundproof.

"Turn around." I breathed.

We adjusted again, him lying beneath me. He looked at me with pure, unfiltered lust and I almost came right there. Slamming my lips to his, we moved together in a fusion of sweat, moans and heavy breathing. His hand hit my stomach as he worked himself under me, and I was so close.

"I'm close." I whispered.

"Me too."

A few thrusts later, we finished together, and I collapsed on top of him. He kissed my shoulder.

"You are amazing." He muttered.

"I know." I replied and he chuckled.

"I love you, Luke."

I met his eyes, shining with his declaration. My heart burst with happiness. He loved me.

"I love you too Miguel."

We grinned at each other. Finally, I retracted from him, but kept him close, snuggling in bed together. I felt like the luckiest person in the whole universe right now. Did this moment have to end? I hoped it didn't. I was content to stay this way forever.

"Luke?"

"Hmm?"

"Will you meet my parents?"

I raised my head. "I thought-?"

"They are dead. But I would like to take you to their grave. They would have loved you, as I do. I know they would."

"Of course, Miguel. Anything for you."

"Thank you." He gave me a soft kiss.

I lay my head on his chest while he played with my hair.

"What were they like?" I asked hesitantly. He paused shortly before answering.

"They were incredible. The kindest people out there, ready to give the shirt off their back if need be. Mother made the best pecan pie. The neighbours use to come by, bringing her the ingredients just so she would make one." He laughed. "My father could have been a comedian; everywhere he went, he made people laugh. He used to tell me jokes when I was sad or angry, and it always made me feel better. He was a true gentleman too, always showing my mother how much she loved him. I always hoped I could be half the mate he was. They really loved each other."

"You are more than half the mate you want to be. You are everything to me. The day I met you was the happiest day of my life, and everyday since." I told him.

"I feel the same for you. I am glad you asked me about them. I have fond memories of them I haven't thought of in a long time."

"Whenever you want, you can talk to me. They sounded like amazing people."

"Thank you." He said again.

I felt someone trying to mind-link me.

*"You left training early?"* Dimitri asked.

*"Yup."*

*"Why?"*

*"To tell my mate I loved him."*

*".... Okay."*

He cut off the link, no reprimands, no scolding. So unlike him. I sent up a silent prayer to the Moon Goddess that Lily and Dimitri could experience what I had.

# CHAPTER 31

Dimitri landed on top of me, his hand around my throat. I pushed him off, groaning.

"Where are you today? That's the tenth time I've taken you down."

I scowled at him. "I'm just not in the mood."

It was just us today. Karla was on border patrol, and I was silently grateful. She'd have my head if she saw how badly I was slacking off this morning. I couldn't focus on anything it seemed. Nightmares had invaded my mind all night, making me feel like I hadn't slept at all. My subconscious kept dredging up my past, making me relive it almost every night. I was exhausted from the effort of trying to deal with it.

Dimitri pursed his lips. "You want to talk about it?"

I shook my head.

He sat next to me. "If you're not up for training, what do you want to do?"

"I-I don't know."

"Why don't we go somewhere?"

"You mean, a run?"

"No. You and me, why don't we go do something together?"

I stared at him, unblinking. Did he just... ask me out?

"You want to do something."

"Yes."

"With me. Together." I clarified.

"Yes."

"Why?"

He shrugged. "Why not?"

I could voice a hundred reasons to that. The only times we spent together, ever, were training and letting our wolves out. We were speaking more, I guess, and considerably more civil with each other. But going out together? Was this even Dimitri next to me?

"Where?" I asked.

"Where would you like to go?"

Was he being considerate? Had this man killed my mate and taken his place?

"I don't know any places here. I haven't gone out much."

He thought for a minute. "I know somewhere. Let's go." He stood and held his hand out to me. I stared at it, confused.

"You're serious about this?"

"Do I look like I'm joking?"

Hesitantly, I took his hand, and he pulled me up. The whole time I followed him back to the packhouse, I searched for any giveaways to say this guy wasn't Dimitri Varlos. He looked like him, and his scent was the same. Perhaps I was still in bed, dreaming? I wouldn't consider this a nightmare, not yet. I looked around, waiting for monsters to come from the forest. Something to prove I wasn't awake.

He led me to a red mustang parked in the drive. Pulling out a set of keys, he unlocked the car, motioning for me to get in.

"Uhm, shouldn't I change first?" I was having Deja- vu. This was like our first encounter, right after our wedding.

"You don't have to, not where we're going."

That response wasn't like the first time. He almost sounded.... nice?

I got in the car, buckling my seatbelt. We drove for about thirty minutes and I couldn't stop starring at him; He turned on the radio, drumming his fingers along with the music, and I think I was slowly going into shock.

"Why are you staring at me?"

"Who are you?" I asked.

"What do you mean?"

"I mean, who are you and what have you done with the real Dimitri?"

He smirked and glanced at me as he turned a corner.

"I'm right here Lily. You didn't want to train, and I don't want to go to do paperwork. This is me trying to do something nice, for once. Can you just go with it?"

"I'm not sure. I'm still deciding if this is real or not."

"Well, if you decide it's not, then stop thinking about it and just have some fun with me. Okay?"

Fun? He knew how to have fun? Yeah, this totally wasn't real.

"Sure..."

"Good, because we're here."

He turned off the ignition, and I finally looked around. Oh, my Goddess.

"You brought me to the beach?"

"I did."

Sand dunes rose in front of us, a small sand covered walkway cutting through. I could hear waves crashing distantly and looked up to see gulls flying overhead. The air smelled sweet and fresh, with a hint of the salty ocean. I'd dreamed of being able to come here, a small wish that was never granted. I unbuckled my seatbelt in a hurry, eager to see what I'd missed out on. Whether or not this was real, I didn't care anymore.

Dimitri followed me as I made my way. I stopped at the end of the path, taking it all in. The sun shining down on the sand, the water. The white tips of the waves before they met the sand. Patches of light green seaweed were dotted near the shore, contrasting with the unbelievably blue water. I could make out a few boats far off, possibly people out fishing. I quickly discarded my shoes and socks and stepped onto the sand, surprised by how warm it was. The grains dipped between my toes as my feet sank in, and I loved the feeling.

Grinning, I grabbed Dimitris hand, pulling him with me. The sparks erupted at our contact, but for once, I didn't ignore them. It only made this experience better. I walked straight to the water, looking in to see small fish swimming around near the shore. Various types of shells were settled in the sand below the water as well, glistening between waves.

There were so many things I wanted to do; I couldn't pick just one. So, I decided to start with the basic. I turned to Dimitri.

"You're going to build a sandcastle with me. Right now."

"Am I?"

"Yes. Let's go."

We settled down with the sun on our backs and got to work. It wasn't the best; in fact it wasn't even great. Dimitri was my go-to guy for running to the waters edge to get the finely packed sand. Together, we constructed an oddly shaped, slightly slanting sandcastle. I wiped my hands together, satisfied with it all the same.

"What now?" He asked.

"Now... we destroy it."

He chuckled, but he helped me kick our creation until there was nothing left. I giggled the whole time.

"Come with me." I took his hand and let him pull me this time. We walked past the many sand dunes to an area where the beach was less sand and more rock. A jagged cliff loomed over us, casting a shadow onto the water. Dimitri led me around the bottom of the cliff to a space where the rocks flattened out into a large open circle. It was filled with small and big pools of water, and when he stopped beside one, I gasped.

Inside was what seemed to be a mini ocean. Tiny fish swam around and around, and starfish clung to the rocks. A crab peered at me, seemingly confused. Barnacles covered the sides and bottom, and bright, colourful anemones swayed back and forth. I walked to the next pool, astounded that so much life could fit in such a tiny amount of water.

"What are these?" I asked Dimitri.

"They're called tide pools. They're pretty, huh?"

"They're beautiful!"

Kneeling down, I examined the little wildlife zoo in front of me more carefully. It was incredible. Dimitri knelt beside me and pointed.

"See that there?"

He pointed to an odd slug looking thing.

"Is that some kind of plant?"

"It's a sea cucumber."

"Seriously? It looks nothing like a cucumber!"

He chuckled. "I didn't name it; I just know what it is. Dried sea cucumbers are actually a delicacy in many Asian cultures."

I wrinkled my nose. "You know this because you've had it?"

"I have. It's not as good as it's made out to be, in my opinion."

"Ew."

"I try everything once. But you're right, it was pretty gross."

I laughed at the look on his face. We stayed and examined each pool, Dimitri pointing out different creatures and giving interesting details about them. He educated me on how you should never pick up a starfish, as it could cause them to suffocate, and how to handle a hermit crab. I picked up various shells that had washed up on the rocks, which ended up in Dimitris pockets since I was wearing leggings.

Once we got back to the main beach, I put them in my shoes so I wouldn't lose them.

"Swimming?!" I asked him excitedly.

"No point in coming to the beach if you're not going into the water, right?"

"I don't know about that. It's been pretty amazing so far."

He smiled and my breath caught.

"Race you?" I suggested.

"You're on."

I took off towards the water with him on my heels. I think he let me win, but I didn't care. I jumped into the water, relishing in the coolness on my skin. I waded in until it was just above my waist, unsure about going further. Where did it drop off?

"Hey, where does the water-" I was interrupted by a splash of water to my face. "Hey!"

Dimitri grinned at me, and I immediately splashed him back. "You're an ass!" I laughed.

"Just trying to give you the full beach experience!"

I chased him around and it didn't take long until we were both soaked and laughing like kids. It was a side of him I'd never seen, but would really like to see more often. He ducked underwater and out of my sight, only to appear right in front of me. I knocked water into his face, and he coughed.

"That's what you get for cheating." I laughed.

"Come here you." His arms snaked around my waist as he lifted me up, flushing my body against his. My arms went around his neck for something to hold onto, bringing our faces very close together. My heart picked up speed as we looked at each other, the waves moving around our bodies effortlessly.

"Did you have fun today?"

"The most. Thank you, so much, for bringing me here. It was the best."

"You're welcome. I think I needed it too, to be honest. But it was more for you."

He tucked a stray piece of hair behind my ear, his hand lingering on my cheek. Unconsciously, I leaned into his touch. He looked into my eyes, and all I wanted was for him to kiss me. His gaze dropped to my lips, his eyes darkening a little. But then he let me go. Disappointment flooded through me, but I kept my face neutral.

"We should head home. I still have that paperwork to do."

"Okay."

We left the water and grabbed our stuff. I tried not feel bad, because at the end of the day, this was still one of the best days of my life. And I got it share it with my mate, which somehow made it better. So, as we drove back home, I leaned my head against the window, a light smile on my face. I would never forget today.

# CHAPTER 32

**DIMITRIS POV**

"So? What happened?" Ben tossed a rolled-up paper at me, and I batted it away.

"Nothing. It was a normal day at the beach. We went swimming, I showed her the tide pools, we built a sandcastle-"

"You built a sandcastle? *You*?" Luke gawked at me.

"She wanted to, so, yes we did."

They looked at each and grinned.

"Why are you smiling like that?" I asked.

"Our boys in love." Sang Ben.

"So in looooove!" Luke chimed in.

"I am not in love! I just did something nice for her. She's never been to the beach."

"Whatever man. I'll remind you of that at your wedding."

"We're already married dumbass."

"A half-ass wedding we weren't even invited to." Luke scoffed.

"You'll have your own wedding. Stop bitching."

They grinned again and I gave up.

"If you two are done grilling me, can we work now?"

"Alright, fine. Just know that we are happy for you, and proud of you. I'm sure Lily won't forget it anytime soon." Ben said as he sat down.

I hid my smile, hoping he was right. I knew I wouldn't forget.

"Are the new security measures in place?"

"All set up and working. We tested them this morning. Everything looks good."

"Great. Have we found anything more on the James situation?"

"Unfortunately, no. But I'm looking." Luke replied.

"Alright, then there's something I want you two to help me with. I want information on Snow Moon. All of it. Especially on the Alpha and his family. Find out everything you can and get it to me as soon as you can."

"We can do that."

"Then get started."

"Wait, now?" Luke asked.

"No, next week. Yes, now!"

"Geez, okay." He held up his hands as he stood, and they left.

Myself, I walked to my desk and opened the bottom drawer. Digging out a stack of papers, I located Alpha Theos number and picked up my phone, dialing.

*"Hello?"*

"Alpha Theo?"

*"Yeah. Who's this?"*

"Alpha Dimitri Varlos."

*"Oh, Alpha! Apologies, I didn't recognize your voice. How can I help you?"*

"I'm calling about Lily."

There was a short pause on his end. *"What has she done?"*

"Why do you assume she's *done* anything?"

*"It's always something with that girl. Are you not satisfied with her? I'm sorry Alpha, but our agreement clearly states that-"*

"I'm not calling to send her back. And yes, I am satisfied with her."

*"Oh. Then why are you calling?"*

His attitude had my back up. Did he have no respect?

"I'm calling because I want help locating her original pack."

*"Like I told you before, we don't know where she came from."*

"She never said anything. Not even a hint?" I pushed.

*"No. She had no memory of a family or any pack when she showed up here."*

I drummed my fingers on my desk, agitated.

\*"Was that everything, Alpha?"*

"Yes."

*"Goodbye then."*

I heard the click followed by the beeping. The fucker hung up on me. I placed the receiver down, an uneasy feeling in my chest. This wasn't the first time I'd asked about Lilys past; I had before I took her from Snow Moon. It was the same answer, nobody knew anything. But now I felt a string of suspicion. I sensed Alpha Theo was hiding something from me, and I was hardly ever wrong when it came to my senses. I just had to find out what it was.

Lily didn't know I was trying to find where she'd come from. I didn't know if she wanted to know or not, but maybe having some answers would help her in the long run. Who knew, maybe she had parents out there somewhere, possibly a sibling? I thought she would be happy if I could find her family. In the meantime, it was time I told her everything I knew so far about James disappearance. I'd wanted more information, but it looked like a dead end for now, so it was time.

*"Greta?"*

*"Yes Alpha?"*

*"Do you know where Lily is right now?"*

*"I do believe I saw her with Hazel a short while ago."*

*"Thanks."*

I cut off the mind-link, opening a new one to Hazel.

*"Hazel, are you with Lily?"*

*"Alpha?"*

*"Yes."*

*"Yes, I'm with her."*

*"Can you let her know to come to my office?"*

*"Sure."*

*"Thanks."*

I leaned back in my chair and waited. Absentmindedly, I pick up the shell Lily had given me and rubbed my hand over the smooth surface. I hadn't missed her disappointment the other day when I didn't kiss her, and I knew she wanted me to. I'd wanted to, badly. But not like that. It was the first time both of our walls were down with each other, the first time it hadn't been awkward. Until the end anyways.

I smiled, picturing the way her face lit up when she saw the ocean. The way she giggled and laughed and just let go and had fun for a while. My heart throbbed when I remembered the way she'd looked with the sun shining down on her, hair fiery and wild, skin glowing. She was beautiful, absolutely beautiful. I'd loved watching her expressions as she took in all the new things, things that I'd always taken for granted. She was innocent and curious about everything. Adorable.

"You wanted to see me?"

I looked up at the sound of her voice. "Yeah. Come on in."

Closing the door behind her, she made her way to her usual spot.

"What's up?"

Not wanting to beat around the bush, I said, "I wanted to update you on James."

Her eyes clouded over in anger when I said his name. "You found something?"

"Yes. A while ago, actually. But nothing new as of yet."

"Go on."

"We're pretty sure James was taken by a Clan Elder. Do you know what that is?" She shook her head. "It's a very powerful witch, or warlock, a leader. Equivalent to an Alpha."

"Okay."

"We figure this person, Gideon? Took James over anyone else because they want information on the pack. On me. Probably because they want me dead."

Lily stood, beginning to pace in front of my desk. "Why didn't you tell me sooner?"

"I wanted more to give you honestly. Luke is researching like crazy, and Ben is out following leads, but we've essentially come to a dead end for now." I recounted everything we'd learned about Clan Elders, their power, and the different theories we had.

"Why would a Clan Elder want you dead though? What did you do?"

I guess it was fair, given my reputation, she automatically assumed *I* was the one at fault.

"I didn't do anything. I've never met any witches, never had any interactions with them."

She looked into my eyes, seemingly deciding I was telling the truth. Then she blew out a long breath, flopping back onto the sofa.

"It doesn't make sense."

"What doesn't?"

"Why take James? Why not take someone closer to you, like me or Ben?"

My heart clenched at the idea of her being taken. Over my dead body.

"Like I said, James is a pack member."

Her forehead creased in thought. "So? He didn't have access to the packhouse, your office, your room. He wasn't ever close to you, he knows nothing about you, not like we do."

When she put it like that, she made a lot of sense.

"But James was the lead warrior- Just one under Ned. He'd be valuable in a fight." I said.

"Even James knows he doesn't stand a chance against you. I'm just saying, it doesn't make sense."

"What are you trying to say, exactly?"

Lily played with her fingers. "What if you're not the target?"

"I'm the Alpha."

"And? I'm Luna. James was taken after assaulting *me*."

My heart started to race in my chest. "I don't-"

"Think about it Dimitri. If *you* wanted you dead, would you kidnap *James*?"

She was right. I hated to admit it, but I knew she was. Looking at it from her perspective, everything came together. Perhaps this Gideon wasn't involved on the attack on Lily, but now he had someone who had proved his hate for her. Someone who knew the pack, knew the schedules. James knew our borders like the back of his hand, he'd been running them for years. He knew which of my warriors were best and also how to take them out. And because of his past, he knew which room my mate was in, and how to get to her.

We stared at each other, both coming to the same conclusion; Lily was in danger.

"What do we do?" She asked me.

"We keep you safe." I deadpanned.

"How? According to you, this person can just take people from wherever they are. I could be in bed, asleep, or out with Hazel, or with you, training!"

I swallowed hard. I wish she would stop being right.

"I-I don't know." I replied uncertainly. And that was extremely hard for me to admit.

The air was tense with frustration and in my case, overwhelming worry. Ajax was pacing with anger at the thought of someone hurting our mate. Even more than that though, our inability to come up with a solution.

"Do you trust me?" Lily asked suddenly.

"Yes." I replied instantly. She seemed surprised but went on.

"Why don't we find a witch to help us? Even the odds a little?"

I pursed my lips. "That's a great idea... if I knew any or knew how to get in contact with any."

"You said Luke was researching and Ben was out looking for leads. One of them must know something."

"Lily, even if we find a witch, it's *highly* unlikely they would help. Wolves and witches hate each other."

"We don't have anything else." She whispered.

For the first time, she looked scared. And it was that that made my decision.

*"Ben?"*

*"Yeah boss?"*

*"Grab Luke and come back to the office. We need to talk."*

# CHAPTER 33

"Let me get this straight. You want me, *by myself*, to go into witch territory, *if* I can even find it, and try and persuade a witch to come help us?" Ben stared around the room, looking at each of us in turn.

"That's the gist of it, yes." Dimitri replied.

"Again, *by myself*?"

"You are my Beta, are you not?"

"Well, yeah, but-"

"It's not with the intent to harm you, Ben." I interrupted him. "They already don't trust us. It would look much worse if it was you and bunch of warriors."

He clenched his jaw and turned to Dimitri. "Am I that replaceable to you?"

"Nobody could replace you, Ben. And nobody is going to. I'm trusting you with this above anyone else because, I know you will be fine. Even if you don't bring a witch back, I'll know you did your best for my ma- for our pack."

Bens eyes softened as he glanced between the two of us, finally sighing heavily.

"I'll go pack. I'll leave in the morning."

"Luke, go with him and draw out some maps from your research."

Both nodded and bowed slightly to Dimitri. Then, surprising me, they gave me the same gesture before leaving. I sent up a prayer to Celeste that, even if he wasn't successful, that Ben would return home to us safely. That's what mattered the most. I stood, every nerve on edge. Going for a run sounded really good right now.

"Want to go for a run?" I asked Dimitri. He perked up almost instantly.

"Absolutely."

Together we left the packhouse and went to our usual spot. I didn't waste anytime finding a tree to change behind, shifting into Aya.

*"Have fun, but don't go too far this time. Okay?"*

*"Like anyone could me down."*

*"Aya."*

*"Alright fine."*

I gave up control and watched silently as her and Ajax played and ran together. They'd made a route through the forest, but it seemed like Ajax was in line with my thinking, not going as far as they usually did. While our wolves spent time together, I thought about my situation. It wasn't hard to figure out why I was the target- I was a Mother Wolf. And clearly this Gideon guy was watching the pack. Or at least the high-ranking wolves. It had me thinking, was that magic? Or was there a mole in our midst, spying on us for him? I really hoped it was magic, but I couldn't rule out any possibilities.

It was troubling, because that meant I didn't know who to trust. If I had to guess anyone, it would obviously be Jennine. She was the one who'd wanted me gone the most. But my dislike for her wasn't proof enough. I thought of my friends, unwillingly, and cringed at the idea that Hazel or Clint could possibly betray me. Greta was simply too kind-hearted; She didn't have a malicious bone in her body. Ben and Luke would do anything for Dimitri, so they were unlikely as well.

And Dimitri? Celeste had told me he'd only wanted a mate to make him stronger. I didn't think he'd get rid of me, not like this anyways. If anything, he'd just send me back to Snow Moon. More than that however, I truly didn't believe Dimitri would cause me any harm. His face when he realized that I was right earlier, that nobody was after *him*... If the solution was to lock me away in the basement for my own safety, I was positive he would do it. He seemed more than willing to do whatever it took to keep me safe.

I didn't know what that meant, for him or for us. Did he care about me? Did he want me? Or was he simply playing nice so he could complete the bond, getting what he wanted? Our day at the beach flashed in my mind; He'd been so amazing. That day, he was everything I wanted in a mate. Playful and caring, sweet and attentive. Loving, almost. But he'd pulled away from me, leaving me confused and hurt. I wasn't going to be an easy lay for him, like so many others. I wanted him to respect me.

*"I'm tired."* Aya panted.

*"Already?"*

*"Lily, it's midnight. You've been in your own world for hours."*

*"Shit. Sorry Aya."*

Running back to our spot, I shifted behind my tree, getting dressed. Dimitri was waiting for me when I walked out, and we walked side by side to the house.

"Thanks. I needed this."

"Me too." He replied.

When we reached our respective doors, I bid him goodnight and entered my room. Only to stop short, my jaw dropping. I surveyed the room, twice. Three times.

Where was my stuff?

"Dimitri?" I called. He appeared in the doorway, leaning against it.

"Oh, that. Yeah, you're not staying in here anymore."

"What?"

"You're staying with me from now on." His tone was nonchalant, like he hadn't just dropped a bomb on me.

"Come again?"

"If someone wants to take you in your sleep, then they'll have to take me too. And no, it's not up for discussion."

"But... I need to shower." I replied stupidly.

"I have a shower. And all your stuff is in there already."

"How-?"

"I asked some Omegas to do it while we were out."

Anxiety pooled in my stomach. Sleeping with him, in his bed? Nu-uh. No way.

*"Can you stop overthinking for once?"* Aya said.

*"Aya, I can't!"*

*"You can. Just close your eyes and sleep like every other night."*

*"With him?!"*

*"Goddess, do I need to take control just so we can sleep beside our mate?! Stop being a baby Lily!"*

I 'hmphed' at her but didn't argue. Dimitri wasn't giving me a choice anyways. He opened the door to his room for me, and his scent hit me like a wall. I inhaled deeply, letting it calm me a little. I found my gaze travelling towards his huge bed again, just like last time. And just like last time, I started to fantasize about all the things we could do on it.

"Bathroom is over there. A pair of your pajamas are laid out on the sink. Take your time." Dimitri moved around the room, taking off his watch, putting his phone on its charger. He seemed totally comfortable, like this wasn't a huge deal.

"Thanks." Did I just squeak?

Ducking my head so he wouldn't see me blush, I dipped into the bathroom and shut the door. His bathroom was almost identical to mine, only bigger. At least I wouldn't have to ask him how to run his shower. However, I was acutely aware that I was naked with my mate only separated by a door. A door I hadn't locked. It made the shower far less relaxing, and I stayed in there longer than I usually would have, playing for time.

*"You can't stay in here all night."*

*"I can try?"*

I could almost see her rolling her eyes at me. Finally, I got out of the shower, taking my time to brush my teeth and putting on my clothes. The anxiety peaked again as I had nothing else to do but walk out and get in bed. With Dimitri. Goddess, help me.

Slowly opening the door, I switched off the light, blinking into the dark room. Dimitri was already in bed, his hands behind his head, staring at the ceiling. His jaw was ticking, and I thought maybe he was as nervous as I was? Crossing the room, I gulped when I saw he had no shirt on, and my eyes trailed down his body of their own accord.

"Coming in?"

His voice was heavy, huskier than usual. It sent a shiver down my spine that I couldn't ignore. Not trusting my voice, I nodded and hesitantly crawled onto the bed, pulling the covers over me. Turning onto my side away from him, I whispered a goodnight.

"Goodnight Lily."

*Just close your eyes and sleep. Just close your eyes and sleep. Just close your eyes-*

I repeated my mantra over and over in my head. At some point, it must have worked because my body relaxed, and I drifted into unconsciousness.

***

Some time later, in the early hours of morning, I woke up covered in sweat, pain radiating throughout my body. My first thought was I had been taken, like James, but my fear was erased when I recognized Dimitris room. Another burst of pain caused a low moan to escape me, stirring my mate from his sleep.

"Lily? What's wrong?" His voice was thick with sleep, sexy as hell, and wetness pooled between my thighs almost immediately at the sound. What was wrong with me?

"I feel- Oww!"

I looked to Dimitri for help. He was awake and alert, his eyes darker than I'd ever seen them.

"Shit! You're in heat."

I was? Well, that sucked.

"What do I do?" I panted.

He bit his lip. The longer I stared at him, the more I thought I knew the answer. Shockingly, I didn't shy away from it.

I wanted it.

I *needed* it.

My mind was clouded with lust and all my fantasies of Dimitri. It gave me a sense of confidence I'd never experienced. Kicking the covers off, I crawled over the bed to him. I straddled his lap, his eyes going wide.

"Lily... I-I shouldn't. You're not thinking clearly."

"So?"

He swallowed, his Adams apples bobbing. "You just need a cold shower. That will help."

"I don't want a cold shower. I want something much, *much* hotter."

Dimitri closed his eyes, breathing hard. I took the opportunity to lean down and lick his neck, right where my mark should be. He growled, placing his hands on my hips. A tiny part of me was wondering where my resolve had gone. A few hours ago, I'd wanted his respect; vowed I wasn't going to be another notch in his headboard. Now, I was ready to take anything he wanted to give me and more. I craved it, like I craved the air to breath. It was all I could think about.

"Come on Dimitri. Show me what my Alpha can do." I breathed into his ear.

# CHAPTER 34

**DIMITRIS POV**

She was killing me, and she didn't even realize it. I shouldn't... no, I couldn't. Lily wasn't in her right mind; she was driven by her heat. This wasn't her.

*"It's part of her. Aya told me about all her fantasies. She totally wants this."*
*"You're not helping!"*

"Come on Dimitri. Show me what my Alpha can do." Lily whispered and I almost lost it. The amount of restraint I was showing right now was nothing short of heroic. Thank the Goddess I was wearing pants; My go-to was just a pair of boxers.

"Lily, we're not. Not for your first time, not like this." I tried to be firm, but somehow my tone came off as more of a plea.

"How do you know it's my first time?"

I growled and she giggled.

"I'm kidding. I've never had sex. Never even been kissed. You could change that though." She ran her hand down my shoulders and over my chest. I caught her wrists and sat up, looking her in the eye.

"I plan to. But not tonight."

Pain flashed across her features. Fuck. I wanted to help her, so damn badly, but if I did, she'd be pissed at me later. I knew she didn't really want this, not now. She only agreed to come to my room because I hadn't given her a choice; there was no way I was taking advantage of her heat.

"It hurts." She whimpered.

"I know. I'll start a shower for you, and then Thara can bring you something-"

"You don't want me."

I saw the pain in her eyes, and I knew it wasn't her heat now.

"That's not why I'm saying no Lily. You'll regret it, later."

"How do you know?" She spat.

"I just know."

She scoffed loudly, looking away from me. "I guess I shouldn't be surprised. You are the one who refused to kiss me after all. Twice."

"Really Lily?"

Yanking her wrists out of my grasp, she hopped off the bed and stalked to the bathroom. A minute later, I heard the shower running. Falling back on my pillows, I covered my face with my hands. The scent of her arousal was thick in the room, drowning me. On top of that, my dick was painfully hard, and all I could think about was joining her in that shower. Ajax was all for it, making me growl.

*"You know we can't. Stop being such a horny beast."*

*"You were the one who told Thara you'd claim her when she healed."*

Shame ran through me as I remembered that.

*"Well, I changed my mind."*

*"She just threw herself at you! What more did you need?"*

*"For her judgement not to be clouded. You're no better than her right now, so I'm ignoring you before you make me do something stupid."*

Effectively blocking him out, I grabbed my pillow and some clothes and quietly left the room, mind linking Thara to bring Lily something for her pain. When I reached Bens room, he was already awake.

"Hey? Something up?" He let me in, taking in my state of undress and pillow.

"Lilys in heat." I grouched.

He raised an eyebrow. "So why are you *here?*"

"Because if I stay there, she's probably going to pounce on me again."

"She's in your room?"

I nodded. "I moved her last night."

Ben let out a low whistle. "Damn, if that doesn't qualify you to be Alpha..."

"Shut up Ben."

"I'm just saying-"

*"Ben."*

He chuckled, holding his hands up. "You get the room to yourself. I was just checking my things over, and then I'm heading out."

"'Kay. Be careful. And come back."

"You sound like *my* mate now. You want me to bring you your favourite cookies on the way back?"

"Fuck off. I just don't want the hassle of replacing you."

"Thought you said I was irreplaceable?"

Picking up my pillow, I chucked it at his head. He caught it, tossing it back. I watched him pack the maps Luke drew up, his phone and various snacks and water bottles into a hiking pack; He gave me a salute and a, "Wish me luck!", before he left. Like a kid going to college for the first time.

Rubbing my eyes, I sat on his bed. I hoped Ben found a witch willing to help us. It was a long shot; we all knew that. But Lilys safety had became a top priority to me, something I had not anticipated. Which brought my thoughts circling back to the girl upstairs, who was probably super pissed at me for leaving. If I remembered correctly, her heat should only last a day. Maybe two, because it was it her first. And what a time for it to happen.

I'd have to make sure someone stayed with her, Hazel or Thara. She couldn't be around the unmated males in the pack. Thara wasn't stupid though- she knew that. I trusted her to make it happen. Since training was obviously out of the question, I decided to go back to sleep. It was rare I got the chance to sleep in, and I was going to take advantage of it.

My dreams stared around Lily and her little show earlier. This time, I didn't say no. I gave her exactly what she wanted, watching the pleasure on her face and listening to her call my name.

*"Oh... Dimitri..."*

*"Dimitri... Dimitri.."*

"Dimitri! Wake up!"

My eyes opened, my body shooting up. "What? What?"

"Calm down, it's just me."

Thara was standing beside the bed, an amused look on her face. I rubbed the sleep from my eyes.

"What time is it?"

"Two."

I blinked at her. "Shit." I sighed.

"Don't worry, nothing important has happened today."

I stretched, climbing out of bed. Thara tossed me my shirt.

"Thanks. How's Lily?"

She smirked. "Angry. But not in pain. Hazel is with her."

"Good."

She continued to stare at me, and it was getting annoying. "Can you stop?" I grumbled.

"I can't help it. Part of me wants to laugh, but the other part is proud."

"Proud?"

"Bro, never in a million years would I have thought you, of all people, would walk away from a she-wolf in heat. The fact that it was your mate is even more shocking. But yes, I am proud of you. You didn't take advantage of her."

"I wouldn't do that."

Thara pursed her lips. "No offence... but there was a time not so long ago when I believed you would."

An argument sat on my tongue, but I killed it. She was right, and I couldn't deny it.

"Things are different now." I mumbled instead.

"I know. Lily told us all about your beach day." She plopped down on the bed I'd vacated. "What else do you planned?"

"Uh..." I rubbed the back of my neck. "I'm not sure? The beach was kind of a spur-of-the-moment thing."

"Well, think it about it. She can't go anywhere for a while anyways. And, like I said, she's angry at you."

I cringed internally. "How angry would you say?"

"She may have threatened to let her wolf out on you. But that's just the heat talking." She waved her hand, but I gulped. Was Aya mad at Ajax too?

*"Oh yeah. I'm officially in the doghouse."* He whined.

*"Poor guy."*

"I'm heading back up. If I were you, I'd confine yourself to your office or in here." She laughed.

"That was the plan."

"Dimitri?"

"Yeah?"

Thara threw her arms around me, forcing me to take a step back. I awkwardly patted her back. She hadn't hugged me in.... When was the last time? Maybe at mom and dad's funeral?

"What was that for?" I asked when she let me go.

"Because I'm happy for you. For both of you."

"Nothing is even going on yet."

*"Yet."* She grinned.

She left cheerfully, promising to update me on Lily when she could. I took a minute to bask in the realization that what I'd said was the truth. I planned on having Lily, on making her happy. I'd finally accepted my mate, finally accepted that I wanted her. My eyes caught a paper blowing in the wind through the window, Bens calendar. Two days until my parents anniversary. I knew what I wanted to tell them this year, and I had a feeling it would make them happy. Make them proud.

# CHAPTER 35

JENNINES POV

I sat at the kitchen table, sipping my coffee, waiting for our guest to arrive. Connor sat across from, his leg irritatingly bouncing up and down while he clicked his tongue. The sound was driving me crazy; I was two seconds away from throwing my drink in his face.

"Would you stop?" I hissed.

"Sorry, I'm just a little nervous." He gave me a sour look.

"Everything is going to go according to plan, okay? As long as you don't wimp out, that is."

"You know Jennine, if I knew you were this much of a bitch, I wouldn't have rejected Silvia." He glared at me and I glared back.

"Your mate was a snivelling little mouse. Useless. It was your choice to reject her."

"Only because you promised *we* would be mates!"

"And I keep my promises Connor. This is just a little test of faith from you."

He scowled at me, and I worried that he was really going to pull out. I couldn't let him; I needed him for this to work. Setting my mug down, I reached across the table, placing my hand on top of his.

"Don't you want her gone? Don't you want her to pay for humiliating you the way she has?" I asked tenderly.

"You know I do. But if anyone finds out... if the Alpha finds out-"

"He won't. We've both been keeping a low profile. They have no reason to suspect us. And the way I have it planned, all the blame will go to Lily."

"I just hope you know what you're doing."

A knock sounded from the back door. I stood up, giving him a kiss as I passed. "Please, trust me." The look in his eyes was uncertain as I moved passed him to open the door. Standing on the porch was a slender girl with medium length brown hair, deep blue eyes and various tattoos on her arms.

"Chanelle." I said.

"Jennine."

"Please, come in." I opened the door all the way, allowing her to walk past me. Connor eyed her up and down when we walked into the kitchen, catching my glare.

"Did anyone see you?" I asked.

"Nobody. I made sure."

"Coffee?"

"Sure, why not?"

Chanelle took my seat across from Connor, who was openly fuming.

"I get you want to catch up with your girlfriend and all, but can we please just talk about the plan? Is she even from our pack?" He eyed Chanelle again.

I gave a sarcastic laugh. "She's not one of my girlfriends. Truth be told, if she didn't owe me a favour, I'd beat the shit out of her right here."

"How you wish you could." Chanelle hissed.

"Wait. We're staking everything on someone you hate? Who hates you? Are you fucking with me Jennine?"

"Nope." I set Chanelle's coffee on front of her. "Like I said, she owes me."

"What the fuck!"

"Would you calm him down? I never would have agreed to this if I'd known he was such a little bitch." She sneered. I coughed to hide my amusement.

"To answer your earlier question, Chanelle isn't part of this pack. She's from Snow Moon."

"Okay?"

I rolled my eyes. "Lilys former pack."

He still looked lost, and Goddess help me, I wanted to strangle him sometimes. There were no brains in that head.

"She's the one who's going to do the job for us."

This time he looked at Chanelle with curiosity. "You?"

She smirked. "Me."

"Have you ever.... done that before?"

"You want a list of names?"

Connor shrank back in his seat. "No, I'm good."

I turned to her, getting to the point. "You have someone set up?"

"Oh yeah. You know her too."

"Tell."

"Remember Paige?"

I smiled and Chanelle looked just as pleased with herself.

"And you can make it look real? Like a Mother Wolf did it?" I asked.

"I had to do some research, but yeah. Shouldn't be too hard. Can *you* get her there?"

"I already have it set up. An Omega in the packhouse told me Dimitri was going to ask her to go to the Ball with him." I clenched my fists under the table. That should have been me at his side.

"Good. I'll update you closer to the date." She stood to leave.

"Wait, that's it?" Connor asked.

"What else do you want?"

"I want to know you're not going to fuck this up. I'm putting a lot on the line here."

Chanelle's claws extended, her eyes going black. "Are you doubting me right now?"

"N-no. I just-"

She turned to me. "He shouldn't be worried about me screwing this up. I'm worried *he* will. You're not the only one putting yourself on the line, bitch." She told him. Was he shaking? Some warrior.

"I'll keep him in check." I assured her. After one more hard look at Connor, she left.

As soon as the door closed, Connor was right in my face.

"I can't do this Jennine."

Rolling my eyes, I pushed past him. "Calm down. Everything is fine."

"It's not fine! Your frenemy there is nuts! How do you know she's not going to turn us in?"

"Because she knows I'll kill her if she does."

"Goddess, listen to yourself! You can't kill someone if your dead Jennine! And Dimitri will *kill* us!"

Resting my hands on the counter, I took a deep breath. Released it.

"I'm not pulling out Connor. Lily needs to go. You agreed not long ago."

"I've changed my mi-"

"No!" I spun around, facing him heatedly. "You haven't changed your mind. You are going to fulfill your part in this. You're so worried about losing your career and your life, but you have already! What are you doing right now, huh?! Getting towels for the boys, giving them water? Yesterday I saw you tying someone's shoes, bent down at his feet like a slave! You've already lost everything Connor!"

Just like I knew it would, anger burned in his eyes. I kept going, strengthening his resolve.

"Who put you in that position?" I threw at him.

"Lily." He spit her name.

"Exactly. Doesn't she deserve to pay for what she's done? Doesn't she need to suffer, like you've suffered? It hurts watching you go through this because of her!" I yelled.

Scrounging up some fake tears, I turned back to the sink and waited. A second later, Connors arms went around me and I smiled.

"She does, and she will. I'm sorry baby, I won't doubt you again. I'm with you." He kissed my head and I sniffled a little.

"Good. Thank you."

His hand travelled down between my thighs, rubbing against my shorts.

"Let me make it up to you. Let me show you how much I love you."

I really didn't want to. But if it kept him from freaking out and screwing everything up....

I lowered my pants and thong, hopping onto the counter. Connor spread my legs and wasted no time sticking his head between my legs. I closed my eyes, picturing Dimitri. Pretending it was his hands on my thighs; his tongue on me. I moaned loudly, biting my lip against saying his name. This was the only way I could get off now. Before, it had been the thrill of sneaking around, but since Connor rejected his mate, I needed something else. And only Dimitri could please me like no one else.

"Goddess, keep going." I breathed.

He hummed against me, picking up the rhythm. I came shortly after, breathing hard. I accepted his kiss, plastering on a smile.

"My turn." He pushed me to my knees and I sighed quietly.

Two weeks until the Ball. Two weeks, and this would be over. I'd have Dimitri back, as it should be, and this little game I was playing with Connor would come to an end.

# CHAPTER 36

LILYS POV

I stood outside Dimitris office, trying to get the words in my head to come together. After my heat broke, I'd avoided him until I no longer felt like a total whore. I mean, I'd thrown myself at him, literally. But he'd been right; I was so happy he hadn't given into me. He'd gained a lot of my respect. I'd slept at Hazels last night, not ready to face him yet, but she encouraged me to just rip the band-aid off. Come and apologize, and leave. Easy.

"Come in."

Taking one more deep breath, I turned the knob and walked in, avoiding his gaze.

"Hey. How are you feeling?"

"Fine." I replied quietly.

He motioned for me to take a seat, so I did. Folding my hands in my lap, I looked at my shoes.

"You wanted something?" Dimitri asked.

My mouth opened. Closed. I licked my dry lips, trying to get myself together.

"I uh,-" I cleared my throat. "I wanted to apologize." I spoke quickly.

"What for?"

"For... you know." My cheeks felt way too hot. I probably looked like a tomato.

Dimitri raised his eyebrows.

"For what happened. The other night."

"When you attacked me in a lust and hormone induced frenzy?" His lips twitched, like he was trying to hide a smile, and impossibly, my face grew redder.

"Yeah." I squeaked. "That."

"Lily, you don't need to apologize. Your heat isn't something you can control. Nor how you act during it."

"Still." I looked at a picture on the wall. "You had to avoid your own room because of me."

"You know why I left."

I chanced a peek at him, seeing that he was gazing at me tenderly.

"Okay. Well, that's all I came to say." Standing, I quickly walked to the door.

"Lily."

*Ah, so close.*

"Dimitri, I really-"

"Lily, look at me."

Slowly, I turned back to him.

"I don't accept your apology, because there's no reason for it. You didn't do anything wrong."

"Sure feels like it." I mumbled and he chuckled quietly.

"Do you wish it had turned out differently?" He asked.

"No. I'm glad you left. Now, anyways." I told him honestly.

"And I knew you would."

I thought for a minute, gathering my courage. "Do you?"

"No." He stood and slowly walked to stand in front of me. "Don't take that the wrong way, please. Just know I would never take advantage of you that way." He tucked my hair behind my ear.

I knew he was referring to me accusing him of not wanting me.

"Thank you. And I do know that. I trust you."

Our eyes met, his surprised.

"You do?"

"Yes."

Perhaps I didn't at first, but now? Okay, I didn't trust him one hundred percent, but what he did couldn't have been easy. It said something about him, about the kind of man he was. And I liked that man more and more. He smiled, happiness shining on his features. The unexpected expression caught me off guard and made my heart throb.

"I want to hold your Luna ceremony tomorrow night." He suddenly dropped on me. "I know it's not much time, but Thara agreed to take you out, get you ready. I'm arranging everything else."

"Uhm, okay." It's not like I could say no.

"Also, before you go..." He walked back to his desk, picking up a peach coloured piece of paper. "This is an invitation to the Alpha Ball."

That rang a dim bell. The Ball was held at Snow Moon one year, some ten years back. I'd been a child, but I remembered admiring all the Lunas, looking stunning in their dresses, like princesses.

"You're attending?" I asked. I took the paper from him, scanning it.

"I have to." His tone said he would rather do anything else. "I was hoping you would go with me? It is customary, but really, I just don't want to attend another one alone. It's brutal."

I pointed to the bottom of the invitation. "Is this the menu?"

"Some of it, yes."

"Yeah, I'll go."

Dimitri laughed openly, the sound like music.

"Anything else?" I smiled at him.

"No, I think that's everything." He sobered. I handed him back the invitation, his hand lingering on mine. "Come back to the room tonight."

"Okay."

I left feeling much lighter than before. On my way down the stairs, I bumped into Silvia.

"Luna Lily!"

"Hi Silvia. How are you?"

"I'm good. Better." She smiled.

"I'm glad to hear it. What are you doing here?"

"The Alpha gave me a job here!" She exclaimed. "Without Connor warrior salary, I had to move back in with my parents. Alpha came to see me, and was kind enough to offer me a job as a maid in the packhouse. I couldn't say no." She grinned.

My heart melted. "That's wonderful Silvia. I'm happy things are looking up for you."

"Thank you Luna. For everything. I don't know what I would have done if you weren't here." She threw her arms around me, surprising me.

"I just did what anyone else would have." I said.

"No, you did more. Much more." She gave me another huge smile when she released me, saying she had to go back to her duties and we would catch up later. I felt a foreign feeling of pride well up inside me. Had I really had that much of an impact on her?

I walked to the pack hospital, a small smile on my face the whole way. Various pack members greeted me, excited by the news of finally having an official Luna.

"Hey you." Thara was signing forms when I located her.

"Hey."

"Come with me. There's a patient in two-oh-six who needs stitches."

I followed her brisk walk, sidestepping gurneys and people waiting to see other patients. Donning a pair of gloves and pumping some sanitization onto my hand, I followed her into a room with a grumpy looking guy, probably in his mid-forties. He had a deep laceration up his right arm, dried blood covering the skin.

"Hello Bill. What happened this time?" Thara asked as she examined the wound.

"That damned chainsaw got away from me again. I swear Thara, I'm going to sue the company!" I blew out angrily, causing his white beard to sway. He kind of reminded me of a not-so-cheery Santa Claus.

"I see Hayley already cleaned the wound. I'll get you fixed up and you'll be perfect in no time. Oh, this is my new assistant, Luna Lily." She gestured to me as she walked around the room gathering supplies.

"Luna?" Bill was surprised.

"Hello Bill." I said politely.

"Now what's the Luna of Blood Moon doing here?"

I shrugged. "I like helping people. Thara is teaching me."

He eyed me for a moment. "Well, pleased to make your acquaintance Luna Lily. Nice to see a fresh face 'round here."

"It sounds like you're here often."

"On a first name basis with most of the staff, it's true." He hissed as Thara applied the ointment to his wound. "Damn woman, that stings!"

"Call me 'woman' again, and I'll pour the whole bottle on it."

Bill laughed heartily while Thara and I smiled.

"Lily, do you want to do this one?"

"Really?"

"I think you're ready. You okay with that Bill?"

"I get the honor of being our Lunas first patient?"

"Yes sir."

"How can I say no to that?"

I sat on the stool, adjusting the light over Bills arm. I worked slowly, precisely. Just like Thara taught me. Pulling the thread through to close the skin, I made sure to keep them an even space apart. Bill was the perfect patient, never twitching or complaining. When I was done, I looked at Thara for approval.

"Very well done Lily. It looks great!"

I beamed.

I went to wash my hands, throwing the gloves in the trash as Thara gave Bill the usual care speech.

"That man really needs a new hobby." She joined me at the sink.

"What does he do?"

"He carves sculptures from wood, huge ones. I don't know how gets anything done though, he's in here all the time."

Leaning against the counter I said, "Dimitri told me you had plans with me."

"I sure do. Meet me by my car tomorrow morning, around eight. No training, we're having a girls day."

"Which entails?"

"Salon, spa, shopping. Not necessarily in that order. And then back here to get you ready for the ceremony."

"Everyone seems to know about it."

"Dimitri sent out a pack wide announcement. Most will be there."

She must have seen the nerves on my face because she placed a hand on my shoulder.

"It'll be fine Lily. I already think of you as my Luna, official or not. You're exactly what this pack needs."

"I'm not so sure."

"Trust me. Put aside your doubts and worries, for one night at least."

"I'll try."

She smiled and handed me a folder for another patient. I scanned it, trying to believe in myself as much as she seemed to.

# CHAPTER 37

**DIMITRIS POV**

When I woke up, a familiar sadness washed over me. July twenty first, the day my parents died. I closed my eyes, anger and resentment and hatred at the world running through me, one after the other. Until a soft snore broke me out of my thoughts. I looked beside me, to my mates sleeping face. Her lips were parted, her hair was messy but she looked completely peaceful. A soft smile appeared on my face as I gazed at her. She was truly adorable.

And just like that, all the horrible things I was feeling moments ago were replaced by calm, joy and happiness. It was the first time ever I'd woken up on this day and didn't feel like shit. All because of the girl sleeping next to me. I spent five minutes more just admiring her before quietly getting out bed and heading to the shower. Thara had gone to our parents graves yesterday so she could take Lily today. We usually went together, but she'd insisted so I didn't argue.

When I returned to the room, Lily was sitting up in bed, rubbing her eyes.

"What time is it?" She yawned.

"A little after seven."

"Ugh." She flopped down again.

"I set an alarm so you can get up to meet Thara." I told her. She gave me a lazy thumbs up in response and I chuckled.

"I have to go. I'll see you tonight."

"Where are you going?"

I paused. She didn't know? I would have thought by now my sister would have told her? I decided to be honest with her.

"I'm going to see my parents graves."

Lily rolled over, peering up at me. So, she really didn't know.

"Your parents?"

I nodded. She cocked her head into the pillow, a question on her face.

"Okay. See you later."

"Later." I touched her head softly before leaving.

The feeling in the house had an air of sadness to it. Everyone here knew what today was, and they all mourned in their own ways. Heading out to my car, I pulled out my phone. Ben had texted me last night, updating me on his location. Nothing new yet, so I threw it onto the passengers seat as I got in. I started the all-too familiar drive, taking my time. The cemetery was located to the south of the pack, just inside the border.

It was unusual doing this without my sister. I stopped to pick up flowers, my moms favourites. Coincidentally, they happened to be Lilies. I smiled, another first for today. When I got to the cemetery, I took my time wandering through the headstones, paying my respects to warriors I'd known who were buried here. Finally, I reached them. Their headstones were larger than most here, intricately carved and beautifully designed. Sitting on the ground between them, I placed half the flowers on my moms grave and the other half on dads. Tharas flowers were still settled there from yesterday.

"Hi Mom. Dad." I looked at their stones in turn. A light breeze blew through, whistling through my hair. "Another year huh? And I still miss you guys like crazy. And it's been a crazy year." Picking up a twig from the ground, I twirled it around in my hands.

"I don't know if you know this, where you are, but I met someone. My mate." I smiled softly. "Her name is Lily. Mom, you would love her. She's amazing. She's cute, and funny and kind and sweet. Nothing like me." I laughed. "Ajax says she reminds him of you. How you were. I can see it, I guess. I think she's going to be a great Luna for the pack. And get this Dad,-" I looked at his stone now. "Lily is a Mother Wolf! I guess all those bedtime stories weren't just stories."

Peeling the bark off the tiny stick, I continued. "I wish you guys were here to meet her. Maybe if you were here, I wouldn't have been such an asshole to her in the beginning. If you saw that, I know you're disappointed in me. You always wanted me to meet my mate." My lower lip trembled slightly. "But I'm going to fix it, if she'll let me. I want her, I want to be the kind of mate she needs. Like you were for each other. I want to make you proud of me again."

My words choked off, a stray tear escaping my eye. I didn't bother to wipe it away.

"I've made a lot of mistakes, and I know if you were here, Mom would have hit me over the head with a frying pan by now. But Dad always told me a real man owns up to his mistakes, and does his best to fix them. So that's what I'm going to do."

I sat for a while longer, telling my parents about Luke finding his mate, and giving them shit if they knew about him when I didn't. I also told them about James disappearing and our crazy idea to find a witch to help us.

"Whoever this Gideon guy is, you can rest assured he'll never hurt Lily. Not under my watch. Do me a favour, and help me watch out for her, please? She seems to have a knack for getting into trouble. I guess we have that in common at least." I stood up, placing my hands on their stones, my eyes wet.

"Next time, I'll bring Lily to meet you. I love you guys."

Shoving my hands in my pockets, I turned and walked away. It was never easy, saying goodbye to them. That's why I only did this once a year. But I was thinking of making an exception this year, for Lily. I got back to my car, wiping my face. Looking over the graves one more time, I turned the key and started the drive home.

***

"Hey man."

Luke greeted me as I entered the packhouse.

"Hey."

"How was it?"

"Honestly? Not as bad this time. Not as hard."

He gave me a smile which I returned.

"I don't know if now is the right time, but I have that information you wanted. It's in your office."

Luke was still gathering the information on Lilys former pack while Ben was away. It was too important to put on hold again.

"How much did you find out?"

"A lot. You might want to leave it until tomorrow."

Thinking it over, I said, "Yeah, you might be right about that."

"I have some stuff to do, so I'll see you tonight."

"Sounds good. Don't be late."

"Never."

Luke was also standing in for Ben tonight, acting as Beta and Gamma. I'd already gotten Bens verbal and written confirmation on accepting Lily as his Luna, but traditionally, both would be here to announce it to the pack. Oh, well. It would be fine. Taking the stairs to my-our-room, I grabbed my clothes for tonight and hung them over my arm. I was giving up my bathroom to my sister for the afternoon so she could 'work her magic' on my mate, as she said. That left me to get ready in Bens room.

I had hours still before the ceremony, so I dropped the clothes and headed to the kitchen, hoping Greta had something to eat. The place was busy; Omegas and cooks bustling around preparing for the dinner after the ceremony. The air smelled of various meats, rice, veggies, potatoes and something garlicy. I spotted Greta amongst the staff and waved.

"Hello dear." She gave me her signature cheeky smile.

"Hi Greta. Think I could grab a sandwich or something?"

"There's a plate for you in the fridge over there." She pointed. "I figured you wouldn't wait until dinner."

"You're the best."

"I know how to take of my boys."

Giving her a quick side hug, I moved through the kitchen to retrieve my plate. Greta was spot on- A turkey and bacon club with potato salad on the side. She knew me well. I grabbed the plate, waving goodbye and left them to their preparations. I ate as I climbed the stairs, going to Bens room. My phone was buzzing on the table when I arrived.

Swallowing quickly, I picked it up. "Hello?"

"It's me." Bens voice sounded distant.

"I can barely hear you."

"Reception out here is shit. This was the best I could do."

"Okay. What's up?"

"You won't fucking believe this, but I found what we're looking for."

I lowered my sandwich. "Already?"

"Pretty good, right?"

"Pretty suspicious."

A loud crash sounded on his end, followed by what sounded like a child laughing.

"Hey! Don't play with that!" Ben shouted. I couldn't make out the reply, but Ben groaned. "I should be home soon. I might actually be there for tonight, if we can catch a last minute flight."

"Alright. I'll alert patrol that you're bringing guests. See you."

"Bye boss."

I hung up, tapping the phone against my thigh. Bens task should have been next to impossible, especially given the circumstances. What witch would go against another? And to help werewolves at that? I had my doubts, and my suspicions, but I would put them to rest until I met whoever he was bringing back. Worst case scenario, I'd send them on their way and we'd start over.

Finishing my lunch, I jumped in the shower again, wanting to be totally refreshed. I had plans for tonight, and not all of them involved just making Lily our Luna. But I'd meant what I'd said to my parents; I was going to try and fix things between Lily and I, starting tonight. I was nervous as hell, and could only hope she would hear me out. While I was brushing my teeth, I mind linked Silvia, Connors former mate, and told her what I had in mind. She gushed at my idea, and promised to have everything ready before time. I'd made a good call with her. She was a nice girl.

Glancing at the time, I started to get ready. I fixed my hair, slicking it back and shaved my ever annoying five-o'clock shadow. My suit was a grey three piece, something Thara had picked out for me. She said it reminded her of the suit Dad wore at our mothers ceremony. It made me wonder what she had in store for Lily.

Luke popped his head in as I was adjusting my tie, Miguel behind him.

"You look very handsome Alpha."

"Thanks Miguel."

"What about me?" Luke pouted.

"*Handsome* is not the word I would use for you." Miguel said and Luke blushed.

"It's almost time. We should go down."

"Right."

As we walked out of the packhouse and made our way to the now transformed training yard, I prayed hard that everything would work out tonight.

# CHAPTER 38

It was official- I was not a fan of malls.

Thara had dragged me around for *hours* today. First we went to a spa, where I'd had oils and lotions and applied to my body, and a very painful waxing experience. *That* was never happening again. Then she'd taken me to a salon, and given specific instructions to the hair dresser, who spent two hours doing my hair. I'd ended up with a half up-do and big, loose curls falling over my shoulder and down my back. After that, we went out for a quick lunch before picking up my dress, something Thara had ordered for me. I hadn't seen it yet, but I was decidedly scared.

I'd begged her to take me home, and she'd finally relented. Now, we were sitting in Dimitris bathroom, (Our bathroom? I wasn't sure), with every possible brand of make-up a girl could hope to own splayed out over the counter. She had brushed, polished and pat. She used things I didn't even know existed until now to make me into the beauty queen she was aiming for. I told her to go light- I wasn't use to wearing make-up. And she wasn't allowing me to look in the mirror, so I could only assume that by now I looked like a clown.

"Stop fidgeting Lily, I'm almost done."

"You said that ten minutes ago. And ten minutes before that."

She rolled her eyes, re-focusing on her masterpiece.

"Your impatience will be rewarded, believe me."

Twenty minutes and a lot of bickering later, she finally declared me done.

"Wait here, and don't you dare look in that mirror. You can't see until your dress is on!" She rushed out of the room. Before I'd taken two breaths, she came breezing back in, a white garment bag in hand. Hanging it on one of the towel hooks, she unzipped it and ordered me to stand. Carefully, she helped me into the dress and zipped up the back, fixing my hair afterwards.

"Let me adjust this... and here....perfect! Okay! You can look now!" She squealed.

Frightfully, I turned to the mirror to see what she'd done. My face morphed into one of pure shock as I took in the girl staring back at me.

She was beautiful.

Long, shiny red hair that was done sophisticated and mature, without overdoing it. Her skin was a light cream colour, a hint of rose on her cheeks. Long lashes framed startling green eyes, made to pop by rose-gold eyeshadow and lightly applied eyeliner. Her lips were plump and red, bringing the whole thing together into a natural but sexy look.

The face was only outdone by the dress. It was form-fitting, slender, a gorgeous pure shade of white. It enhanced the cleavage, without being slutty, and accentuated every curve. It had off the shoulder half sleeves that had intricate lace designs cut into them with little gemstones woven in.

"Well? What do you think?" Thara asked me.

"Thara..." I swallowed. "I...I don't have the words..."

"You look stunning." She replied smugly.

I nodded mutely. I'd never doubt her again.

"Originally, this was suppose to periwinkle,-" She touched my dress. "-But I thought, since your wolf is white..."

"It's perfect. You are, without a doubt, the best sister-in-law in the whole wide world." I beamed at her.

"I'm glad you like it." She grinned. Her eyes clouded over momentarily before clearing again. "Hazel is on her way up. Come on, let's get you into some shoes and then it's time to go."

Taking one last look in the mirror, I followed her out. Hazel stood in the middle of the room, wearing a light blue dress that reached just passed her knees, her usual hair-do twisted up into a tight crown on her head. When she saw me, her mouth hit the floor.

"Lily? Oh my Goddess! You look amazing!" She exclaimed.

"Thanks."

Thara handed me a pair of white flats and I slipped them on. It was surprising how well I could move in this dress- It gave the impression of being tight, but I felt no different than wearing my jeans.

"Alright, let's go! You're going to be so happy with what we've done in the training yard!" Hazel gushed.

Apparently the yard was the only space large enough to hold almost all, if not the entire, pack.

"I have no doubt." I smiled at her.

The girls talked as we made our way out of the packhouse, excitement vibing between them. Me? I was a puddle of anxiety. I'd never been good with large crowds, and now I had all of Blood Moon, (Or most of it), waiting to see me. I was not use to being the center of attention, always trying to be invisible in an attempt to avoid it. More than that though, with every step I took, my fears grew. From the moment I found out I was an Alphas mate, I never believed I'd be worthy of being a Luna. It didn't matter that it was Blood Moon; It could have been anywhere, and I would have felt the same.

I had grown up a slave. Unloved, uncared for. Now I had an entire pack to care for, and the weight on my shoulders felt crushing. How could I be everything they wanted me to be?

*"You're a slave pretending to be a Luna."*

Jennine's hateful words echoed through my mind, strongly reinforcing my thoughts. Who was I trying to kid?

"Lily?"

I met Hazels eyes, some distance away. I hadn't realized I'd stopped walking.

"What's wrong?" Thara asked.

"I... I can't do this."

"Hey, none of that. You'll do fine. It's just a few oaths, and the cut doesn't even hurt." She reassured me.

I shook my head. "No, I mean *this*. I'm not... I mean, I can't be..." My breathing started to come faster and I felt dizzy.

"Lily." Hazel put her hands on my shoulders. "Stop. Take a deep breath. In. Now out. Again. In. And out. Good. Now, listen to me. You can do this. You *can*. No, don't shake your head at me. I know you can do this, and you want to know why?"

I didn't reply, so she went on.

"You are kind. Smart. Caring. Loving. Attentive."

"Strong. Wise. Friendly." Thara chimed in.

"And you are a good person. You have a good heart, a good soul. I know, people say that all the time, but *that* is what counts here. You went through so fucking much Lily, I don't even know the half of it, because you won't tell us. But you're standing here, on the other side of whatever you went through. You're standing here, tall and head held high. Because you were meant to come out stronger. You are the best choice for this pack, the best choice to be our Luna and lead us."

Thara put her hand on my back. "You can't see it the way we do Lily, but you've done so much good for us already. My brother is no longer the merciless tyrant he once was. He's smiling again, laughing again. He's looking after the pack fairly and justly, just like our Dad did." Tears brimmed her eyes. "You're bringing out the good in him, which can only bring out the best in all of us. You were meant to do this. So, do it proudly."

I looked between them, the fog clearing. They really believed in me. They accepted me, trusted me. Sincerity rang in their words and their faces, breaking through the last of my remaining fear.

"Okay. Let's go." I whispered.

"That's my girl." They quickly enveloped me in group hug before pulling me along with them.

When we finally reached the training yard, I was as Hazel predicted, incredibly happy. Twinkle lights had been strung from the trees, casting a soft glow over the faces of the pack members. Beyond them was a small platform with a table. I could make out a large golden bowl and two golden goblets resting atop it. Tables lined with white cloth had been placed in various areas, filled with all manner of food and drink, which people helped themselves to. The mats and equipment had been removed, replaced by dining area of tables and chairs. A larger table faced the rest, decorated with vases of flowers. My eyes caught a Blue Star Gazer Lily, and I smiled. That would have been Greta, for sure.

"Where's Dimitri?" I asked.

"He's here. Somewhere." Thara answered.

"What do I do now?" I asked her.

"You come with me, I have to be up there too since I'm Dimitris family. Luke is standing in for Ben."

"Oh no, he's not."

We turned to see a very out of breath, very disgruntled Ben behind us.

"I'm here, and the show can go on." He gasped.

"You made it!" Thara exclaimed.

"'Course I did."

"I'm happy you're here Ben." I gave him a warm smile.

"Me too munchkin. I would hug you, but I haven't showered in days."

"I can smell." I teased him.

"Doesn't matter. I made it. I wouldn't miss it for the world. I'm gunna go find Dimitri." He waved and disappeared into the crowd.

"I'll see you afterwards." Hazel gave me a hug before leaving as well, probably to find Clint.

"Come on." I followed Thara behind a black curtain I hadn't noticed before set to the right of the platform. It was positioned to block us from the crowd and the stage. I peeked around, looking for a sign of my mate.

"This feels more like a wedding than a Luna ceremony." I commented.

"Perhaps my brother is trying to make up for your guys' wedding."

That brought a blush to my cheeks.

A few minutes later, Ben and Luke joined us behind the curtain. Luke gushed over me, complimenting Tharas handy work.

"Dimitri says we're about to start." Ben said. I took a deep breath, trying to steady my nerves. Remembering my friends words, I held my head high. Then we heard Dimitris voice.

"Welcome, Blood Moon Pack! Thank you, so much, for coming out tonight and helping us celebrate. In a few moments, you will finally get to welcome your new Luna!"

# CHAPTER 39

**LILYS POV**

"Thara Mary Elena Varlos, please join me." Dimitri called. Thara gave me a quick pat before stepping out from the curtain and joining her brother.

"Beta Benjamin Griffin Hayes, please join me."

"You're middle name is *Griffin*?" I snickered. Ben put a finger to my lips, going to join Dimitri.

"Gamma Lucas Erik Michael Turne, please join me."

I peeked through a slit in the curtain, seeing Thara, Ben and Luke standing behind Dimitri.

"Lily Varlos, please join us."

My ears perked at the name. Nobody had ever used my new legal name until now. It sounded odd, weird. But strangely good.

*"We can do this."* Aya reminded me. I nodded and stepped from behind the curtain.

My gaze locked with Dimitris, the look on his face faltering my steps momentarily.

*"Is something wrong?"* I asked Aya.

*"Nothing at all. They're just in shock."* She chuckled.

Walking carefully up the three steps, I moved across the platform until I was standing in front of my mate. His eyes roamed over me, lingering on my hips, my cleavage and finally, my face. His expression was comical, to say the least, like it was the first time he'd seen someone of the opposite sex. A few people in the crowd cleared their throats loudly.

"Right. Let's begin." Dimitris voice was thick and deep as he turned to his sister, who was smirking at him, unashamed.

"Thara."

She joined us the table, offering him her hand, palm turned up. Dimitri picked up a long blade, the hilt encrusted with a giant red stone. He ran it quickly over he skin, drawing a thin line of blood. Thara squeezed her hand over the golden bowl, allowing a few drops to drip into it. I hadn't noticed before, it was filled with some sort of clear drink. Wine perhaps? Tharas blood sank into it, swirling around.

"Ben."

The same process was repeated with Ben, and then Luke. And then Dimitri held his hand out to me. Softly placing my hand in his, he turned my palm up and placed the tip of the knife just below my thumb. I kept my face neutral as he drew it across quickly. Remembering Tharas instructions, I waited until he cut his own hand and clasped it with mine, our blood mixing together.

"Do you Lily Varlos, promise to lead the Blood Moon Pack justly and fairly, without intent of malice and harm?" Dimitris voice boomed across the clearing.

"I do."

"Do you, Lily Varlos, promise to uphold our laws and our beliefs with kindness and without bias?"

"I do."

"Do you, Lily Varlos, promise to accept me as your Alpha, and do you accept the privilege and responsibility of ruling the Blood Moon Pack by my side?"

Meeting his heavy stare, I answered loudly. "I do."

He turned to our friends. "Do you accept your new Luna wholeheartedly, without objection or question?" He asked.

"I do." Their voices rang out together, filled with happiness.

Squeezing our hands together, our mixed blood fell into the bowl, mixing with the others. Dimitri released my hand and picked up one of the goblets, motioning subtly for me to do the same. Dipping it into the wine, we drank the concoction, a warm feeling spreading through my veins and into my stomach. It vaguely reminded me of shifting.

"I, Alpha Dimitri Harold Varlos, accept you, Lily Varlos, as my mate and Luna of the Blood Moon Pack."

As soon as he'd finished speaking, I felt a bond separate from ours click into place. At the same time, my mind was instantly overwhelmed with hundreds of voices, the chaos causing my knees to wobble and my eyes to shut tightly against the noise. I realized it was pack members, all of them. I was officially connected to them, able to mind-link.

Dimitri gave me a moment to right myself before taking my hand again and pulling me close. He turned to the crowd and said, "Welcome your new Luna Blood Moon!"

Clapping and cheers and utter pandemonium erupted from the crowd, deafening me. The overwhelming acceptance was so unexpected that tears sprang to my eyes. I the most surprising one for me though was the man standing next to me. Becoming his official Luna had almost completed our bond. I could feel waves of happiness and pride radiating off him. He was glad his pack accepted me so fully, I could tell. Our pack, now.

"There is plenty of food, and you're all welcome to stay and celebrate with us. Enjoy yourselves." Dimitri said to the crowd before leading me off the stage, followed by Thara, Ben and Luke.

"You did so well Lily! I'm so happy!" Thara gripped me in a tight hug.

"You really did. I am proud to officially call you my Luna." Ben smiled.

"Me too." Luke agreed.

I grinned at all of them.

"Thank you, you guys. I'm proud to be your Luna too."

"Come on. I'm starving." Thara took my hand, pulling me with her to the dining area. I took the seat she indicated, she sitting next to me. We chatted until the boys joined us, Dimitri setting a plate full of food in front of me.

"Thank you." I told him.

He gave me a gorgeous smile, taking my hand on the table. I was in too good a mood to analyze his actions so I simply accepted it and chatted with his sister as I ate. Laughter and excitement could be heard from every direction, the pack as happy as I'd ever seen them. Some time later, Luke left us to find his mate and Ben went with him. Thara claimed to be tired, and took her leave as well. Which left me sitting alone with my mate, still holding hands. I decided it was the perfect time to try.

*"Dimitri?"* I sent out a hesitant mind-link, giggling when he jumped a little before looking at me.

*"That's going to take some getting use to."* He smiled softly.

Hearing his voice in my mind... it was so different. I loved it.

*"I like it."*

*"Me too. And there's someone who wants to say hi."*

I raised an eyebrow.

*"Hello mate."*

A voice that didn't belong to Dimitri floated into my head.

*"Ajax?"*

*"Yes. It's nice to finally be able to contact you."*

I furrowed my brows. *"You couldn't before?"* I simply assumed he'd never tried, not that he couldn't.

*"No, though I do not know why. Aya was able to talk to Dimitri, but I could not reach you, even in wolf form. Perhaps it is because you are a Mother Wolf."*

*"Huh. Weird. Well, it's nice to finally meet you."*

*"And you. I want to thank you Lily, for showing us kindness. Even when my human did not quite deserve it. You are truly a perfect mate."*

I blushed. *"I see why Aya is so enamoured with you. Shame that Dimitri did not get your manners."*

*"He is trying. I will give him back control now."*

*"Bye Ajax."*

I watched as Dimitris eyes cleared and he sighed. "Everyone likes him more than me." He grumbled. I laughed.

"He is quite charming."

He rolled his eyes.

"I like you too, you know." I told him shyly.

"Really?"

"Really." I squeezed his hand on mine. "You're not... as much of a monster as I thought you were." I said slowly.

His face softened.

"Thank you." His tone said my words meant a lot to him.

We made small talk, laughing here and there, and it felt so nice. A few pack members came to congratulate me, telling me how happy they were to have me as Luna. I accepted everyone graciously, feeling every bit the Luna I now was.

"I have something for you." Dimitri told me an hour later. The celebration was still in full swing-these people knew how to have a good time, obviously.

"For me?"

He nodded. "It's in our room. We can wait a while if you want to stay longer though."

I hadn't missed the way he'd said 'our room'. Thinking about it, my curiosity got the better of me.

"We can go."

Pulling me to my feet, we said a fond farewell, assuring everyone they were welcome to stay as they liked. We walked together back to the house, him still refusing to release my hand.

"Did you have fun?" He asked.

I nodded. "It was incredible."

When we got upstairs, I got confused as he led me past his door.

"I thought you said-?"

"I did. Just wait."

We walked past his office, turning the corner. I'd always assumed this way led to more bedrooms, but the hallway came to a sudden stop in front of just one door. I looked at him questioningly.

"This is the Alpha and Lunas suite. I've never used it, you weren't here yet. It can be our new room, if you want."

"You want me to move in with you, officially?"

"Yes."

Excitement bubbled inside me, but I tried to contain it. "Okay."

Dimitri beamed. Like I'd just given him the best Christmas present. His behaviour today was so unusual, I'd never seen him smile this much. But I liked it, hoping it would last.

"Close your eyes."

I gave him a look.

"Trust me."

I did as he asked, hearing the door open. He came to stand behind me, guiding me forward. The door closed behind us. Different smells drifted around the room. Rose... Lilies...and was that smoke? Angling me slightly to the right, he leant down to my ear, "Okay."

I slowly opened my eyes, gasping as I took in the room. The first thing I saw was the huge bed, as big as the one in his room. It had a soft looking gold comforter with white pillows laced with gold trim. Two wooden night tables sat on either side of the bed, both with huge white vases filled with roses and lilies. I saw a double door that I assumed was the closet. An open kitchen was placed to the left of that, a small dining table and chairs seated close by. That was also adorned by flowers.

There was an old fashioned stone fireplace opposite the bed, a giant plush rug on the floor in front of it. A fire was already roaring inside, sparks crackling in the air. An open doorway led to a bathroom, looking every bit as polished and fine as the ones I'd used so far. Looking up, I noticed a beautiful chandelier hanging from the high ceiling. The walls were the same dark colour as Dimitris room, familiar.

It was a lot to take in.

"Wow." I breathed.

# CHAPTER 40

## DIMITRIS POV

"You like it?"

Lily nodded. "I love it. It's beautiful."

"So are you." I said softly. She blushed from the unexpected compliment.

"What's gotten into you?" She mumbled.

Wrapping my arms around her from behind, I laid my chin on shoulder. "Can I be honest with you?"

"Please."

*Here goes nothing.*

"Ever since my parents died, I've been making mistake after mistake. I was cold, angry. Heartless. I was running the pack, but not as well as I could have been. My people didn't trust me; they feared me. I pushed everyone away, closed myself off from the world. And then out of nowhere, a girl with red hair and startling green eyes entered my life, and started to make me feel again."

Lilys chest moved up and down rapidly as I talked. Slowly, I turned her in my arms, resting my hands lightly on her back.

"You made me remember what it felt to feel happy. To smile and laugh. You showed me how to let go of my anger and have fun again. I've made a lot of mistakes with you, Lily. Now I'm standing here, asking if you'll give me a second chance."

I could practically see the wheels turning in her head. I waited patiently, giving her time to organize her thoughts.

"Is this real? Or do you only want me for your original reasons?" She asked finally.

"I'm being serious. I know I was selfish. And stupid. I wanted you for only one reason, but now I want you for many."

"Such as?"

"The way I feel when I'm with you. The way you can make me laugh, just by being yourself. Your kindness and caring. I wanted you to make me stronger, and you have in the most unexpected ways. I can't go back to a life without you in it Lily."

A stray tear ran from the corner of her eye and onto her cheek. I wiped it away with my thumb.

"I want you. *For you.* You're the most beautiful person I've ever met, inside and out. I want us to start over, have a new beginning. Just know that if you say no, I'll spend the rest of my life trying to make up for my shitty choices until you change your mind. You're worth every second."

I watched her anxiously, hoping with everything inside me that she wanted me like I wanted her.

"Having you begging for my forgiveness for a whole lifetime is pretty tempting." She mused. "But being happy with you, as mates, sounds even better."

My heart cracked, pouring out so much happiness I thought I'd faint. Placing my hands on her cheeks, I brought my lips down on hers, kissing her with everything I had. Sparks shot through me at the contact, stronger than I'd ever felt before. Lilys arms went around my neck, pulling me closer. It was far too long overdue, but she was so worth the wait. It was the best kiss I'd had ever have, and it also felt like the first. It was *her* first, and I thanked the Goddess it was I who shared it with her.

She pulled us to the bed, never removing her lips from mine. I kicked off my shoes, running my hands down the soft material of her dress. Gently lying her back, I took a minute to gaze at her beautiful face. She was glowing, pure joy shining in her eyes. Swiftly, I undid her hair, letting it fall onto the bed and frame her face.

Lily reached up, her small hand cupping my cheek softly.

"I want you Dimitri."

My mind stuttered, my heart beat picking up.

"I didn't do this so you would sleep with me Lily."

"I know." She smiled. "But I want to."

"But-"

"Don't make me attack you again." She threatened.

I raised an eyebrow. "Would you?"

"Without hesitation."

Pulling me down by my collar, she whispered in my ear, "Come on. Show me what my Alpha can do." And every ounce of self control I had was gone. My lips slammed down on hers and I kissed her with a hunger of a man starved. Lily broke the kiss, gasping in air. I simply moved my lips down her jaw. Over her neck. Kissing and gently biting the swell of breasts. I had to remember that everything that was going to happen was all new to her- I needed to take my time.

Her first time should be as special as she was. It was going to hurt; there was nothing I could do about that. But I could try and prepare her as much as possible. With that thought in mind, I slid my arm under back and pulled her into my lap. I used my free hand to slowly unzip her dress, letting the sleeves slip off her shoulders. I attacked the newly showing skin, eager to taste of every inch of her. I grazed her marking spot with my teeth, and her hips bucked.

Placing her hands on my shoulders, she gently pushed me back. Her eyes were alive with a confidence I'd only seen once before, during her heat. standing on the bed, she pushed the sleeves down and let her dress slide off her body to land at her feet. She wasn't wearing a bra, only a thin layer of white silk panties that had me drooling. I didn't have words to describe how she looked. Beautiful seemed too mild.

Discarding her clothes to the floor, I pulled her back down.

"You're making it very difficult to go slow with you." I told her.

"I'm really not sorry."

"I know you're not." I kissed her, taking her lower lip between my teeth. "Tell me if anything makes you uncomfortable, okay?"

"Mhmm."

My eyes never leaving hers, I lowered my head running my tongue over her nipple before taking it in my mouth. A soft moan left her lips, the sound heading straight to my dick. I licked and teased her before moving to give her other nipple the same attention. Her breath was coming rapidly and the scent of her arousal hung thickly in the air. It was hard to leave her gorgeous mounds; I could stay like this all night. Still, she was eager and so was I. I sat back on my heels, undoing my belt. Lily watched my movements with a curious and excited expression.

Relief washed through me as I took off my pants; They'd been far too tight. The relief was replaced by amusement as I watched my mates face morph from curious to shock and then doubt.

"Hey."

She met my eyes.

"Do you trust me?"

"Yes." She answered immediately.

I took off my shirt, throwing it to the floor. Leaning over her, I placed a kiss on her nose.

"I won't hurt you. Not intentionally. But this doesn't have to happen if you're not ready. You can *always* tell me stop, and I will, no questions asked. I promise."

After a minute, she said, "I'm ready. I want you Dimitri."

Leaving a trail of kisses down her body, I hooked my fingers in her panties and pulled them off. Then I spread her legs and settled my head between her thighs. She was already so wet, the sight making my dick throb. Flicking my tongue out, I ran it quickly over her slit, savouring her taste. It was incredible. Her hips lifted at the contact, a hiss coming between her teeth. Repeating the action, I got the same response. Holding her hips in place, my tongue ran all the way up, teasing her clit. And again.

"Dimitri!" Lilys voice was raspy, breathy. It only turned me on more.

I teased her for several minutes more before finally taking her clit in my mouth, sucking on it hard. She moaned loudly, encouraging me to go further. I inserted one finger, all the way until I felt a wall. She winced a little so I pulled out, adjusting so I wouldn't hurt her. Her hips started moving, grinding against my face as I licked and sucked and bit gently. When I thought she was ready, I added another finger.

"D-Dimitri..."

"Hmm?"

"You're going to... make me..."

"Mhmm." I hummed. A minute later, she did, my name leaving her lips, sounding like music to my ears. I licked her juices, not able to get enough of the delicious taste.

"Oh my Goddess."

Positioning myself over her, I gave her a long kiss. "Are you ready?"

"Yes."

Wrapping one arm under her neck, I positioned myself at her entrance. I pushed in an inch, stopping when she winced. When she nodded, I went a little further. Fuck, she was *tight*. It was incredibly hard to take it as slow as I was, no pun intended.

"Breathe Lily."

Lily took a deep breath under me. When she released it, I pushed in again. We went like that until I hit her wall again.

"This is going to hurt." I warned her.

"I know. It's okay."

I kissed her, and feeling like a total asshole, pushed through the resistance inside her. She screamed into my mouth, biting my lip. I think she drew blood.

"I'm sorry. Are you okay?" I asked her worriedly.

"When exactly does it start to feel good?" She hissed through clenched teeth.

"Soon. I promise."

Two tears fell onto her cheeks and I kissed them away. I stayed perfectly still, just letting her breath and relax.

"I'm okay, I think. You can move now."

Keeping my eyes on her, I started to move in and out. After a few minutes, the pain on her face was replaced with a look of awe.

"Oh.." She moaned softly and I smiled.

"Better?"

"Much."

I picked up the speed a little, Lilys mouth forming a small 'O'. Her fingers ran across the skin of my back, nails digging in. Everywhere she touched, fire erupted on my skin.

*"Faster. Please."*

Lilys voice was mixed with her wolves in my head. Her eyes were flashing from green to black and back again.

"You really want to see what your Alpha can do?" I growled.

Something between a growl and moan was my response. I started giving her my best, not my all, but enough to give her the pleasure I wanted her to have. I'd save the rest for another time. Ajax pushed himself to the surface. I knew what he wanted, I did too. Tilting her chin away from me, I exposed her neck. My canines extended, my wolf ready to take over and complete our mating.

*"Mine."* Ajax's voice came from my mouth before my teeth sunk into neck. I felt Lily bite me almost instantly after. I couldn't describe what happened next, not in a million years. The closest I could come to was saying I felt something like our souls coming together, intertwining. At the same time, I felt my mate clench around me, almost painfully tightly. With one powerful thrust, I came undone inside her, experiencing the best orgasm of my entire life.

Together we released each other and fell to the bed exhausted.

# CHAPTER 41

**BENS POV**

I left Luke with Miguel, making an excuse about needing to shower. Okay, it wasn't really an excuse; I *did* need one. Pack members were actively avoiding me, telling me all I needed to know about my stench. I just really wanted to get back to the packhouse. I'd left the witch, Clara, in my room with a short promise to return as soon as possible.

She wasn't like anything I'd been expecting. I'd found her in the southern region of our state, guided by the humans rumors of a witch who lived in the forest. I'd been prepared for an old hag-like woman that I'd have to fight tooth and nail to convince to come with me. Not a beautiful blonde with shimmering brown eyes and her four year old daughter.

And certainly not a mate.

At first, I'd thought it was some magic she'd spelled me with. I couldn't be mated to a witch- that just didn't happen. But she was as shocked as I was, breaking down on the porch and cursing to any deity that came to mind. I told her to reject me, earning myself a slap. Apparently witches couldn't reject their other halves without giving up their magic. Who knew? And who knew that witches had mates to begin with?

And how the Hell was I suppose to explain this Dimitri and the others? Sighing, I entered my room.

"It's about time. What took you so long?" Clara stood, crossing her arms.

"I couldn't just leave. That would have looked weird."

"Isabelle fell asleep hours ago. I had nowhere else to put her." She pointed to my bed where her daughter was curled up, hugging my pillow.

"I'm sorry, okay? You can stay here for tonight. I'll find somewhere else. Just let me grab some clothes."

"Where are you going to go?"

I shrugged. " I don't know. I'll find an empty room or something."

"Yeah. Right." She rolled her eyes.

"What's that suppose to mean?"

"Nothing. Just go." She sank into the armchair, glaring out the window. I stared at her, not understanding where her anger was coming from.

"Would you rather sleep somewhere else?" I asked.

"And what? Wake her up? She won't go back to sleep for hours if I do that."

I threw my hands up. "So you're angry if I leave, and you're angry if you have to. And you've made really clear you don't want to be around me, so we can't stay here together. Why are you making this so damn difficult?"

"*I'm* making this difficult?! I didn't ask for you to show up at my door! I didn't ask for a werewolf mate!" She whisper-yelled.

"And I didn't ask for my mate to be a witch! I guess the Goddess has a sick sense of humor!"

Shock appeared on her face, followed immediately by hurt.

Fuck.

Pinching the bridge of my nose, I sighed heavily. "I'm sorry. That was out of line. We're both just really tense, this is a weird situation. I'm going to grab some clothes so I can shower and I'll come find you in the morning."

She didn't answer, so I quickly gathered my things and turned to leave.

"Ben?"

I looked over my shoulder.

"Are you...Are you going to find a she-wolf to spend the night with?"

"What?" No. I'm going to find a room to shower and sleep. By myself."

"Okay. Fine." Sitting back in the chair, she avoided my gaze.

"Clara, whether you like it or not, you're my mate. I have no desire to seek out some random girl with my mate sleeping in the same house. If you're not going to reject me, then at least have some faith in me. I may be part beast, but I'm not a monster." With that, I shut the door and left. What on Earth had made her ask me that?

"*Isn't it obvious?*" My wolf, Jude, asked.

"*Uh, no?*"

"*Wow, you really* are *dumb sometimes.*"

"*Are you going to tell me or not?*"

"*I was, but now I want to see if you can figure it out yourself.*"

"*I hate you.*"

I did find an empty room, thankfully. Dumping my clothes on the bed, I stripped out of my dirty ones and threw them in the corner. Jumping in the shower, I let days of dirt and sweat run off me. I felt a million times already. Focusing my mind on my mates question, I turned over different theories. Was she worried about losing her magic? Would that happen if I slept with someone else? Not that it mattered, because I wouldn't. Or was she just worried about Isabelle? Did she think I was the type to parade different women around in front of her and her daughter?

*"Oh my Goddess, you idiot. She's been cheated on!"* Jude yelled at me.

*"Huh?"*

*"No woman asks that out of the blue unless it's happened before. How do you not know this?"*

*"How do you* know *this?"*

*"Because I'm not stupid."*

I hmphed at him. *"But I would never do that."*

*"I know that. But whoever hurt her really took a toll. My guess would be it was Isabelle's Dad."*

It made sense, looking at it from his perspective.

*"Okay Mr. Expert On Women. What do I do?"*

*"Nothing you can do bud. Except give her time and show her you're not that type of guy. She'll come around."*

*"Really? All you've got is 'she'll come around'?"*

*"Yes. And maybe work the kid in our favour too."*

*"You want me to use my mates kid to manipulate her into liking us?"* I scoffed. He was unbelievable.

*"It's not manipulation. Clara is our mate, so Isabelle is our pup. And she already likes you."*

*"That just seems wrong dude."*

*"If Clara came to us right now and accepted us, would we or would we not accept Isabelle too?"*

*"Okay, yeah. I see your point. I just don't like the way you worded it."*

It was true, Isabelle took to me almost instantly. While her mom was packing, she'd asked me endless questions about what it was like being a werewolf. She had a curious mind and a wild imagination. The kid was also a little ball of energy; Like a battery that never lost it's charge. Isabelle needed to see everything, know what it was, and then ask fifty questions of how's and why's.

I smiled, remembering when we were at the airport. Isabelle had been *fascinated* by the planes.

### ***FLASHBACK***

*"Mama, how do they stay up? What makes them fly?"*

*"Uh... mechanics?" Clara had no idea.*

*"What kind?"*

*"The..mechanical...kind." I bit my lip to keep from laughing. Isabelle, clearly not satisfied with her moms answer, turned to me.*

*"What your mom is trying to say is there is a whole lot of science that goes into airplanes. It's super complicated and involves a lot of math."*

*Her little nose scrunched up with disdain. I'd learned very quickly that Isabelle hated math, avoiding it when she could.*

*"Never mind."*

*Clara looked at me, lips pursed. By now, I wasn't expecting a thank you. And I didn't receive one.*

*"Mama! Mama, why is that ladies belly so fat when the rest of her skinny?!" Isabelle was pointing to a pregnant women standing about five feet away. Her voice carried loudly around the area, making the women turn and raise her eyebrows.*

*"Because I'm having a baby." The woman told her.*

*Isabelle's eyes lit up. "Really? How did it get in there?"*

*Clara just about choked when her daughter looked at her for an answer. This time I couldn't hold back my laugh, earning myself a cold glare.*

*"Well... uh...you see sweetie..." Clara fumbled for words, coming up empty.*

*"She ate a watermelon seed Isabelle. The seed is growing in her belly, and it turns into a baby." I said.*

*"Really?!" Clara hissed at me.*

*"Yup, really."*

*"Wow!" Isabelle turned to examine the woman's stomach again.*

*"You know that now I can never give her watermelon again." Clara said lowly to me.*

*"Tell her it's not the baby kind, and you'll be fine. That's what my mom did with us."*

*"You're unbelievable."*

*"You want to tell her the truth instead?"*

*She blushed adorably, shaking her head frantically.*

**\*\*\*END FLASHBACK\*\*\***

My dick hardened, picturing my mates face all flushed. I groaned. Why did it have to be this way? Why did the Moon Goddess do this to me? I was a nice guy- I was loyal and hard working. Never asked for much. So why couldn't my mate be a she-wolf, like everyone else?

*"We don't get to choose that. And you're being pretty selfish right now."* Jude huffed.

*"I just want my mate. And I want her to want me too. How is that selfish?"*

*"Don't you think she feels the same way? All anyone wants is to be loved."*

If Clara wanted to be loved, why was she pushing me away? We were literally made for each other- she was the other half to my soul. I could say it was because she was protecting Isabelle, but it felt more personal to me than that. Maybe my wolf was right, and whoever she let in before had hurt her so bad that she didn't want to let anyone in again, mate or not.

I sighed heavily. Why couldn't anything just ever be easy?

# CHAPTER 42

I woke up to a very happy, very energetic Dimitri planting kisses along the beck of my neck. The feeling sent shivers down my spine.

"Good morning." He spoke deeply between kisses.

"Good morning to you." I giggled.

"How did you sleep?"

I turned over, facing him. "Very well. You?"

"Best sleep I've ever had." He grinned down at me. His hair was mussed sexily, eyes shining as he gazed at me. I pulled him down for a quick kiss, unprepared for the way he attacked my lips hungrily.

"Dimitri!" I laughed. "I have to use the bathroom."

He groaned. "Can't you hold it?"

"Not for what you have in mind."

Releasing me, I slipped off the bed. I did my business and then brushed my teeth. My reflection smiled back at me, my cheeks glowing and my eyes bright. A hint of red caught my eye and I looked down to see dried blood coating the inside of my thighs. Well, that was embarrassing. Turning on the shower, I half stepped in when the door opened.

"Women really do take forever in the bathroom." He said.

"I uh, have to wash myself. After last night." I blushed. His face dropped, and it took me a second to hear what he'd heard in my words. "Not because of you!" I pointed to the blood.

"Oh. Right, sorry. I forgot that happens with virgins." He smirked.

Stepping under the water, I reach for my body wash. "I'm thinking the sheets need to be replaced."

"Probably." His voice came from behind me, startling me.

"What are you doing?"

"Joining you in the shower. I thought that was obvious, since you didn't want to come back to bed."

He stepped into the spray, my eyes travelling down his chest, over his abs and stopping at his member. This man would be the death of me, I swear. While I was busy ogling him, he took the bottle from my hands, squirting some of my lavender wash into his hands. Without saying a word he proceeded to start rubbing it over me, my shoulders, my arms.

"I'm liking the service this room offers." I giggled.

"Do you now?"

"Very much. It's highly pleasurable."

His eyes darkened as his hands went over my breasts, pausing to tweak my nipples once. I bit back a moan.

"Turn around."

I did as he asked, feeling his front flush my with my back, his erection poking me in the butt. His hands wandered over my stomach, the soap sliding down my body if a foamy soothing manner. He washed my back and then kneeled to wash each of my legs int turn. While he did that, I washed my hair. I peeked down at him while I rinsed, raw need written all over his face. That look alone had me turned on, the scent of my arousal wafting over us. First, however, I wanted to return his favour.

Grabbing the bottle of men's wash, I applied a generous amount to my hands, lathering it up. It smelled really good, like pine. Dimitri stood, allowing me to run my hands all over his body. His natural scent mixed with that of the soap and it was intoxicating. He washed his while I worked, groaning when I stroked his member. Quickly, I bent the way he had and washed his legs, peering up at him. An idea was taking form in my mind, but I was nervous to try it. I figured it was going to happen someday, so I might as well rip the band-aid off, right?

"I want to try something." I said shyly to him.

"Oh?" He raised an eyebrow.

Tentatively, I reached my hand up and gently took hold of him. Despite being in the shower, my lips were dry with anxiety. Would I be any good at this? Would he like it?

Not meeting his eyes, I hesitantly rose up on my knees and licked the tip of his shaft. His hissed at the contact. This was more difficult than I thought-he was a lot taller than me, even more so with me on my knees. It would be too embarrassing to crouch like a crab though.

Feeling my frustration, Dimitri lifted me to my feet. "Come here." He sat down on the low bench attached to the wall. I got on my knees again; Much better. Taking him in my hand, I licked his tip again. It was smooth, soft- Not what I'd expected.

*"Just look at his face. You totally own him right now."*

Aya's words boosted my confidence. She was right; Dimitri was giving me *that* look, the same one he'd had after I shifted the first time. This time, instead of making me angry, it made me feel sexy. Confident. My anxiety washed away with the water and I used my tongue to slowly lick from the base of his shaft to the tip before taking him in my mouth.

"Fuck Lily..." His eyes closed, his head dropping back.

I took him as far as I could, which was not even half. His hand went to my hair, gently twisting into it while he guided my movements. I flicked my tongue over him as I went up and down, feeling get impossibly harder in my mouth.

"If you don't stop now, I'm going to come in your mouth." He warned.

Our eyes met, his black as night. I continued to bob up and down on him, wanting to experience it. I wanted to taste him; He'd tasted me, it was only fair. I started to stroke him as I went, a growl erupting throughout the room. Two seconds later, I felt his dick twitch and unload in my mouth. It was salty, with a hint of sweetness. I swallowed everything, proudly. Sitting back on my heels, I smiled at him.

It didn't take him long to recover. Dimitri picked me up, wrapping my legs around his waist. My back hit the wall as he entered me in swift movement.

"I want that every morning." He breathed.

"Every morning?"

"*Every* morning." He thrust into me hard.

"No promises." I gasped. Dimitri kissed me, long and hard, continuing to slam into me. It wasn't long before I was a moaning, incoherent mess.

He grunted. "Ben wants us downstairs to meet-"

"He can wait!"

Hips meeting mine again and again, I felt my insides clench. My world exploded as I came undone around him, gasping his name at the same time he growled out mine. He finished closely behind me, both of breathing hard. I kissed him passionately, over the moon and feeling a little giddy.

"That was the dirtiest shower I've ever had." I giggled and he smirked.

"Better get used to it darling." Dimitri kissed my nose and set me on my feet. My legs were a little wobbly but I didn't mind.

I washed one more time before grabbing a towel and stepping out.

"So, Ben wants to see us?" I asked as I wrapped my hair.

"To meet the witch he brought back, yes."

"Give me five minutes to get ready." I said as I headed into the closet. Pulling out some clothes, I dressed quickly and brushed my hair. I threw it into a bun and met him in the room. He looked at his watch.

"That was exactly five minutes?"

"So?"

"You might be the only girl I've ever met that says she'll be ready in five minutes and is actually ready in five minutes."

I laughed. "I'm not really the dress-up, fancy everyday type."

"I know. That's one thing I lo-like about you."

I blinked. Was he about to say love?

"Come on. Everyone is gathered in my office." He took my hand and we left together.

Did Dimitri love me?

Did I love him?

Looking up at his smiling face, feeling the way my heart melted, I thought maybe I might.

# CHAPTER 43

**DIMITRIS POV**

Together, Lily and I stepped into my office. Ben, Luke, and Thara were already there, along with a short blonde women I assumed to be our witch. A little girl who looked just like her stood behind her, peering at me with a curious expression. Every pair of eyes except the two zeroed in our joined hands, then simultaneously went to Lily and I's new marks. The room was dead silent for a one heartbeat. Then-

"*Ahhh!*" My sister squealed and rushed us, enveloping us in a tight hug. My Beta and Gamma jumped slightly and the women and girl looked at her like she was crazy. "*Finally!* I am so happy for you guys!"

"Thanks Thara." Lily patted her back.

Releasing us, Thara pointed a finger at me. "You better have a re-do on your wedding. Her Luna ceremony doesn't count! I want the chance to stand at the altar with my sister-in-law."

I rubbed the back of neck. "I'll think about it."

"What is going on?" The witch whispered to Ben.

"I'll explain later." He told her. He then stepped around my siter to give me a bro-hug. "Congrats man. I'm happy for you."

"Me too. Took long enough." Luke said from behind him.

"Can we get on with business please?" I asked eagerly. I was unbelievably happy that I finally got to be with my mate, but my friends, and especially my sister, were known for being nosy. They would undoubtedly want details of what happened between us to lead us being together at last, but there were more pressing matters to be dealt with. And, there was a child in the room.

"I think that's a good idea." Lily said, squeezing my hand.

"Fine." Thara rolled her eyes.

I sat down at my desk, pulling Lily with me. She perched on my lap, my arms going around her waist. Everyone gawked at us until I cleared my throat.

"Ben?"

"Right. Everyone, this is Clara Whitethorn, and her daughter, Isabelle. Clara, Isabelle, this is our Alpha Dimitri, his Luna and mate, Lily, and our Gamma Luke."

"Ahem!"

"And that's Dimitris sister, Thara. Though I'm not sure why she's even here. Shouldn't you be at work?" He asked her.

Thara shrugged. "I'm allowed to take days off. And I'm part of the Alpha family, I have a right to be here too."

"Whatever." Now Ben rolled his eyes. He seemed to be on edge.

I ignored them, turning to Clara. "Welcome to Blood Moon. Thank you for agreeing to come."

"I didn't have much choice." She scowled at Ben, who paled. I looked between them, confusion gnawing at me.

"What do you mean by that?" I asked.

She glanced down at her daughter, pressing her lips together.

"Isabelle, wasn't it?" Lily untangled herself from me, going to kneel in front of the girl. I saw Clara tense. "We have a terrific game room in the packhouse. Would you like to see it?"

"I don't-" Clara began.

"Okay!" Isabelle exclaimed. She took Lilys hand as she stood up.

"I'll have some of warriors watch over here. Please, don't worry." Lily said gently to Clara. Finally, she relented. "I'll be right back."

Watching the way she smiled at the little girl, the way Isabelle immediately warmed up to her made my heart flutter. I couldn't wait to have my own pups with her; Lily was going to make an amazing mother.

"Will she be safe?" Clara looked at Ben, eyes wide with worry.

"Completely. Our warriors are the very best. Nobody will touch her."

My Beta had a look on his face that I couldn't really place. He was usually the joker amongst us, always happy; Right now he was unusually tense. Part of me acknowledged that he was just as concerned for Isabelle as her mother.

"Is there something I should know? I asked the two of them. "About Isabelle?"

"What are you implying?" Clara glared at me.

"Is she a witch?"

"Obviously."

"Is she dangerous?"

Clara looked ready to explode. "There is nothing wrong with my daughter!" She yelled at me. Ajax growled in my head.

"He didn't mean that Clara." Ben put his hand on her shoulder, effectively calming her down.

"Okay, what is going on?" Luke was looking between our friend and the witch, over and over. Suddenly, his eyes widened, jaw dropping. "No..."

Ben paled even more. "Yup."

"It's not possible!"

"Well, obviously, it is." Ben huffed.

"Someone want to include me in the loop?" I asked, annoyed.

"Oh for fucks sake." Clara threw her hands up. "He's my mate. There, I said it."

My eyebrows shot up so high, they all but disappeared into my hair.

"What?"

"It's true." Ben said. "She's my mate."

I shook my head, trying to make sense of their words. "But she's a witch..."

"Thank you, Captain Obvious." Clara sneered.

The snarky remark was lost on me, I was in too much shock. How was this possible?

"What'd I miss?" Lily came waltzing back into the room, stopping to take in our expressions and the tense atmosphere. "What happened?"

"Ben found his mate." Thara said quietly. I'd almost forgotten she was here.

"Really? Who is it?" Lily looked excitedly at Ben, who was looking at Clara, who was looking at the wall angrily. Connecting the dots, my mate did what none of us expected. As usual.

"That's amazing!" She gushed as she hugged Ben around the waist.

Clara spun around, only to be tackled by Lily in a giant hug. The anger on her face was replaced by surprise with a hint of uncertainty. Probably regarding Lilys mental health.

"Isn't it?!" Lily looked around the room. "Guys?"

"Uhm..." Luke seemed at a loss for words.

"Sure, why not?" Thara said.

Lily looked to Ben. "Are you not happy?" She asked him.

"I... uh..." He stuttered and Clara and Lilys faces fell.

"That's definitely not the right answer." My sister scoffed.

"I'm just... still trying to process it." He blew out a breath. "It's complicated."

"You can say that again." Clara said.

I held up my hands. "Okay, why don't we put this...development aside for now? There's other things we need to talk about."

"Sounds good." Ben said and Clara threw him a dirty look.

I looked at her. "I'm assuming he told you about why we needed you to come here?"

She nodded. "I'm afraid I can't help you."

I blinked at her. "Then why did you agree to come?"

"Like I said, I didn't have a choice." She glanced at her mate. "We're not like you, witches. If we reject our mate, we lose our magic. It's a punishment for rejecting the bond, a gift from the Goddess. Besides that, witches have a much harder time than wolves do staying away from their mates. It's painful and it effects our abilities."

Huh. Interesting. By the look on Luke's face, he thought so too. I'd have to keep him from interrogating Clara about her species; I really didn't want her to turn him into a toad or something.

"Is there anything you can do to help us?" I asked.

"Ben said you think you're dealing with a Clan Elder. If that's true, there is nothing I can do. My magic is nowhere near that strong."

"Great." I sighed in frustration.

"So, we just find another witch." Thara piped in.

"There's no point. Only another Clan Elder would be powerful enough to help you, and you know as well as I do they won't even consider it. If my situation wasn't what it is, I wouldn't have even come here."

Ben flinched at her words, hurt passing over his face.

"There has to be a way to get to him." Lily drummed her fingers on my desk, thinking.

Clara turned to her. "Him? You know which Elder it is?"

Lily shook her head. "We only know his name. Gideon."

Confusion swept over Clara's face. "There is no Elder Gideon."

"What?" Luke, Lily and I asked in unison.

"There are four Elders, Cidion, Alyssia, Tate and Rythe. They've been in power for a long time, since before I was born."

I looked at Luke for answers.

"I don't know. I thought for sure..."

"Why did you think it was an Elder?" Clara asked him. He told her about James disappearance from the dungeon.

"Ah. He is very powerful then. Just like you, we do have our handful of rogues. Witches who are not part of any Clan, who live by themselves. Unlike wolves, however, not all the rogues are bad. We retain our humanity, even though we live separate from the others. That being said, not all of them are good either."

"You talk like you're one of them." I commented.

"I am. I am not part of any of the four Clans. It is just my daughter and I."

"May I ask why?" Lily asked her.

"No, you may not." Clara snapped. I growled at her disrespect towards my mate, though it didn't seem to effect her. "It sounds like you are dealing with a Dark Witch, someone who specializes in using the Dark Arts. And my guess would be they are after you because you're a Mother Wolf."

# CHAPTER 44

I threw Ben a look, but he held his hands up.

"I didn't tell her that! I just told her about Gideon!" He defended himself.

"He didn't need to tell me." Clara scoffed. "The power radiating from you is so thick, you could cut it like butter. No ordinary wolf, not even an Alpha, has that power."

"There are Jade wolves, though. Even Amethyst wolves. How did you guess she was a Mother Wolf?" Dimitri asked. I didn't know what either of those things he said were.

"Believe it or not, I've met both Jade and Amethyst wolves. Neither had the aura your mate has. She would crush them under that alone."

Luke whistled lowly, glancing at me with admiration.

"Care to explain?" I asked him.

"Jade wolves are rare, though not as rare as you. Maybe born once every fifty years or so. They're bigger than Alphas, but again, nowhere near you. Amethyst wolves are much the same, but less rare. There's a handful of them alive today. I think only one Jade wolf though."

"What makes them special? Different from you guys?" I asked curiously.

"Jade wolves have control over the elements. Usually, just one element, but sometimes two. Amethyst wolves are telepathic, they can hear peoples thoughts all the time without mind-linking. They can also control the mind, to an extent. Compel others to think or do things."

"Wow." I said.

"I doubt any Amethyst wolf could do that to you." Clara commented.

"You think?"

"You don't have any idea how powerful you are, do you?" She cocked her head to the side.

"Uhm, well I know I'm big. Aya is bigger than any wolf here, bigger than Dimitris wolf."

She turned to Ben and Luke. "You don't have books on Mother Wolves here?"

"We went through everything we could find. Most of it is old stories, folklore."

"All myths stem from some truth."

Luke rolled his eyes. "By that logic, Lily should be able to sprout angel wings and fly."

"I didn't say they were all true." Clara snapped at him. "But she hasn't even tested her abilities because she didn't know she had any."

"How would I do that?" I asked before they could start fighting.

Clara pursed her lips. After a minute, she sighed. "I can show you." Her tone said she really didn't want to. But I was excited. Maybe, if I could unlock whatever hidden powers I didn't know I had, I could use them to protect the pack against our threat. Protect my friends. My mate. The people I cared about.

"When can we start?" I asked eagerly.

"I have a daughter too. I need to work around her schedule."

"We have a care facility here." Dimitri said. "For pups. I'm sure your daughter would love it there."

"A daycare for wolves is not where Isabelle belongs." Clara huffed.

"Clara." Ben took a step in her direction. "You can't keep her locked up in the packhouse. Isabelle needs to make friends. Who cares if they're wolves? It won't make a difference to her."

"Your mate is a wolf." Thara added. "You shouldn't teach your daughter to be prejudiced against us."

Clara turned on her. "I'm not! I have no problems with wolves! It's *you* who have the problem with *us*! I don't want my daughter picked on and bullied because she is the only who is different!"

"We can't promise that won't happen. Kids are mean to each other at times. But do you really think I would let it slide if someone was picking on her? Mistreating her?" Ben asked.

"What's your plan Benjamin? Are you going to beat up every little kid who is mean to her?"

I held back a laugh when Clara used his full name. She sounded like *his* mother, scolding him.

"Of course not! But that doesn't mean I can't have a talk with them." He let off some of his Beta aura, making Clara's eyes widen. A hint of lust crossed her face, which she unsuccessfully tried to hide.

"I don't know..."

"Come on. For Isabelle." He pleaded with her.

Chewing it over for a bit, she finally nodded. I released a breath. The air was tense, emotions running high.

"Why don't you two take Isabelle tomorrow, and we can meet after?" I suggested.

"Fine." She obviously was still very hesitant.

"Alright. Clara, I'll have a room arranged for you and your daughter. Now if you'll all excuse me, I would like some privacy with Lily." Dimitri stood up.

Everyone filed out, Thara eyeing Bens mate doubtfully. It was clear she didn't like her, but I hoped they would grow to at least be civil with each other. It would be less of a headache in the future. When the door closed, Dimitris arms snaked around my waist, his chin resting on my shoulder.

"You really want to work with her?" He asked.

"I think of it more as training. A different type of training. And yes, I do."

"She's not very nice."

I barked a hard laugh. "Neither were you, not so long ago."

"Fair enough. Just be careful." He kissed my cheek.

"You don't trust her?"

"Not entirely. She admitted to being a rogue witch; She even said not all of them are good."

"She's not a Dark Witch." I said with certainty. "The Goddess would not do that to Ben. She's just protective of her daughter, as any mother would be. And even you can't blame her for being hesitant towards ben. The situation is extremely odd and, I'm assuming, rare?"

"Maybe rarer than you."

I raised my eyebrows. "Has this really never happened before? A witch and wolf being mates?"

"Not that I'm aware of. I guess the only person who would know for sure is the Moon Goddess."

"Well, I think it's a step in the right direction."

Dimitri lifted me up and placed me on his desk. He stepped between my legs, brushing the hair out of my eyes.

"What step would that be?"

"The step to heal the rift between our species. I think Ben and Clara being mates is proof that a better future is on the horizon, for all of us. A future without hate."

He searched my eyes for a time, before smiling gently. "You really do have a heart of gold, you know? I feel so proud to have you as my Luna. My mate." He kissed me softly. "If anyone could bring about an alliance between species, it would be you."

"Not all me. My mate is a wolf after all."

"Hmm." Dimitri kissed down my jaw and across my collarbone, making my breath hitch.

"Who knew you could be so affectionate?" I giggled breathlessly.

"Just making up for lost time." He said against my skin.

I brought his lips back to mine for a short kiss before pulling away.

"Make up for it later. I'm starving."

"Later." His voice held a promise. "Let's get you fed."

We left the office, chatting about inconsequential things. Breakfast was over, but I had every intention of raiding the kitchen. At some point, I'd have to make use of the smaller kitchen in our room. Maybe I could make Dimitris favourite, whatever it was. I realized how very little I knew about him, even now. Well, that was going to change, and soon.

Entering the kitchen, I looked around for my favourite cook, spotting her whistling near the sink.

"Morning Greta." I beamed.

"Oh! Good morning dear! What brings you down?"

"Just hungry. Anything left from breakfast?"

"Always." She laughed. She proceeded to fill two plates with hashbrowns, bacon, waffles, and a side of fruit for me. Dimitri had the same, except with a side of wedges. Greta tossed me a bottle of syrup and the salt. "I'll come up later to stock your fridge. Anything in specific I should put in there?"

"I'd love some of your homemade strawberry jam, if you have any."

"Definitely." Dimitri agreed.

"You're in luck, I just made a fresh batch." Greta grinned at us.

"You are the best Greta." I returned her smile.

She turned to Dimitri. "I made you a sandwich for lunch. I'll put it there too."

He looked so happy by the news, like a little boy. It melted my heart.

"Go on you two and eat. I have some dishes to finish up." Greta shooed us away, but I stayed behind.

"Go on. I'll meet you in a minute." I told him. Taking his plate, he left the kitchen and I joined Greta at the sink.

"Need something else dear?"

"Yes actually. I was hoping you could leave me a list of Dimitris favourite foods? While your stocking our kitchen. I'd love to make him something, surprise him."

"I would be happy to, of course."

"Thank you Greta. I appreciate it." I said goodbye, meeting Dimitri in the empty cafeteria. It looked much bigger when it wasn't packed with pack members. We ate in silence for a few minutes, enjoying each others company.

"What's your favourite colour?" Dimitri asked at the same time I asked him, "What's your favourite movie?"

We laughed together, him pulling me into his side. We took turns asking each questions after that. I learned his favourite colour was green, same as mine. He was a actually a huge fan of reading, mostly murder mysteries. I recommended some books for him to read, and his favourite movie was anything with Ryan Reynolds. His favourite sandwich was a turkey bacon club with potato salad on the side. We finished eating, Dimitri going back to his office to do some work. I made my way to the hospital in search of Thara, and the questions I had for about my future in the pack. I hadn't told Dimitri, it was another surprise I had for him.

Hopefully it worked out in my favour.

# CHAPTER 45

**CLARAS POV**

I watched as my little girl ran around with a few kids who were about her age. The daycare was exceptional, I'll admit. Almost as big as the main floor of the packhouse, with brightly coloured walls with all sorts of different themes. There was an endless supply of books, which was great; Isabelle loved to read. Or look at the pictures, as her reading skills were only just developing. Ben had brought me to the room designated for Isa's age group, but across the hall there were toddlers running around, pulling on the workers clothes and occasionally throwing food. How I did not miss that stage. Down the hall a ways was the room assigned for newborns and babies. And how I dearly missed *that* stage.

Now my little snuggler was her own person, with her own thoughts and feelings and limitations. I missed being the person she relied on for everything, but at the same time, I was so damn proud of her everyday, as she learned new things and grew. Still, I wished I could just make it stop, and keep her as my little girl forever. And then there were days, after tantrums and tears, after fights to put shoes on, wrestling to get her clothes on and for her to *keep* them on, I prayed she was old enough to live on her own soon. Being a mother was a terrible mess of emotions that no book or pamphlet had prepared me for.

I wouldn't change it for anything in the world.

So, needless to say that it was very, very, *very* hard to watch Isabelle walk away from me into a group of werewolf pups, who may or may not treat her as an equal.

"Your daughter will be very safe here, and she will have lots of fun. She is in the best of hands." The women, Sarah I think her name was, was smiling at me in I guess what was supposed to be a reassuring manner. She looked friendly enough, an open face that had fine lines around her eyes and mouth. I put her at around fifty years old, but with wolves, who knew?

She could have been ninety. Regardless, the sincerity in her light blue eyes calmed me some.

"And Ben... I mean, the Beta... he explained our situation?" I asked her.

She nodded. "He did. And you need not worry about it. I would not care if your daughter was a dragon, I would treat her the same as I would any pup here. And I will make sure that the children do too."

I let out a breath. "Thank you."

"I do need to ask though, as Beta Ben didn't know. Has Isabelle ever been in a school-like setting?"

"No. I was home-schooling for the last year or so." I paused. "Is that okay?"

"It is. I will just have to get her acclimated one step at a time. But I am confident she will learn it all in no time." Sarah beamed towards my daughter, playing with blocks on the ground with a little brunette. "She seems to draw people to her. Amara is usually so quiet, a shy girl. I'm so happy to see her playing with someone else for a change."

I smiled proudly. "She is special." I said.

"That she is."

I startled, turning to look at Ben beside me. I hadn't even noticed he was here! He wasn't looking at me though; He was gazing at my daughter with a mixture of awe and pride. Exactly what I was feeling inside. It made my heartbeat stutter.

"What are you doing here?" I meant to be stern, and failed miserably.

When his piercing gaze finally met mine, I had to work to keep myself in check. This man had such an effect on me, it was insane. His wavy hair just begged for me to run my fingers through it. His eyes were the colour of chocolate milk, warm and relaxing, but easy to get lost in. And I never thought I'd be the type to like facial hair, but Ben pulled it off very well. Standing next to him, I felt like a midget, but I also felt safe; protected. Ben was sexy as Hell, and that was not helping me to stay resilient towards him. Stupid hormones.

"I'm taking you to meet Lily. I didn't want you to get lost."

"Well, off you go then. I need to start todays sing-along shortly." Sarah said to us. With one last look at my girl, I forced myself to walk out the door with Ben. The urge to run back to her was almost overwhelming.

"Hey."

Having been so absorbed in my thoughts, I'd missed that Ben had stopped walking. I almost ran into the back of him.

"What?"

"She's going to be fine Clara. I can see how worried you are, but remember what I said. If anyone messes with Isabelle, they will have me to deal with."

"I know." I sighed. "You can't possibly imagine how hard it is for me right now though. I've never been away from her."

"Ever?"

"Never."

"Then I think this will be good for the both of you. You need to have a life outside being a mom, and Isabelle needs to explore, make friends and learn what it's like to be independent."

I knew he was right. I did. My brain agreed with him, but my heart was telling me to go back and not let my child out of my sight. We started walking again, our arms occasionally brushing against each other. I felt tingles every time; I'd heard the bond wasn't as strong for witches as it was for wolves, but experiencing it now, I wasn't sure I agreed.

"When was the last time you went out?" Ben asked me suddenly.

"Out?"

"Yeah. Like, to the movies or out for dinner or something."

"I don't know. Probably before Isabelle was born?"

"Uhm, okay. Wow."

"Why?" I peered at him curiously. Was he nervous?

"Well, I was thinking... there's a great movie theater here. And we also have some pretty great restaurants, nothing too fancy though. There's also burger joints if you're into that-"

*Oh my Goddess.*

"Ben." I interrupted his rambling. "We can't." I shook my head.

He sighed sadly. Then a look of something close to determination entered his eyes. "I'm trying here Clara. I know neither one of us expected this. But I don't want to spend all our time fighting, or avoiding each other."

"I'm not ready to... be your mate, not the way you want. I don't know if I ever will be." I admitted.

"You know what, that's fine with me. But we *are* mates, so we should try and make this work so some degree, don't you think? Maybe, I don't know... we can just be friends for now?"

"You just asked me out." I pointed out to him.

"Friends can go to the movies together. And grab dinner. I do it with Dimitri and Luke all the time."

My eyebrows raised in surprise. "Your Alpha goes to the movies?"

"Well, not lately."

I bit the inside of my cheek, thinking about it. He had a point. Being mates meant that no matter how much I tried, I wanted to be around him. And he wanted to be around me, which meant he was going to be around Isa. I couldn't spend all my time fighting with him, not in front of her. That was no good, and truthfully, it upset me as well. It was just easier to be angry with him, for any reason, even if it was stupid. But that's not the example I wanted for my daughter.

"Okay." I said slowly. "We can be friends. But only for Isabelle." I clarified.

"Great!" He grinned and I couldn't help a little smile in return.

We walked in silence for a while. It felt odd being close to him; Odd because it was nice. I felt calm, carefree. Something I'd not felt in four years.

"Speaking of Isabelle..." Ben trailed off.

"What about her?"

"I'd like to get to know her a little better. Spend some time with her. With your permission and supervision of course."

I couldn't bring myself to say no. "I suppose it's inevitable anyways."

Ben simply nodded, looking overjoyed. His reaction sent a pang of hurt through my chest. This man who barely knew us was more invested in my daughter than her own father had ever been. It wasn't fair.

Then again, maybe it wasn't fair to compare the two.

"Here we are."

When had we gone into the forest? Damn, I really needed to pay better attention! We stood in a little clearing, some distance from the packhouse. Lily was leaning against a tree, waving at us frantically. I gave her a short wave back.

"I'll come by when you're done to take you back to the daycare."

"That's really not necessary." I protested.

"Think of it as a friendly gesture." He winked and my lips went dry. I watched him walk away, admiring the way his muscles moved under his shirt. Damn.

"So, what's on the agenda for today?" Lily skipped over to me, a huge smile on her face.

*Focus Clara.*

Turning away from my mate, I said, "First things first. You need to shift."

# CHAPTER 46

I watched Clara drool over Bens retreating form, a little smile on my face. Oh yeah, she totally wanted him! And knowing Ben, he had something up his sleeve to make her realize it. Hopefully it wasn't too idiotic; I'd hate to have kick his ass.

"So, what's on the agenda for today?" I joined Clara, pretending I didn't notice the way her cheeks were flushed bright red.

"First things first. You need to shift."

I paused.

"If I shift, how will we communicate?"

Now it was her turn to pause.

"Shit. I should have asked Ben to stay, translate for you." Her forehead creased in thought.

"I can call him back." I said, ready to send out a mind-link.

"No, it's fine. We'll figure it out."

"Clara-"

"Just shift, Lily."

I sighed. However, I did as she asked, first taking some steps back. A few seconds later, I was looking down at her from Aya's eyes.

"Whoa." Clara breathed.

I realized, apart from Dimitri, Clara was the only one who had seen my wolf. Our friends knew I was big, but I wondered if their reactions would be the same when they actually *saw* me. Clara took a few minutes just staring at me before focusing on the task at hand.

"Okay Lily. And Lilys wolf. I want you to close your eyes. Focus on each other, on your bond as wolf and human. Cancel out everything else, except the sound of my voice."

*"This sounds like a hypno-session. I hope she doesn't make us believe we're a chicken."* Aya snorted.

*"You're not focusing Aya."*

227

*"Right. Sorry."*

It was hard; It went against all my instincts to turn off my senses. It left us defenseless, open to any attack. I worked for several minutes on tuning out the forest around me, the birds and squirrels, the trickling of the nearby stream, the leaves rustling in the breeze. Finally, all I could hear was the sound of my heartbeat, slow and steady and Clara's breathing. I focused on her scent alone, turning my mind inwards and connecting with Aya.

"I can sense your aura... that should be sufficient as communication." Clara said. "Keep focusing on your wolf. You're trying to become one being, instead of two individuals in one shell."

I kind of got what she meant. After a while, I could feel it. It felt like a thick cord of steel, the thing that connected my wolf and I. Like I could feel my soul, see the very fabrics that bound us together.

"Good Lily. Reach for that, your connection. See it, embrace it." Clara's voice sounded distant, so far was I into my own self.

And then suddenly, I *could* see it. A ball of white light, glowing and alive inside me. Inside *us*. I could see myself, and Aya. Surprisingly, I could even see Ajax and Dimitri. I guess that only made sense; They were our mates, literally a part of us now. I'd known it, but it was something else entirely to physically see the part of the soul your mate gave to you. It was beautiful, raw. Pure. Hesitantly, I reached out with my consciousness, touching the light, curious what it felt like.

Instead of the light touch I'd intended, I was pulled into it, forcefully. Like a wave being sucked back into the ocean. I gasped, instinctively fighting back.

"Don't! Don't fight Lily!" I heard Clara's voice, but it sounded like a whisper. I was caught inside myself, trying to understand what was happening. Images flashed around me, so quickly I couldn't make sense of them. Voices drummed into my ears, some I recognized, others I didn't have time to place. I felt as though my whole body, mind and soul were being flung apart at the seams, and then put back together again, over and over. It was confusing, disorienting. But surprisingly, and thankfully, not painful.

A force was trying to break free from me, but I didn't know where from. My mind? My body? Both? I couldn't focus on anything, while trying to hold onto to something sustainable. Something solid. Desperately, I reached for that force. It seemed to be the only thing not moving, only growing. I grabbed it, holding on for dear life. Still, it built and grew until it hit a wall, almost knocking me off.

*"Let go Lily."*

*"Celeste?!"*

*"Trust me. Let go. Now!"*

The next few seconds I couldn't describe if I tried. There weren't words. The next thing I knew, I was looking at Clara's face hovering over me, my breathing rapid and erratic.

"Are you okay?" I read the words on her lips. My ears felt like they'd been filled with cotton balls.

"I-I-I...." I gasped. I couldn't push the air out of my lungs enough to form words.

Worry creased over Clara's forehead as she looked down at me. Ripping off a piece from the bottom of her shirt, she waved her hand over it. The fabric twisted and pulsated until it fell to the ground in a heap. Quickly, Clara used the magic-built blanket to cover my naked body, helping me to sit up. My vision blurred as my head spun wildly; I leaned against her for support.

"Goddess Lily. I'm so sorry! I didn't think that would happen!" Clara sounded as if she was close to tears, but her words confused me.

"W-what-" I tried my voice again, only to be interrupted by the sound of thundering paws.

Ajax burst into the clearing, his ears pressed against his skull and teeth bared. His eyes zeroed in on me, his tail twitching. When he looked at Clara, a vicious snarl erupted from him. I felt her flinch against me, frightened.

*"What happened?!"* Dimitri and Ajax yelled in my head at the same time. It was loud, much too loud. I winced.

*"Clara didn't do anything. Don't be angry with her."* I pled to them. At least I could mind-link.

Ajax trotted over to me, sniffing my hair, my face, my neck. He scanned every visible inch of me, snorting in relief when he saw I was unharmed.

*"I thought you were dying Lily. My heart... no, my soul! It was... I don't know. It didn't hurt, but-"*

*"I know. I'm sorry. I didn't know you would feel it too."* I apologized.

*"Are you okay?"* He asked anxiously.

*"I'm fine. I think. I think I just need to sleep. That was... intense."*

He walked away to shift. When he came back, he was donning a pair of men's shorts. Clara instantly started sobbing, startling me.

"I'm so sorry Alpha! I tried to call out to her, but she couldn't hear me. And then she started to change, and I panicked, and-"

"What are you talking about? What do you mean she 'changed'?" Dimitri demanded.

"H-her fur... it was white and then it started to grow black...."

I blinked at her, shocked. Clara sniffled, wiping her eyes. Ben chose that moment to run into the clearing, Luke right on his heels. As soon as he saw Clara, he was by her side in an instant, wrapping her in his arms, and shoving me to the side.

"Ben!" Dimitri roared. He caught me before the blanket could fall, exposing me.

"Sorry." Ben rushed an apology to his Alpha before focusing on his mate. "Are you okay?! Why are you crying? What happened?"

"Lily..." Clara mumbled.

"Did she hurt you?"

A growl tore through the clearing, louder than I'd ever heard before. Dimitris eyes turned black as he glared at his Beta.

"How dare you-"

*"Stop!"*

I mind-linked Dimitri but every head snapped in my direction, shock dominating their features.

"Did she just...?"

"How?"

"What the fuck?"

Dimitri didn't say anything, simply staring at me with his mouth open. *"What?"*

"Lily... did you just mind-link *the whole pack?*" Dimitri gasped. Huh?

*"No?"* It came off as a question. Had I? And even I did... *"But you do it all the time?"*

"Because I'm the Alpha. But you shouldn't be able to."

"It wasn't just your pack. I heard it too." Clara said. Now everyone turned to her. "It must be one of your abilities. To mind-link with other species."

Nobody seemed to know what to say. We all just stared at each other, eyes wide. At least, theirs were. Mine were drooping more every second. I rested my head on Dimitris chest.

"Tired." I whispered. My voice sounded raspy. I needed a drink badly.

"I'll take you home."

Carefully, he picked me up, making sure not to uncover me. I snuggled into his warm embrace, sighing. The others talked while we walked, but I didn't pay much attention. I did hear Dimitri apologize to Clara, and Ben apologize to my mate. After that, I tuned out completely, inhaling Dimitris scent. I called out to Aya, wondering if she was okay.

*"I'm here."*

*"Oh, thank Goddess. Are you good?"*

*"Yeah. It took more of a toll of you than it did me. But I'm just as tired. Can we talk later?"*

*"Sure."*

I felt a light imprint on my forehead, probably Dimitris lips, before I gave myself over to sleep.

# CHAPTER 47

**DIMITRIS POV**

Lily was already asleep when I laid her in bed. I sat down beside her, gazing at her face. My guts were clenching, still wanting to be one hundred and fifty percent sure she wasn't hurt. If she felt more than what I had, it was no wonder she was so exhausted. I was only on my feet now because of my Alpha blood. And probably a shit ton of adrenaline.

I'd been holding the file Luke had got on Snow Moon, debating whether I was in the mood to read it or not, when I'd felt the strangest sensation go through me. Soon, I was collapsed over my desk, gasping for air. I hadn't known what was happening, only that it was connected to Lily. As soon as I was able, I used all my speed to go to her. I'd almost fainted with relief when I saw her in the clearing, clearly exhausted, but alive.

Now I sat wondering. Lily could mind-link out of our species. I was amazed and awed, shocked and honestly, anxious. What else could she do? I didn't want to think like this, but it was built into me, into my very DNA. I had to look after my pack, and while I trusted Lily heart and soul, I needed to know she wasn't a danger.

*"You know she would never hurt anyone."* Ajax said quietly.

*"I know. I do. But you know I can't help thinking like that."*

*"You're thinking like an Alpha. And that's fine, as long as she knows you trust her."*

I laid down beside my mate, playing with her hair. At some point, I fell asleep too, my arm over her stomach. I woke up to the now familiar sparks of our bond. Opening one eye, I looked at my mate as she trailed her fingertips over my cheek.

"I didn't mean to wake you." She said quietly.

"Don't worry about it. How are you feeling?"

"Much better."

"Good." I kissed her lightly. "I think we should talk."

"I saw you." She smiled softly.

"What?"

"I saw my soul Dimitri. I saw my bond with Aya, and with you and Ajax. You literally gave me a part of your soul, and I know I gave you a part of mine. I could see it, feel it. It was so beautiful."

I stared at her, amazed. Was that what I felt when we marked each other?

"What else?" I asked curiously.

"I don't remember all of it. But it came back, when I was sleeping. I saw my past... Snow Moon. And the things they did to me." Her bottom lip trembled slightly. "I saw you, when you met me the first time. I felt your anger."

I flinched.

"But I also saw you now. I see that you do really want me, you accept me. I know you really, truly want this to work between us."

"I really do."

"And I know that you love me."

Well, shit. It wasn't like I didn't know it. I'd almost said it to her, before catching myself. I wanted to say it at the right time, and when I was sure she felt the same. Her eyes held such certainty though, it wasn't like I could deny it. She knew.

"I do love you." I told her.

She grinned, pulling me in for a sweet kiss that took my breath away.

"I love you too." She whispered against my lips.

Joy burst from my chest, radiating throughout my entire body. How great it was to hear her say those words! We kissed again, letting our love pour through the bond between us. It felt incredible. So good, that I had a hard time pulling away. When I finally managed, my breathing was harder.

"We still need to talk."

"I know."

I cupped her cheek gently. "I'm not trying to be an asshole-"

"But you need to ensure the safety of our pack." She finished for me.

"Uh, yeah."

"I'm worried about it too Dimitri. I don't know how to explain it... I just *feel* like... like there's more I can do, I just don't know what yet. And I totally get where you're coming from. As long as we can go through it together, with trust and honesty, I'm happy."

"We will. But Lily-"

She placed a finger on my lips, silencing me. "If... if something happens, and I become..." She paused, blowing out a breath. "I'll leave. I won't put you or the pack in danger. I promise. I would never do that. But you have to promise me, that if that happens, you won't try and stop me. It's what's best, the right choice."

I couldn't believe it. She was willing to leave, to abandon everything and everyone she cared about, just to keep us safe? I couldn't make her that promise though. My heart shattered at the very idea of her not being here, not being with me.

"Dimitri." She forced me to look at her. "Promise me."

*"Don't you dare!"* Ajax howled in my head.

"I... I promise." I whispered.

Lily smiled, even as a tear ran down her cheek. I wiped it away, caressing her face.

"It won't come to that though. I know you; You would never hurt anyone, not without a good reason. You're not a bad person Lily." I brought her into my arms, rubbing her back. "You're my girl. The best girl in the world, and I love you. I'll help you, support you. You can count on me."

"I do." I felt her smile against my chest. "But you're kind of weirding me out. You're not usually so mushy."

"That's what happens when you speak from the heart darling."

Lily laughed, making me smile. "Goddess, there are times when I miss asshole-Dimitri."

I leaned away to look at her. "Seriously?"

"Seriously. I'd never admit it to you then, but asshole-Dimitri can be really sexy."

"I don't know what to say to that."

Suddenly, I felt her hand on my groin, rubbing over my pants. I instantly loss blood supply from my brain.

"When you take control-", She kissed my jawbone, "-And show your dominance-", Her tiny hands skillfully undid my belt, pulling down my zipper, "-It makes me have all sorts of dirty thoughts." She pushed my pants down, grabbing me softly.

"Like what?" I breathed.

Her hand moved agonizingly slowly, torturing me. I'd discarded the blanket from Clara when I'd put her to bed, so she was completely naked. I glanced down at her hard nipples, just begging to be in my mouth.

"Let me show you."

I wasn't sure we should after what she'd been through today, but I couldn't say no. All I could do was watch as she straddled me, placing my tip at her entrance. She rubbed it against her slick core, the feeling bringing a low groan out of me. My hands automatically went to her hips as she lowered herself onto me, inch by inch, until she had taken all of me. To say I was impressed didn't even cover it. I was so fucking turned on, I didn't know how long I would last right now. Just the sight of her on top of me was enough to make me come. And she thought *I* was the dominating one?

I wanted to give her the chance to get adjusted to the new position, when she suddenly lifted herself up and slammed down on me. The feeling was unlike anything I'd ever felt.

"Holy fuck." I growled.

Lily repeated the action, almost lifting herself off me. She was glorious, so hot. I couldn't believe she'd never done this before. I started moving my hips, guiding her and soon we found a steady rhythm. It was new for her, but it felt like it was for me too. Wanting to show her more, give her more, I sat up, keeping my hold on her. She wrapped her arms around my neck as I gently started moving her hips back and forth, griding against me.

"Oh... Goddess that feels good!" She whispered breathlessly.

Soon, she took over by herself, finding her own pace. I sucked one of her delicious nipples into my mouth and at the same time used my hand to roll and knead the other. Lilys head fell back, lost in pleasure. She rolled her hips deliciously, giving me a sensation I'd never felt before.

"Dimitri... Oh..."

She started to move faster, rougher. I brought my lips down on hers and she rode me, gently biting her lip. Bringing my hips up, she growled in pleasure as she took me deeper. Her walls clenched around me, fluttering. I kissed her deeply, recklessly. When she came, I lost my grip on reality. I'd pay any amount of money to experience this feeling again. Lily exploded around me, half moaning-half screaming into my mouth. I followed right behind her, wrapping her in my arms tightly.

We fell back, her landing on top of me. After several minutes of heavy breathing, I kissed her mark, feeling her shudder.

"So, what other fantasies do you have about me?" I smirked.

# CHAPTER 48

LILYS POV

Dimitri had made love to me for the rest of the day and well into the night. I couldn't feel my legs; It felt like I was walking on wood. But I didn't care. We'd lived out most of the fantasies I'd had about him, and even a few he'd had about me. He showed me the utmost love and care, being gentle when I needed it, and complying with me heartily when I wanted more. We'd fallen asleep wrapped in each others arms with whispered 'I love you's'.

Because of that, I couldn't stop smiling. Throughout my breakfast, which I'd decided to have with Hazel and Clint. Throughout training with Dimitri and Karla, lunch, and now in Tharas office. I sat waiting for her, my goofy grin plastered on my face.

"Someone's in a good mood." Thara said as she entered.

"Yeah." I agreed.

"Something happen? Other than gaining a super cool power, I mean?" She smiled. I'd told her, along with my other friends. I trusted them, and knew they wouldn't look at me any differently.

"I love your brother." I blurted out. Thara paused halfway seated in her chair.

"Does my brother know that?"

I nodded. "And guess what?"

"What?"

"He loves me too!" I laughed.

Once again, my sister-in-law turned into a jumping, squealing mess. We hugged tightly.

"Finally! I could have you two that a long time ago! I'm so happy for you guys!"

"Thanks." I beamed. "I'm hoping you're here to make me happy though? Or happier, I guess."

"Today is just your day girl. You're going to be over the moon." She passed over a thick book.

"This is all?" I asked confused.

"This is not like human hospitals. We don't get sick like they do, their diseases don't effect us. Where humans have to go school for years to be a doctor, it's a significantly much shorter process for werewolves."

"So, how does this work?" I held up the book.

"That's one of five books on werewolf anatomy. There is an exam at the end of each, which you will take with me in the room. If you pass all five exams, you get to train with one of us here in the hospital for a year before you can take the final exam to be a doctor. If you fail that, you have to train another full year before taking it again."

"You make it sound so easy."

"It's not. I failed my third exam, had to re-take it, and then failed the final exam once. True, it's not years of school, but it's not easy either."

"I'll do my best." I promised her.

"When are you going to tell Dimitri?"

"I was thinking I'd do it tonight, at dinner. He wants to run through the guest list for Alpha Ball with me, familiarize me with it."

An odd look passed over face, and then she was smiling again. "I'm sure he'll be proud of you. I know I am."

"Thanks Thara. I couldn't have done this without you."

"Thank me once it's official, in a years time."

We left her office together, chatting until she had to see a patient. I was taking time off from working with her to start studying. Hopefully soon, I would be training under her for real, not just in my spare time as a hobby. Textbook under my arm, I made my way back to the packhouse. I had a special dinner planned for Dimitri and I tonight, and I wanted to get started.

"Luna!"

I turned to see Connor walking towards me. I hadn't seen him since the day he rejected Silvia, though I'd had reports from Luke and Ben both that he was suffering during training. Good.

"Connor." I nodded stiffly at him. He stopped a few feet away, nodding back. "Can I help you?"

"I wanted to talk to you."

I raised an eyebrow. "Go ahead."

"Don't you think I've suffered enough Luna? Are you ever going to lift my punishment? I'm losing out on training, and you know the pack need all it's warriors."

"I suppose my answer would depend on your answer."

"My answer to what?"

"Do you think Silvia has suffered enough? Has she moved on yet? Gotten over what you did to her?"

"I-I really couldn't say. I haven't talked to her."

I mulled it over in my head. "Tell you what, Connor. I'll offer you a proposition. You apologize to Silvia, in front of everyone, and then she will make the call whether or not you've learned your lesson."

"Is that really necessary?" He growled.

"Yes, it is." I growled back. "Besides, she knows you better than I do. If you simply put on an act, she'll know. So I'm leaving it up to her."

"Why do I have to do it front of everyone?"

I scoffed. "Why did you have to reject her in front of everyone? Honestly, this is far less embarrassing. That's my deal, take it leave it." I tapped my foot, waiting for him to make a decision.

"Fine!" He crossed his arms.

"I'll let her know. I have things to do though. Bye."

I walked away without a backwards glance. I had a feeling Silvia wasn't going to let him off the hook; He didn't look very sorry to me. As I entered the packhouse, my mood dampened again. Jennine was standing by the stairs with her friends, dressed in what could be considered a bathing suit. Who walked around like that in the open, for real? Did she have absolutely *no* shame? Without hesitation, I marched up to the three women, planting myself in front of them.

Jennine glared at me hatefully. "Can I help you?" She sneered.

"You could help a lot of us by putting more clothes on." I replied.

"Sorry, but you don't have the power to dictate how I dress."

"I wasn't trying to. It was merely a suggestion. What are you doing here?"

All three stared at me. "Excuse me?"

"What are you doing here, in the packhouse?" I clarified.

"I have as much right to be here as you!"

I shook my head. "You may have, once. But you and Dimitri are no longer together. The packhouse is for Omegas who work here, warriors and their mates, and the ranked wolves. You are none of the above. Yet, you continue to hang around."

Her eyes flashed with coldness. However, it was her friend who answered.

"There are a lot of people who hang out in the packhouse. Your friend Hazel for example?" Red Streaks said.

"Yeah, even before she found her mate." Red Hair added.

"Hazel worked in the gardens, in case you forgot. Aside from that, she was always here with an invitation extended by me."

Judging by their faces, none of them knew that Hazel had worked at the pack house. I hadn't known it either for a while, until I joined her one day out of boredom.

"That being said, I'll ask again. What are you doing here?"

"I'm here to see Dimitri." Jennine answered cooly. "I'm here to put in a complaint."

I rolled my eyes. "Then submit a form like everyone else."

She scoffed. "I'm not like everyone else. Dimitri always-"

I'd had enough. Of her, of her attitude, and the way she still thought she had a claim on my mate. Anger coursed through me when she said his name, like she had the right to. My Luna aura spread out around me, effectively cutting off her words. It was the first time I'd ever used it.

"First off, he is not Dimitri, at least not to you. He is your Alpha, and you will address him as such. Second, if you think for one second that I, his *mate*, am going to let another woman dressed like this-," I waved my hand at her body, ",- near my mate, you are out of your fucking mind. Third, you *are* like everyone else Jennine. You are not a ranked wolf, nor do you work here! You have no mate either. Therefore, you have no business here. So *leave.*"

The last of my words were laced with command, something I'd only seen Dimitri do. The twins bowed their heads in submission, but Jennine just glared at me. I could tell she was fighting the urge to submit to me. Truthfully, I didn't care if she did or not, I just wanted her gone. Roughly hitting my shoulder with hers, she stormed past me, her friends following quickly. Jennine slammed the front door harshly, the sound bouncing off the walls. It was then that I scented him. Looking up the stairs, my mate was gazing down at me, shock and amusement on his face.

"Hi." I said.

"Hi." He came down the steps, eyes locked with mine. "It seems we've discovered another talent of yours."

"I didn't mean to. It just... happened."

"Well, they deserved it anyways." He kissed my nose. "I'm glad you finally discovered your Luna tone. It was quite a turn on to see."

"You mean that wasn't part of my abilities?"

"Nope. Every Luna can do that darling. Just like Alphas can."

"Awesome." I grinned and Dimitri chuckled. Then his face clouded.

"However, it's not normal that Jennine didn't submit to you like the other two. I've never seen that happen before." His forehead creased in confusion.

"I'm chalking it up to her incredibly stubborn and bow-down-to-me attitude."

"Maybe you're right." He still looked concerned though. "What's that?" He changed the subject abruptly, eyeing the book in my hand. Quickly, I shoved it behind my back.

"It's a surprise!" I squeaked. "For later."

"Oh?"

I nodded. "I'll tell you at dinner. Six thirty, don't be late, okay?"

"Wouldn't dream of it." He bent to give me a quick kiss. "See you later sweetheart."

My cheeks flushed at the term of endearment. He'd changed so much in such a short time. Yet, he was still the same. I realized that it wasn't so much that he'd changed-this Dimitri was always inside of him, just buried. I just happened to be the one to bring him out. Just like I knew he was responsible for bringing me out my shell into the confident women I was now. I watched him walk away, a content smile on my face.

I took the stairs up to our room, unaware of someone far worse than Jennine plotting against us.

# CHAPTER 49

**LILYS POV**

I had just finished setting the table when Dimitri walked in. His head lifted, sniffing the air.

"It smells amazing in here."

"Thank you." I smiled.

I'd spent the rest of the day preparing our dinner. We had medium-rare steaks, homemade potato salad, regular salad with cucumbers, carrots and tomatoes, freshly made dinner rolls,(Compliments of Greta), and a huge bowl of mashed potatoes. I'd also set a bottle of his favourite red wine on the table.

"I asked Greta for a list of your favourites." I told him as he took a seat.

"Everything looks and smells incredible. Thank you so much." He pulled me in for a lingering kiss that made my heart race.

"I hope it tastes just as good." I replied.

Dimitri wasted no time at all filling his plate. His eyes widened slightly as he chewed his steak, making me a little nervous.

"Wow. That is... Wow."

"Good?"

"The best I've ever had!" He exclaimed. "You should be a chef Lily, honestly."

I smiled. I had thought about it, but after spending my life cooking for Snow Moon, with much less gratitude than he was giving me now, a career in cooking just didn't excite me. I felt much happier working with Thara.

"How was your day?" I asked him.

"Alright. Alpha Killian of Harvest Moon requested to come here sometime in the following weeks. He wants to set up a trade-deal with us that I'm still considering."

"What sort of deal?" I asked curiously.

Dimitri took a bite of the potato salad, moaning loudly. "Did you make this?"

242

"Yes."

"Don't tell Greta I said this, but this is better than hers."

I laughed. "My lips are sealed."

He took a sip of wine, returning to our original conversation. "Blood Moon trades with various packs. Killian wants to negotiate the expansion of his pack, but that would place them right on our borders. Possibly closer, I might have to give up some land." He swirled the liquid in his glass. "I'm not sure I'm comfortable having them that close."

"Do you not trust this Alpha?"

"I do. He's actually a good friend. But I have to think of the bigger picture, I have to think of the pack."

"What is he proposing?"

"In exchange for the land, he's offering us access to his warriors if we need them, and weapon resources." He sighed, taking another bite of his food. "It's a tempting offer."

I bit my lip, unsure if he was looking for a second opinion. I think he felt my hesitation because he reached over the table, placing his hand on mine.

"What do you think?" Dimitri asked.

"I think your right. It is a tempting offer, and one I think you should take." He raised his eyebrows. "I understand your hesitation. But this sounds like a good alliance, and from an Alpha you already trust. Our warriors are the best around, but it never hurts to have more people fighting on your side right? And, Blood Moon doesn't have much in the way of weapons, I've noticed. We focus on hand-to-hand combat. It could be a useful skill for them to learn, in the long-run. I think that's worth giving up a small space of land."

I poured my thoughts out, hoping I didn't sound like an idiot. I had no past involvement in pack politics or anything of the sort. I held my breath, waiting for him to say something. Finally, he smiled, squeezing my hand.

"How did I get so lucky to have you as my mate?" He sighed and I blushed. "You're right, and I think this will be a good thing for Blood Moon, in the long run."

I released the breath I'd been holding, content that I'd helped him with an important matter. More, that my opinion mattered to him. We talked some more over our dinner, enjoying each others company. I brought out his favourite dessert afterwards, pecan pie with vanilla ice cream. I swear he almost drooled.

"Before I forget." Dimitri wiped his mouth, finishing his third slice. I had a feeling I was going to be making a lot of pies. "I have something for you." He reached into his jacket, bringing out a sleek black cellphone.

"A phone?"

"I did ask my sister to get you one, but I guess she forgot. I've already added the necessary numbers, mine, Bens, Lukes. And Tharas."

He passed it over. "Thank you." I turned the screen on, looking over all the little apps. I'd never owned a phone before.

"We don't use them much, but I feel better knowing you have one. Plus, Candy Crush is a great game."

I laughed, seeing he'd already installed it. This man could be so adorable sometimes.

"Now, I believe you had a surprise for me?" Dimitri leaned back in his chair, gazing at me expectantly.

"I do. Close your eyes."

He did as I asked. I walked to the bedside table, pulling out my textbook from the drawer. Setting it in front of him, I told him he could look. His eyes landed on the book, confusion crossing his face.

"Where did you get this?" He picked up the book.

"From Thara."

"Because...?"

His tone was not disapproving-he was genuinely confused.

"Because I'm going to start my studies to become a Doctor in the pack." I said.

The confusion was swept away instantly. Surprise and pride lit up Dimitris face.

"Really?"

I shrugged. "Well, I'm going to try anyways." I rocked back on my heels. "What do you think?"

His face transfixed with the biggest smile, stopping my heart. I was wrapped in his arms before I knew it, his lips moving against mine.

"I love it. You're going to do amazing, I have no doubt."

"You're okay with this?"

"You don't need my permission Lily. If this is what you want to do, I would never stand in your way. You're so good at taking care of people, I can't think of anything better for you."

"I thought you said I should be a chef." I smirked.

"You definitely could be. But if this is what you choose, I'll support you all the way."

"Thank you. I love you."

"I love you too."

We kissed again, the atmosphere quickly changing into need. I'd only started undoing the buttons on his shirt when Dimitri tensed, causing me to freeze. His eyes were glazed over, mind-linking someone. He growled with annoyance, gently removing my hands but keeping hold of one.

"We need to go." He pulled me out the door, fixing his shirt as he walked.

"What happened?" I asked.

"Rogues." He spat.

Anxiety pooled in my stomach. Together, we ran outside, meeting a group of warriors. Bens brother walked by our side, filling Dimitri in on the situation.

"A group was spotted coming in on the East border. We met them before they got too far, but another group caught us by surprise. I'm getting reports of a third group as well."

Dimitri swore under his breath. "They've never attacked with this many before. What is going on?"

We ran through the trees, and I caught the sound of fighting. The smell of blood was getting stronger the closer we got, and so was the stench of rogues. My face twisted into disgust at the rotten smell; It smelled like rotting flesh. I broke through the thicket, every cell in my body on high alert. Wolves were everywhere, snapping and snarling at each other. I recognized Bens wolf, Jude. He was going head to head with a small brown wolf while another snuck up behind him.

Dimitri shifted, rushing towards them and taking down the second wolf easily. Our men shifted, running around me to join the fight. I got ready to do the same when a dozen or so more rogues jumped from the trees. That would be the other group Ned had talked about. One ran in my direction, yellow teeth bared dangerously. Letting Aya come forward, my clothes shredded as I shifted, letting out a fierce, guttural snarl towards my opponent. He stopped immediately, taking in my size with raw undiluted fear.

In fact, everyone stopped. The rogues halted their attack, our warriors staring at me in awe. I'd been planning on making the truth known to the pack soon, we couldn't keep them in the dark forever. But this worked too, I guess. I crouched, ready to attack the wolf in front of me, our men getting ready to follow my lead. Suddenly, he threw back his head and howled loudly. Distant howls sounded off in the distance. To my utter shock, the rogues started retreating, running through the forest away from us. Alarm bells went off in my head.

What had just happened?

*"Don't let them leave!"* Dimitri commanded the group. *"Bring back at least one, alive."*

The warriors took off after the rogues. I was about to follow them when Dimitri stepped in front of me, shaking his head. He shifted back, so I did too.

"Are we not going with them?" I demanded.

He looked out into the forest. "That was a signal, I know it. It's a trap."

"Trap or not, we can't just stand here-"

"I know. I'm going with them. You're going home. Please don't argue either."

"Dimitri I'm not some damn damsel in distress. I can help, you know I can!"

"I'm not doubting you Lily, I'm trying to keep you safe! They only retreated after seeing you. This attack is different from before, and I think it's connected to Gideon."

My argument died on my lips.

"Please, go home. I'll be back shortly, I promise." He kissed me quickly before running after his men, shifting back into Ajax on the way.

I hated that he was right; Hated that I couldn't help my mate and my pack. Not wanting to be caught out here alone, I let my wolf out once more and ran through the trees heading home.

# CHAPTER 50

**DIMITRIS POV**

"Almost ready to go?" I glanced at Lily.

"Mhmm." She didn't even look at me.

I sighed. She was angry with me, still. She'd been like this since the night of the attack. When I'd got home, pissed as fuck, I'd found a just as angry mate waiting for me. It was the first fight we'd had since truly accepting each other, and I guess it was true what they said; Women really could hold a grudge.

We'd chased those fucking rogues for two miles outside of our border until they disappeared. Literally. A whole fucking group of wolves just up and vanished into thin air, confirming my suspicions about Gideon being behind the attack in the first place. What really pissed me off was we didn't have a live prisoner to interrogate.

But Lily was convinced she could have helped. She was pissed I sent her home, but I couldn't do anything else. As soon as I'd realized it was a trap, everything inside me screamed to get her to safety. I couldn't turn it off, and I couldn't ignore it. As a result, my mate had barely talked to me since.

I'd also been confused when she'd shifted. Hadn't Clara said she was black now? Aya was still white, with the same soft glow. Perhaps Clara had been mistaken in panic.

Today, we were in our room, getting ready separately for this stupid Alpha Ball. As if I needed another thing to stress about. I watched as Lily applied her lipstick carefully; I decided to try again.

"You look beautiful by the way." And I wasn't lying. She was wearing a floor length green dress that brought out the red in her hair and outlined her curves. Her hair was left down, but curled in loose waves that brushed over her back.

"Thanks." She replied curtly.

My jaw ticked. "How long are you going to keep this up?"

She pursed her lips, setting her make-up down. She didn't answer me, just walked past me to put her shoes on. My patience snapped at the silent treatment. I walked over and took the shoes from her hands, throwing them on the bed.

"Dimitri!"

Turning her to face me, I held her chin, meeting her eyes.

"I know you're pissed. But you know why I had to do it."

Lily yanked herself out of my grasp. "No, I don't actually. All I know is you didn't trust me enough to look after myself. Instead, you sent me back here to hide in the packhouse. I'm sure the warriors think so highly of me now, their cowering Luna!"

"That's what you're worried about?"

She grabbed her shoes angrily off the bed. "Yes! I'm suppose to help protect this pack, and you had me run away! What is the point of all my training if you're going to send me away to hide every time there's a fight?! I'm not some useless, weak slave anymore Dimitri! But you acted as though I was." She snapped.

I was taken aback by her outburst. Did I really make her feel that way?

"I don't think of you like that Lily. I just didn't want you to get hurt." I took a deep breath. "I don't know what I would do if you got hurt. I can't even think about it." I admitted.

Her eyes softened a bit. "You don't think I feel the same way? Do you know how hard it was to watch you leave without me? I worried just as much about you. But I also know how capable you are, so I trusted you to come back. You didn't even give me the chance."

*"She's right. I hate it, but it's the truth."* Ajax said.

Crossing the room to her, I took her in my arms and kissed her head. "You're right. I'm sorry. I should have had more faith in you, but I screwed up. Next time, we'll fight together, as equals." Everything inside me went against having her in danger, but she had a point. The pack would never respect her as Luna if she hid every time trouble came knocking.

I felt her arms wrap around my waist. "That's the way it's supposed to be. Now, can you kiss me please? It's been hard, ignoring you."

I chuckled, pressing my lips to hers. "Next time, don't ignore me." I said against her mouth.

"Next time, don't be an idiot." She bit my bottom lip gently, pressing her body against mine.

"We should go. If we stay here, like this, we won't be leaving this room for at least a few hours."

"Hmm, that doesn't too bad actually."

Groaning, I pulled away. She radiated smugness, knowing exactly what she does to me. Bending over to put her shoes on, I almost changed my mind.

"Knock knock." Ben opened the door, poking his head inside. "You guys ready?"

"Coming." Lily said. She gave me an innocent smile, running her hand over my chest as she passed me. I bit back a growl, giving her a look.

Ben looked between us. "Something up?" He asked.

"Dimitris just having a hard time containing his excitement." Lily said. She walked past him out the door, leaving me to face my Beta. He gave me a knowing look, unsuccessfully hiding his smirk,

"Shut up." I snapped.

"You ready to go, or do you need a couple minutes to yourself?" He chuckled.

"I swear, if you weren't one of my best friends..." I nudged him out of the way, closing the door.

"I see you two made up." He bit his cheek.

"Ben, seriously, let it go."

"But it's so much fun annoying you."

I sent a punch to his arm, which he neatly dodged.

"Did you tell her yet?"

"No. I will, in the car."

His question brought my blood to a boil. I'd finally read the file Luke had given me on Snow Moon. Turns out people really like to gossip in that pack; Everyone knew about Lily, and what she was going through. They knew she was whipped, beat, cut with silver. The things I'd read were horrific, worse than I'd ever imagined. What kind of people could do that to someone else, with no conscious or remorse? The worst part, in my opinion, was everyone knew, but nobody ever stepped in. In fact, it seemed most of the pack helped in torturing my mate. I wanted to that pathetic excuse for an Alpha to feel everything Lily had felt, only worse.

We got into Bens SUV, Lily sitting in the back humming to herself. She seemed to be in a better mood now, and I hated myself for what I had to tell her.

"Sweetheart, we need to talk."

She turned away from the window to look at me. Ben started driving, glancing at her in the mirror.

"I should have told you before. There's going to be some people at the Ball that you don't want to see."

I watched as the light bulb went off. "Alpha Theo."

I nodded. "And his Luna, and probably their daughter."

Lilys face paled a bit. Then she raised her chin and said, "It doesn't matter. They have no power over me anymore."

Ben smiled and so did I. She most definitely was not weak; She was the strongest person I knew.

"I'll make sure nothing happens." I promised.

"Me too. One of us will always be with you." Ben added.

"Thank you guys. I love you."

"You mean me, right?"

"No, Ben too. He's the big brother I never had."

"Awe. Thanks munchkin. I love you too."

I growled and they both laughed at me.

***

## LILYS POV

I felt like an idiot for not realizing that my former Alpha would also be attending this Ball. They were the last people I wanted to see, ever again. However, what I said was the truth. They *didn't* have power over me anymore, they could no longer hurt me. Dimitri would never allow it to happen, nor Ben. I was safe.

That's what got me through the two hour car-ride, and enabled me to take Dimitris hand and walk with him into the hall, head held high. With him by my side, nobody could touch me. We were at StoneLake

Pack, where the Ball was being held this year. It was a beautiful pack, with modern houses and lush gardens. True to it's name, a large lake spread out behind the packhouse, reflecting the clouds in the sky. It was a place I'd like to visit again.

The Alpha had opted to use his training gym for the Ball. It was decorated stunningly with whites and golds and silvers. Flowers and vines were everywhere, giving the feeling of being outside. It was comfortable, nice. I moved along at Dimitris side, taking it all in. How different this experience was compared to the one I'd had as a child. This time, I was one of the Lunas I'd admired so long ago. It felt surreal.

"Alpha Dimitri Varlos, how good it is to see you!" A tall, broad shouldered man came forward to shake my mates hand. He had red hair, and an equally red beard. He stood almost as tall as Dimitri, and just as muscular. The hair colour told me this was our host.

"Alpha Phillip. It's good to see you too." Dimitri said.

"And who is this lovely woman?"

"This is Lily, my mate."

"I'd heard you finally found your mate! Congratulations to both you!"

"Thank you."

"It's a pleasure to meet you Lily." Alpha Phillip stuck out his hand, and we shook. I liked him already. He had a very positive vibe about him.

"It's nice to meet you too Alpha Phillip. You have a lovely pack."

"Why, thank you dear. I have my Luna to thank for that." He smiled proudly. "She really brought out the best of StoneLake."

"I didn't know you found your mate as well." Ben said.

"Oh yes. I couldn't be happier Beta. She is nothing short of a miracle sent into my life."

"Is she here?" I asked. She sounded like someone I could get along with, and Alpha Phillip was clearly over the moon for her.

"Ah, here she is! Come here baby, I want to introduce you to someone."

I looked over my shoulder, my smile dropping from my face. She was wearing a gorgeous pink dress that sparkled under the lights. Her blonde hair was tightly secured on her head, and a gold chain with a blue gemstone hung on her neck. When our eyes met, she froze, mouth gaping open.

"Lily?" She gasped.

"Evelyn."

# CHAPTER 51

**LILYS POV**

Alpha Phillip looked between the two of us, clearly trying to understand the situation.

"You two know each other?" He asked.

My mouth pinched into a thin line. So, she hadn't told him then. Why would she? Who wanted to admit they abused and tortured someone for years? I wondered how she got him to believe she was this sweet, innocent girl when she was anything but.

"Lily was a member of my former pack." Evelyn walked to us, taking her mates hand. Her mate. How was someone like her mated to someone like him? He seemed so nice and she was.... *her.*

"Oh, that's nice!"

I gave him a tight smile, trying to keep my emotions under control.

"I should circulate, greet some more people. I'll leave you two to catch up."

"I'll go with you." Evelyn offered quickly.

"No, dear, it's fine. You stay here, talk to your friend."

*Friend?*

He moved away, leaving us alone. Dimitri squeezed my hand, but I couldn't focus on him. I stared at Evelyn, who seemed to be having a hard time meeting my eyes. Eventually, I found my voice.

"So, you're mated to an Alpha. You're parents must be so happy." My tone was harsher than I intended.

She shrugged. "Yeah, they are."

"Great."

Evelyn looked around the room, everywhere but me. It was starting to piss me off. She could beat me, make my life a living Hell for years, and now she couldn't look at me?

"The place looks beautiful." I said. "I'm a little surprised though. I would have thought you'd gone darker, to match your soul."

253

She flinched at my words, finally looking directly at me. I couldn't contain my hatred, letting it show on my face.

"Can we talk? Privately?" She whispered.

"No." Dimitri spoke up beside me.

"I meant all of us. I didn't think you'd let her come with me alone." She walked away. I looked at my mate and my friend.

"You don't have to." Dimitri told me.

"Might as well get it over with. She'll find a time to say whatever she wants to say anyways."

We followed Evelyn outside, into one of the many gardens. The many different species of flowers made the place bright, colourful. They're scents mixed together beautifully, wafting around us. Evelyn stopped near a huge rose bush, turning to face me.

"I didn't know if you'd be here, but I'm glad you came." She said. "I've been wanting to reach out to you for a while now."

I crossed my arms. "Why? To tell me you're a Luna now? I really don't care."

She shook her head. "Can you hear me out? Please?"

I really didn't want to. But I'd made the choice to follow her out here. "Fine."

"This is harder than I thought." She laughed quietly. Running her hand over a rose, she blew out a breath. "When we were little, when you first came to the Snow Moon... I tried to be your friend. Do you remember that?"

I blinked. Searching my memories, I thought I did. Hadn't she tried to play some board game with me?

"Kind of." I admitted.

"Do you remember what happened when my mom caught us?"

That, I did remember. I'd forgotten it was Evelyn though. Luna Esther had broken the game and screamed at me. I'd ended up with a broken wrist that day.

"Yes." I swallowed. "What's your point?"

"After mom punished you, she punished me too. She told me to stay away from you, not to talk to you. She hated you for no reason, and I learned to too. I was told that every time you got punished, it was because you deserved it. I started to think like my parents. I found reasons to hurt you, to get you in trouble. I never knew why my parents hated you so much, but it was easier for me to let the blame fall on you for everything. If I stayed out late, or came home drunk, it didn't matter. They wouldn't do anything to me, they would take their anger out on you."

She was bringing back painful memories, ones I didn't want to see. "I'm well aware you used me as a scapegoat to do whatever you wanted Evelyn." I snapped.

"And that was wrong."

Huh? Did I hear her correctly?

"Ever since I met Phillip,-" She smiled to herself, ",-I've gained a lot of perspective. About who I am, who I was. And who I want to be. I don't want to turn out like my parents. I don't want to live my life full of hate and anger. What I'm trying to say is, I'm sorry Lily. For everything, everything I put you through. Everything Snow Moon put you through. I know, it doesn't even begin to make up for what I've done. But I needed you to know anyways. I'm trying to do better, be a better person."

Never in a million years did I think Evelyn would say those words. I didn't think she was capable of apologizing, for anything. To say I was shocked would be an understatement; Part of me was totally convinced I was dreaming.

"One apology does make up for a lifetime of abuse." Dimitri snarled.

Evelyn looked at the ground. "I know. I know it doesn't. That's not what I'm trying to do."

"Then what are you trying to do?" I asked. "Dimitri is right; I still have nightmares about everything that happened. And I don't even know if I can trust that what you're saying is truth."

"You have every reason not to believe me."

"Are you doing this for Lily, or for yourself? Because it kind of seems like your trying to justify everything by apologizing now." Ben said.

"I'm doing it for Lily. I swear. But we really should get back, Phillip will be wondering where I am."

She patted my shoulder lightly as she passed, and I didn't even flinch at the contact. I didn't know what to think; Could she have changed that much? Could her mate have brought out the goodness in her? It seemed unbelievable. Not possible. Then again, I was a mythical wolf; I guess anything was possible, wasn't it?

"Come on, let's go." Dimitri pulled my hand, effectively also pulling me out my thoughts. We walked slowly back to the hall, my eyes catching Evelyn and Phillip laughing with a group with people. Comparing this Evelyn from the one at Snow Moon, she did seem different. Relaxed, happier.

"Let's not dwell on this all night. Let's have some drinks." Ben thrust a glass into my hand. I drank mechanically, not really paying attention.

For a while, we mingled. I was introduced to different Alphas and their Lunas. I met Alpha Killian, and was more convinced than ever that his trade agreement was the right move. He was an explosively happy individual, always cracking jokes. I didn't think I'd ever laughed so hard before. His size and strength were equal to my mates, telling me he could also be dangerous. He would be a valuable ally, I was sure.

"Oh, Goddess help us. Look who's here." Killian jerked his chin over Dimitris shoulder. I glanced back and tensed as Alpha Theo and his Luna entered the room. They were dressed like a King and Queen, outdoing most everyone here. Luna Esther strode to her daughter, who had a tight smile on her face. Huh.

Alpha Theo on the other hand, caught sight of Dimitri. I immediately turned around, avoiding his eyes. What were the chances he wouldn't come over here?

"Alpha Dimitri. Killian."

I suppose that answered my question.

His voice grated against my nerves, causing all sorts of painful flashbacks. I ground my teeth together, fighting the urge to run away.

*He has no power over me. I am safe. Dimitri and Ben are here. I'm safe.*

"Theo." Killian greeted my former Alpha, leaving out his title. I liked him more and more.

"Where is your mate Dimitri?" I heard him take a sip of his drink. "Though I guess I understand you not wanting to bring her *here*, of all places. That would be quite embarrassing!" He chuckled. "Who is this lovely girl?"

I felt Dimitri tense. I squeezed his hand tightly while taking a deep breath. Then I slowly turned around, meeting Alpha Theos eyes. He gazed at me for a moment, cocking his head to the side. I could almost hear the *click* as he finally recognized me. To my utter disgust, his beady eyes roamed over my body, lingering on my chest. I wanted to throw up and punch him at the same time. My eyes glanced to the side. Evelyn was watching us with a little frown, eyeing her father coldly.

"Lily?"

My attention was pulled back to the man in front of me. I didn't have it in me to greet him, even without his title.

"My, my. You certainly have changed. I didn't even recognize you."

"I guess that's what happens when one has *proper* care." I replied.

His eyes narrowed. I knew that look. I knew that if I looked down, his hand would be twitching, ready to strike.

"I see you're attitude hasn't changed as much as your face."

"On the contrary, my attitude has changed a great deal since leaving your 'pack'." My confidence was growing every minute, fueled by my hatred of this man. "I've learned what my worth is, what I'm capable of. It's been quite an experience."

His jaw ticked angrily. "Well, isn't that something." He sneered.

"Dear, you'll never guess who I ran int- Oh." Luna Esther appeared, looking me over. Her eyes widened when she realized who I was. "What on Earth are you doing here?" She spit.

"She is the Luna of Blood Moon. Did you not expect her to be here?" Ben asked.

"Certainly not! This is no place for someone like you!"

"Alpha, you may want to reign in your Luna." Dimitri hissed. His whole body was rigid with anger. I rubbed his back gently, trying to calm him down. Killian stood to the side, watching the whole thing while nursing his drink. I almost asked if he wanted some popcorn to go with the show.

"I cannot believe you, a respectable Alpha, would bring her here." Luna Esther continued. "One would think you would care about your reputation."

"*My* reputation?" Dimitri gave a hard, humorless laugh. "What about *your* reputation Luna? And you, Theo?"

"What the devil are you on about?" Alpha Theo scowled.

"I'm talking about the years of abuse you put my mate through."

# CHAPTER 52

**DIMITRIS POV**

"Excuse me?" Killian rounded on me, before looking at Lily.

Luna Esther waved her hand dismissively. "Nonsense! That girl is a known liar, always has been."

"We treated Lily with the utmost care and respect in our pack. Whatever she told you is a lie." Theo added.

"Oh really? Is that why she came to my home dehydrated, underweight and with marks covering every inch of her body? Was that care I saw when her cheeks were bruised and her lip was bleeding at our *wedding?*" I nearly shouted. Lily shifted uncomfortably beside me, and Ben threw me a look. I'd attracted the attention of some other guests, looking at us curiously. But I couldn't contain my anger, not with these people. The people who tortured and hurt my mate endlessly.

"Any marks she had were her own doing. The girl has problems."

"Yes, I'm sure she willingly took a silver knife to her own back." I spat.

*"What?"* Killian gasped.

"Dimitri, stop. Please." Lily whispered.

"What a load! Silver doesn't fade, and I saw no marks on her back."

"What lies have you been spreading about us?" Esther glared at Lily.

"I always knew you were ungrateful, but I never imagined you would tarnish my name like this!" Theo took a threatening step towards her.

I stepped into his path. "Back off. Now." I growled.

By now, almost everyone was listening to us, watching us. Evelyn pushed her way through the crowd, Phillip right behind her.

"What is going on?" Phillip demanded.

"Mom! Dad! What the hell?" Evelyn exclaimed at the same time.

"It's not us Evelyn! This one,-" She pointed at Lily,"-Has been telling tales about us! We're only defending ourselves!"

I scoffed loudly.

"Mom." Evelyn ground out, her jaw clenched. "Just leave it. Walk away."

Luna Esther grew red in the face. "I most certainly will not! I won't stand here and be accused of such horrid things!"

"It's not accusations if it's the truth!" Evelyn yelled. People around us gasped at her words.

"Evelyn!" Her mom said her name with horror; Theo said it with an undertone of warning.

"What? It *is* true! Lily was abused at our pack. By you, by dad, and by me." Phillips head swung to his mate, disappointment and shock on his face. "We beat her, whipped her, used silver on her. Dad even used a lighter to burn her hair off once. I'm not going to deny anything, not anymore."

*That* wasn't in the file I had. I wondered briefly if Ben had a lighter on him. Unlikely, since he didn't smoke, but I could hope.

"Evelyn, what are you doing?" Esther hissed.

"I'm telling the truth Mom. Lily didn't deserve anything we did to her. The best thing you guys ever did for her was letting her go to Blood Moon."

"You stupid little bitch!" Theo shouted at his daughter. "I gave you everything, treated you like a fucking princess, and this is how you repay me?!"

Before she could respond, he rounded on Lily. "And you! You just couldn't keep your mouth shut could you?! No, you had to cry and snivel to your mate like the pathetic little weakling you are!"

Killian shoved Theo by his shoulders roughly. "Says the man who had to beat a little girl! What kind of Alpha are you?!"

Lily yanked her hand out my grasp. I finally looked at her, my heart wrenching as I saw her cheeks washed with tears.

Fuck.

"Lily-"

"Don't."

She walked away from me, grabbing Evelyn of all people, pulling her out of the room.

"You see! She claims abuse, but leaves with my daughter! She's clearly lying!" Esther continued to try and save herself.

"Your daughter apologized to Lily before you even got here!" Ben snapped. "*She* at least has some remorse, some sort of conscious!"

That got Phillips attention. "She apologized?" He asked.

"She did." I confirmed.

Hope sparked in his eyes.

"Leave." Theo turned his angry glare on me. "Get out. And don't ever cross my path again. Because if you do, I promise I will make you endure everything my mate endured by your hands, tenfold."

Fear clouded his eyes, before flattening back to anger. He grabbed his mates hand and started to drag her with him.

"Theo!" Phillip called.

"What?!"

"Consider this the end of our alliance."

He turned so sharply, he almost threw his Luna. "You're married to my daughter!" He shouted.

"And I will stay married to her. But I want nothing to do with you, not anymore. You two are banned from my pack, and our trade agreement ends tonight. Get out of my territory." He snarled.

"Same goes for me!" Alpha Julian stepped forward, his Luna nodding her agreement. "I don't want to be associated with an Alpha like you."

"Me either!"

"Or me!"

A few other Alphas shouted out. Theo looked around the same before his eyes landed on me. Unfiltered hatred radiated from him.

"You'll pay for this. You and that little bitch mate of yours."

"*LEAVE!*" Phillip thundered.

Theo glared me a second more. Then he stormed off, nearly taking the door off in his haste. The room erupted with voices, questions and general disgust for the Alpha and Luna of Snow Moon. It wasn't the revenge I'd hoped for, but it was enough.

"Go. Find Lily, make sure she's okay." Ben nudged me. I nodded.

"Thanks. You too Killian."

"He had it coming for a while. I knew there was something off about that guy. What a piece of shit." Killian spit.

I left them together, focusing on finding my mate. I was glad Theo finally got called out on his shit, but I could feel that Lily was hurting over it. I couldn't even say I was sorry, because I wasn't. Killian was right; Theo had it coming. I exited the building, looking for any sign of Lily or Evelyn.

I caught her sweet scent, following it. It led me through the same garden we were in before, further in. I found the girls sitting on a bench together, talking quietly. To make my presence known, I cleared my throat.

"Can I talk to you?" I looked at Lily.

"I guess."

"I'll leave. I need to find Phillip anyways, explain to him." Her heels clicked on the stones as she walked past me. I took the seat she vacated, adjusting myself so I was facing Lily.

"I'm sorry." She said it before I'd even opened my mouth.

"What? No, you didn't do anything wrong."

"I overreacted. I was just embarrassed that my life was being put out there for everyone to see. I shouldn't have stormed off, I'm sorry."

"I understand."

She narrowed her eyes at me. "You're not going to apologize?"

"Nope. I'm sorry that you were upset, and that I didn't get to wring his useless neck. But that's all I'm sorry for."

She sighed. "What happened?"

"Well, Phillip is going to stay with Evelyn, but he banned her parents from StoneLake. He also cut off their alliance, along with everyone else who was associated with them."

"Really?"

"It was incredibly satisfying to witness."

"Damn. Now I really wish I'd stayed." She laughed. I tucked her into my side, kissing her hair.

"Thank you. For being there for me, for having my back. I love you."

"I'll always be there for you Lily. I love you too."

"And you told me the Alpha Ball was boring."

"It usually is. This is by far the most fun I've ever had at this thing."

She smacked my arm, both of us laughing quietly. She grabbed my hand, playing with my fingers.

"I have a new ability." She whispered.

"What?"

"I think... I'm not sure, but it seems like I discover them when I'm emotional. It came out of nowhere."

"What is it?"

"I'll show you."

She sat up, climbing onto my lap. Taking my face in her small hands, she closed her eyes. I waited, curious. Then, an odd humming sounded in my ears. Lily scrunched her eyes tighter, concentrating hard. Suddenly my vision clouded, going black. I couldn't see anything, but I could feel *everything*. It was mildly uncomfortable, like touching a sunburn. I didn't understand what this ability was supposed to be until I felt a wave of emotions. Lilys emotions. They hit me as hard as a truck, more intense than even the mate bond. Instinctively, I knew she could feel everything from me as well.

I gasped for breath when my vision cleared, the garden surrounding us once more. Lily sat back, wiping sweat from her forehead.

"What was that?" I asked breathlessly.

"The best way I can describe it, is now I know Evelyn was telling the truth. I could feel her emotions, her intents. She really is sorry about how she treated me all those years, she really is trying to become better. Just like I know that you really aren't sorry about what happened with Alpha Theo. And I know there's something you're hiding from me."

She looked at me expectantly.

"I'm not hiding anything."

"Please don't make me do that again. It's exhausting."

"Fine." I sighed. "I got Luke to get information on Snow Moon. About your past. I'm sure there's more than what he found out, but I read enough to get the gist. I didn't want you to know, I figured you'd talk to me about it all when you were ready."

"You could have just asked me." She frowned.

"You haven't talked to anyone since you got here about it, not even my sister. I didn't think you'd talk to me, even if I asked."

Lily bit her lip. "You're right. I wouldn't have. But I will. Someday."

"No rush sweetheart. But you know it's not good to keep all of that inside. And I'm here for you."

"I know." She kissed my cheek lightly.

We stood together. I was going to suggest finding Ben and getting a drink but as I opened my mouth, a piercing scream echoed through the garden. A second later, the smell of blood coated the air around us.

# CHAPTER 53

The smell of blood hit me, forcefully. I acted quickly, shoving Dimitri away from me towards the hall.

"Go! Find Ben and Killian and bring them back!"

He nodded, running away through the bushes. I took a second to acknowledge that he was actually trusting me this time. Then I was running in the opposite direction, kicking off my heels into the bushes so they wouldn't slow me down. The garden abruptly ended, giving way to a spacious field of grass. The forest lay beyond, dark with looming shadows. I hardly paid attention though, as I followed my nose to the body lying on the ground. Her eyes were wide and staring, but seeing nothing. her once ash blonde hair was matted with the blood that pooled from her grotesquely slashed neck. Her midsection has also been ripped open, intestines spilling out.

My stomach rolled, bringing up everything I'd had to eat or drink. I doubled over, retching violently onto the ground beside the mutilated corpse.

*"You need to calm down! We are not alone."* Aya warned me.

I wiped my mouth with a shaking hand. My wolf pushed forward as my eyes roamed over the trees, through the shadows. Sure enough, a figure stepped out in my direction. It was a large grey wolf, one I was sure I'd never seen before. He snapped his jaws at me, growling.

*"He is not a rogue?"*

*"No."*

Whoever he was, he clearly wanted a fight. I shifted quickly, my clothes a lost cause. I looked down at his grey self, baring my teeth. To my surprise, he let a wolfish grin spread across his face. Then he turned and ran into the forest. Just like before, red flags popped up. Something was wrong.

I looked down at the girl in the grass. My heart wrenched as I realized how beautiful she was, had been. And so young too.

264

"Paige!"

Alphas and Lunas and the like were hurrying towards us. Most everyone was stopped, staring at me. Except one man, who ran to the girls body. Throwing himself onto the ground next to her, he started to sob brokenly.

"Paige! My daughter, my sweet daughter."

I took a couple steps away, wanting to give him space.

"Who is responsible for this?!" The Alpha barked. His eyes landed on me and narrowed into slits. "You! Monster!"

I whimpered, stung by the word.

"It was not Lily!" Dimitri shouted, but the man did not listen.

"Shift beast!"

I instantly did as he asked. His face was torn with grief and rage. Using his Alpha speed, he jumped to his feet only to slap me hard across the face. Tears jumped into my eyes. Dimitri was in front of me in less than second, his hand around the Alphas throat.

"You dare protect her!? Look at my daughter! Look at what she did!"

"Calm down Richard! It could not have been Lily. She was with me when we heard your daughter scream." Dimitri shoved him away from us.

"Of course you would defend her! She is your mate! I don't believe you!"

I got my voice back, leaning around Dimitri to look at Alpha Richard.

"Alpha, I swear, I didn't. I would never! There was another wolf, a big grey one-"

"Bullshit!" He shouted. "You lie! I know what you are." He glared at my mate. "You should have warned all of us about her! Mother Wolves are monsters, untameable. She will kill again, just like tonight. She should be put to death!"

My heart started to race in my chest. I was horrified that everywhere I looked, people looked back at me with worry and fear. Disgust even. Like I was indeed a monster, out for blood.

"I-I didn't..." I tried again. I was scared. Would these people turn on me? Even Dimitri couldn't hold them all back, not even with the help of Ben or Killian. They wanted answers, answers I couldn't give. Alpha Richard wanted blood, blood for his lost daughter. Undoubtedly mine

I felt an odd sensation growing inside me, and panic took over. *Now* was not the time for me to show I had abilities! I couldn't contain it though, the feeling only being fueled by my feelings.

*"Aya! Help me! Stop this, please!"*

*"I can't Lily. This needs to happen."*

*"No!"* I shouted.

My legs gave out, the voices that were shouting around me drowned out. My vision tunnelled, going black around the edges. I fought it back with everything I had, but it wasn't enough. My nails dug into the Earth, ripping out the grass. My eye caught sight of my arm, beyond shocked that it had a light golden glow around it.

*"Give me control."* Aya demanded. I didn't argue, just let myself be shoved to the back of our mind.

I watched as we stood up, walking towards Paige's body.

"What are you doing?! Get away from her!" Alpha Richard shouted, but made no move to stop me. Like everyone else, his eyes were wide with fear, afraid of what I would do next.

"I will reveal what truly happened here." Aya voice came from my lips.

Kneeling beside Paige, Aya placed our hands on her forehead. The glow around us peaked, grew until it was shone. Gasps and shouts came from the crowd. Then, an image slowly materialized in front of us. It was hazy, reminding me of a mirage. Shadowy figures moved around, their voices muffled. And then, as if a veil had been lifted, the image became clear for all to see.

Two people stood embracing. One was Paige, and unexpectedly, the other was Connor. Questions danced on my tongue, but I kept them in, watching from inside my mind.

"I am so happy you came to see me! I missed you." Paige said.

"I as well. You are very important to me Paige."

She smiled, her whole face lighting up. "I think I might be in love with you Connor. I truly hope we are mates."

I almost puked again. She wasn't even eighteen?! They kissed again, heatedly. I watched as Connors body tensed. Another person entered the vision, a girl I did not know. She was tall, strong looking. She carried some sort of stick with her. Long metal daggers were attached to the end, hooked at the ends like claws. She walked casually towards the unlikely couple, a smug smile on her face.

"I am sorry for this Paige."

"Sorry for what?"

Connor pushed her away from him roughly, shifting into his wolf. His grey wolf. I was screaming inside my head, wanting to prevent what I knew was going to happen next. Aya held me back, reminding me it was already done. I watched helplessly as Paige turned to the mystery girl. Her eyes opened wide, a terrified scream leaving her mouth. The scream Dimitri and I had heard. The sound was cut off with a choked gurgle as her throat was slashed and ripped open. Paige fell to the ground, holding her neck.

"W-W-W-" She looked at Connor, tears running down her face. Her expression was utterly heartbreaking. Unconcerned, Connor used his paw to push her to the ground, and watched as her insides were torn out. He turned away from the girl who had moments before professed her love for him, eyeing the woman who'd murdered her in cold blood.

"You know what to do. Get into the trees and wait for Lily."

What the fuck?

Connor nodded once, racing off.

"That was gruesome."

A voice floated through the image to my ears, instantly making my blood boil. Jennine appeared, kneeling down beside Paige's body.

"It looks good. Disgusting, but good."

"It's sad you still doubt me."

"Whatever. Get lost, before someone sees you."

"Let me know how everything works out." She walked off, swinging her makeshift weapon over her shoulder. As if she hadn't just brutally murdered someone. And I was the monster?

Jennine stood, stepping away from Paige's body, her face radiating smugness. "Sorry girl. I feel kind of bad, having Connor play with you like this. But Dimitri is more important, even more than your life." She walked away, into the forest.

Everyone watched as I ran into the vision. They saw Connors wolf appear, and me shifting. It ended with Alpha Richard kneeling by his daughter, dissolving into the air like smoke. Abruptly, Aya gave me back control, and I slumped over the girl under me, every ounce of energy leaving my body. I felt the sparks as Dimitri lifted me away from her, cradling me into his arms.

Nobody moved. Nobody talked. The only distinguishable sound was that of Alpha Richards sobs. They filled the air, gut wrenching to hear. Alpha Killian and Ben moved to him, patting his back and trying to console the broken man.

I felt wetness land on my cheek. I looked up into my mates face, my heart twisting when I saw the tears running from his eyes.

"This is my fault." He choked out.

I opened my mouth to deny it, to tell him it was nobodies fault but Jennine's, when her voice broke through the clearing.

"You're right. It is!"

Every head turned to her. She stalked out of the forest, her hand tightly grasped onto something. A noise I'd never made before left my mouth when I realized it was Connors head. His mouth hung open, his eyes glassy. Blood dripped from his severed neck, staining the grass. Jennine tossed the head towards us, letting it come to a stop in front of Ben.

"Why?" I asked her.

Her laugh filled the emptiness, the sound crawling down my spine. She sounded insane.

"Why?! Because of you!" She pointed at me. "You waltzed into my home, took everything, *everything* away from me! Do you even know how hard I worked to get where I was? How many women I had to get rid of?!"

She turned her mad eyes on Dimitri.

"And you just threw it all away, threw *me* away, for a slave! I could have ruled Blood Moon by your side. I could have brought our pack to fruition, made it the very best. I would have helped you be the most powerful Alpha around. I would have killed for you!" She shrieked. "I did kill for you!"

Dimitri shook his head. "Not for me. You did this for you."

Was I the only one who noticed Alpha Richard had stopped crying? He was starring at Jennine with more hate and rage I'd ever seen on anyone. His body was shaking, vibrating. I saw his claws extend.

"Everything I did was for you! I had to endure sleeping with hat useless mutt-," She pointed to Connors head,"- for you! I had this bitch killed, for *you*!"

A terrifying roar echoed around us at her words. A giant brown wolf stood where Alpha Richard had sat, his eyes flat and teeth bared. With no hesitation, he rushed Jennine, claws aimed for her face.

And she disappeared.

Richards wolf landed on the other side of where she once stood, falling to a heap on the ground. He jumped to his feet, looking around for his prey. But she was gone.

In her place however, now stood a tall, finely dressed man. He had salt and pepper hair, and a sophisticated trimmed goatee. Alpha Richard snarled at him, snapping his jaw. The man waved his hand lazily towards the wolf. I watched with a horrified face as his eyes grew heavy and he slumped to the ground, unconscious. Ben and Killian were at our side in seconds, both taking fighting stances. The man turned to us, eyes going straight to me.

"Gideon." I whispered.

# CHAPTER 54

**JENNINES POV**

Everything had failed. I'd planned this so carefully, even Connors death. I was happy to be rid of him, finally. The last step in an otherwise perfect plan. But that bitch had ruined everything.

And I was going to die for it.

I watched as Alpha Richards wolf lunger at me, claws extended. I wasn't scared though; I knew I was going to die as soon Lily revealed the truth. I didn't plan on begging for my life either, I was better than that. And I didn't have regrets. Standing calmy, I waited for the burn of claws piercing through my skin; It never came.

Instead, I was violently ripped away from the clearing, my vision blacking out. I felt as though my body was being pulled from every direction, stretched and put back together. I landed hard on a cold surface, the wind knocked out of me. Despite having no air, I rolled to the side, vomiting everywhere.

What the fuck just happened? Was that death? Then why did I feel like shit?

"I apologize. The first time transporting can be harsh on ones system."

A velvet, smooth voice drifted to my ears. The sound alone sent shivers down my spine, and heat pooling between my legs. I looked up to find the sexiest man I'd ever seen staring down at me. His face had to have been carved by angels, every inch of it perfectly proportioned. His lips were full and red, set in a soft smile. His nose was long, straight, proud. And his eyes... so dark they were almost black. Greedily eyeing the rest of him, saliva filled my mouth as I took in his white button down shirt that did nothing to hide how fit he was, and the pants that gave a clear outline of his dick. I licked my lips at the sight.

Air finally filled my lungs again, and I used it to ask him where I was.

"You are in the land of witches."

"How did I get here?"

"I brought you here."

"Why?"

"Because I need you."

My face flushed with heat, my arousal growing stronger.

"Who are you?" I asked.

"Someone who wants to help you get what you want. What we both want. Your plan to get rid of the Mother Wolf was alright... but it had many flaws."

I straightened my spine, climbing to my feet. I didn't care how gorgeous this creature was, nobody criticized me.

"What do you know?" I hissed at him.

"I know that I have a better idea. One that will actually work." He was in front of me so fast, I didn't even have time to blink. His hand cupped my cheek, spreading warmth over my face.

"Who are you?" I asked again. My voice sounded weaker, and I cursed myself.

"You may call Bastian."

"Bastian." I tested it out on my tongue. I liked it. "You want to get rid of Lily too? Why?"

"That, you will learn later, after you have proven your loyalty to me. I'm not sure you will want to, after learning my intentions."

"I'm with anyone who helps me get rid of that bitch."

"Even if I want to get rid of her mate as well?"

I gasped quietly. I couldn't do that. Everything I did would have been for nothing!

"I can't help you hurt Dimitri. I love him."

Bastian scoffed, the softness on his face replaced with dark humor.

"Come now, don't be so foolish girl! That man does not want you, does not love you. If I had not taken you away when I did, he would have happily watched you die, glad to be rid of you!"

Tears sprang to my eyes at his words. The worst part was I knew he was right. Dimitri hadn't even tried to save me, too focused on his pathetic mate.

"Join me, and I will give you everything. Together, will take revenge on those who have wronged you. I will do better than make you a Luna; I will make you a Queen. Join me, and rule by my side."

I thought of the way Dimitri had shoved me aside. The way he'd played with me, toyed with me. All the times he paraded Lily around in front of me, as if she was the Goddess herself. I thought of the way he'd looked at me tonight, with disgust and hatred. The way he was going to let me die. Anger coursed through me, strong and ripe. I would join Bastian, and I would get my revenge. Dimitri and Lily would have no shred of happiness, not after I was done with them. I would destroy them.

"How should I prove my loyalty?" I asked Bastian.

He smirked. "I have a few ideas. But for now..."

He pressed his lips against mine, guiding my hand to his pants. I gasped at his size. If this is how he wanted it, proving myself to him would be truly easy. I was more than eager.

"If you do this, there is no going back. I will kill you if you betray me." He whispered into my ear.

"I will not betray you." I promised.

He ripped my shirt open, leaning down to bite the skin above my breast. I moaned.

"I do not believe you." He muttered against me.

"How? How can I prove it?" I breathed. He discarded my bra and took my nipple in his mouth, my hand caressing him over his pants.

"Let me strip you of your wolf."

I jerked in his arms. Bastian grabbed my face, meeting my eyes.

"You want to get rid of my wolf?" I exclaimed.

"I have no use for your kind. In exchange for your wolf, I will give you magic. I will make you strong. Stronger than you've ever been. You do not need a wolf."

"Don't! Don't let him do this, he's evil!" My wolf shrieked in my head, trying to force her way out. I shoved her to the back of my mind, forcefully. She whimpered, struggling against me.

"Yes. Do it." I agreed.

Bastian searched my eyes, looking for any hint of hesitation. There was none. I was willing to do whatever it took to get my revenge.

"You are off to a good start." He smiled.

Carefully, I unzipped his pants, sliding them down. I sank to my knees, my eyes never lifting from his.

"I will not betray you." I repeated. "But if you double-cross me, I will kill you. Nobody will stand in my way this time." I promised before I took him in my mouth.

# CHAPTER 55

**DIMITRIS POV**

It had been one month since we captured Gideon and brought him to Blood Moon. Though 'captured' might be the wrong word. He'd willingly surrendered to us, not putting up an ounce of fight. His new home was the dungeon, obviously. Occasionally, he would leave, transporting himself to his home, wherever that was. The first time he did it, I lost my mind.

"I do need to change clothes, you know." He'd said.

The frustrating part was, I couldn't stop him. I could chain him to the wall but it wouldn't make a difference. The confusing part though, was that he always came back. He'd be gone for thirty minutes or so, long enough to clean up, and reappear in his cell. I asked myself countless times, why bother? Was this a way to taunt me? To show me he could escape anytime he wanted, and I couldn't do shit about it? The whole situation put me on edge.

Today, myself along with my Beta Ben and Gamma Luke, and Bens mate Clara were going to interrogate Gideon. Again. Every time I'd tried, he would studiously ignore me, whistling to himself or reading a book he'd brought back with him. I was starting to contemplate violence.

"I hope you know there is nothing I can do to really help here. He outclasses me in so many ways." Clara said now.

I nodded to a few of the gardeners who were hard at work. "I don't know what else to try." I replied to her.

"You think the three of us are enough to intimidate him into talking?" Luke asked.

"Maybe."

"Why doesn't Lily-"

"No!" I interrupted Ben harshly.

I knew what he was going to suggest. Lily herself had offered to do it, but I'd shut down the idea. I didn't want my mate within hundred feet of this guy. He'd already taken two pack members, he could easily kidnap Lily too. We entered the dungeon, all four of us wrinkling our noses at the smell. A few rogues we'd captured glared at us as we passed, others shrinking away into the corners.

"This place is disgusting." Clara commented behind me.

"That's kind of the point." Luke muttered. She shot him a dirty look. Those two were always bickering; They reminded me of siblings.

I led my group to the very back of the dungeon where Gideon was housed. His cell was medium sized, but just as dirty and dark as the others. I stopped in front of the bars, glaring inside. He was dressed in a black t-shirt and jeans with white sneakers. His salt and pepper hair was freshly washed and combed; His goatee as well. As usual, he had a book in his hand, flipping the pages lazily. He was definitely the cleanest prisoner here, and it pissed me off. I tapped on the bars, averting his attention.

"Hello Alpha." His tone was polite, not at all scared the way it should be.

"I'm here to-"

"Question me. I know. I thought it was obvious by now that I won't answer you."

"Then why do you keep coming back?" I growled.

He shrugged. "I have my reasons."

Scanning my handprint of the pad beside his cell, the door creaked open. Gideon looked at me over his book, his eyebrows raised. I stepped into the space, Ben and Luke and Clara behind me. There was barely enough room to fit all five of us, especially with how big we wolves were. Gideon closed his book, swinging his legs to face us.

"This is new. Are you planning to beat the answers out of me?" He smirked a little.

"If that's what it takes." I threatened.

"You know I could transport myself out of here to safety as soon as you lay a hand on me?"

Ben stepped forward, shuffling me off to the side. "What is even the point of this?" He snarled. "What's your plan? To live down here forever?"

"Not forever. Just until I get what I want."

"Which is?" Clara asked from behind us.

"Ah, the witch. I was wondering when we'd meet."

"Don't talk to her." Bens eyes grew black.

Gideon looked between Ben and the sound of Clara's voice. Honestly, she was basically hidden behind the three of us in the small space. "She's your mate." He stated.

Neither Ben nor Clara confirmed it, but a slow smile spread of Gideons face. He seemed genuinely happy that my Beta was mated to a witch.

"She asked you a question. Answer it." Luke snapped.

Gideon focused back on me. "I want to talk to Lily."

Of course he did. "No." I deadpanned.

"Then I have nothing else to say." He leaned back against the wall, picking up his novel. My patience snapped, and I had him a foot off the ground by his throat a second a later.

"Stop playing with me!" I shouted. "You think I couldn't snap your pathetic neck in an instant? You might have magic, but that won't save you. That won't stop me from ending your useless existence!"

A hint of anger touched his eyes. "I've been lenient with you Alpha, but you're really starting to test my patience. I've told you what I wanted."

"No way in Hell are you getting near my mate." I spit at him.

"Fine. But that's the only way I'm going to talk."

"Why?" Ben asked.

"That's my business."

I squeezed my hand tighter. "Wrong. I'm her mate, her husband. Anything to do with her has to do with me."

"Really? Where was that attitude when you were pretending she didn't exist? Except when it benefited you, of course."

My wolf, Ajax, pushed forward forcefully. My fist connected with his nose, blood immediately gushing out. Part of me acknowledged that even though he'd stated he could, he didn't leave the cell. He simply crouched on the ground, cursing under his breath as he righted his broken nose. Clenching my fists tightly, I held Ajax back from coming forward fully to do worse.

"Perhaps that was out of line." Gideon muttered.

"I want answers." I ground out. "Or she is going to give me a truth serum that I will shove down your throat." I jerked my thumb over my shoulder to where Clara was standing.

"I'll take it willingly."

"What?" Luke asked.

Gideon nodded. "But only in front of Lily."

My teeth snapped together with anger. "I told you-"

"I'm not negotiating Alpha. Either I talk to Lily, or you get nothing from me at all." He snapped.

"Why haven't you just transported yourself to her? If you're so adamant about this?" Clara spoke up. Ben looked at her wide-eyed, shaking his head back forth quickly. She was treading into dangerous territory and he knew it. However, Gideon shook his head at her.

"I won't do that. She won't listen to me if I force her to. I need her to be willing to hear me out."

Luke placed a hand on my shoulder. "Come on. This is pointless right now."

Ben agreed, already moving his mate out of the cell and away from me. Giving Gideon one more hard stare, I followed my friends, slamming his cell shut on my way out. I didn't care if it locked or not; He could leave either way so what was the point in double checking? I stalked past the other prisoners, leaving my friends behind. I was beyond angry.

When I got outside, I rounded on Clara.

"Why the fuck would you suggest something like that?!" I roared. Ben stepped closer to her protectively, but Clara just crossed her arms and met my gaze.

"It wasn't a suggestion; It was a question. And I don't think you need to worry anyways. If he wanted to take Lily, he would have by now."

"You don't know that!"

"No, I don't. But I think you should let him and Lily talk."

"Are you insane?" I snapped at her.

"That man down there is powerful, as powerful as any Clan Elder! If he was a Dark witch, he would have killed you in your sleep already and taken your mate. He must have another reason for being here."

"Wait." Ben said. "Are you saying Gideon is not a Dark witch?"

"I don't think so. I've not met any, but I've heard they have a disturbing aura about them. I felt how powerful Gideon is, but I felt no darkness from him."

I ran my hands through my hair roughly. There were too many 'buts' and too many 'ifs' here. How could I, in good conscious, allow Lily to put herself in danger without all the facts in place beforehand?

"He agreed to take the serum Dimitri. And we have nothing else, no other ideas. He's clearly not going to talk to us." Luke said.

"And Lily already agreed, a while ago." Clara added.

My eyes went to my Beta. "I agree." He said.

Groaning, I kicked a rock in my path, sending it flying into the forest. Pushing past them, I stormed back into the dungeon, growling the whole way to Gideons cell. Yanking open the cell door, I planted myself in front of him.

"You will come to the packhouse tomorrow at noon. You will take the truth serum, a double dose if I see fit to administer it. You will not speak to Lily alone! And if you try anything, anything at all, I will remove your head faster than you can snap your fingers. Do you understand me?"

Gideon blinked at me for a few seconds. "Why the packhouse?" He asked.

"One because I can't fit all the necessary protection for my mate down here. And two, because she hates coming down here."

He nodded. "Understood. I will see you tomorrow."

I left, a feeling of unease and regret moving over me. I already knew this was a bad idea.

# CHAPTER 56

LILYS POV

"I need to talk to you."

I was sitting on our bed, playing Candy Crush when Dimitri slammed into our room. He looked angry, tense. He'd been this way for the last month, thanks to our new prisoner. I prisoner I'd offered to interrogate, many times, but Dimitri wasn't having it. I understood his point of view, but at the same time, he wasn't getting anywhere with Gideon. He couldn't force him to talk and I didn't have to. I simply had to touch him to know everything we wanted to know.

My abilities had grown over the course of these few weeks. I wouldn't say I was close to mastering them, but using them no longer exhausted me to the point of almost fainting. I'd taken to adding extra training during my days, my normal exercise and sparing with Dimitri in the morning and practicing with my gifts in the afternoons or evenings. Clara liked to help out with that; We'd become closer recently, working our ways to becoming friends. I liked Bens mate a lot, and I enjoyed spending time with her and her daughter, Isabelle.

"About?" I focused my attention back to my mate. He was pacing the room, his jaw ticking.

"That bastard won't talk to anyone but you."

Setting my phone down, I sat up and crossed my legs. "By 'that bastard', I'm assuming you mean Gideon?"

He nodded. "I'm out of ideas." He sighed.

"So, let me talk to him. I already said I would."

"I told him to come here tomorrow, at noon."

My eyebrows shot up. "You did?"

"Yes, and I'm having Ned here as well. And some warriors. And myself, Ben and Luke. Clara too." He ground out her name, making me wonder if they'd had a fight.

"Okay, slow down. What happened? Why did you change your mind?" I pat the spot next to me, inviting him to sit.

Ignoring my request, he quickened his steps while he talked. "Clara doesn't think Gideon is a Dark witch. He agreed to take a truth serum, but only if you're there, only if he can talk to you. And I fucking hate that I agreed to this!"

He was making me dizzy, watching him pace like that. I slid off the bed, taking his wrist as he turned to make another round. The sparks from our bond zinged through my hand and up my arm, causing my heart to flutter.

"Dimitri, stop. Breath. You're talking too fast, and not making a lot of sense."

Pulling him to the bed, I pushed him down and climbed into his lap. His face pressed against my neck, over the spot where his mark lay, inhaling deeply. I rubbed his back in soothing circles; After a few minutes I felt his muscles release and relax.

"Better?" I asked him.

"Much. I'm sorry. I'm just so pissed."

"I couldn't tell." I chuckled. "Now, start over for me."

He told me everything that transpired with Gideon, explaining why Clara didn't believe he was a Dark witch, and that he agreed to take the truth serum if he could talk to me. Admittedly, I agreed with Clara; Gideon had already proven he could come and go as he pleases. He could have taken me anytime he wished.

"But just because he might not be a Dark witch, doesn't mean he's not dangerous. He's already taken two of our people; That's why I'm having Ned and the warriors here tomorrow as well." He finished.

"I don't think that's necessary." I replied.

"Of course it is! I won't let you near him without protection!"

"That's why I have you. And Luke and Ben and Clara."

"I'd feel better having more of my men there."

"Dimitri, Connor plotted against us for who knows how long with Jennine. And he was one of your warriors. I think it's safe to say that we don't know who we can trust right now."

I was right, and he knew it; I could see it in his eyes. Since we found out Jennine was even more psychotic than we thought, murdering an innocent girl in cold blood with the help of Connor, I'd kept to myself and the people I knew beyond a doubt I could trust. I hadn't gone out of my way to make new friends for that reason, though I still attended to my Luna duties. It was hard for me, and I knew for Dimitri too, having the knowledge that people in our pack, our home, might be conspiring to kill us.

The few people that knew exactly what had gone on at the Alpha Ball, and everything since were my friends and mates Hazel and Clint, Dimitris sister Thara, and of course Ben and Luke and Clara. Of course, all the Alphas and Lunas who were at the Ball knew, and our friend Alpha Killian. Rumors travelled like wildfire, but so far, most of the our pack only speculated as to what really happened. The hard truth that everyone knew though, was that I was a Mother Wolf. That information spread faster than wildfire, branching out and taking life.

I'd known it would happen, but it still hurt a bit that pack members looked at me differently now. They were wary, careful. They acknowledged me as their Luna, but I think it was more out of fear than respect now. I knew my secret couldn't stay hidden forever, but I had been hoping to lessen the blow when it came out. Preferably not attached to the fact that I had been assumed to have killed Alpha Richards daughter because I was suppose to be a wild, bloody thirsty monster. Nothing I could do about it now though.

"Lily?"

"Huh? Sorry, I zoned out."

Dimitri brushed his fingers across my cheek. "You don't have to do this."

"I do, actually. We need answers. You don't want me to do it, but it's need to happen."

He sighed. "If he hurts you..."

"Then you have my full permission to go big bad Alpha wolf on him." I kissed his nose.

"I don't need your permission for that darling."

Dimitri wrapped his arms around my waist, flipping me onto the bed so I was under him. He kissed me lovingly, leaving me breathless.

"Nothing is going to happen. I trust you to have my back." I said quietly.

"Always." He promised. We kissed again, the tension in his body quickly turning into lust. I was naked before I knew it, my mates head between my legs. I let out a content sigh as he pleasured me.

"I have studying to do you know." I said.

"Don't care." His tongue flicked out and I bit back a moan.

"Dimitri, I have my first exam in a week." I gasped.

"Really don't care."

"Dimitri." I'd meant to sound firm, but it came out as more of a plea.

He hummed against me, adding extra pleasure with his fingers. It was a wonder I ever got anything done around here with his seemingly insatiable need for me. Finally, I gave in, giving myself to the feelings only he could ignite within me; We exhausted ourselves together, falling asleep in each others arms.

I woke some time later, glancing at the clock on the bedside table. Four in the morning? Goddess. Way too early. Rolling over, I snuggled into Dimitris back. But sleep didn't come; In fact, I was oddly alert. Had Dimitri turned up the heat? I kicked off the blankets, letting the breeze from the open windows cool my body. A minute later though, I was too cold. Frustrated, I sat up. The minute I moved, my stomach rolled violently. Hand covering my mouth, I was off the bed and running to the bathroom as fast as my feet would carry me. Attempting to hold my hair back, I let out my dinner into the toilet, groaning.

"Lily?"

Dimitri entered the bathroom, coming to kneel beside me.

"Are you okay sweetheart?" He put his hand to my forehead as I flushed the toilet.

"I'm fine, now. I don't know what that was." My voice was raspy. "Can you get me some water, please?"

He brought back a large glass and I downed it.

"Maybe I should get Thara up here." Dimitri offered.

"No, don't wake her. I'm fine, really."

"Lily, you just puked."

"I feel better now. Don't bother your sister, I'm sure it was just something I ate."

He looked doubtful, with good reason. Greta had made us dinner, and nobody ever got sick off her cooking. It was next level work.

"Let's just go back to bed. I'm tired." He helped me stand and watched me like a hawk all the way to bed. Pulling the covers over us, Dimitri hugged me close. I fell asleep soon after, wondering why I didn't feel uncomfortable now. I assumed getting sick must have drained me.

When we woke a few hours later, I still felt fine. I made us breakfast; Scrambled eggs, french toast, hashbrowns, muffins and bacon. Lots of bacon. I filled my plate mostly with meat, Dimitri eyeing me as I poured syrup over everything.

"What's gotten into you?" He asked.

"I'm hungry."

"You never put syrup on eggs."

I shrugged, taking a bite. He shook his head at me.

"You're feeling better then, I take it."

"I told you, it was probably weird I ate. I'm fine. Stop worrying."

"It's my job to worry about you. One I take very seriously." He leaned over to kiss me.

I finished my breakfast, my eyes drooping tiredly. Not bothering to take my dishes to the sink, I crawled back into bed.

"We have training." Dimitri said.

I was so tired, I simply waived him off. "Not today."

He paused. "Okay." He kissed my forehead gently. "I'll wake you up in a bit."

He might have said something else, but I was already asleep.

# CHAPTER 57

**LILYS POV**

Dimitri woke me up at ten thirty. I was groggy, and starving. I asked him to make me a sandwich with a side of potato salad while I showered. The look he gave me was justified; Wolves ate more than humans in general, but this appetite was unusual for me. Not to mention the fatigue. Perhaps my mate was right, and I should visit Thara. I didn't feel sick, but I didn't feel like myself either.

"I made you a turkey bacon club." Dimitri mind-linked me.

I smiled as I rinsed my hair. "Perfect. Thank you."

Turning off the water, I dried myself hastily, eager to get to the food awaiting me. I haphazardly wrapped my hair and strode out of the washroom completely naked. Dimitris eyes widened as I sat down and grabbed the sandwich, taking a huge bite.

"This might be the hottest thing you've ever done." He gazed at me.

"Don't even think about it. I'm way too hungry for sex."

He smirked, taking my words the wrong way. I rolled my eyes while I continued to devour my meal.

"I'm going to find the guys. Meet you downstairs?" He pecked my cheek. The little touch sent heat pooling in my stomach. My arousal drifted between us and clearly showed on my face.

"You know, maybe I changed my mind about the sex." I bit my lip.

"Best thing I've heard all morning."

I jumped at him, catching him by surprise. The towel unwrapped from my still wet hair, falling to the ground. My lips met his in a rough heated kiss, which he returned happily. Part of me wondered if I was going into heat; I wasn't usually this horny. But, no, I just had my heat, hadn't I? I shouldn't have another one for six months. Was it different for me, being a Mother Wolf? I stopped pondering when Dimitris hand slipped between my legs. My head fell back with a loud moan.

By the time I was completely satisfied, it was fifteen minutes until twelve. I left my mate breathing hard on the bed to get dressed. I opted for something I could move easily in, in case this meeting went badly. Dimitri joined me in the closet to get new clothes; His were a lost cause, shredded in my need to have his skin on mine. Scraps of the remnants were scattered across the bed and floor. I wasn't even sorry.

"Gideon just arrived. Ben is escorting him inside."

"Where are we meeting?" I asked as I tugged my shirt on.

"The common room. I've made it clear nobody is allowed in there today."

I nodded. "Good. Let's go."

"I need pants Lily."

"But you look so much better without them."

"I think the guys would disagree with you."

I actually pouted when he grabbed a pair of black jeans. Goddess, I needed to get myself under control.

"Later." He promised. My mood instantly brightened.

"I'm holding you to that."

Taking my hand, we went together to the common room. I eyed the artwork that decorated the walls in the packhouse. I'd been here for a while now, and still I couldn't get used to the beauty of this place. Not just the packhouse, but the pack itself. I was lucky to be able to call Blood Moon my home. Dimitri opened the door for me, allowing me walk in first. My eyes immediately sought out Gideon, standing near one of the many bookshelves. He seemed quite impressed at the collection.

Ben stood near him, watching him closely. Clara was sitting on one of the plush, grey sectionals, and Luke was leaning against the redbrick fireplace set on the far wall. To my surprise, others were here too. Alpha Killian looked up as we entered, a man I didn't know standing next to him. He nodded a greeting at us. Even Hazel and Clint were here, sitting at a small table tucked into the corner.

"Thanks for coming." Dimitri said.

"You said be here at noon." Gideon replied.

"I wasn't talking to you. I was talking to him." He gestured to his Alpha friend. Gideon shrugged, continuing to scan the books.

"Why are you all here?" I asked.

"You didn't want the warriors here, but I still wanted extra protection." He glared across the room. "We trust everyone here, without a doubt. Right?"

"Right."

"With one obvious exception." Killian said.

"It's nice to see you again Alpha." I smiled.

"You can call me Killian Lily. No titles amongst friends."

"Alright. And this is?" I nodded to the man next to him.

"This is my Beta, Julian."

"Pleased to meet you Luna." Julian offered his hand. I met him halfway, and we shook.

"You as well."

I cast my eyes to the side, having the sensation of being watched. Gideon was staring at me, a strange look on his face. It almost looked like pride.

"It's amazing how well you can ignore the elephant in the room." Killian commented.

"And with that being said, let's get on with this." Dimitri announced. He hadn't left my side since entered the room.

I looked at Gideon for the first time properly. Dimitri had been right; He was freshly clothed, cleaned and shaven. It sparked annoyance in me. He was a prisoner, for the time being. He should act like one. After all, he had surrendered to us

"I was told you would willingly take a truth serum." I didn't phrase it as a question.

Gideon nodded. "I will. Under the condition-"

"We met your condition! You get to talk to Lily; You don't get anything else!" Dimitri snarled.

"As I was saying-," He acted as if my mate hadn't spoken, stirring anger in the air,"- Under the condition that only you, Luna, ask the questions."

"Why?" I asked.

"Because only you will ask the right ones."

He wasn't making any sense, but I didn't push it. I looked at the faces of my friends, and my mate. "Anybody have a problem with that?"

"No."

"Nope."

"No."

Dimitri shook his head mutely. "Okay. Clara?"

She stood, reaching into her pocket and producing a small, thin vial with gold liquid. We'd had the opportunity to test this batch, on Luke. Clara hadn't made a truth serum since before Isabelle was born; She wanted to make sure she got it right. I'd learned many interesting things about my friend, mostly due to Ben and Dimitri asking him embarrassing questions. He could be sure that I would remember everything, and he would never live it down.

Ben shadowed his mate as she walked to Gideon, stopping two feet away. She tossed him the vial, crossing her arms. I was surprised when he popped open the lid and downed it one go. Part of me honestly expected him to screw us over, to take the potion and vanish. It's not like it wouldn't come in handy in the future; The Devil himself would spill his darkest and most intimate secrets. Gideon shuddered slightly, his pupils dilating. Clara had told us it could take up to three minutes for it to take effect, so I counted in my head. When I got to three minutes exactly, I asked my first question.

"What is your name?"

"Gideon Abraham Whitethorn."

His last name rang a dim bell, for Goddess knows what reason. Whitethorn was not a name I'd ever known.

"Are you a Dark Witch?"

"No."

"Told you." I heard Clara mutter to Ben.

"If you're not a Dark witch, why did you take James and Jennine?"

"I only took James. I did not take Jennine, though I meant to."

My forehead creased in confusion.

"Where is James?"

"Dead."

My mouth dropped open. That was the last thing I expected to hear.

"But... Margie told me that you'd offered him a deal, something about getting revenge on Dimitri and I? That the Alpha and Luna would pay?"

"I did offer him revenge, but it was only a pretense. I am powerful, but because I do not practice the Dark Arts, James had to agree to be transported to me."

"You... You don't want to hurt us? Me? Or Dimitri?"

"No."

"Then why did you kill James?!" I demanded. I couldn't honestly say I was sad over his death, but coming from a man who just claimed he had no ill will towards us, it was a little strange.

"Because he hurt you." Gideon said nonchalantly. I was taken aback by his confession.

"Why does that matter to you? You don't even know me."

"I do know you. I've always known you Lily. I've been keeping watch over you your whole life."

My heart started to race. Suddenly, I wanted to leave the room, to be done with this. Yet, despite my inner turmoil, my mouth opened and asked the question I wasn't sure I wanted the answer to. But it seemed inevitable; If not here, now, I would find out some other way. Unavoidable.

"Why?"

Gideons eyes looked shinier, as if he was fighting back tears. But he answered in a calm, confident tone.

"How could I not watch over my own daughter?"

# CHAPTER 58

"Excuse me?" I gasped.

I could feel the shock in the air, the growing tension. The words were out there now, almost visible, yet unbelievable.

"You are my daughter." Gideon repeated sincerely.

My breath was coming hard; My mind wasn't processing his words. Finally, it clicked and I exploded.

"I can't be your daughter! I'm a werewolf!"

"It was always a fifty, fifty chance of which way you would turn out."

"You're lying!" I shouted.

"Sweetheart, he's not. He can't." Dimitri reminded me. Angrily, I turned on my mate. His expression radiated worry.

"The serum must have worn off." I said.

"It hasn't. It won't for at least another hour." Clara spoke quietly.

"Then... then he is tricking us. He tampered with it!" I continued to grasp at illogical theories, unwilling to accept that this was my fate. My friends stared at me silently, not wanting to push me further.

"I can show you proof." Gideon suddenly said.

"I don't want your proof!" I screamed at him. He flinched, obviously hurt by my words. I didn't give a fuck.

Without another word, I turned and left the room, slamming the door behind me. It had to be a trick; He'd outsmarted us somehow. He was powerful, more powerful than Clara. He had to have done something to either himself or the serum. He was lying, toying with us. With me.

"He's not." Aya whispered in my mind.

"He has to be!"

"You want him to be lying Lily, because that's easier than accepting the truth. Go back, let him show us whatever proof he has."

"I can't. I just can't."

"Why?"

I ran my hands through my hair, pulling it in frustration. "Because if it is true, that means I not only have a father, but that he abandoned me as well! And it means I have a mother who did the same! I don't want to hear how they didn't want me!"

"I understand Lily. But we need to do this. I can feel that. You can't avoid this and sweep it under the carpet like you're doing with everything else. Life has many challenges, but I'm here with you to face them together."

I hated that she was right. I also hated that a big part of wanted to see his 'proof'. I wanted to know just as much as I didn't. I practiced calming my breathing, making sure I was relatively calm, before I opened the door and strode back inside. Every pair of eyes were on me, but I only had eyes for the man claiming to be my Dad.

"Show me." I demanded. My tone was harsh, hopefully covering up how scared I was right now.

"Lily-"

I held my hand up, silencing Dimitri. It was disrespectful, for sure. But if I didn't do this now, in this mindset, I would leave again and never come back.

Gideon nodded. "I will need something from home." He said.

"Make it quick!" I snapped.

He snapped his fingers, vanishing. I blinked and he was back. In his hands was a thick book, with a worn black cover and yellowing pages. He flipped halfway through before setting it on one of the tables. Curiosity guiding me, I inched closer to peek. The writing was not English. It was a series of strokes and dots and symbols I'd never seen before.

"It is the language of witches." Gideon explained. I glanced at Clara, who peered over my shoulder, nodding to confirm what he said.

Gideon placed his hand on the page and began to mumble under his breath. I caught some of it, though it made no sense to me. The words started to glow under his palm, brighter and brighter until they were a shining white gold light. Abruptly, the scene around us changed. The common room disappeared, leaving us standing in a lush meadow. A gentle breeze blew through the grass, but I couldn't feel it on my skin. I had a moment of Deja vu. This place oddly reminded me of my one meeting with the Moon Goddess.

"What the fuck?!"

"Where are we?"

I looked around to my friends. Everyone aside from Clara and Gideon and myself were looking around in shock and amazement. Luke reached out trying to touch the now non-existent fireplace, jumping back when he couldn't find it.

"This is way too freaky." He gulped.

"Shh! Watch." Gideon said.

He was looking out over the meadow expectantly. I followed his gaze, my heart thumping in my chest. A soft giggle floated towards us before a woman and a man appeared, chasing each other through the grass. As they came closer, smiling and laughing, I felt tears form in my eyes. The man was Gideon, younger, livelier. His hair was pure black, no hint of grey. The goatee was missing, his face clean and happy. The woman was beautiful. Long red hair that reached her waist, pale flawless skin. Her lips were full and redder than roses. I small sound left my mouth as she turned, her eyes sweeping over us, through us. They were green, a duller shade than mine, by far, but I knew it.

This was my Mother.

The young Gideon caught her around the waist, quickly pulling her in for a kiss. The love surrounding them was raw, pure. It was so obvious, anybody could see it.

"I should go." The woman said.

"No, not yet. I hardly ever get to see you Rose."

Rose? My mothers name was Rose?

"Short for Rosalie." Present day Gideon muttered to me. He was tense as he watched the scene with us.

"I know." Rose caressed young Gideons face. "But you know we cannot risk getting caught. You know what will happen."

"I hate this!"

"I do too. I wish I'd be been born a witch. Or you a wolf. Life is so unfair."

"I could-"

"No! You mustn't Gideon! I could not bear to see you shrouded in Darkness. I love you too much."

He looked heartbroken, utterly lost. I heard Clara gasp behind me.

"You were going to...?" She whispered.

"Yes."

The younger version of my parents kissed again and Gideon snapped his fingers. The scene dissolved, changed. I gave him a sharp look.

"Did you want to watch yourself being conceived?" He asked.

Oh. No thanks. I shook my head, looking away.

We were in the same meadow, but it was now night. A beautiful full moon hung in the sky, stars dancing around it. It cast a light glow over the trees, the grass, the flowers. Rose sat on the ground, crying silently. My heart lurched, and I took a hesitant step towards her. A figure stepped through me, literally right through me, making my body wave and shimmer. I jumped back with a yelp.

"My love, why are you crying? What's wrong?" Young Gideon pulled my mother into his arms, stroking her hair.

"I have ruined everything." She sobbed.

"You could never ruin anything. You are too perfect for that. Tell me what has upset you like this."

"I....I...." She hid her face in her hands. "I am pregnant!" She cried.

I winced. Pain ran through my chest as I watched the woman who carried me in her womb cry her heart out. She'd said she'd ruined everything, because of me? She hated me that much already?

"Pregnant?" Young Gideon breathed. Rose nodded.

"I am s-sorry Gideon. So sorry!"

"Don't be!" His face was transfixed with a warm bright smile. His face was full of joy. "Rose, this hasn't ruined anything. It's only made it better!"

"How can you say that?!" She hissed. The knife drove itself deeper into my heart. "My father will kill you, he will kill this child!"

Wait, what?

"I won't let him! Let's go Rose, let's run away. We will have our baby, we will love them. Together."

"You... you would do that for me? For us? You would become a rogue?"

"I would do anything for you. And for our child."

My mother stood, wiping her tears. "Yes. I will go with you. I love you Gideon." She jumped into his arms, embracing him.

A snap of fingers and the scene changed again. A large gate loomed over us, attached to a pale stone wall. Beyond, I could see a magnificent mansion with white siding and large windows. Rose bushes were planted upfront, being tended to by various people.

"You are making a mistake Rosalie!"

A loud, booming voice resonated over my ears. I finally noticed my mother was walking down the stone path, leading away from the mansion. Following behind her was a large man in an expensive looking suit. He had wavy brown hair and cold light blue eyes. He grabbed Rose by the shoulder, turning her to face him.

"You can't do this! You're throwing your life away and for what?! A witch?! You are not thinking straight girl!"

"I am not throwing anything away Father!"

I gasped. This cold angry man was my grandfather?

"I love Gideon, and he loves me. This is the most sure thing I have ever done, or will ever do." Rose continued.

"Are you really that dumb! He's bewitched you Rosalie!"

She smiled softly. "Yes, he has. There is nothing you can do Father. I won't reject my mate, not even for you."

Two separate gasps sounded behind me. I knew it was Ben and Clara.

"Y-your mate?"

"Yes. Gideon is my fated mate. I do not question the Goddess's choices. We are meant to be together, and we will be."

"If you do this, you can never come back here. I won't allow it!" My grandfather thundered.

My mother straightened her spine, lifting her chin. "I, Rosalie Lillian Green, hereby cut all ties to the Crescent Moon Pack."

"I accept!" My grandfather spit. They both winced, my mothers hand clutching her chest. After a minute, she straightened again and turned away from him.

"Goodbye Father."

"You will regret this Rosalie! You and that witch! I'll make you regret it!"

She pushed the gate open, ignoring the threats behind her. I thought she might look sad, or even hesitant. But my mother walked proudly away from her pack, officially a rogue, caressing her belly lightly.

# CHAPTER 59

**DIMITRIS POV**

I was stunned. Our group stood together, watching everything Gideon had to show us. My eyes were constantly going to my mates face, analyzing the play of emotions there. This was hurting her, and I wanted to stop it. But I also knew that she needed this, needed to see it. I would help her through the aftermath, as best I could.

The image changed again, and honestly, it was starting to make me dizzy. This entire time, I'd been feeling odd; The air felt sticky on my skin, too thick. I noticed a while ago that the others were visibly uncomfortable as well, apart from Clara, Gideon and Lily. The witches made sense, but Lily was a wolf like me. I figured it must be because she was half witch.

"That doesn't change anything." Ajax said.

"No, it doesn't. I'd love her if she were part chicken."

A scream interrupted us, and I instantly pulled my mate closer, looking around. We were in a house, a small house. The younger version of Gideon paced in front of a room, worry and anxiousness set in his features. He looked more like the man standing in front of me now; A short black beard had grown on his face, and he looked more mature. Another scream echoed through the door and he cringed. A few minutes later, the cry of a baby was heard. Warmth spread through my chest; Lily had just been born.

A man stepped through the door, old with half moon glasses. He looked drained, but he wore a big smile.

"Congratulations Gideon. You have a beautiful, healthy baby girl."

"I daughter?"

"Yes sir. She was a big one too, nine pounds, three ounces."

"How is Rose?"

"Tired, but relieved." The man chuckled. "Give my wife a few minutes to clean her up, then you can go see your family."

"My family..." Young Gideon grinned. "Thank you. So much Peter. I don't know how I can ever repay you for everything you've done for us."

295

"All I require is you bring that little girl over to see her papa. That is payment enough."

"And her nana." A short, blonde woman exited the room, her front stained with blood and some form of goop. I internally cringed, like the typical man I was.

"Of course. Once Rose is feeling up to it, we will come by."

"She is feeding the little one now. You can go in."

I gave the men around a hard stare. Quickly, they all averted their eyes. It may have been a memory, but I was still pretty certain Lily, and Gideon for that matter, did not want this many people seeing that.

Young Gideon pushed the door open, and we followed him into a bedroom. I looked at the painting on the wall, Clara looked at the ceiling, and the rest gazed at their shoes. The sound of baby Lily feeding was the only sound in the room.

"Rose...." Young Gideon choked back tears. "She's beautiful. Perfect."

"I know. Just wait, she is even more special than we thought."

I heard a tiny burp and a few seconds later Lily nudged me. Rose had swaddled her, tucking her into her arm. Curiously, I moved a bit closer. Lily opened her eyes, the colour shining brightly against her pink skin. She looked curiously at her Father before letting out a huge yawn and falling asleep instantaneously.

"What... What..." Young Gideon seemed to be at a loss for words.

"I met the Moon Goddess Gideon." Rose said.

"What?" He repeated.

Tears left her eyes silently as she gazed at her baby. "Our daughter is special. She is chosen by Celeste herself to do great things. I am sorry, I cannot explain more to you."

"I trust you." Rose smiled at him. "Can I?"

"You have to ask? She is your daughter silly."

Young Gideon gazed at the sleeping infant in his arms. "What should we call her?"

"I was thinking Lillian... Lily."

"Your mother?"

"She would have loved her. She would have accepted her, and us. I know it."

"I love it. My little Lily." He kissed her nose. "I love you so much my little girl."

Gideon snapped his fingers silently. I briefly wondered if he relived these memories often, or if this was the first time.

"Lily! Where are you?"

We were in a forest, the sun shining high in the sky. Rose was wandering through the trees, Gideon walking behind her. They both looked older now.

"Lily, come on out. Your Mom is worrying." Gideon called.

I heard a giggle behind me. I stepped out of the way as a whirlwind of red hair ran past me, jumping into her mothers arms.

"There you are!" Rose nuzzled her daughters neck, tickling her. I smiled as my mates child self erupted into fits of laughter.

"Mama, stop!"

She was set on her feet and Gideon took her hand.

"Lily, you know you shouldn't run off."

"Sorry Daddy."

"You worry us when you disappear. Stay with us from now on, okay?"

"Okay Daddy. I love you."

"I love you too pumpkin."

Gideon snapped his fingers, harshly and turned away. I jumped to the side as fire erupted beside me, almost knocking over Clara. It couldn't hurt me, of course, but it was so different from the happy scene a few seconds ago. I watched in horror as the forest around us burned and smoldered. Smoke filled the air, thick and strong. Squirrels and rabbits ran for their lives through the thicket, birds screaming in the trees.

"Take her Gideon!" I turned to see Rose shoving her daughter into Gideons arms.

"Rose, please! Don't do this!"

"Mama, stay with me!" Lily cried.

"I have to, Gideon. I will lead them away, and then I will find you. Take her, now!" Not giving him a chance to refuse again, she ran away, shifting into a beautiful white wolf with black boots.

"Mama!" Lily jumped from her fathers arms, racing after her mother. My heart was hurting at the scene.

"Lily, no! Come with me, come on. We have to go. Mommy will come back." He scooped her up and ran past our group, out of sight. We were left standing in the middle of a burning forest. I was confused why Gideon didn't take us elsewhere until a howl pierced through the air. It grated against my nerves, cut into my heart. The sound abruptly cut off, followed by a heavy silence.

Clara was crying silently beside me, wrapped under one of Bens arms. Lily stood in front of me, a look of denial on her face. I brought her back against me, rubbing her shoulders. There was nothing I could say, nothing I could do. Not even the mate bond could ease the pain of knowing her mother was gone. Gideon hadn't watched the vision with us, still turned away, looking into the smoky bush. His shoulders moved, indicating he too was crying. Another snap, and we were transported once more.

I looked around, recognition washing over me. We stood on the border of Snow Moon. Lily sat on the ground under a tree, crying. Gideon kneeled in front of her, smoothing her hair.

"I want Mommy." She sniffled.

"I know pumpkin. I know. It's going to be okay."

"You said she would come back."

He didn't answer her. Instead, he hugged her close, kissing her hair. "I love you so much Lily. And Mom does too. I'm so sorry."

"Sorry for what?"

His hand started to glow with a light blue hue. He placed it on her small head, mumbling under his breath. Tears streamed down his face and he choked on the words. Finally, he released her. The child who stared at him now had a blank face. She clearly didn't know who he was.

"Your name is Lily. You are five years old. Say it."

"My name is Lily, I am five years old."

"You are a werewolf."

"I am a werewolf."

"You..." Young Gideon choked on a sob. "You are an orphan." He managed.

"I am an orphan?"

"Yes. Say it Lily."

"I am an orphan."

"Go into this pack. They will look after you until I find you again." He hugged her one more time. "I love you, so, so much. Now go. Go!" He pushed her towards the border lightly. She looked back at him once before running through the forest. Her father watched her, fists clenched, heart on his sleeve. Screaming into the night air, he vanished. The trees started to spin, colours mixing together. I shut my eyes and when I opened them, we were back in the packhouse common room.

Clara stepped away from Ben, wiping her eyes. Luke sat heavily on the sectional, putting his head in his hands. Killian and his Beta just stared, absorbing everything they'd witnessed. Hazel was curled up with Clint, and Gideon slammed his old black book shut. I searched my mind, trying to come up with anything to say to Lily; I came up blank. What could I possibly say to her?

"You *asshole*!"

# CHAPTER 60

**DIMITRIS POV**

Lily sprang from my grasp, lunging at Gideon. His eyes widened before her fist connected with his jaw. He fell to the floor, staring at her in surprise.

"How could you do that?! How could you leave me there, with those people?!" She screamed.

"Lily-"

"Do you know what they did to me?! Do you know what I went through because of you?!" She started to sob. "You abandoned me into the hands of the Devil, and you just left! Why? Why didn't you take me with you?!"

"It was too dangerous! I couldn't lose you too!" He shouted.

"You're lying! You said you've watched over me all my life? So you just let them beat me, whip me, cut me with silver? You stood by when they burned me, tortured me, broke me from the inside out! And you didn't do anything!"

"I couldn't."

"Bullshit!" Aya's voice mixed with Lilys. "You couldn't handle the death of your mate, so you dumped me at the first pack you found! And you took my memories! You're not my father. I want nothing to do with you. I hate you!" She screamed.

Gideon cringed at her words forcefully, like she'd given him another blow. Chest heaving, my mate ran from the room. Her emotions were hitting me like a train. Despair, grief, heartache. And blinding rage. I believed in that moment, she truly did hate Gideon.

He sat on the floor, looking utterly miserable.

"Why did you do it?" Killian asked before I could.

"I had to find her mother."

"But Rose.... we all saw." Clara said.

Gideon shook his head. "She's not dead."

"What?" Our voices echoed together.

300

He looked Clara in the eye. "You should have figured that out. I still have my magic. The bond never broke."

Her eyes widened. "So, wait. What happened to her? Where is she?"

"I don't know."

"Her father.." I started but he shook his head again.

"He died shortly after Rose left. His Beta took over as Alpha, a nice man. They never came looking for us."

"Then who attacked you? Who was Rose leading off?" Ben asked.

"My brother."

"What?" We all repeated.

Gideon sighed. "It's a long story. One I was hoping to explain to Lily." He looked towards the door sadly. "But I always knew she would probably hate me for what I did."

"I will talk to her." Hazels said softly.

"I don't think there's any point. She has every reason to be angry."

"You did what you thought was right. You were a father trying to protect his daughter. I'd do the same for my child, in that situation." She patted her stomach, and my jaw dropped.

"Your pregnant?" I gasped.

"We just found out." She smiled at Clint. "I'll go find Lily. I need to lie down anyways." She kissed her mate quickly before leaving to search for mine.

"Congrats." I nodded to Clint.

"Thanks Alpha." He beamed.

"Okay, this is great and good for you, but I'm still really needing answers." Clara said.

"Same." Luke said.

"Sorry to take away your thunder dude, but I agree." Ben said.

"No worries. I'm sitting on the edge of my seat too."

We all looked at Gideon who sighed again.

"You've told them about the Dark Arts?" He asked Clara.

"To a point."

"Okay. Well, my brother is a rogue, like me, but for very different reasons. He's always had a fascination with Dark witches. I tried to steer him away from it, down the right path. But he is greedy, selfish. I knew he'd gone too far when I caught him raping a girl from our Clan. He... he was going to use the blood from her virginity for a ritual." He cringed and the rest of us did too. "I reported him to the Elders. He was banished, exiled. I was hurt, but I thought I was doing the right thing."

"You did." Clara said.

"You saw as clearly as everyone else what happened to my family. Bastian sought me out, wanting to take his revenge."

"Hold on! Your brother is Bastian? Bastian Whitethorn?!"

"In name only, but yes."

"You know him?" Ben turned to his mate.

"Everyone knows him. Among witches anyways. He has decimated villages, killed hundreds of innocent people..." She gulped, her face pale.

"Yes, he's made quite a name for himself." Gideon said sarcastically.

"How does someone that dangerous go unnoticed by us?" Luke wondered aloud.

"How often do you wolves involve yourself in other species issues?"

"Okay, true point."

"Anyways, Bastian had been keeping an eye on me. He found out that Lily was special, though none of us, except maybe Rose, knew just how special she was. The night we were attacked, it was because he wanted Lily. He set our house on fire while we slept. I held him off as long as I could while Rose got Lily outside. He reminded me of his promise for revenge, saying he was going to use Lily to make him the most powerful witch in existence." His fists clenched tightly. "Instead, he got my mate, and I was forced to hide Lily in a random pack I came across."

"How do you know he still has her?" I asked.

"Bastian is a cruel son of a bitch. I've lived all this time, all these years, feeling Roses emotions. I feel when he hits her. I feel when he touches her. I have tried to follow the bond, but I always come to a dead end. It's as if she's here with me, but out of my reach. It's fucking Hell!" He slammed his fist on the ground.

My stomach rolled. I couldn't even imagine going through that, let alone for years. How had he not gone insane yet? I shared a look with Killian, knowing we were thinking the same thing. Any wolf would have gone feral by now.

"Question, why didn't you go back for Lily? When she was older?" Luke asked Gideon.

"I wanted to. So badly. She is right, I saw everything those wretched people did to her, If I had known what they were like beforehand, I never would have left her there. I would have found another pack. But I knew Bastian was looking for her as well. I didn't want to give her away, lead him to her. So I watched her grow up through my Orb, keeping an eye on her."

"Orb?" I questioned.

"Like a crystal ball." Clara explained.

"Ah. Still, you could have taken her with you. You could have searched for Rose together." I snapped.

"You all think I'm strong, but Bastian is stronger. She was protected, invisible from him. The minute I took her back, he would have known and he would have come for her. Do you have any idea what happens to us when we dally with the Dark Arts? What happens when we give ourselves over to it?"

"You lose your soul." Luke said. His research into different species was paying off.

Gideon gave a hard nod. "Right. My brother has no soul. No conscious, no sense of right or wrong. He has magic I could only dream about. I cannot defeat him, and because I am a rogue, I have no help from the Clans or the Elders."

I wanted to yell at him, accuse him, but I couldn't. He was caught in an impossible situation, with no way out. I wanted to hate him for leaving my mate at the hands of Snow Moon, but I understood why he did, and why he never went back. Whereas before I saw my enemy, now I saw a broken, hopeless man who only wanted his family back after years of suffering. I couldn't help but feel sorry for him.

Lily was going to eat me alive for this.

"We will help you find Rose." I stated.

Gideons head snapped up, eyes meeting mine. "I didn't come here to ask you for your help."

"Then why did you?" Clint asked. "You just said Bastian would know if you were with Lily. Yet, you came here willingly. What's the deal?"

"Lily has a strong mate and a pack who loves her now. She is far more protected here than she was at Snow Moon, or even by herself with me. I can be with her now, as long as she has you." He looked at me. "She's been here for months, and he hasn't tried to take her." He sounded like it should have already happened, which concerned me a lot.

"I think you're forgetting what happens to us when we use Dark magic for so long." Clara scoffed. "Isn't it obvious? He's weakened."

"How so?" Clint asked.

"According to you,-" She gestured to Gideon, "- He's been using Dark magic for over a decade. He gave up his soul a long time ago. Losing your soul takes a huge toll on you; Our souls are our essence, our bodies only the shells that carry them. Bastian will literally wither away into nothing sooner or later."

"I... I didn't know that." Gideon gulped.

Clara gaped at him. "How are you more powerful than me?!"

"Then why don't we just wait it out? Wait until he dies?" Ben suggested.

"We can't." I said. "If he's weak, then he'll be more desperate."

Gideon nodded. "He's already started his attack."

"What do you mean? Killian demanded.

"I took James for what he did to Lily. And yes, I killed him. I meant to grab Jennine too, but..."

The blood drained from my face. "Bastian got her first." I stated.

"Yes. And based on what I saw from her time here, I have no doubt she will help him destroy Blood Moon."

# CHAPTER 61

I ran, and I didn't stop until I was in my room. I raced to the bathroom, crouching over the toilet and becoming violently sick. My tears never ceased, the sobs breaking from my chest making it a painful experience. Eventually, I had nothing left to bring up. Exhausted and overwhelmed, I sat back, screaming into the empty space. I was dizzy, lightheaded. My body swayed, slumping to the floor.

"Fuck!"

A pair of hands caught me before my head hit the floor.

"Hazel?"

"I'm here Lily. Come on, let's get you to bed."

I let her help me stand, wrapping my arm around her shoulders. I felt so weak, so tired. And, super strangely, hungry. How could I even think of being hungry right now?

"Hazel."

"Yes?"

"I'm hungry." I said sheepishly.

"I will make you something. Lay down."

She arranged the pillows for me, covering me with the blanket. I grabbed Dimitris pillow, bringing it to my nose and inhaling his scent; It did wonders at calming my nerves. Hazel came back with a bowl of Greta's chicken noddle soup. She handed it to me and I eagerly dove in; Hazel sat beside me and raised her eyebrows. I finished the soup in no time, placing the bowl and spoon on the bedside table.

"You were hungry, weren't you?"

I nodded. "It's weird."

"Probably a symptom of the stress." She patted my hand. "How are you feeling now?"

"I don't know Hazel." I blew out a breath. "Angry. Betrayed. Heartbroken... to name a few."

"I understand."

We sat in silence for a while, lost in our own thoughts.

"I'm pregnant." She suddenly announced.

My eyes widened and I pulled her in for a huge hug. "Really?! Oh my gosh! Congratulations Hazel!"

"Thanks Lily." She returned my smile. Her eyes clouded over, letting me know someone was mind-linking her. When her eyes cleared, she grasped my hand. "You'll want to mind-link Dimitri." Her tone was soft, but commanding. I did what she asked without questioning her.

"Dimitri?"

"Lily! Are you okay?"

"No."

"I'll come find you soon darling. But you need to hear this."

He told me everything that had been discussed since I left. I swore at least a dozen times, and when he finished, I swore again.

"So I have a crazy grandfather who hated my parents, and an even crazier Uncle who wants to use me? Probably kill me?"

"I'm sorry Lily."

"And he's working with Jennine. Wonderful."

"We'll come up with a plan. Nobody is going to hurt you."

"Come up soon. I need some serious cuddles."

"Whatever you want darling. I love you."

"I love you too."

I cut off the mind-link, seeing Hazels eyes clear as well. Her expression said Clint had also filled her in on what we'd missed.

"Goddess, Jennine is just digging her own grave." Hazel mused.

"I'd rather dig it for her. And put her in it." I snarled. Hazel pursed her lips in agreement.

"The good news is that your Mom is still alive. That's a miracle, you must be happy about that."

I was. Truthfully, that information spread warmth throughout me. I had a Mother, a Mother who loved me. I would do anything to get her back, to bring her home.

"I need to come up with a plan, to get her back." I told Hazel.

"You? Don't you mean 'we'?"

"I don't need Gideons help."

Hazel sighed. "Lily, he did it to protect you. You heard what Dimitri said- Bastian would have found you already if Gideon had taken you away. It wasn't an ideal situation, but I believe he made the right choice."

My jaw dropped. "You can't be serious?! Hazel, the man abandoned me with no memories! He watched me become a human punching bag for an entire pack!" I seethed.

"I know it's hard to understand. And I know I'm not a Mom yet... but even now, everything in me is telling me to protect my pup. If I was faced with a choice like Gideons, I would leave my child too, if it mean they'd be safe."

"Then you're as bad a parent as he is!"

The words left me mouth before I could stop them. Instantly, my hand went over my mouth as Hazels face crumpled in hurt. What the hell was wrong with me?!

My friend stood, making her way to the door.

"Hazel, wait! I didn't mean-"

"I'll come see you later, when you're in a better mood." And she left.

"Aaaarrgggghhhh!" My head fell into my hands. I was horrible; Was there anything worse I could have said? I wouldn't be surprised if Hazel never talked to me again. I wouldn't if I was her. Tears fell from my eyes, catching in my palms.

I felt ridiculously sad. Not just remorseful, though I was. I cried for half an hour on the bed, until my stomach grumbled. Sniffling, I made my way to the kitchen where I grabbed a package of bacon from the fridge. Throwing into a pan, I turned it on high letting the juicy meat get crispy. I cooked the whole package and grabbed another. Setting my heaping pile on a plate, I brought it back to the bed and snuggled under the covers.

Munching on my odd snack, I put on a movie Dimitri and I had already watched. My thoughts wandered in circles as the characters own dramas played on the screen. Was I suppose to forgive Gideon? Just like that? Nobody here knew the extent of what I'd endured at Snow Moon; Nobody knew how many times I'd contemplated ending my own life. Okay, so that was my doing, I never talked to anybody about it. Not even my mate. But the difference was that Gideon had seen it all and never stepped in.

He killed James because of what he did, but what about the rest? What about everyone else who'd hurt me? How was that right? Part of me wanted to believe that if my Mother hadn't been kidnapped, she would never have agreed to what he did. Mate or not, she would have protected me, wouldn't she?

The memory of my birth played in my head. Gideon holding me for the first time, love and happiness shining on his face. With that image came a string of guilt. I didn't want to believe Hazel, didn't want to see it from his point of view. That would make what he did okay, and it wasn't okay.

At some point, I fell asleep, completely drained. I woke up to the sparks of my mate holding me close.

"Did I wake you?" He whispered.

"No. I have to pee."

He let me go, allowing me to slide off the bed and go do my business. I washed my hands, noticing my plate on the table. I'd only eaten half the bacon I'd made; Hopping back into bed, I picked up the plate and resumed finishing it. Dimitri reached for a piece, pulling his hand back when I slapped it.

"Don't you dare."

He shrugged. "I already had three anyways."

I scowled at him. "What time is it?"

"Almost dinner. You slept most of the afternoon."

I didn't know what to say to that, so I said nothing.

"How are you feeling?"

"Fine."

"Lily."

"Okay, I'm confused and angry and honestly, I'm still tired. And I'm angry. I just want things to go back to normal; No, I want things to be normal. I want to not be some mythic legendary wolf with all these problems. I just want to live my life with you, happily. Is that too much to ask?"

"I get what you're saying, but life isn't always that easy Lily. Everyone has challenges, some more than others. I too wish you didn't have to go through all this, but it is what it is. All we can do now is be prepared."

"Like we were prepared the first time?" I scoffed.

"We have foresight this time around. And we know what our enemy is after. That makes everything a little easier." He brushed my hair behind my ear. I caught his hand, the sparks setting off a different kind of hunger in me.

Dimitri registered my mood a second before my lips were on his, my hands tugging open his shirt. To my surprise, and disappointment, he pulled away.

"What's wrong?" I asked.

"I asked Greta to bring us dinner tonight so you didn't have to cook. I'd feel pretty awful if I scarred the poor woman this way."

I was seriously thinking about mind-linking Greta to hold off with our food until a knock sounded at the door.

"Come in." Dimitri called and I reluctantly climbed off him.

"Hello dears! I hope you're hungry." Greta wheeled in a trolley loaded with food.

"It looks amazing Greta, thank you so much." Dimitri gave her a side hug.

"Anything for my favourite Alpha and Luna. Enjoy loves." She left with a cheeky grin.

We ate until we couldn't anymore, settling back against the pillows. Dimitri rested his hands behind his head, closing his eyes.

"That woman can make anything out of potatoes, I swear." He sighed happily.

"It was delicious." I agreed.

"Speaking of things that are delicious, are you still in the mood-"

I silenced him with a heated kiss, pulling him to me. He grinned against my lips, his hands coming up to remove my shirt. Together, we worked off any possible calories from our dinner until well after midnight.

# CHAPTER 62

I lay in my mates arms for hours, finally somewhat content. The stress of everything in my life seemed to wash away for now. But just like the changing tides, everything came crashing back; In my case though, it was Dimitri who spoiled my mood.

"You should talk to him." He said. I'd thought he was asleep, my hand running over his chest. It came to a halt at his words.

"Excuse me?" I scoffed.

"You heard me. Lily." He rolled over, hovering above me, eyes meeting mine. There was no hint of sarcasm or joking in his depths. "I have lived without my Dad for so long now. Not a day goes by where I don't wish he was still here with me, Mom too. But my parents are never coming back." He swallowed hard, his Adam's apple bobbing. "Trust me when I tell you, you shouldn't give up this chance. Don't push him away."

"There's a difference though. Your parents didn't want to leave you." I snapped.

"Neither did yours!"

I rolled my eyes heavily.

"I'm not saying don't be mad. You have a right to be mad. But don't hate him for his mistakes. He hates himself enough for both of you."

My eyes narrowed at him. "You don't hate him, do you?" I gritted my teeth. Wasn't he supposed to be on my side?

"No, I don't. I can't. I can't hate him because he helped bring you into this world." He kissed my cheek.

"What about him abandoning me?!"

"I can't hate him for that either. Okay, maybe a little. But if he hadn't left you there, I probably wouldn't have found you. You don't seem to realize that he could have dropped you anywhere, the other side of the world even. If he hadn't left you at Snow Moon, we never would have met."

Okay, he had a point. A bit, I guess. But that didn't mean that I was going to rush off to my Fathers arms and forgive him for everything. Part of me wished I still had scars on my body, my back. The sadistic side of me wanted him to see proof of what he'd left me to face by myself. And a whole other part of me, mostly my wolf, *wanted* to give in and finally have the fatherly love I'd always wanted. I'd scolded Aya, but I couldn't fault her- even though Gideon wasn't a wolf, he was my Dad. And so Aya felt a connection with him. Nothing like the mate bond, but a family bond. Since regaining my memories, she recognized him, wanting to be with our family.

I sighed. "Can we just not talk about this right now?" I pleaded with Dimitri.

His eyes hardened. "You can't run away from all your problems Lily."

"I'm not." I replied sharply.

"You are. You never want to talk about anything, nothing hard. Your past, your traumas, your abuse. You put it all on the back burner, locking it away. I'm your mate; You should trust me to talk to, to be open with me."

Anger bubbled up at his words. "Why can't you just drop it?!" I growled. "And you can't talk anyways! Have you ever explained the reasoning behind your behaviour towards me in the beginning? No! So don't preach to me what you can't practice!"

As soon as the words were out, Dimitri rolled off me. I was too angry to feel guilty. He sat with his back against the headboard, breathing hard while I made to get out of bed; I was hungry. But his words froze me in place half on and half off the mattress.

"I killed my grandfather." He deadpanned.

Slowly, I turned to look at him.

"What?" I whispered.

Dimitri gave me a hard look, anger and an array of other emotions burning in his eyes.

"My grandmother was my grandfathers fated mate. They met when she turned eighteen, she was an Omega in the pack. She worked in the kitchens, she made the best chocolate cake. Grandpa went down that night for a midnight snack and she was making a cake for another girl who had the same birthday."

"That's sweet." I mumbled.

But Dimitri scoffed loudly. "Not so much, actually." My eyebrows furrowed at his words. "Grandpa was disgusted to have such a weak mate. How could she be Luna, when she was simply an Omega? Not good for anything other than housework?"

He rolled his eyes, and I could tell he was quoting his grandfathers past words.

"He made it clear as soon as they accepted each other that she was his mate in name only. She was there to serve one purpose, and that was to make him a stronger Alpha. She would continue to work in the kitchens accept when he required her to be in his bed. She would produce him pups, but if they turned out to be weak like her, he would kill them."

I gasped audibly.

"Fortunately, grandma only had two children, two sons. My Dad, and his brother a year later. My uncle died when he was sixteen, at the hand of rogues. My Dad went on to become Alpha. His whole life, he watched his mother suffer when her mate screwed other women, hit her, raped her even. She was never seen as Luna of the pack, never given the respect and love she deserved. When my Dad met his mate, he promised he would break the cycle. My mother was from a different pack, she was the daughter of the Gamma. Still low-class in grandpas eyes. He wanted Dad to treat her the same way he treated grandma. To teach her, her place, to be seen and not heard."

Bile rose in my throat, and I had a hard time swallowing it down.

"Grandpa threatened to take the Alpha title away from my Dad if he didn't comply. He was adamant that Lunas were more of a hindrance to a pack than a blessing. If an Alpha loses his Luna, it could literally drive him insane. He ordered my Dad to keep his mate around to make him stronger, and that was all. But Dad didn't want that. He loved grandma, he didn't want his mate to have the same lonely life. And when they had me, he tried to shield me as much as possible from grandpas skewed views."

Dimitri took a long breath, blowing it out slowly before continuing.

"I didn't spend a lot of time with my grandpa. Or grandma. My parents made sure of that. The older I got, the more I understood why my parents wanted it that way. I thought he was sick, to have mistreated his mate so badly. A couple months before my parents died... I killed him."

"Why?" My voice was barely audible. Dimitris eyes held mine, holding me in place. I'd never seen to much hatred in them before.

"Because he killed grandma."

My eyes widened, the exclamation stuck in my throat.

"I was walking around in the woods when I stumbled on them. He was beating her mercilessly. After so long, so many years, she finally tried to reject him. And he killed her for it. I'm not sure why she did it then, instead of before. Maybe it was because of her kids, maybe it was because her grandkids. I never got the answer before she was murdered. He made she to accept the rejection before he did it too, so her death wouldn't affect him. He looked me in the eye standing over her corpse and said 'A mate is only good for one thing, to make you stronger. Your father is a fool; Sooner or later, that bitch will be the cause of his downfall.'" Dimitris eyes closed with the memory. His hands shook, balling into fists. "I didn't care if he was right or wrong, all I knew was he took the life of his mate. The one he'd abused for years. In a way, I think she might have been happy it was finally over. I remember warriors and my Dad bursting in on the scene. I'll never forget the look on his face as he looked at his mothers dead body lying on the ground. I'll never forget his screams either. He loved her, unlike her mate. He ordered his owns fathers execution right there. But he was so shaken with grief, he couldn't do it. So I did. I slit his throat and watched him die."

Tears welled in my eyes throughout his story. It was no wonder Thara and him were always so private about their family life. After learning their parents were dead, I simply assumed it was too painful to talk about, so I never pushed the subject.

"What about Thara?" I asked.

"She was far more protected than I was. Mom kept her around almost twenty-four seven, except for school. She didn't see or hear as much as I did growing up, thank the Goddess. She still knows everything, but I guess it affected her less than it did me."

I nodded, not sure what to say. But Dimitri wasn't done with his story.

"When my parents died, I spent a lot of time blaming myself. If I had been with them, maybe I could have stopped them from being killed. Or at least one of them. I don't know. As the future Alpha, it was my job to protect members of the pack. And I failed. The two most important people in my life, aside from my sister, were ripped away from me, and... I got mad. At them, for leaving. At the Goddess for taking them. The rogues who killed them. Myself for not preventing it. I was just mad at everything, the world. I had to take on a huge pack way before I was ready, all by myself. So then I got angry at you, my would-be mate, for not being there to help me when I needed it. I searched for a long time to find you, until I figured out the Goddess was punishing me for my parents deaths. She didn't intend to give me a mate. So I stopped looking.

My grandfathers twisted beliefs started to make sense to me. The world was cruel, heartless. It didn't care about my happiness. I strived to be the best damn Alpha for Blood Moon. I was merciless with our warriors, I whipped them into the best fucking army this side of the world. I took this pack to a whole other level, by myself. The only thing that would make us stronger was having a Luna. And when you finally came into my life, I was still so fucking angry at you for not being there before. And then I was angry that you were so weak, so fragile. Angry that I needed a strong Luna, and you were anything but. I didn't even want you anymore, you hadn't helped me achieve anything. I'd done it myself. You were here to serve one purpose."

"To make you stronger." I said. My voice was weak, his words were breaking my heart. I knew he loved me, but hearing how much he loathed me at first was hard.

"Yes." Dimitri paused. "But you weren't what I expected. I told you that Ajax says you remind him of my mother. But honestly, you remind me more of my grandmother. She was never overly strong, physically. But she was fiery, she had a fierce attitude. Throughout all her abuse, she never lost her spark, her spirit. She had no problem calling us out on our bullshit, and at the same time, she would tend to us if we were hurt or scared. She loved my mother like the daughter she never had, while grandpa brushed my mother off. The little time I spent with her, I grew to love her a lot. You have the same spirit, the same spark. But just like her, you hide your trauma and focus on everyone else."

# CHAPTER 63

## DIMITRIS POV

It was so fucking hard talking about all this. Even with Lily. I hated the pity in her eyes, but she had a point; I couldn't ask for something I wouldn't give her. So I laid it all out in the open, hoping it was a stepping stone for her.

"I don't know what you want me to do." Lily choked out.

I let my face soften. "I want you to open up Lily. I want you to talk to me, to trust me. Just like I did with you, just now. If not to me, then to my sister. Or take her offer, and see a therapist. I know you hate the idea, but if you keep everything inside forever, it will eat at you forever. I love you; I don't want you to be held back because of your past."

Her hands knotted the blanket, her teeth rolling over her bottom lip.

"Did it help you?" She mumbled finally.

"Talking to you?"

She nodded.

I thought about it for a minute. "It did. I'll be honest, I could do without the pity I'm getting from you. But I guess that means you care. But I feel...lighter." I admitted. In all truth, it felt like a huge weight was lifted from shoulders. She was the only person I'd confided all that to. The way I felt, my inner thoughts and demons. And it felt good. I only wanted the same for her.

"I don't know how." She finally said. "I don't...I don't want you to look at me different. I don't want you to see me... the same way as before."

I shook my head. "I won't. I'm sorry I hurt you. I'm sorry my past affected our relationship. And I'm sorry I couldn't get past it until now." I took her hand and pulled her over to me, wrapping my arms around her waist. "I guess I lied, kind of. It's not that I didn't want you, I always wanted you. I was just too much of an idiot to admit it, to want to admit it. Even to myself. But I always knew how strong you really were, deep inside. Ajax definitely knew. I promise I won't judge you, or look at you differently

315

than I do now. I just want you to be safe, happy. And healthy, and keeping everything inside isn't safe, happy, or healthy."

She stared at me with wide, glassy eyes. Her bottom lip quivered slightly. Lying her head against my chest, she started to talk. A little at first, and then waves of tears streamed down her cheeks and onto my skin, mixing with her words as her story poured out of her.

"On my ninth birthday, I got a piece of moldy bread and sour milk. Theo ordered a big cake to be made, enough to feed the whole packhouse. I was ordered to serve it, and then sit in the corner and watch as they celebrated my birthday without me. I got sick from the bread and milk, and they just dumped me in the basement. I was forced to work the next day even though I was sick... I threw up all day. I threw up in the kitchen when I was making lunch and Esther... she... she.. I got twenty lashes for it."

I held her tightly, not once interrupting and trying so fucking hard to keep my emotions at bay. She could feel them through our bond, and I didn't want her to know just how angry I was. I should have killed those two when I had the chance.

"Theo used a silver knife on me for the first time when I was twelve." She stopped and I waited. The tears never stopped, and I tensed.

"Why?" I asked as calmly as I could, but she shook her head. I didn't want to push her, but she was finally talking, finally letting it out. "Why?" I asked again.

Lily choked on her breath, burying her face so hard into the crook of my shoulder that it hurt.

"I-I asked him if... if I could have one o-of Evelyn's old b-bras. I was starting to.... develop. H-he... He... told me to.. prove it."

My hands fisted behind her back, Ajax jumping to the surface. I held him back by inches.

"I d-didn't want to. I refused. H-he said I-I was lying a-and he... he r-ripped my shirt off. I covered m-myself." Her voice lowered against my skin. "Because I wouldn't... he cut me." Her tiny voice cut on a sob.

I was fuming, not even able to keep it from her. The anger was so fierce, it travelled through the bond like fire. But I had to know.

"Did he ever... did *anyone* ever.. touch you?" I ground the words out. I knew she was a virgin, or had been, but if they forced her to other things... I swear, I would run to that pack tonight with my warriors...

"No." Lily hiccupped against me. "I never let it happen."

Thank the Goddess for that small mercy. However, Theos fate was now sealed. I wouldn't hunt him down, I didn't have to, but he was a dead man walking. His days of breathing and tainting perfectly good air were officially numbered.

After a couple minutes, Lily continued. I listened intently, stroking her back, her hair, her arms. By the time she finished, her cheeks were raw and her voice was hoarse. The things I'd heard tonight would haunt me forever. My mate cried for another hour and a half, screaming through her tears and I let her. She was a tornado of emotions that she deserved to be allowed to finally release. Throughout the storm, I offered her unlimited support anyway she wanted it. And when she finally fell into an exhausted sleep, I simply covered her with the blanket and kissed her forehead before lying beside her.

I'd been wrong before; She was stronger than grandma. I doubt even she could have survived what Lily had. Hell, *I* would given up long before this. It was a miracle she was here, in my bed alive and breathing. The thought made me pull her closer, wanting to protect her from everything. I felt guilty pushing her to do this; it might have been unfair. But she'd held it all in for so, so long. I could only hope she felt better in the morning.

For me though, sleep was impossible. I spent the night staring at my mate. While I did that, I planned different ways I was going to kill Theo and his mate. Perhaps not their daughter though, if she truly showed she regretted everything she did. And honestly, she didn't do half of what her parents did. A misled child, forced to act in ways she didn't understand because that's what she'd been taught. Still, she had a lot to make up for.

It was around four in the morning when Lily suddenly shot straight up. Immediately, I looked around the room, searching for any signs of danger.

"What? What's wrong?" I asked panicked.

Lily didn't answer me. Instead, she jumped off the bed and ran to the bathroom. A second later, I heard the sound of her vomiting. I was right behind her in a matter of seconds, holding her hair.

"Are you okay?" I asked anxiously. Fuck, had I stressed her that much? Was this my fault?

"Water. Please." She panted.

"Hang on."

I ran to the kitchen, getting her an unopened water bottle. She took a couple small sips when I brought it to her.

"It's so fucking cold in here." She muttered.

"Do you want me to run you a bath? Or a shower?"

"Hmm...maybe. I don't know." She sighed, leaning her head against the toilet seat. "I'm so tired now. Fuck."

"Come on." I capped the water and scooped her up, waiting to see if she felt sick again. When she nodded the okay, I walked her back to bed and covered her back up. She was out in seconds, the water bottle resting against her cheek.

She'd been getting sick a lot lately. Was she this stressed out? My stomach knotted all over again with the fact that I'd forced her to relive her worst memories hours after she got the shock of meeting her Father. Goddess, was I the stupidest mate ever? It could have fucking waited. Feeling like shit, I crawled in beside her, wrapping my arms around her and giving her my warmth.

At some point, shadows from the rising sun streaked across the room; I hadn't slept a wink. Lily stirred in my arms, her arms stretching out.

"Mmgry." She mumbled sleepily.

"What?" I chuckled.

"I'm hungry." She announced clearly this time.

"You feel okay to eat?"

"Mhmm." She rolled over, kissing me heartily. "How about we start with a snack before breakfast?"

I raised my eyebrows. "Seriously? You were puking not five hours ago."

"I'm not puking now." Her lips moved to the mark on my neck, biting gently. My dick instantly stood at attention.

"Maybe you should eat first." I gulped.

"Okay."

With a cheeky smirk, my mate lowered herself slowly until she had me in her mouth. Not what I meant, but I'd take it happily.

# CHAPTER 64

It had been one week since Gideon had shown up. I still hadn't talked to him, still hadn't seen him. After pouring my soul out to Dimitri, I felt even more anger towards him. I'll be honest here, I felt better, so much better, having Dimitri know everything. More so, finally letting everything out. I guess he'd been right about that part; my past had been destroying me from the inside, like a disease. But now I didn't have to carry the burden by myself. And that was something nobody could put a price on. I was extremely lucky to have Dimitri.

We'd discussed it the morning after, after I'd had my 'snack'. That had lasted a whole hour before Dimitri finally convinced me to eat breakfast. I'd finally agreed to talk to someone, other than him. But he assured me he'd always be there to talk to anyways. I still wasn't sure about meeting with a therapist, but I was willing to give it a try. Anything to make our relationship better, to make it work. I loved him enough to do this for us. So he was reaching out to the very best people, and it would be my decision who I saw in the end.

Which brought my thoughts back to Gideon. I hadn't even started trying to sort out my feelings about him. I guess that was something I could try in therapy? I snickered to myself; the Luna who needed therapy. Goddess, help me. I was playing a game on my phone, thinking all this through when I knock sounded on the door.

"Come in."

To my surprise, Hazel opened the door. I sat up, chucking my phone to the side. She was wearing a yellow sundress that brought out her eyes and her hair was in a messy bun. She looked cute.

"Hey." I said.

"Hey."

She stood by the door, a white shopping bag in hand. I bit my lip, feeling a bit awkward. We hadn't spoken since my outburst, which I still felt like shit for.

"Are you busy?" She asked.

"Not at all. Come on in."

"Thanks." She shut the door made her way to the bed. Sitting on the edge, she looked around the room.

"How have you been?" I asked timidly.

"Good. You?"

"Fine."

Hazel glanced at me sideways. "Just fine?"

I shrugged. Silence fell. Awkward, again. I took a breath.

"Hazel, I'm sorry. So sorry. I didn't mean what I said. I just... No, nothing can justify that. You're going to be a great mother, you already are! I am sorry, please forgive me!" I begged.

A small smile spread on her lips. "I already forgave you Lily. I know you didn't mean it."

"Still. If I'm ever that way again, I give you full permission to slap some sense into me!"

She laughed. "I'll remember that."

"What's that?" I pointed to the shopping bag.

"Some anti-nausea medication. I've been having some morning sickness."

"Got extras? I'm tired of puking too."

Her eyes widened. "You're...?!"

"Oh, no! I've just been really stressed lately, it's taking a toll on me."

Her head cocked to the side. "You sure? I haven't seen you train in a while."

"I've been sleeping in a lot. Like I said, stress."

Her eyes landed on the plate of bacon on the table.

"Stress eating?"

"I guess. I like bacon." I was starting to get irritated. Why? I had no idea.

"Whatever you say." Hazels tone held sarcasm, and I snapped.

"Look, I'd know if I was fucking pregnant okay?"

Hey eyebrow raised, and I covered my mouth. Good Goddess, what was wrong with me?! I'd just apologized to the girl, and here I was biting her head off again! Over nothing!

"Hazel, I'm so sorry!" I blurted.

To my surprise, she burst out laughing. She laughed for a full minute, wiping tears before she stood up.

"Here." She reached into her bag, holding out a small pink bottle. "Come with me."

I followed her into the bathroom. She dug into the bag again, placing a rectangular box on the sink.

"Why do you have a pregnancy test? You already know you're pregnant?"

"I picked it up for one of Clints friends. They're trying for a pup, but I'll get another one later. You are taking this one." She pointed to the box and I swallowed.

"But I don't have to pee." I blurted out stupidly.

"That's fine. We can wait."

"Hazel-"

"Look, no offense Lily, but you're moody and sleeping and puking. And I'm guessing that isn't your first plate of bacon. If I'm right, I want bragging rights that I was the first to know." She smirked.

I rolled my eyes. "Fine. But don't get your hopes up!"

We chatted for a while, catching up. It was a little odd doing it in my bathroom, but whatever. Finally, I had the urge to pee. Hazel turned around while I tried to get the test out of the stupid packaging. Eventually, I just used my teeth to rip it open before I squatted over the toilet and tried my best to aim for the end of the stick. Putting the cap back on, I laid it on the sink while I cleaned up and flushed. Hazel rushed to my side, practically vibrating.

"Dude, would you calm down?"

"Nope. I have a feeling." She gushed. "Will you be excited if you are?"

"You have no idea."

My whole life I dreamed about having a baby. I promised myself I would shower them with love and attention, everything I'd never had. Or I hadn't remembered I'd had, anyways. The time I didn't believe I had a wolf,

I still dreamt of running away, meeting a human and falling in love. Starting a family. It was the only thing I really wanted, to have the chance to give someone what I didn't. If I was ever lucky enough for that dream to become reality, I would give it my all and nothing less.

I waited anxiously, chewing on my thumbnail while I watched the test work. It was one of those digital ones, the ones that are suppose to say 'Pregnant' or 'Not-Pregnant'. The instructions said it would take around three minutes for the results to appear, but it felt like three hours. I couldn't take my eyes away from the small test laying on the huge sink. Finally, bold letters appeared on the screen and I felt like my world tilted on its axis.

**Pregnant**

Hazel shrieked in my ear. "Stress my ass! Congratulations!" She threw her arms around me as tears welled in my eyes.

I was pregnant. We were going to have a baby. Oh my Goddess.

"Holy shit." I breathed. I picked up the test, analyzing it from every angle. But the result didn't change. I was pregnant!

"How are you going to do this?!"

"Huh?" I was caught up in my shock.

"How are you going to tell Dimitri?!"

Oh. "Uh... I don't know."

Hazel bounced around me, her grin wider than I'd ever seen it. The shock wore off, and I joined her, both of us bouncing around the bathroom like idiots.

"I can't believe it!" I squealed, hugging her tightly. "Okay, you're right, I need to plan. I want him to be surprised."

"Oh girl, trust me, he's going to be." Hazel chuckled.

I walked out of the bathroom, the test in my hand. Turning abruptly, Hazel almost ran into me. I thrust the test into her hand.

"Take this. I don't want him to see it. Just, I don't know, bury it in the woods or something."

"Seriously?"

"Just get rid of it so he doesn't find it!" I laughed. I sat on the bed, my hand going to my tummy. "Okay so, what about giving Dimitri a onesie?"

Hazel shook her head. "Too common. What about a basket of baby stuff?"

Now I shook my head. "Nah. How about...?"

We bounced ideas off each other for a while, neither of us coming up with anything good. I was starting to get frustrated when a knock sounded.

"What?" I yelled.

Ben poked his head in. "Hey. It's lunchtime, you hungry?"

I stared at him, an idea popping into my head. I mind-linked Hazel, and she grinned. Ben looked between us.

"Why are you staring at me like that? What's up with you two?"

"Ben, come in and close the door." I said.

He did as I said, looking at me suspiciously while Hazel snickered. Oh, he was going to hate me. I told him I was pregnant, and at first he was super happy. Like, completely thrilled. Of course, that didn't last long when I told him what I had in mind. He gaped at me, mouth flapping.

"No! No way!"

"Come on Ben! Please?" I begged.

"Look, I love you like a sister Lily, but there is no fucking way I am doing that!" He crossed his arms.

"What if I gave you incentive to do it?"

"There is nothing you could possibly offer." He scoffed.

"How about a raise?"

"Nope."

"A new car?"

"Nope."

"There must be something you want!" I groaned.

"What if we talked to Clara?" Hazel suggested.

"Yes!" I nodded eagerly.

Ben simply stared at us, his eyes narrowing.

"We could butter you up. Take Isabelle more often so you guys can have alone time. Take her out on dates."

"I could take Isabelle every weekend!" I offered.

Ben groaned, even louder than me.

"I hate you." He sighed.

"Is that a yes?" I exclaimed hopefully.

"Yes! But you owe me! *Big time!* And you better hold up your end of the deal because you know I'll never live this down."

I squealed, rushing to envelope him in a huge hug. "Thank you Ben!"
"I'm regretting this already." But he hugged me back.

# CHAPTER 65

**DIMITRIS POV**

It was one of those rare weekends where I'd opted to be in charge of group training. Luke kept ditching to be with Miguel, and honestly, I found myself wishing the honeymoon phase was over with already. I got it; It was hard to be away from your mate. But he had responsibilities in this pack, he wasn't my Gamma for nothing. So this morning I was heading to his room to pull him out of bed and get his ass to the training yard. He couldn't skip out with me there. Standing in front of his door, I knocked three times loudly. No response.

"Luke! Get up and let's go!" I yelled.

Sounds of rustling and groaning drifted to me through the door. A second later, Miguel opened the door dressed in sweatpants and a backwards t-shirt. It was obvious I'd woken him up.

"Good morning Alpha." He yawned.

"Morning. Can you fetch your mate for me? It's time for training."

"Sorry Alpha but Luke is not here. I believe he already went down to the yard."

My eyebrows scrunched together. Luke got up before me? Did Hell freeze over?

"Uhm, okay. Thanks. Sorry I woke you."

"Do not worry about it." He smiled and waved before closing the door.

Still extremely confused, I made my way through the house, stopping by the kitchen to grab a banana and water. I'd been up thirty minutes and already it was a weird morning.

*"I love you."* A mind-link came from Lily, catching me by surprise.

*"I love you too. Why are you up so early?"*

*"I woke up when you were in the shower."*

*"Oh. I didn't mean to wake you."*

*"It's fine. I'm going back to sleep for a while. Just wanted to tell you that I love you."*

I could feel the smile in her voice, one of my own appearing on my face. She cut off the link and I waltzed through the front door, munching on my breakfast. The closer I got to the yard, the more the air smelled of sweat. Spotting Luke, I joined him looking over the groups of maybe warriors. They were in rows of five, everyone down doing sets of push-ups. I noticed some were having more difficulty than others. One kid looked like he was ready to pass out already.

"Who is that?" I pointed.

"Greg Bannerman. The group puker."

I made a face. "Why haven't you cut him yet?"

"You'll see why when they spar."

I shrugged. The guy had good muscle tone, even if he was on the heavier side. He'd be a big dude after he shifted.

"Can't believe you got here before me." I said to my Gamma.

"I have a feeling it's going to be an eventful day." He replied.

"What does that even mean?"

"Well, eventful is an adjective, commonly known as events or incidents, especially of a striking character. For example-"

"Alright smartass. Just focus on the exercises." I rolled my eyes and he chuckled.

I'd given Ned the day off as I was going to be here. Together, Luke and I ran the kids through the regular exercises and then laps. As promised, Greg vomited thirty four laps in. Apparently, it was a new record for him; Most days he didn't last past twenty five. Stopping beside him, I handed him my water, telling him to keep it. Greg was tall, taller than most here. His face still held some of his youth, sweat pouring down his face and from his pits. He was breathing like he'd run a thousand laps instead of just over thirty.

"Thank you...Alpha." He huffed as he chugged the water.

"How old are you?" I asked.

"Seventeen sir."

"Can I ask you something Greg?"

"Sure Alpha."

I moved him off to the side of the track, away from the others running. I studied him quizzically. "Why are you here?"

"Uhm? I train every morning, like everyone else?" He was confused.

"No, I mean why are you still training? No offense kid, but you don't seem cut out to be a warrior. Why do you come back everyday?"

He straightened at my question, his brown eyes growing lighter in the sun.

"I come back everyday because I'm not a quitter. Blood Moon needs the best to protect us, and I intend to be the best. I know I don't look like much, now, but I've been training for years before this with my Dad. I have what he calls the 'fat gene.'" He laughed once. "I've always been a bigger guy. So was Dad, before he shifted."

I rubbed my chin thoughtfully. "Who's your Dad?"

"Jake Bannerman Alpha."

My eyebrows raised. I knew his last name was familiar. Jake was indeed one of my best. If not Ned, I would have put him as head of the warriors. Ned just happened to be a little better, but I knew they trained together themselves. I was surprised when Ned had beat him all those years ago. Looking at his son now, I could see the resemblance.

"My Gamma says your a fair fighter."

Greg shrugged. "My size helps a lot."

"Your Dad is right, this-" I waved my hand around us, "- Becomes easier after we shift. Our stamina goes up, and our endurance. Can I give you a little advice though?"

"O-of course Alpha. I'd really appreciate that." He seemed stunned that I, of all people would give him advice. Was I that out of touch with my own pack?

"Judging by the er, pile there." I gestured to his vomit. "I'd say your eating a hearty breakfast."

"Always Alpha."

I shook my head. "Not a good idea. Before I train, I have one bottle of water and one piece of fruit. You shouldn't eat a full meal before training, especially the way Blood Moon does it."

He nodded softly. "I'll remember that. Thank you Alpha."

I gave him a small smile. "I look forward to seeing you spar. Now come on, only sixteen more laps to go."

I kept pace with him while we ran, encouraging him. Luke watched me with raised brows, as did many of the others, but I didn't care. This was the type of Alpha I strived to be; I just lost my way somewhere. When we finished, I handed Greg another water and patted him on the back.

"You've got heart kid." He gave me a grin and Luke announced the next set of drills. The scent of wildflowers invaded my nose and I turned to see my mate. She smiled brightly at me, looking all sorts of adorable in red sundress and black flats.

"What are you doing out here?" I asked her.

"I needed some fresh air. And I couldn't resist coming to see you." She walked in front of me, wrapping her arms around my neck and bringing me down for a lingering kiss.

"If you keep doing that, I'm going to have to take you upstairs. And that would be counterproductive, since I'm here to make sure Luke doesn't skip training. Again."

She sucked my bottom lip between her teeth, biting gently. I growled lowly, gripping her waist.

"Sorry, I can't it." She giggled. Pulling out of my arms, she looked to where Luke was setting up teams to start sparring. "Can I watch too?"

"Sure. Come on." I took her hand and pulled her over. "Everyone, say hello to our Luna. She'll be observing as well today."

"Hello Luna." They chorused. A few offered her smiles and Lily waved to them.

"Alright. Everyone in position? Good. The aim is to take down your opponent quickly and effectively. The longer you draw it out, the more chance there is for someone to sneak up behind you, or from the side. Try to never give an enemy that advantage."

The kids nodded at me, facing their partners. I signaled for them start, keeping an eye on mistakes and openings they left. I was impressed by how well some did, and disappointed by others. One particular girl caught my eye, she looked a lot like Karla. This must be her younger sister, Kaitlin. She was around the same height as Karla, and moved just as quick. For sure, she'd picked up some moves from her sister. My gaze travelled to Greg, who was throwing punches and rib jabs faster than I expected. He took down his partner with ease, before helping him up.

"Greg!" I called. He halted mid kick, looking over to me. I motioned for him to join me.

"Yes Alpha? Hello Luna." He nodded respectfully to Lily.

"Hello."

"Greg, I want you to partner with Kaitlin." I said.

"W-what?! Kaitlin? But she's... and I'm..." He gestured down his body.

"I know. That's why I want you two to spar. You won't always fight someone your size you know."

He gulped loudly. "But what if I hurt her? She's so tiny."

"Occupational hazard Greg. Now go." I shooed him away. He looked terrified. I watched as he tapped Kaitlin on the shoulder; She had to crane her neck to look him in the eye. He gestured to me and she shrugged. Her partner walked off to join Greg's former opponent and the two took fighting stances. Lily squeezed my hand.

"I hope you're sure about this." She said.

# CHAPTER 66

**DIMITRIS POV**

Luke, Lily and I watched intently as Kaitlin and Greg eyed each other. Greg looked horrified he had to fight such a tiny woman, while Kaitlin looked focused and serious. Suddenly, she struck, catching him off guard with a quick punch to the gut. Greg grunted, throwing a punch to her face, missing completely. A dazed look came over him; He'd aimed too high. Taking advantage his confusion, Kaitlin landed a kick to his knee, dropping him on one leg. Two punches to the face came next and a swift drop kick on his back. She stood over him, smug. Greg rolled over, getting to his feet. Re-taking their positions, this time he didn't hesitate. He rushed her, attempting to get his arms around her. Kaitlin dodged and slid under his legs, bringing her foot up to kick him from behind. I laughed loudly; *That* she definitely learned from her sister!

"I think Greg has hearts in his eyes." Lily commented.

"He always does when it comes to Kaitlin." Luke chuckled.

"She's pretty cute!"

I jerked my eyes to where Hazel and Clint now stood beside us.

"When did you get here?"

"Just now Alpha." Hazel replied.

"Okay, *why* are you here?"

She simply smiled at me. Clint chuckled and Lily giggled. I looked to Luke who had a huge grin on his face. What the hell was happening?

"Someone want to clue me in?" I asked.

"Patience dear. Goods things come to those who wait."

I looked over my shoulder to see Greta, Miguel, and Clara and Isabelle, and Thara.

"What... Shouldn't she be in daycare?" I pointed at Isabelle who pouted at me.

"I would never let her miss this." Clara smirked.

"Miss what?"

"Uhm, Alpha?" Greg called to me. Turning back to him, I saw all the kids had stopped. Some were pointing, others were whispering and they were all laughing. Greg pointed, and I followed his direction until my eyes landed on the single weirdest thing I'd ever seen in my whole life.

Ben was walking from the direction of the packhouse. He wearing a very tight fitting green onesie, the kind babies wore. It molded to his skin, showing off his muscles in a very odd way. His hairy legs were on full display, and a soother hung from his neck. The outfit was completed by a matching green bonnet that tied under his chin. He looked utterly miserable as the fits of laughter grew louder around us.

"What the fuck?!"

Luke was losing his mind beside me, holding his phone to video my Beta. Lily and Hazel snickered uncontrollably, Thara was crying she was laughing so hard, and even Greta was holding her belly, doubled over in laughter. Ben stopped in front of me, looking down at a paper I hadn't noticed before. What the actual shit was happening right now? This was not normal.

Ben took a breath and began to read;
*"I'm so happy that you're my dad;*
*You're one in a million Pop!*
*When it comes to first-class fathers,*
*You're the absolute cream of the crop!*
*You love me no matter what,*
*Whether I'm a goodie or a baddie;*
*I really love you, Pa;*
*You're a fine and fantabulous daddy!"*

My jaw was hanging open, my eyes practically falling out of their sockets. Ben was red as a tomato, shifting awkwardly on his feet. I had no idea what the hell was going on. I looked around for answers, only to find everyone smiling at me. Lily tugged on my hand, a bright happy grin on her face. One by one, Bens words sank into my brain. Daddy. He'd said daddy. But I wasn't...

"No." I breathed. Pulling Lily to my chest, I cupped her face in my hands.

"Congratulations." She whispered.

"Really?!" I exclaimed.

"Really." She laughed.

"Yes!" I yelled. I picked Lily up, swinging her around. "I'm going to be a Dad!"

The kids cheered and clapped, calling out their congratulations. Our friends gathered around us when I set my mate back on her feet and kissed her lovingly. The happiness surrounding us right now was nearly tangible; I felt as if I could reach out and grasp it, lock it away. Ajax was howling in my head, sharing in the joy and reaching out to Aya. Their happiness flexed through the bond, adding to the moment.

"I love you so much." I told Lily.

"I love you too." She brought me in for another kiss.

"Can I *please* go change now?" Ben muttered behind me.

"Awwe, I think you look cute." Clara giggled.

"You look silly!" Isabelle snickered.

"I think this should be your new everyday attire." Thara said and Luke busted up again.

I hugged Lily close to me, a movement catching my eye over her shoulder. Gideon stood some distance away, a small happy smile on his face. He nodded to me, mouthing 'Congrats'. I nodded back, wondering why he was here. Not that I disagreed; He was Lilys Dad. I just didn't think she would invite him. She glanced over her shoulder, tensing when she caught sight of him and feeling my confusion through the bond. She sighed.

"Aya wouldn't let me not tell him. He agreed to give us space though." She said.

"So, I am the last one to know?" I tilted her chin so she was looking at me again.

"Well, out of those close to us, yes. The rest of the pack doesn't know."

"I don't care. This is the best day of my life. Even better because you somehow got Ben to agree to something so fucking outrageous!"

"You're really happy?" She asked.

"I am truly, really, over the moon. You're going to be a kick-ass mother." I told her and she blushed. I turned us so we faced everyone. "You know what, you can all go home. Take today off, and tomorrow!"

The kids cheered and together they ran off. I had no doubt each and every one of them would spread the news. The pack would probably know by dinner time. Thara jumped on my back, wrapping her arms around my neck.

"I'm so happy for you bro! I can't believe I'm going to be an Aunt!" She squealed.

"The best Aunt of all time." I grinned.

"Do you two want to know how far along you are?"

"Can we?" Lily asked excitedly.

"Of course! I took the morning off for this. We can do it right now." She let me go, sliding down my back. Lily turned to Ben.

"Thank you. You made this memorable for us."

"That's for sure!" Luke said.

"Please don't ask me to do anything like this again. My ego is wounded, badly." Ben sniffed dramatically.

"Man, go change. I can see the outline of your-"

"Language!" Clara snapped.

"His what?" Isabelle looked around at the adults.

"Never mind. Let's go Lily." I interlocked our fingers, swinging our hands between us. Our friends chattered amongst themselves behind us. I couldn't keep the smile off my face, not even when we passed Gideon.

"Congratulations Lily." He offered her his hand. She looked at it, then him. Hesitantly, she placed her hand in his, shaking once.

"Thanks." She mumbled. "We have to go." And she yanked my arm, walking us away from him. I gave him a look over my shoulder, which he understood. 'Give her time', it said.

Thara and Lily chatted as we walked, making plans to go shopping for baby stuff. Lily included me in the plans, giving my heart a tug. I couldn't wait to do the things she was planning; I wanted to be involved in everything. I wondered what we would have; I was good with either gender. As long as they were healthy, I didn't care. I also wondered if they would be a Mother Wolf, like Lily. Was that genetic? If so, would she be able to carry the pup to term? It was hard enough carrying an Alpha pup; they tended to be bigger than others. This baby was an Alpha *and* had Lilys Mother Wolf genes. I started to get nervous thinking about it.

"Will I be able to carry the baby? Because... you know." Lily asked my sister. Our line of thinking was once again the same.

"I think so. We'll keep a close eye on it; You'll need more ultrasounds than a regular pregnancy. If he or she becomes too big, you might have to ride out the rest of the pregnancy in wolf form and give birth that way."

"Well that sucks! I'll have to live outside, Aya is too big to fit in the packhouse." Lily frowned.

"We'll make it work. You're not going to live outside." I assured her.

"We could make you a really big doghouse." Thara giggled. "Like Clifford the Big Red Dog!"

"Who?"

"I'll show you later." Thara led us into the hospital. A couple nurses smiled at me, earning low growls from my mate. I tucked her under my arm, rubbing her shoulder. I'd heard she-wolves got more possessive when they were pregnant. Admittedly, it was rather fun seeing this side of her. We entered a vacant room, with one bed and a whole lot of machines.

"I'll go get the ultrasound machine. Be right back." My sister zipped out of the room.

"Are you excited?" Lily asked me as she climbed on the bed and laid down.

"Very." I stood next to her, taking her hand. We waited exactly three minutes before Thara returned, pushing the machine ahead of her. It looked like a computer on wheels, with lots of cords and wires and a keyboard. She flicked the lights off after closing the door.

"Okay, I'm going to do an internal ultrasound. I don't think you're very far along yet, so that's the best way to get a clear picture."

"Sounds good." Lily started pushing her underwear down.

"Whoa! What is going on?" I grabbed her hand.

"An internal ultrasound means she has to put the wand in me Dimitri." Lily explained. Thara held up the 'wand', a long white thing that looked like a sex toy. I shuddered a bit, making both girls roll their eyes.

"Better get over your aversion to stuff like this bro. The birth isn't going to a picnic you know."

I scowled at her while Lily finished removing her underwear. Thara helped her place her feet and asked her to spread her legs, ankles together. I was thankful it was my sister doing this, but at the same time, it was weird that my sister was doing this.

"Would you relax?! Goddess, Dimitri. Okay Lily, this is going to be a little cold." She clicked the keyboard, the screen turning to a blank grey colour. Lily let out a small gasp as Thara inserted the wand, her legs automatically twitching to close. Thara placed a hand on one of her knees, urging her to relax. Clicking another key, the screen changed. It was fuzzy looking, with a black circle in the middle. Everything kept moving, shifting around.

"Okay. There's your uterus." She angled the device slightly to the right. "Hmm. Now where are you... Ah ha! Found you." Thara smiled at the screen. She clicked around on the keyboard for a minute before angling the position again. Her forehead creased and her lips pursed.

"Is something wrong?" Lily asked.

"Uhm....."

# CHAPTER 67

**BASTIANS POV**

My hands came slamming down on the table, knocking the Orb off its holder. It rolled off the table and crashed to the floor, glass shattering everywhere. A piece stuck in my foot; I barely felt the pain. Anger burned through my veins, making my vision turn red. She was pregnant. Fucking pregnant! This is not the way I had planned things! I couldn't use her now, her blood was tainted, mixed with the babies. *Fuck!*

"What's wrong love?"

I barely suppressed the shudder at Jennine's voice behind me. I hated her. She was annoying, stupid, immature; She never thought of the bigger picture. Her main goal was to kill Lily, take her revenge. She didn't realize I needed her alive, I needed her blood. She was useless if she was dead. Of course, I didn't tell Jennine that. It was safer to let her believe I wanted the same thing. Jennine was a means to an end, and when she had fulfilled her purpose, *she* would end. I could barely tolerate her now.

"Nothing." I snapped.

"You're bleeding."

"I'm fine."

"But-"

"I said I'm *fine*!"

"Don't talk to me like that." She replied coldly.

Running my hand down my face, I let out an exasperated groan.

"What do you want Jennine?"

She didn't answer, and I felt her irritation in the air. Like I cared. I thought she was a bitch before? Ever since I took her wolf and made her into a witch, she was worse. She acted as though *I* should be the one bowing down to *her*. As if she were the Goddess herself. If only she knew she wasn't as powerful as I told her she was. I'd given her a fraction of my magic, enough for the simplest and most basic of spells. I suppose to her, that was enough to feel invincible. If she were a true witch, a born witch, she would know I could crush her with a snap of my fingers. The thought was tempting too.

"Well?" I turned to face her. Her hair was cascaded down her back, her face plastered in cheap make-up. She wore a long black dress that was see-through, leaving absolutely nothing to the imagination. She crossed the room to the bed, settling herself on its dark red comforter. I knew where this was going.

"Why don't you come join me? You seem tense." She purred.

"I'm not in the mood." I turned away from her.

"You never are anymore." She huffed. I rolled my eyes.

"Jennine, I'm busy. Why don't you go down to the kitchens and-"

"Talk to your whore?" She interrupted me. I slowly turned back to face her.

"Excuse me?"

She studied her nails, an ugly smirk on her face. "I'm not stupid Bastian. I saw Layla leaving her last night before I came to bed. In *my* underwear. Did you think you could hide it from me?"

I'd tried. Not because I didn't want to hurt her; I could give two fucks if she was hurt. I simply didn't want to deal with her attitude or a tantrum. I'd fucking told Layla to leave earlier, but she wasn't done with me. She'd left later than I'd planned, and now I was going to face the consequences. Fuck me.

"Well? Aren't you going to defend yourself?" Jennine asked.

I crossed my arms. "Why should I?"

"So you fucked her."

"Yes."

"In *our* bed." She ground out.

"Three times."

Her hands started to a glow a dull orange. Jennine had absolutely no control over her magic, and I doubt she ever would. Her emotions controlled her, making her lash out. She was as useless as a witch as she was a wolf.

"How could you!?" She screamed.

"Oh please. You think you are the only one who can satisfy me? While we're taking a ride on the truth train, I might as well tell you; I've been fucking a different girl every night since you got here."

"Son of a bitch!" A small fireball appeared in her hand. "You promised to make me your Queen! And your sticking your dick in dirty, disgusting rogues?!"

"Calm down." I hissed.

"Fuck you!" She flung her hand out, hurling her pathetic little fire at me. With a wave of my hand, I dissolved it easily. I called the shadows, directing them towards the girl on the bed. They slithered across the floor like snakes, winding around the bedposts and striking out to wrap around Jennine. She gasped and struggled against them. Fear replaced her anger when she looked at me. Taking calculated steps, I stopped in front of her, roughly grabbing her chin.

"You did not just attack me." I spat in her face. A whimper left her lips in response. "Do you not realize I could kill you? Do you not remember that if it weren't for me, you would have already been killed? I brought you into my home, gave you power. This is how you repay me?!" I shouted.

"What about me? I've been nothing but loyal to you. And you betrayed me."

"You have other things to worry about other than who I fuck." Like whether or not I could continue to be around her without killing her.

"You promised to make me your Queen." She repeated.

"And I will. But even a Queen does not question her King. You need to learn to be compliant, or I will find someone more suitable to rule at my side."

"I won't stand by while you fuck diseased she-wolves! You said you had no use for my kind!"

A cruel smile landed on my face. "They are no longer your kind. And the only use I have for them is to use them, in any way I see fit. If you can't live with it, tell me now and we can end this little arrangement."

Hate and resentment filled her eyes. Her lips pressed into a thin line, making her look like a pinched gargoyle. Truly, I hoped she would choose to end this. There were many more women among my army of rogue wolves that I could replace her with. I'd only chosen her because she'd been close to Dimitri and a member of Blood Moon. I needed her insight. But I could manage without her.

To my intense disappointment, Jennine jerked out of my grasp and said, "I am loyal to you. As long as I get my revenge."

Covering up my true feelings, I patted her cheek once. "Good." I straightened, glaring down at her. "As punishment for attacking your King, you will work in the kitchens for three days. Go."

Her jaw fell slack. "You can't be serious!"

"Did I fucking stutter? Get out of my sight!" I roared. "Perhaps this will teach you to learn your place, and not question me!"

Scrambling off the bed, she threw me a look of complete contempt before heading to the door.

"Oh and while your down there, send Layla up." I threw at her casually. She muttered something under her breath, slamming the door hard as she left. She really was a child.

Walking to my cabinet, I took a replacement Orb from the top shelf, setting it in the holder on the table. My plan was falling apart already. I'd attempted to take Lily a long time ago, when I first realized what she was. Unfortunately for me, I couldn't teleport her here. I tried many times, each time failing. Finally, I concluded it was because she was a Mother Wolf. How typical, the girl whose blood I needed to live was the one person I couldn't teleport. Now I had to resort to more complicated methods, such as finding a way into Blood Moon and taking her physically. And I'd finally come up with the perfect idea.

I faced the middle of the room, concentrating on her. With a snap of my fingers, she appeared in front of me, the tray she'd been carrying crashing to the ground. Cups and plates scattered across the floor, cracking and breaking. Rosalie turned slowly, her usual cold glare pinning me.

"*Why* do you insist on doing that?" She hissed.

"Because I can."

"What do you want now Bastian?"

"I have a surprise for you Rosie."

"*Don't call me that!*"

Her thin frame vibrated with anger. Rosalie used to be quite beautiful, before I brought her here. She still I was, I suppose; She was just severely underweight and filthy. The resemblance to Lily when she'd first arrived at Blood Moon was uncanny. However, her spirit never broke, no matter what I did. A fire lived in her eyes, undying and strong. She truly believed she would leave here someday, reunite with her family. How sad.

"I think I've denied you your family long enough." I said nonchalantly.

Rosalie's raised one brow, caution in her eyes now.

"What are you talking about?"

I gestured to the Orb. "Would you like to see your daughter?"

"What trick is this?"

"No tricks this time, I promise." I grabbed her arm, pulling her to the table. Placing both my hands on the glass, Rosalie watched as colours swirled inside, slowly taking shape in the forms of people. Lily was walking with her mate and his sister, all smiles and joy; She was glowing under the sun, her life at this moment perfect. Two spots appeared on the table and I looked up to see Rosalie crying steadily.

"She's beautiful, isn't she? A perfect picture of you." I said.

"W-why are you d-doing this?" She sobbed.

"Didn't you want to see your daughter?" I walked around her, tucking her hair behind her ear. "Haven't you said over and over that she was the highlight of your life? Aren't you happy to see her?" I drew in close, my front flushed with her back.

"This is cruel. The cruelest thing you've done to me yet." She hissed. Yet her voice wavered, it had lost some it's sharpness.

"Oh sweetheart. This isn't cruelty. Not compared to what I have in mind."

Rosalie didn't take her eyes off the Orb, captivated by the images of Lily.

"I already told you. I won't help you Bastian. You'll have to kill me."

"No, I don't think so." I leaned in, whispering in her ear. "How will you see your daughter again if I kill you?"

She sucked in a breath, turning quickly. Her hand made contact with my cheek, the resounding slap echoing around the room. I laughed loudly.

"I won't help you hurt Lily! Never!" She shouted at me. The next second, I had my hand around her throat, squeezing tightly.

"You're going to help me get your precious daughter. You're going to help me bring her back here. Because if you don't-," I tightened my hold, her face going from red to purple, "-I will kill her instead. And I will take her unborn child for myself."

Despite being strangled, her eyes widened in horror. Then they shut tightly, and she gave a soft nod. I released her, dropping her to the ground where she coughed and cried. Smirking at her, I turned and walked away. Jennine wasn't going to send Layla, obviously. I'd have to go find her myself.

# CHAPTER 68

**LILYS POV**

"Thara, you're freaking me out. Would you just tell us?!" I almost yelled.

"Calm down, there's nothing *wrong*. I'm just wondering how many kids you two planned to have?" She looked between Dimitri and I.

I looked up at my mate, confused. He seemed equally confused as he stared at his sister with irritation and anxiety.

"I hadn't really thought about. But I kind of always wanted a big family." I said.

"Me too." Dimitri agreed.

Thara sighed, smiling softly.

"Well, that's great. Because you're having twins."

Dimitris hand slipped out of mine, his body faltering a few steps before he hit the wall. Thara made to stand up, stopping when I gasped. The wand was still inside me; She's yanked it into a fairly uncomfortable position.

"Sorry Lily. You okay Dimitri? Do I need to get a nurse in here?"

"No. No. I just... twins? Are you sure?" He asked.

"See for yourself."

She turned the screen towards us. I'd seen many ultrasound images while studying to become a doctor here, so I knew what to look for. Dimitri on the other hand, was lost. Right away I spotted a white line with a little irregular ball at the end. Thara angled the wand slightly and another little ball appeared just to the left of the first one. Fraternal twins. My babies. Our babies.

"Oh my Goddess." I whispered. Tears sprung to my eyes and I didn't even bother holding them back. "Dimitri, those are our babies!" I gasped.

"Here?" He pointed to one of the pups. I nodded.

"And here." I pointed out the second.

"Whoa." He breathed and I laughed. He looked so bewildered.

"Quick training time. Lily., how far along would you say you are?" Thara questioned me.

342

I scanned the image, noting the measurements she'd taken and the date. I did some quick mental math, biting my lip.

"Nine weeks?" I said.

"Perfect! Nine weeks and three days exactly." We smiled at each other.

"When can we tell the genders?" Dimitri asked.

"Probably in two weeks." She removed the wand from me, the screen going black. Sadness surged through me; I could spend all day looking at my pups.

"I thought it was twenty?" Dimitri asked.

"That's human pregnancies bro."

"Oh"

"There's some things we need to discuss." Thara removed her gloves, leaning against the wall. "You need to start taking prenatal vitamins. I'll get you some before you leave. And you need to keep up a healthy diet. Since you're carrying twins, you're due date probably won't be exact either."

"You mean I'll deliver early?" I asked nervously.

"It happens with multiples, a lot. You're almost three months now. I'm guessing instead of the regular five months for us, you'll deliver in your fourth month."

What?! That only gave me a month and a half to prepare! That wasn't nearly enough time!

"Why aren't I showing yet?"

"Uhm... well. You kind of are. I didn't want to say anything; Nobody likes to be told they're putting on weight. But at least now we know the cause."

"And here I thought it was all that bacon you've been eating." Dimitri chuckled. I slapped his arm playfully.

"Shut up."

"I'll go get you the vitamins. Be right back." Thara left, closing the door behind her. I put my underwear back on and sat up, on edge and full of nerves.

"We need a nursery." I said.

"I know. I was thinking about your old room, but it's too far from ours."

"It's right down the hall."

"Too far." He shook his head and I laughed.

"Hmm... What if we converted your office? It's big enough. And you could move your office to my old room?"

He thought about it. "That could work actually. I'll get someone on it right away." He walked to stand between my legs, tilting my face up. "I love you."

"I love you too." He brought his lips down to mine. Immediately, my hands ran over the front of his pants. I guess I knew why I was always so horny now.

"Really? Right here? My sister will be back any second."

"Lock the door." I grinned.

"Lily." He shook his head scornfully. I pouted. "When we get back to the house. Okay?"

"Fiiiiiiine."

Dimitri laughed as Thara walked back in. She set a bag on the end of the bed and handed me an envelope.

"Ultrasound pictures." She grinned.

"Thank you Thara."

"I got you enough vitamins to last the pregnancy. Take one a day, either morning or night, though I suggest night. They make you sleepy."

"Got it." I grabbed Dimitris hand while he grabbed the bag. I practically dragged him out of the room.

"Someone's eager."

"Yes, yes I am."

We'd only made it three steps in the packhouse before we were overrun by the staff. Everyone was there to congratulate us. I was hugged by at least ten people before Dimitri pulled me back to his side.

"When is the due date dear?" Greta asked excitedly.

Dimitri beamed. "Sometime in the next month and a half. *They* will be coming soon, so we need to be prepared."

The group got intensely quiet at his words. Two heartbeats later, Greta had gathered us both in her arms.

"Oh Goddess! How many?!"

"Twins." I replied.

*"Twins!"* She gushed, and the staff took up her cheer. We were re-congratulated, hugged again. I appreciated the enthusiasm, but I really wanted some peace and quiet with my mate.

*"Dimitri..."*

*"I know darling."*

He held up his hand, silencing the house. "Thank you all very much. I'm sure we are as excited as all of you. But our Luna is tired, so we'll be retiring to our room now."

We walked off to the stairs together. Whispers and murmurs fell behind us; The ache in my nerves was growing more intense as we climbed each step. When we hit our floor, I almost ran to the bedroom, Dimitri right on my heels. As soon as the door closed, I rounded on him. His shirt tore beneath my hands, his lips finding mine in a feverish kiss. Coolness touched my back, feeling good against my overheated skin. Somehow we'd reached the bed, my fingers desperately trying to undo his belt. I succeeded and pulled it off, throwing it across the room; My bra joined it a second later. What had happened to my dress? Oh, well I didn't care.

Dimitri was muttering something about being gentle for the babies, causing me to snarl at him. I silenced his words by invading his mouth with my tongue, exploring every inch of it. He groaned loudly, only adding fuel to the fire inside me. My thighs were already coated with my wetness, my scent the strongest in the room. I needed him. Now. Grasping his shoulders, I laid back on the bed, pulling him with me. I wrapped my legs around his waist, feeling him at my entrance. Aya pushed forward, but I held her back. I wanted him to myself. Both of them, Dimitri and Ajax.

"Take me." I growled. "Now."

He entered me roughly, the feeling indescribable. I moaned into his mouth, lifting my hips to match his thrusts. When I pulled away for air, his lips immediately sought out my mark, nibbling and licking. My vision tunneled at the sensation. I was absolutely primal; I wanted more. I wanted what I'd never had before.

"Ajax." I called his wolf, feeling him tense over me. Dimitri met my eyes, but it wasn't Dimitri now. I gazed into pools of black, and when he spoke, it was an echo of my mates voice, dominated by his wolfs.

"You want me?" He asked.

"Yes." I breathed.

He growled, thrusting into me harder than ever. My eyes rolled back into my skull. The animal that he was, he pulled out momentarily to flip me over and bring me to all fours. When he slammed into me, I screamed. My head hit the blanket, my ass in the air. Ajax never let up, growling and snarling; The sounds were undeniably sexy. He reached around to find my clit, pulling and teasing until I came undone around him.

Ajax put me into all kinds of positions, and after the fourth orgasm, I stopped counting and gave myself over to him completely. At least until he finally spent himself inside me, giving Dimitri back control. We lay together, bodies entwined, breathing heavily and raggedly.

"That was new." Dimitri finally managed.

"Yeah." Was my witty response.

He kissed me softly, nuzzling my nose. "Don't tell me you like sex better with him now."

I giggled. "No. But that is definitely happening again."

"He's pretty damn proud of himself right now."

"As he should be."

We cuddled until my stomach rumbled. Dimitri pulled on a pair of sweatpants, intent on making me food. I was so worn out, I didn't even argue. I watched him buzz around the kitchen, admiring his toned body when out of nowhere, a wave of dizziness hit me. It was so fucking extreme that I swayed while I was lying down. I must have called out because the last thing I saw before everything went black was my mate dropping everything in his hands and rushing towards me.

# CHAPTER 69

It was weird. You know those nights where you close your eyes, intending to sleep, and the next thing you know, it's morning? Almost like you simply blinked? That was me. One minute, I was recovering from Ajax ravaging me, the next I was stumbling around the woods. Aya was not present; I couldn't feel her in my head at all. I looked at the dense bush around me; I wasn't in Blood Moon anymore. The trees were too green, covered in moss. Large rocks jutted up from the ground, also covered. The air smelled fresh, unpolluted, and it was a little chilly. Birds squalled above me, an owl hooted somewhere in the distance.

Had I been kidnapped? Had Bastian finally made his move?

"No child. I am very much the opposite of that man."

I spun so fast I almost tripped. Celeste stood before me, looking otherworldly amongst the trees and rocks. A soft smile played on her lips, her eyes warm and loving. Having her so near filled my with a sense of peace.

"Why are we here?" I asked.

"Because I need to talk to you."

"No, I mean *here*. Last time you brought me to a meadow."

"A change of scenery is sometimes healthy. But we can go to the meadow, if you prefer."

"Uh, that's okay." If she liked the mossy forest, who was I to complain? "So... what's up?"

"Walk with me Lily."

Without waiting for a reply, she turned and began walking away from me through the trees. She made no noise, as if she wasn't touching the Earth beneath her. Shaking my head of distracting thoughts, I made my feet move after her. We walked for a while in silence, me stealing glances at her every so often. Did the Moon Goddess call me away for a leisurely stroll through the woods? That seemed unlikely, but I guess anything was possible. Ten minutes later, I was about to ask her why I was here when she finally spoke.

"I can see you liked my gift." She eyed me.

"Your gift?" Her gaze went to my stomach. "Oh. Yes. I mean, yes, very much. I don't know how to thank you. I'm so happy." A huge grin broke out on my face.

"You're children will do great things." She replied. "I wonder though, if you would consider doing me a favour? The choice is up to you."

"Of course." How strange it was, the Moon Goddess asking *me* for a favour. Celeste looked into the woods, her eyes landing on a particular spot. I followed her gaze, squinting into the bushes. After a few moments, a beautiful wolf appeared some distance away. It was sleek, quick, and an irregular colour of black and white. Celeste held out her hand as the wolf stopped in front of us; I noticed it was a female. She sniffed the Goddess's hand before pushing against her adorably.

"Lily, I would like you to meet Nia. Jennine's former wolf."

I stopped breathing for a second. This was Jennine's wolf? How could something so beautiful live alongside someone so ugly? I felt bad for her, having to put up with a human as disturbed as Jennine.

"Did you say former? Wait, does that mean Jennine is dead?" I asked.

"No. She still lives." Celeste answered.

My forehead creased. "If she's alive, why is her wolf here?"

Tears gathered in Celeste's eyes, stunning me. Her next words, even more.

"Because Jennine killed her."

The noise I made was foreign to my ears. It was somewhere between a gasp and a scream. She killed her wolf? Her *wolf*?! How? Why? Our wolves were a part of us, a part of our very souls. I knew; I'd seen it! Aya was as much a part of me as Dimitri and Ajax now were. How could Jennine rip out a piece of her soul? Nobody was *that* cruel. Were they? Tears ran down my cheeks as I looked at the magnificent creature in front of me.

"Why?" I whispered.

"Purely selfish reasons. But it is done. Jennine made her choice, and Nia was sent back to me, long before she was meant to."

"That's...I can't believe it."

"I could not either." Nia looked between us, sitting back on her legs. "I chose Nia for Jennine in the hopes that she would take her down the right path. She is a calm wolf, a peaceful one. But smart, and strong. It seems my effort was wasted though." Celeste frowned. "But I would remedy my mistake, if you will allow it."

"Jennine does not deserve to have her wolf back." I spat.

"No, she does not. Nia deserves someone who will love her, appreciate her. That is the favour I'm asking you."

I blinked a couple times. "You... you want to replace Aya?" My heart hurt at the thought.

"Of course not dear. I would never separate you from Aya. You two were made for each other. What I am asking is if you will allow Nia to become your pups wolf."

"Which one?"

"Whichever you choose."

"What about my other pup?"

"You believe I will give the other a wolf less than this one?"

I shook my head frantically. "No, no. I know you wouldn't."

"All I seek is a good person for her." Celeste waved her hand toward Nia. "A second chance. She has been through so much, so much unnecessary pain. It is your choice, as I've said. I will not be offended if you decide not to; I would understand, given everything her former half has done to you."

I bit my nail, thinking it through. "Will Nia remember Jennine?"

"No. I will give her a fresh start. There is no need for her to have those memories, to suffer over them. But her personality will remain the same."

I looked at Nia, really looked at her. Her eyes were sad, full of pain. Clearly, she still remembered everything right now. How much pain did Jennine inflict on her in order to remove her? The thought made my stomach roll. Celeste was right; Jennine was selfish. She never should have gotten the privilege of having her wolf in the first place. She would have faired better as a human. I couldn't talk to Aya, but I knew what she would say if she were here. I knew I was making the right choice.

"I'll do it." I said firmly. Celeste beamed, pride filling her eyes. Nia jumped at me, licking my face with her huge tongue. I laughed, scratching her behind the ear. "Welcome to the family Nia."

"I cannot tell you how happy I am Lily." Celeste said.

"It was an easy choice." I replied truthfully. I looked her in the eye over the wolfs head. "Will she have the same name?"

"No. But you will find out in eighteen years."

"I can't wait."

"There are struggles ahead Lily. Remember that I am always with you. I love you, my child."

Just like our last meeting, Celeste leaned in and kissed my forehead. The next thing I was aware of was an icy cold wetness drenching my face. I scrunched my eyes, raising my hands to shield from the uncomfortable feeling.

"Lily? Lily! Darling, please open your eyes!" Dimitris voice pounded into my ears and bounced around my head. Ouch.

"Quiet." I mumbled.

"What?"

"Voice. Down. Quiet!"

"Sorry. Here." I felt his hands on my back, helping me to sit up. Opening my eyes was a *bad* idea; Covering them with my hands, I begged him to turn them off. Sparks went up my arms as he removed my hands, cupping my face. I was still in bed, but someone had thrown one of his shirts over me. Thara stood beside me, worry etched onto her face.

"Are you okay? You fainted." Dimitri said.

"I'm fine."

"I'm going to take your blood pressure." Thara went to move away, but I caught her wrist.

"I am *fine*. Honest."

"Lily, you fucking passed out. You've been out for almost ten minutes!" Dimitri's voice shook. I placed my hands over his on my face, trying to reassure him.

"Dimitri, listen to me. I didn't faint. I was... I guess you could say I was called away?"

"What are you talking about?" Thara asked.

I smiled. "Celeste."

"Celeste? You mean, the Moon Goddess?"

I nodded. I told them everything, from the first time she'd summoned me during my first shift and now. Dimitri and Thara stared at me with wide eyes, mouths dropped to the floor. I grabbed my mates hand, explaining what Jennine had done, and that I'd chosen to give her wolf to one of our pups.

"She... she killed her wolf?" Thara whispered.

"That's fucking sick!" Dimitri was horrified.

"I know. But you'll see her again. Dimitri, she's so beautiful. I couldn't ask for a better wolf for our pup. Whichever one she goes to. And Celeste promised the other baby would get a wolf just as good. I couldn't pass her up, I just couldn't."

"I'm not mad darling. If anything, I'm extremely proud that you gave her a second chance. It sounds like she deserved it."

Thara scoffed. "Anyone would, having that bitch as their other half! Goddess, I can't even process this!" She paced beside the bed. "How sick in the head do you have fucking be to do something like that?! I swear, if I ever get my hands on Jennine, I'm going to fucking wring her neck!"

"Calm down Thara." Dimitri tried to soothe his siter but she shrugged him off.

"I will *not* calm down! I hope she suffered so much more than that wolf! And why is it so fucking hot in here Dimitri?! Goddess, open a window or something!"

I looked at my mate, then at the open balcony doors. At the same time, a familiar scent drifted to me. I opened my mouth to tell him to wait; I wanted to calm Thara down first. But Killian threw open the door, startling all of us. His eyes were big, focused on my sister-in-law. He was sweating buckets, breathing in shorts gasps. Thara stopped mid-pace, staring at him like I stared at bacon nowadays.

# CHAPTER 70

**DIMITRIS POV**

I watched as my sister ran to her newfound mate, jumping into his arms. I let out a harsh, loud growl that had them both freezing.

"Dimitri!" Lily scolded beside me.

I couldn't help it. The bond I felt with my sister, my family, urged me to protect her. Killian was a good friend, an ally; Still all I saw was his arms around my sister. Thara was all I had left, now she was leaving me too.

"Easy Dimitri. I'm not going to hurt her." Killian said gently.

"Dimitri, he's my mate. It's fine. I'm okay."

*"We can't let her leave! She's the only family we have left!"* Ajax howled in my head.

I stood, using my Alpha speed to grab my sister out of Killian's arms. She looked at me with anger and shock, but Killian growled fiercely, his eyes changing colour.

"Give me my mate!" His wolf snarled.

"Dimitri, stop. What are you doing?" Lily asked nervously.

"I can't let her leave. I can't." I turned to Thara. "I can't lose you too."

Her face softened; She looked like Mom right now. "You're not losing me. Ever. Please Dimitri, I didn't think I'd ever get this chance again. Please, don't take this away from me." She begged. My heart rippled in my chest.

"What if-"

"He won't. Can't you see how much he wants me?"

Killian had inched closer, the urge to be near his mate overwhelming him. He placed a hand on my shoulder, his wolf at bay now.

"We will make this work. I would never take her away from you. I've waited so long to find her, please."

I met his eyes, my Alpha aura seeping out around us. "Don't hurt her." I commanded. Even though I knew it wouldn't effect him, I needed him to know how serious I was. Friend or not, I would remove his soul from his body if he hurt my sister.

"Never." He promised. Killian held out his arms, and Thara walked around me into them. "I am taking her tonight though. Not to my pack, we will stay here. We can figure this out in the morning."

Everyone looked at me, so I nodded. I needed time to process. Thara gave me a big hug before they left together, leaving my mate gazing at me questioningly.

"What the Hell was that all about?" Lily demanded.

"Thara never told you." It wasn't really a question.

"Tell me what?"

"It's not really for me to say."

"Damnit Dimitri! You can't say something like that and not tell me!"

I sighed, sitting heavily on the edge of the bed. "Fine, but if she gets mad, you forced me to tell you."

"I am forcing you. Now explain."

No point in beating around the bush. "Killian is Tharas second chance mate."

Lilys jaw dropped. "She had a mate before?"

I nodded. "He rejected her."

"*What?!*"

I leant forward, my hands cupping my chin. I hated talking about this, albeit, not as much as Thara. It was hard controlling my anger when I thought about her first 'mate'.

"When she turned eighteen, our parents threw a big party. They invited all the neighbouring packs. My Mom was good friends with the Luna of Crescent Moon; She had a son, William." I said his name like a curse. "William was Tharas first mate. Luna Sarah brought him along, and that was that."

"What happened?" Lily asked. She had tears in her eyes; She loved Thara as much as I did.

I threw myself onto my back staring angrily at the ceiling above. "They accepted each other. The plan was for Thara to go live at Crescent Moon, become the future Luna. But as soon as that bastard got what he wanted from her, he rejected her. He didn't even mark her."

"What the fuck?!"

"Thara was heartbroken. Luna Sarah apologized for her son, but I could tell she didn't really mean it. I still believe that she never intended to give up her position; She seemed happy that she would remain Luna. William, on the other hand, he didn't apologize. He took my sisters virginity, and then threw her away like garbage. It took *months* for Thara to even come out of her bedroom after that. She wouldn't eat, she wasn't sleeping. She wasn't living."

"Killian would never do that." She sounded confident.

"How can I be sure?"

"I didn't feel any ill intent towards Thara from him. He just wants his mate."

My head rolled so I could meet her eyes. "I thought you had to be touching someone to feel their intentions?"

Lily bit her lip, looking away from me, at the wall. "I've uh, been practicing. With Hazel. And sometimes Clint too. It's not perfect, but I can kind of reach out with my mind... or maybe my aura? I don't know. It's hard to do, and it tires me out. But I'm getting better."

"Why didn't you tell me?"

She shrugged. "I don't know."

"I can that's a lie even without your gifts darling."

Lily blushed softly. "Okay, fine. It's just... I don't know how you feel, being mated to me. No offense, but we both know I'm more powerful than you. And then I have powers on top of that... I didn't know if you'd feel bad, or start resenting me. So I kept it quiet."

I guess it made sense. Sort of. If I thought about it from her perspective; And there were many Alphas who would feel that way. I could actually name a few off the top of my head. However, I wasn't one of them, and she needed to know that.

"Lily, I'm proud that you're learning to control your gifts. Proud that you're taking the initiative to do so. Maybe other men would feel emasculated, but not me. If anything, it just adds to who you are."

"Are you just saying that?"

"No, I'm not. Here, try it on me. I can help you with this training too."

"You sure?"

I nodded. "Go ahead. I'm ready."

She gave me her loving smile before closing her eyes. I waited, trying to prepare myself for that tidal wave feeling like the first time. This time though, it wasn't as strong. It still left me somewhat breathless, but I could focus around it. After a minute, Lily opened her eyes, the feeling abating when she did. She was also breathing harder, her hand coming up to rub her forehead. Despite that, she was smiling.

"You really do love me." She said.

"Of course I do, silly girl."

"Thank you."

"For loving you?" I laughed.

She shook her head. "For loving all of me. For accepting me for who I am."

I sat up, scooting closer. "You don't need to thank me for that. I love you, all three of you." I rubbed her belly.

Before she could reply, I was hit with a mind-link.

*"Dimitri!"* Ben shouted in my head.

*"What?"*

*"You need to get down here! Now!"*

*"What's going on?"*

*"Oh my Goddess!"*

Those words came from my mate. She was out of bed before I knew what was happening, running to the door. I followed as fast as I could, but she was already running down the hall.

"Lily! Wait!"

I scrambled after her, my heart racing as she jumped down the stairs. I nearly collided with Luke on my way down after her. At the bottom I caught sight of Ben and Clara. They were standing with Gideon in the entrance hall, all three facing the door. Miguel came running in from the hall to the kitchens, and Killian and Thara peered over the banister on the floor above me. Lily stopped beside my Beta, clutching his arm tightly. Nobody said a word, though I was screaming inside for someone to tell me what was happening.

When I finally reached the bottom step, an unfamiliar scent hit me. I was positive I'd never smelled it before, but it reminded me faintly of Lilys wildflower and citrus smell. My eyes travelled until I found the source; A woman stood before us, her face caked in dirt and her hair unwashed and greasy. She was skin and bone, wearing an equally dirty dress that I thought was once white. Despite never seeing her before, not in person, I knew exactly who she was.

"Rosalie." Gideon sobbed.

Lilys mother looked at her mate, tears welling and spilling over. She gave him a small smile before looking to Lily.

"Lily." Rosalie held out her arms. Alarm bells went off in my head. But I was too late; my mate ran into her Mothers arms, nearly tackling her to the floor. They embraced, crying together. And then she spoke.

"I'm so sorry."

I blinked, and they were gone. Just gone. I blinked again. And again. I must have looked half an idiot the way I stood completely still, not breathing, just blinking. Maybe if I repeated the action enough times, she would reappear.

But she didn't.

Ajax roared in my head at the same time my muscles unlocked. I was across the room and out the door in seconds, eyes scanning every inch of the grounds, looking for my mate.

"LILY!"

She couldn't be gone. Not her; Not our pups!

Reality came crashing down hard; I felt myself falling. My clothes shredded as I shifted, bones snapping. Distantly, I heard the others calling to me, but I couldn't listen. I had to find them. I had to find my family.

# CHAPTER 71

LILYS POV

My heart galloped in my chest as I ran down the stairs. It couldn't be true. She couldn't be here. I'd been thinking of all sorts of different ways to rescue my mother, coming up empty. If Gideon couldn't find her after all this time, how could I? But I was willing to try, until my last breath if necessary. When I reached the entrance hall, I grabbed Bens arm, searching for the impossible.

And, impossibly, she was standing in front of me. I blinked the tears away, afraid they would make her disappear. Her scent hit me strongly, and Aya lurched to the surface wanting to be with her mother. Our mother. Part of me, a small part, took in her gangly appearance; She looked something awful, dirty and underweight. The larger part of me was reeling from the fact that she was truly, really here. Gideon choked out his long lost mates name, but she barely spared him a glance. Her arms rose feebly, extending towards me.

"Lily."

Unthinkingly, I ran into her, colliding with her roughly. Sobs broke from my chest as I inhaled again and again, clutching her to me. I couldn't let her go. Not again. I opened my mouth to tell her how much I missed her, how happy I was she was here when she said something unexpected.

"I'm so sorry."

I tried to pull away, instinct telling me to back off, but she held to me tightly. And then my world was spinning; Upside down, right, left, backwards, horizontally. My stomach heaved, but I didn't know if I vomited or not. If I did, it got lost somewhere in this crazy vortex of wind and churning. Finally, I landed on something hard, my arm breaking my fall. Pain radiated from my wrist to my shoulder, making my yelp. Closing my eyes, I took a few minutes to breath deeply, trying to understand what the fuck just happened.

"Good job Rosie. I wasn't sure if that would work."

357

A deep voice spoke somewhere beside me; It made my skin crawl. Instantly I became alert, my eyes shooting open. The first thing I noticed was the cobblestone floor under me. No wonder that hurt so much, I probably broke my arm when I hit it. A giant fireplace was built into the wall in front of me, the fire roaring inside. Glancing to my right, I saw a large wooden table, big enough to seat at least ten people, though only two chairs were seated at it, one at each end. Beyond that was a four poster bed, with black curtains hanging around it. Various types of artwork hung on the walls, the biggest set over the fireplace. The piece reminded me of the Celeste's meadow.

"I was hoping it wouldn't!"

I turned my head to the right, where my mother sat on the floor. She was holding her head, probably trying to get her bearings as well. Standing in front of her was Gideon. No... I shook my head, the rest of the fog clearing from my head. Not Gideon, but a man who looked a lot like him. There were subtle differences, this man was taller, and his eyes were different. The aura around him was also darker, much, much darker. This was Gideons brother.

Bastian.

Ignoring the pain in my arm, I forced myself to sit up, staring at my mother. She had helped kidnap me, taken me away from my pack, my friends. My mate. My heart shattered in my chest, leaving me gasping for air. How could she do this?

"Why?" I whispered to her. She reached out to me, but I flinched away. Goddess, did neither one of my parents care about my well being?

"Don't blame Rosie. She only helped me because I forced her to." Bastian stepped in front of her, crouching down so we were eye level.

"You must be Bastian." I said.

The corner of his lips twitched. "Ah, so you know me. Good. Then we can skip the introductions, thankfully." He raised his hand to my face, and I slapped it away.

"Don't touch me!" I spat.

"Hmm. You truly are mother and daughter." He looked between us. "She has the same fire in her eyes." He told my mother.

Concentrating, I felt Aya push forward, ready to rip this guys head off. Bastian looked at me with amusement before snapping his fingers. I screamed as I felt my wolf being thrown into the recesses of my mind. It was like someone punched me from inside my soul; The pain ripped through my entire body like fire. I called to Aya frantically, but she didn't answer.

"What the Hell did you do!" I shrieked.

"I simply restrained the beast inside you."

"You bastard!" Throwing my body towards him, I aimed my good hand for his face. Bastian caught my wrist easily, as if I was no more than a child lashing out in anger.

"Don't touch her!" My mother screamed.

"Back off Rosalie. You're no longer needed here, so go."

"I'm not leaving my daughter with you!"

"Very well." He snapped his fingers again, and she disappeared.

"Where did you send her?"

"Back to her room. That woman can be so stubborn." He rolled his eyes. "Now, hold still and don't attack me."

When he grabbed my bad shoulder, I gasped in pain, immediately struggling to get away from him. He only held me tighter. His aura grew stronger, washing over me. It was disgusting, like walking through spider webs. Despite that, my arm started to feel warm; Too warm, verging on hot. Just when I thought he was going to burn me, he pulled away. I stretched experimentally; My arm was fine. He'd healed me.

Big mistake.

Without hesitation, I leaned back on my hands, kicking him under the chin. Bastian flew backwards, landing in a heap. Jumping up, I spotted a big wooden door across the room. I'd just grasped the handle when his arms snaked around my waist, pulling me back. I threw my elbow towards his face, satisfied when it connected with his nose. His grip loosened, enough to allow me to turn; Cocking my knee back, I brought it up into his groin as hard as I could.

"*Fuck!*" Bastian fell to the ground, hands on his jewels. I ripped the door open, racing down the stone corridor. What the fuck was this place, a castle? Old fashioned fire torches lined the walls, the windows made of thick stained glass. I ran and ran, but the hall never seemed to stop. And there was no place to turn. Eventually, completely out of breath, I stopped and looked around. Only to find the door I'd run out of six feet behind me. How was that *possible?!*

"So much like your mother." Bastian's voice came from behind me. I spun, trying to punch him in the face but he dodged neatly. "She used that same move on me when I first brought her here."

"Stupid of you not to expect it then." I hissed.

"You might be right about that." Bastian stalked towards me, backing me into the room. He kicked the door shut, the lock clicking into place. Like that mattered, if there was nowhere to go?

"What do you even want with me? I won't help you, I won't let you use me." I told him.

"You say that like you have a choice. You don't. Whether you like it or not, I will use your blood to make myself stronger again." His face fixed into a sneer. "Of course, now I have to wait. Your blood is useless right now."

Instinctively, I placed my hand over my stomach. Terror shot through me as I realized my situation. I was trapped, I had nowhere to run.

"You have to let me go." I whispered.

Bastian laughed. "Why? Because you're pregnant?"

"I need proper care!" I shouted.

"Not my babies, not my problem." He shrugged.

Why was I surprised? This man was a monster. And they said Dimitri was heartless? Bastian outdid him a hundred times over.

"You're evil." I deadpanned.

Bastian smiled wickedly. "That's what they say. You'll get used to it."

"Dimitri-"

"Will never be able to find you. Your own father has wasted too many years trying, you don't really think a simple werewolf can?"

"He's not a 'simple werewolf'. He's an Alpha, and my mate. And when he finds me, you can be assured I won't stop him from ripping you to pieces." I said venomously.

Bastian's eyes darkened at my words. He was in front of me in a second; How did he move so fast? Or was he teleporting? His hand went round the back of my neck, bringing my face inches from his. His other hand ran into my hair, pulling it back harshly. I bit my lip against the pain.

"The day I come face to face with your pathetic mate is the day I will rip his heart out in front of you. But not before I show him that I've brought you to my side, that you belong to me."

"I will never belong to you."

"You will. Either willingly or forced, but you will be mine." Something sharp pressed against my belly. I glanced down to see Bastian holding a long blade. "You wouldn't want me to cut out those babies, would you?"

I sucked in a shuddering breath. "You would kill two innocent babies?"

"You're the one who pointed out that I was evil Lily. I just don't think you realize how evil I actually am."

I shook in his arms. He wasn't giving me a choice; I had to protect my pups. A thought struck me, something to hopefully distract him, even for a minute.

"Where is Jennine?" I asked.

My question obviously caught him off guard. "Why?"

"She killed her wolf, right?"

The blade moved from my torso, allowing me to breath a little easier. Bastian looked at me suspiciously.

"How do you know that?" He demanded.

"I have my sources." He didn't like my answer; Anger took over his features. "How did she do it? It's next to impossible to kill our wolves."

"She didn't. I did. She allowed me to."

"So, you made her a human?"

"Enough questions!" He shouted.

A tiny hint of fear sparked in his eyes. He blinked it away, but I knew; He didn't like that I knew things I shouldn't. He was scared his plan was going to fail. That's all I needed to endure this, to wait until someone came for me.

# CHAPTER 72

Bastian had left me, promising to have someone bring me food later. That around six hours ago. And as promised, food had arrived, delivered by a young girl with curly blonde hair. She'd kept her head down, placing the tray on the table and leaving quickly. And that's where it still sat now. I wasn't touching anything he had made for me; For all I knew it had poison in it. Even if he didn't want to kill *me*, Bastian had been very clear how he felt about my children. I wasn't going to risk something that would harm them. Sure, I was starving, but I ignored it as best I could.

Instead, I passed the time trying to contact my wolf. I could feel she was there still, just very deep down.

*"Aya, if you can hear me, focus on the pups. Protect them. I can bear anything he does, but I'm counting on you to look after our babies."*

Nothing. No hint of acknowledgment, not even a whisper. I could only pray she heard me, and would do what I asked. Curling up on the bed, I eventually fell into an uneasy sleep. Dreams of my mate and friends plagued my mind; Even in sleep, my heart ached. I missed them so much. I just wanted to go home!

I woke up crying, my tears staining the pillow. I wouldn't claim it as mine; Nothing here belonged to me, and I didn't plan to stay long enough for that to change. The smell of potatoes had my stomach rumbling loudly, and I sat up to see a very unwelcome sight. Bastian was sitting at one end of the long table which was now covered in different food. He had his hands clasped under his chin, staring at me intently. Fucking creep.

"Why didn't you eat lunch?" He asked.

I lay back down, turning away from him. "Not hungry."

"Yes, you are."

"I'm not eating that food."

His chair squeaked as he pushed it back. I listened to his footsteps as he approached the bed, coming to stand in front of me. I simply turned my back to him, just wishing he would make the mistake of touching me. He'd have one less arm.

"So, you're plan is to starve yourself then?"

I didn't answer.

"There is nothing in your food. I'm eating it too."

Still, I remained silent. Could he not take a hint?

"What would be the point of killing you? Honestly."

"It's not me I'm concerned about." I said.

"I gain nothing from killing your children."

That got my attention. Reluctantly, I looked over my shoulder at him. "You didn't seem to have that mindset when you held a knife to my stomach." I hissed.

Bastian crossed his arms. "I've been thinking about it. What are the chances your children, even one of them, are as special as you?"

My face paled, all the blood draining to my toes. He smirked.

"I'd rather wait and see if I'm right. If so, you're of more use to me than I first hoped. Now, come eat."

He walked back to the table casually. I stared after him, wanting nothing more than to drive a knife through his twisted, dark heart. Over my dead body would he ever use my pups that way! I was about to go off on him, maybe shove a hot plate in his face when the door burst open and my second worst nightmare stormed in. Instantly, I was on my feet, backed against the wall in a defensive position. Jennine found me immediately, her eyes narrowing to slits. She didn't look much different than the last time I'd seen her. The only big difference was the way I perceived her, the selfish bitch who'd willingly killed her other half and submitted to the Devil.

"So it's true. You brought her here." She turned to Bastian, who was calmy slicing his meat.

"Yes." He replied nonchalantly.

"And you're having dinner with her?!" She shouted at him.

"Yes."

"I've been waiting an hour for you in our room!"

"I never said I was coming back tonight."

Jennine looked ready to explode. "You're not spending the night with *her*!" Ugh. Her voice was as grating and annoying as ever. Bastian slammed down his utensils, the table quaking under the force. He stood slowly, turning his glare on Jennine.

"Are you giving me orders?" His voice was low, dangerous.

"It doesn't matter." I said before she could reply. "You're *not* spending the night here, and I'm not having dinner with you."

His glare fell on me now. "Stay out of this."

"You think I want to be in the middle of your little lovers quarrel? I didn't invite you here; Go back to your own room." I crossed my arms.

"This is my home. I'll be where I want to be. And you." He looked at Jennine. "You need to leave. Now."

"Are you serious?! You're really going to stay here with her?"

"My patience is wearing thin Jennine. Go!"

To my surprise, she actually left. I stared at the door, wondering how she could leave when I couldn't. Clearly, the door led somewhere, it just wasn't accessible to me. There must be someway to get around that magic? Someway to break the spell so I could escape.

"Eat." Bastian sat back down, picking up his fork. I shook my head.

"Go to Hell."

"*Damnit!*" He shot to his feet again, pointing at the chair meant to occupy me. "*Sit the fuck down and eat!*"

I smirked. It was idiotic of me, but I got a little satisfaction watching him lose control. He was going to learn sooner or later that I wasn't just as stubborn as my mother; I was way worse. I would fight him on everything, even the little things. To make my point clear, I sat on the bed, looking away from him. He appeared in front of me, his hand gripping my chin painfully. I met his eyes, letting the hate I felt for him show vividly.

"Did you not hear me when I said my patience was wearing thin?" He snarled.

"I did. Did it looked like a gave a shit?"

My face whipped to the side, my cheek stinging from his slap. The metallic taste of blood hit my tongue, and I spit the blood onto the floor. I lifted my head and laughed; Bastian's face transfixed into surprise.

"What do you think hitting me with accomplish? Do you know anything about me? I spent most of my life as a human punching bag. Pain is nothing new to me."

His face darkened, something that was getting old. His anger did nothing to intimidate me. What I did fear, was the calculating look in his eyes. He turned, snapping his fingers. Rosalie appeared, letting out a gasp as she looked around. Before she could comprehend where she was all of a sudden, Bastian walked to her side and slapped her.

"What are you doing!?" I rushed to my mothers side, catching her before she fell.

"Eat." Bastian said.

"You're a sick person!" I shouted at him.

"Eat, or I'll make her unrecognizable."

I was so fucking pissed when I looked into my mothers face. Her cheek had the imprint of his hand on it, already turning a nasty shade of blue. I placed my hand over it, wiping away her tears.

"I'm waiting Lily." Bastian tapped his foot beside us.

"I'm sorry." I whispered to Rosalie.

"It's fine." She squeezed my hand.

I stood, slowly making my way to the table. When I looked back, my mother was gone and Bastian was taking his seat once more. I took a small portion of mashed potatoes and vegetables. Hesitantly, I lifted the food to my mouth, not tasting it, just swallowing it whole.

"Just know that from now on, if you disobey me, your mother will suffer the consequences."

My hand froze halfway to my mouth. Bastian smiled at me, a smile full of promise. Taking a deep breath, I focused my attention on maybe getting some answers.

"So, why now?" I threw at him.

"Excuse me?"

"Why did you decide to take me now? Why didn't you before?"

He studied me for a moment. Finally, he shrugged. "I couldn't before. Not for lack of trying though."

"What does that mean?"

"It means I attempted to bring you here when you first shifted and I knew what you were. But I couldn't. Don't ask me why, because I don't know."

"But you did bring me here." I said confusedly.

"No, I brought Rosie. She just happened to be holding you. I guess you could call it a loophole, a grey area."

"So you can't teleport me, but you can teleport other people?" I confirmed. "Then why didn't you take me when I was hugging my friends, or in the arms of my mate?"

"Because then I would have to kill them, and that wasn't ideal. I have other plans for your friends. And some fun plans for your mate." He mused while I tried to keep my anger under control.

"Like what?"

"Ah, no. That would spoil the surprise." Bastian winked.

"Why are you doing this?" I set my fork down, leaning over the table. "All this, and why? Because you were exiled? That was your fault."

His eyes flashed up to mine. "You think this is some sort of revenge thing on Gideon?" He answered his own question. "It's not. I always knew that I could become more. More powerful than him, more powerful than the Elders. Your idiot father wasted his time trying to steer me away from Dark Magic, but it was useless. Honestly, I couldn't care less that he got me exiled; I was leaving anyways. The only reason that you're my target, my dear, is because of what you are. The fact that you are Gideons daughter is just a bonus."

"You know, that's really sick. Technically, you're my Uncle. Yet you want me to be yours? That's insanely messed up." My face screwed up with disgust.

Bastian laughed, loudly. I stared at him like he was insane; Which he was, of course.

"He didn't tell you the full story, did he?" He laughed again. "Well, allow me to enlighten you."

# CHAPTER 73

BASTIANS POV
**WARNING; THIS CHAPTER INCLUDES SEXUAL ASSAULT**

"Tell me, do you know how many Clans there are?" I asked Lily. Her face turned thoughtful before she answered.

"Four."

"Correct. However, there use to be five." I took a drink of my wine, the cool liquid coating my tongue. "I was born into that fifth Clan, Yellowcreek."

"Clara never said there was a fifth Clan."

"Probably because she wasn't born yet. It is not talked about amongst our kind."

"The Clan?" She looked confused.

"The destruction of it."

Her face paled. I poured myself more of the delicious drink, my thoughts going back to my earliest memories.

"Yellowcreek's Elder wasn't like the others. He thought witches were the superior species, that we should rule over the others. He wanted to go to war, to claim the werewolf lands, eradicate that humans, make slaves of the vampires."

"There are vampires?!" Lily exclaimed. I raised a brow at her.

"How do you not know that?" I asked curiously.

"I didn't go to school." She huffed.

"Well, yes vampires exist, the few that are left anyways. They've all but wiped themselves out. Anyways, Yerik, Yellowcreek's Elder, was overruled by the others. He was furious. Instead of settling things diplomatically, he turned to the Dark Arts."

Despite her hatred for me, Lily was listening intently. One hand was cupping her chin, the other placed on the table. Her eyes were focused as she listened to my sad tale.

"You clearly see where this is heading. The others gathered to overthrow Yerik, bringing death upon the entire Clan for we were, as they said, 'tainted'. They burned buildings, flooded the fields. Killed gruesomely and without mercy. People who ran were hunted and slaughtered; Children were ripped away from mothers, families thrown together into seemingly bottomless pits. None escaped the Elders wrath. No one but me."

"How?" She whispered.

"Pure dumb luck. I was four years old at the time, visiting my Aunt in the neighbouring Clan. When the news reached us, she took me in and lied, saying I was her son. But people started to talk, people who knew her. So she sent me to her friends in the Eastern Clan; Gideons family. It was just convenient that him and I looked so alike, people really thought we were brothers. Nobody suspected a thing."

"Does Gideon know?" Lily asked.

"Yes. When we were older, his parents told him everything. It was after that that he started to watch me more closely, began not to trust me."

"You never considered them family?"

"Never." I spat. "My family was murdered. The people who took me in were always wary of me, always watching me. Always treating me like the outsider I was. They kept the secret about who I was, where I came from. But they never loved me." I sat back in my chair, eyeing her across the table. "And before you go off and try to appeal to my good side, save it. I don't crave love like everybody else; I crave power. Yerik had the right idea, just the wrong execution. And he didn't have a Mother Wolf by his side." I downed my drink with my words.

"I'm not by your side Bastian. And I wasn't going to appeal to your good side; I don't believe you have one."

"Good, then we're on the same page. So, does that answer your questions? Truthfully, I'm surprised Gideon didn't tell you the truth about me."

I could tell she was too. What was the point in hiding it? The only answer I could come up with was that he was ashamed, like he always had been. Still, it made no difference to me. If anything, it had only awarded me some time talking to Lily, and time away from the harpy Jennine. Even when she was attacking me, Lily was still far better company. Was there even a point in keeping Jennine around now? Surely I could go ahead without her?

"Why does Gideon still refer to you as his brother then?" Lily pulled me out of my thoughts.

I shrugged. "Old habits die hard, I guess. We were forced to call each other brother for a long time. Even I slip up occasionally still."

"How do I know you're not lying to me?"

"Now, that's just insulting. I may be a monster, I may be evil, but even I won't commit incest. There are things in this world that gross me out too. But if you want, I can order a DNA test?"

Her face became impossibly paler.

"Fine. Do that."

I stood, grabbing a bowl of rolls. I overturned it, dumping them onto the table. Waving my hand over the bowl, water appeared, filling it halfway. Taking my knife, I picked the end of my forefinger, drawing blood.

"Come here." I ordered her. She remained seated and I glared at her. "Don't make me bring your mother back Lily."

She scowled before standing and coming to my side. I grabbed her hand, drawing blood from her finger as well. Squeezing her finger, I let three drops fall into the bowl.

"What are you doing?"

"A DNA test."

Placing both my hands on the bowl, I explained to her.

"If our blood mixes together, we are related in one way or another. If it doesn't, we are not." Her mouth opened to protest, but I interrupted her. "You should know that blood magic doesn't lie. After all, it is what tied you to your pack."

I said the required words, and waited. Lily leaned over the bowl, watching the water intently. Our blood had swirled together a little already, but it was now separating. It was pulled to opposite ends of the water, the result very clear. Lily drew in a sharp breath as I stepped back and behind her. She turned away from the table, pushing against my chest.

"Don't. " She snapped.

"I just proved we're not related."

"I don't care! That doesn't change anything! I don't want you, I'll never want you!"

I placed my hands on the table, trapping her between them. Leaning in, I caught the fear in her eyes, could feel her shaking. This was so much better; I liked a challenge every once in a while.

"Remember what I told you? You will be mine, but I would prefer if it was willingly on your part. It makes it so much better."

"No!" Lily pushed me again, and this time I caught her wrists. Spinning her around, I brought her back to my front, holding her hands securely. Still, she fought back and I was growing impatient. I called the shadows, the snake-like creatures darting out from the corners of the room; They crawled up our bodies, replacing my hands on her. Lily shrieked and pulled against the Darkness.

"That's extremely Dark Magic sweetheart. You won't be able to break it." I kissed the back of her neck.

"Don't touch me!"

"You don't want me to force you Lily. Come to me, it's so much easier."

"Fuck you! I'll kill you!"

My hand went over her mouth, my lips at her ear. "I'd like to see you try." My other hand ran up her side, stopping at her breast. She whimpered under my touch, attempting to bite me. I'd given her clothes when she arrived here, but right now I wanted her out of them. But something inside me wanted her to want it too. She wasn't giving me any more options.

"Remember, you chose this." I whispered in her ear. I took the vial out of my pocket, uncapping it. I forced her head backwards, quickly removing my hand and emptying the contents down her throat. She sputtered and coughed, trying to spit it out; I covered her mouth again before she could, waiting.

Her body froze, becoming entirely still. Even her breathing stopped. For a second, I wondered if I fucked up, if I'd given her too much. I never got spells wrong, but she was like a statue. Three seconds ticked by and Lily finally lowered her head. I uncovered her mouth, turning her body to face me. When our eyes met, hers were no longer filled with hatred. They were calm, a soft smile on her face. I smiled in return; Nothing could stand in my way now. Lily held out her hands, glancing at the shadows still restraining her. I shooed them off, pleasantly surprised when she wrapped them around my neck.

"Do you know who I am?" I asked her.

"Bastian."

"And who is your mate?"

Her eyebrows furrowed. "I don't have a mate."

I smiled. "That's right. Because you belong to *me*."

"Yes. I belong to you." She pulled me down, my lips meeting hers.

# CHAPTER 74

## DIMITRIS POV

I was in the kitchen, going over a map of the surrounding areas with Ben, Luke, Killian, Miguel and Gideon. My office was uninhabitable; My whole floor was actually. Staff were working to repair the mess I'd caused, making me feel even shittier. I'd run for hours with no sign of my mate. Eventually, Ajax had gotten through to me, telling me to go home and work out a plan of action. But when I'd gotten here, Gideon was waiting with more bad news. As if the worst hadn't happened already, I had more shit added on top.

Somehow, word had gotten out about Lilys kidnapping. The entire pack was in panic, rumors spreading that we were to be attacked. The fucked up part? I couldn't tell them they were wrong, because I didn't know. The thing that pissed me off more was that I had loose tongue in the packhouse, someone who couldn't keep their mouth shut. More than likely, it was one of the staff, and when I found out who it was, they were gone. I'd had enough bullshit.

"You can look at all the maps you want." Gideon said to me now. "It won't help. I've searched this area. And the ones beyond. I've been to different states even."

"Well, what do you expect me to do?!" I snarled. "I can't just sit around with my thumb up my ass! Why don't you stop being so damn pessimistic and fucking help!"

"Why can't you just see where she is through your Orb thingy?" Luke asked.

"You don't think I've tried?" Gideon threw back at him.

"Well, what *haven't* you tried?" Ben threw his hands up in exasperation.

"I don't know what you want from me. I've tried everything within my limits over the years, and I never found him, or my mate! You don't think I'm just as desperate as you are?! Do you not remember that that bastard now has my mate *and* my daughter?!" Gideon shouted.

"All the more reason for you to stop doubting yourself, and help us come up with something to find them!" Ben shouted back.

"All of you, *calm down.*"

We turned to see Clara entering the kitchen with Thara, and Isabelle trailing behind. What the fuck? This wasn't a meeting for children. Aside from that, looking at her innocent face just brought to life the fact that my children were in danger and I was helpless to find them. That wasn't Isabelle's fault, but I didn't want her around me right now.

"What is she doing here?" I asked Clara.

"Everyone in the house is in a state, and Ben is with you. I had nobody to leave her with."

"Hazel-"

"Is on her way here with Clint." She interrupted me. Sure enough, the couple walked in a second later. I sighed.

"Fine. Whatever." I refocused on the task at hand. "Maybe you can give us some new ideas." I shot a dirty look at Gideon who returned it with an equally nasty one.

"First, you all need to stop fighting with each other. We won't find Lily or Rosalie if we're spending time being at each others throats." Clara glared at all of us.

Ben picked up Isabelle at her request. Her tiny face examined each of us in turn, taking in the tension in the room. Her gaze landed on me.

"Your mate is missing." She stated.

"Yes." I ground out.

She looked at her mother. "So use a locator spell, like you did for Charlie."

Clara shook her head. "It's not that simple sweetie."

"Why not?" I asked.

"That's too easy. Bastian wouldn't leave a giant hole like that. And Gideon already tried."

My face fell. It was starting to feel like Lily was lost to me for good.

"Why are you looking like that?"

I looked at Killian, who was looking at Gideon. He was shuffling his feet, looking at the ground.

"Wait, *have* you tried that already?" Hazel asked.

"Uhm, no."

*"What?!", "Why?!"*

Everyone shouted at him in outrage. I knocked the map off the steel counter, ready to jump over and strangle him. Clara looked like she wanted to set him on fire, and Thara had her fists balled at her sides.

"Why the fuck not?!" I roared at him. Isabelle covered her ears, hiding her face in Bens shoulder. I attempted to control my anger.

"Because of what you just said!" Gideon told Clara. "There's no way he would make it that easy."

She threw her hands up. "That is literally the *first* thing you should have tried, you fucking moron!"

"Mama, don't swear." Isabelle scowled.

"Sorry Isa." She bent down, scooping the map I had off the floor. Examining it, she looked at me. "Do you have a world map? Or a globe?"

"There's a globe in the library." Thara answered.

"I need it."

Thara nodded, racing out of the kitchen. I pinned Gideon with a cold stare.

"Anything else we should know?" I spat.

Pain ripped through just then, radiating out of my chest. I gasped, clutching the counter for support. It was so strong, I felt like my bones were on fire.

"Dimitri?!"

Luke grabbed my one arm and Miguel caught the other. Together, they lowered me to the floor where I sat, dazed. What was happening to me? Another wave hit me and I screamed, clutching my chest. It hurt so much, I would gladly rip my heart out to escape this pain.

"It hurts!" I shouted. Suddenly, Clara's face appeared before me. The expression on her face said she knew exactly what was happening to me. "Make it stop!" I begged her.

"I will." She placed her hands on either side of my head and closed her eyes. After an excruciating minute, the pain eased, faded, and then stopped altogether. Sweat coated my body, running into my eyes; My whole body shook.

"What... what was that?" I gasped.

Clara looked at me with sympathy. "That's what happens when your mate is intimate with someone else." She whispered.

Her words clicked into my brain, one by one. But I still didn't process them. Lily wouldn't do to that to me. She wouldn't. No, someone had to have forced her... I didn't realize I speaking out loud until Ben spoke.

"She was willing. You and I both know mates don't feel pain if the other is forced." He spoke to me, but his eyes were on his mate.

"It's true. It's the choice to stray from your bond that causes the pain for the other person. Rape isn't a choice. I'm sorry." Clara said.

"I don't believe it. Dimitri is right, Lily wouldn't cheat on him."

"Especially not with Bastian. Isn't he her Uncle? She would never consent to that." Clint spoke for the first time.

"Well." We all looked at Gideon, who was taking measured steps away from me. "He's not her Uncle *biologically*."

Luke was tossed backwards, along with his mate as I jumped over Clara. I propelling myself over the counter and tackled him to the ground, my hands around his throat.

"Talk! *NOW!*" The walls shook under my wrath.

"Ben, give me Isa." I briefly acknowledged him passing her off and Clara leaving the room. But my main focus was on the asshole underneath me.

"He's adopted. He came to live with us when I was little. I didn't think it was relevant!" Gideon rasped.

"Not *relevant?!* The fucking prick is sleeping with my mate!" I roared.

"Maybe! You'd feel the same pain even if they just kissed..."

I punched him so hard he was out cold. Useless, he was fucking useless. I looked at Ben.

"Go out with Isabelle. I need Clara in here." I ordered. He nodded, walking away.

Thara came in as he left, holding the globe I kept in the library. Clara came in after her, both looking at the passed out man at my feet. My sister raised her eyebrows but didn't comment; She simply set the globe on the counter and went to stand with Killian. Clara motioned for me to join her, holding her hand out to me. I placed my hand in her smaller one, waiting for instructions on how this worked.

"Since you're Lilys mate, you're the best thing to find her; You hold a piece of each others souls. There is nothing stronger than that, so it will make this easier, if it works."

"*If?*"

"It is possible to block your location from this type of spell. Still, he should have tried it." She shook her head at Gideon. "Okay, I want you to close your eyes and focus on Lily. Think of the best memories you have with her, her face, her smile, everything that draws you to her. And, most importantly, focus on your bond. Let your wolf help you if you have to."

She closed her eyes and I did the same. I brought up Lilys face, smiling at me the way she did when she was happy. I heard her laugh, her giggle. The way she looked when she told me about the pregnancy; How much she was over the moon that we were starting a family together. Ajax helped by remembering the way she felt in our arms when she'd called on him to make love to her. The way it felt when him and Aya chased each other through the forest. Cuddling under the stars and nuzzling each other. I remembered the first time I saw her, a mixed memory. The way she outshone everyone in the room, and how her eyes captivated me. Even if I hadn't wanted her then, I knew inside she was the one who was going to bring me back to myself.

Together, Ajax and I let the bond flow, remembering every happy moment, some of the not so nice ones, and how much we loved her. Everything that made us, us. The day at the beach. Lilys Luna ceremony. The first time she told me off. Everything.

"Dimitri."

Clara called me out of my reminiscing. She was looking at the globe, eyes wide. A spot on the sphere was glowing slightly; I leaned closer, dropping her hand.

**ISLE OF SKYE**

"She's in Scotland." Clara whispered.

"Then that's where we're going." I replied.

# CHAPTER 75

**BEN'S POV**

"Gregory! You're slower than syrup on paper man, come on! *Move!*" I shouted. Gregory shoved past me, muttering under his breath. Perhaps it was a good thing I was too distracted to focus on his words; I doubt Dimitri would put up with a brawl right now. Clara's magic seemed to be keeping him pain free, but for how long? I had to keep reminding myself that Lily would do anything to survive, for her pups and for Dimitri. Even if that meant having to be intimate with someone who wasn't her mate. I just hoped she knew what she was doing.

"Are you okay?"

I glanced over my shoulder to see my mate. I can't remember the last time she looked so concerned about me, if ever. My heart stirred at the sight of her beautiful eyes gazing into mine.

"Fine. Just thinking." I replied.

"I'm sure Lily is fine. From what I've seen, she's a tough girl."

"I know. It's just..." I blew out a breath, leaving my words to trail.

Sparks erupted as Clara placed her hand on my shoulder. I looked down at her.

"You're trying to understand why she would cause your Alpha so much pain." She said. It wasn't a question, but I nodded anyways. "I'm going with the assumption that she had no choice. We don't know the situation over there, but I know she would never do that on purpose. She would never betray your Alpha that way."

We looked around at the men and women boarding the plane. The plane that was to take our small army to Scotland. Gregory had disappeared inside, and I spotted his son a few meters away. Clara squeezed my shoulder, making to move past me. Instantly, I had my arm wrapped around her waist, holding her back.

"Where are you going?" I asked.

She blinked at me. "I'm getting on the plane."

"No, you're not."

Her eyes clouded over in anger. "Excuse me?"

"Do you not know what is coming? There's going to be a fight, a bad one. I don't want you anywhere near that!"

She gripped my arm, causing me to yelp and release her. I rubbed where she'd burnt me. Damn.

"I'll have you know that I am not some poor, defenceless woman Benjamin. *That,-*" she pointed to my arm,"-is just a taste of what I can do. I may not be as powerful as Gideon, but I am far from helpless. You'd do well to remember that."

I watched as she stormed off, stomping angrily past the wolves and on board. A tiny smile appeared on my face. My mate was feisty girl, I'd give her that.

"Something funny?"

Dimitri appeared beside me, looking worn and worried. I put my smile away and grew as serious as the situation.

"Just Clara being... Clara."

"Ah. Well, let's go."

"Right." I turned to the rest of the men. "Everybody, let's move! We take off in one hour!"

"Yes Beta!" they shouted back to me. I followed Dimitri across the pavement and to the steps. Ducking my head, we entered the plane and looked around. It was a military jet, filled with our top warriors. The rest of our army was still at the pack, with Gideon. I knew we didn't have enough men here, not even close. But we had the best. The rest would be joining us via portal, which Gideon would open when we contacted him from the island. The element of surprise would, hopefully, turn the odds in our favour. I glanced at Clara, turning the jade necklace Gideon had given her in her fingers; He held an identical piece, a way to keep the portal open once he opened it.

I leaned down as we passed her. "Where's Isabelle?"

"At home." She snapped. The next second, her eyes went wide and her hand flew to her mouth. I smirked. "I mean-"

"I know what you meant." I pecked her on the cheek, enjoying the blush that followed. "Glad you finally consider it your home."

Before she could comment, or deny it, I straightened and continued walking. Dimitri was already seated, his leg anxiously tapping up and down. I took the seat next to him, running my hands through my hair. I went over every detail of our plan in my head, looking for weak points, for any flaws. We'd stayed up all night figuring this out. Best case scenario- We get to Lily without much fuss, get her home, and take care of Bastian. Worse case scenario- We would have to fight Lily herself, if he'd done something to her. *That* was going to be a tough one, given she was a Mother Wolf. And our Luna.

The plane was starting to fill up and slowly, I could see Dimitri starting to calm down. I knew him too well; This is what he did. He was a fighter. Never the one to sit on the sidelines, but be in the middle of the battle, bloody and bruised. He'd never fought for anything for himself up until this point though, and that worried me. As if he could hear my thoughts, he turned and met my eyes.

"The reason doesn't change anything Ben."

"You've never had a weakness before." I mumbled.

"Weakness." He laughed quietly. "Lily is not my weakness. She is my strength. My hope, my goodness, my heart and soul. She lifts me up, even when I was the one to bring her down. She's done more for me, and this pack, than I ever thought possible. She's worth fighting for, worth dying for."

I nodded slowly. I caught Clara's eyes briefly before she looked away.

"I know what you mean." I replied.

Luke and Miguel took the seats across from us. I nodded at them. "You ready?"

"Born ready." Luke grinned.

"So cocky." Miguel nudged him.

"Only for you." Luke winked.

"Guys. Please." Dimitri snapped at them. They both muttered apologies.

We sat in silence while everyone boarded. At last, the doors swung shut and we were instructed to buckle up. The air was thick was tension and nerves, but also determination. I looked around at the men, each one worth their weight in a fight, each one having proven themselves at one point or another. I sent up a silent prayer as we took off that we didn't have to bury any of them when this was over.

We'd barely gotten a decent amount of height when I heard Dimitris phone ringing. He glanced at the screen with confusion before pressing send.

"Who's this?"

Being this close, I heard everything, and the reply sent a wave of shock through me.

"Hello Dimitri. Miss me?"

His hand clenched so tightly over the device, I worried he would smash it.

"You'd better have a good fucking reason for calling me Jennine." He growled.

She laughed, and I cringed at the sound. "Oh, I do. Unless you don't want to know where your mate is?"

Dimitri was breathing heavily, rage and hatred on his face. I felt Clara come up behind me, and I put a finger to my lips in a gesture for her to keep quiet.

"I already know where she is." Dimitri was saying.

"Oh, do you?"

"She's in Scotland. The Isle of Skye."

Jennine laughed again. "At the castle."

"Yes."

"Do you happen to know *which* castle?"

"What are you talking about?!"

"There are seven castles on this island Dimitri."

He glanced at Clara who had gone pale. At that moment, I honestly worried for my mates safety. Before he could explode, though, Jennine spoke again.

"I'll tell you where she is."

That got our attention.

"Why? And why would I believe you?"

"That's up to you. My motives are my own, but if you don't want the information..."

"Tell me!" He practically shouted.

Silence. I could see him starting to lose control, almost on the verge of shifting. I was about to take the phone away from him when she answered.

"You'll find her at the most southern castle. It looks ruined, but it's a spell, an illusion."

"You better not be lying to me Jennine. I swear to the Goddess I'll-"

"I'm giving you this information because I want something in exchange Dimitri."

"Like fuck! I owe you nothing!"

"Relax. It's something you already want. All I want is for you to kill Bastian. Deal?"

"What?"

"You heard me."

"I think I'll just kill you both."

"Oh no. I'm already gone Alpha. But we'll meet again, don't worry."

"Is that a threat?"

"A promise. Goodbye Dimitri."

The line went dead. We all looked at each other, confused.

"Are we suppose to trust her?" Luke asked.

"Do we have a choice?" I looked at my Alpha. "Do you believe her?"

He tapped the phone against his leg. "Like you said, we don't have a choice."

"I'll go inform our pilot." Miguel stood and walked off.

"What are you thinking?" I asked Clara, who was sitting beside me with her eyebrows scrunched together.

"That I hope this isn't a trap." She whispered. I knew what she was thinking about; Isabelle. Reaching over, I took my mates hands in mine.

"We'll make it through this. And then we can go home to our daughter."

Her eyes went wide, as did mine. Oh shit.

"I didn't mean-"

She put her hand over my mouth. " I know what you meant." She gave me a warm smile and a kiss on the cheek before going back to her seat. I caught Luke's smirking expression and shot him the finger.

"Shut up." I said.

# CHAPTER 76

**DIMITRIS POV**

The closer we got to our destination, the angrier I was becoming. Usually, I would take this time to go over the plan, the details. Encourage the men. This time, I was silent, introverted. I could feel that it was putting off the men, but I couldn't find it in myself to give some grand speech. What would I say anyways? "We get my mate back or I'll kill all of you in a blind rage"? Yeah, sure. This was different than any other fight I'd ever been in. Too much was at stake; There was too much that could be lost. For me, for the pack. That wasn't the cause of my anger though.

All I could think about was what that piece of shit might be doing with my a Lily. Because of Clara's magic, I couldn't feel if she was betraying me or not. And if that's what she had to do to survive, I couldn't fault her for it. But that didn't mean I was okay with it either. Just the thought of him touching what was mine, kissing her, feeling her body... it made my blood boil in my veins. Jennine hadn't had the need to make any deals about Bastian's death. In my eyes, he was already a dead man. And if she was telling the truth, he was a dead men sooner than I hoped.

"We're about half an hour out. You want to say anything to the men?" Ben whispered to me.

"You do it."

"Uh... alright."

I felt him stand and watched him stand in front of our group. I felt like a shitty Alpha right now, but at the same time, I didn't care much. I'm sure any man in my position would feel much the same. I looked down at my knees as my Beta talked.

" You all know why we're here. To get our Luna back." He paused. "I'll be honest with you all, we don't know if our Luna is under the influence of magic. If she is, there is a chance she will fight against us. I don't need to tell you the consequences if she gets hurt."

A snarl ripped it's way out of me, audible to everyone.

"If that so happens to be the case, the *only* course of action to take is to subdue her. To get her safely through the portal and back home. You all know how these things go. There will be blood. There will be death. But let's make it so it belongs to other side. Each and every one of you has proven yourselves the finest warriors of Blood Moon. I want to see you uphold that honor, and bring our Luna home. You with us?"

Shouts went up around the cabin of agreement. Ben sat down, sighing loudly.

"Good job." I said.

"Thanks."

"It was very moving. You should write poetry." Luke pretended to wipe away a tear.

"You're always such a dick before a fight." Ben scoffed.

"It's the energy man. Can't help it."

I ignored their bantering as I felt the plane tip. We must have been closer than Ben thought. The pilots voice came over the speakers, ordering everyone to strap in for landing. I looked around, noticing only one person who looked more nervous than excited for the coming battle. But I trusted Ben to take care of his mate so she could go home to her daughter. I had my own mate to worry about for now. My stomach lurched as we descended; admittedly, I had never been a good flyer, but sometimes it was necessary. I looked out the window, seeing the tops of trees appear, and the ocean below us.

Far out in the distance, I caught site of what looked like an abandoned ruin. I kept my eyes trained on that until the trees blocked my view and I felt the wheels hit the pavement. The landing was rough, and everyone sighed in relief when we finally came to a full stop.

"I am never getting on of these things again." Miguel muttered. He had a green undertone to his face as he stood on wobbly legs.

"Not even for our honeymoon? I was going to take you to Greece." Luke said.

"I'll swim."

I stood and made my way to the exit. Ben and Luke followed behind me with their mates, and the rest followed after us. I took the time to look around, get my bearings. We'd landed in what seemed like a large area of bare forest. All around us were great giants of trees. It was quiet, except for our breathing and the sounds of the ocean. Ben, Luke and I scanned the area for any signs of danger, any signs of a trap. I was more than shocked that we didn't find any; Perhaps Jennine had told the truth. Looking in the direction of the old ruins I'd seen, I signaled to the group snow standing before me.

"You all know the plan. Three groups. One with me, one with the Beta, and one with the Gamma. Let's go!" I barked.

Men started filing in around me, but I couldn't focus on them. Lily was here, I knew it. I could feel it. Our bond felt stronger, almost like a pull. Before everyone was situated, I started walking towards the trees, anxious to get to my mate. Ben caught me before I hit the tree line.

"I know you want to get this done. I know. But Dimitri, you have to think. We can't just storm the place."

"What are you implying?" I snapped.

"Nothing. Just that you need to calm down and stick to the plan. Don't act on impulse."

I took a deep breath. He was right.

"You're right. I just... I just want her back."

"So do we. So let's do this, rationally."

I nodded. "Let's do this."

He clapped me on the back once. "I'll go get Clara to call Gideon."

I waited until my group formed behind me and for Ben to give me the thumbs up. When all was ready, I stepped into the trees and let our bond pull me forward. Ben and Luke split with their groups on either side of us, covering from all sides. We walked silently for about twenty minutes before I stopped.

"Alright. Wait here until night. Keep your eyes and ears open. Collin, tell the others we've stopped."

"Yes Alpha." I looked at the sky; The sun was setting, not long to wait now.

*"I can feel her."* Ajax said.

*"Me too."*

*"Hmm."*

*"What?"*

*"I can feel Aya, but I can't reach her."*

*"You can't talk to her?"*

*"No. It feels... it feels like there's a wall up. Like she's blocking me out."*

My guts twisted uncomfortably. *"What does that mean?"*

*"I'm not sure."*

*"Can you reach Lily?"*

*"I think so. But I don't think I should try, in case she's..."*

*"Right. Better leave it then."*

I grit my teeth painfully; I couldn't even tell my own mate I was here to save her because she might have turned against me. The fact that I couldn't trust her right now hurt badly.

"Alpha, Beta Ben says they have movement where they are." Collin spoke up suddenly. I spun to face him.

"How many?"

"Five, in wolf form."

"Tell them to take them out, quietly. And hide the bodies if they can."

His eyes glazed over. When they cleared, he nodded at me, indicating it was done. I nodded back and looked around. More than likely they were out hunting, but what if Bastian knew we were here? That wasn't a risk I was willing to take. The sun was nearly set now, and I wasn't waiting anymore.

"Tell the others we're moving in."

His wolf nodded at me while my men took their positions. Silently, we stalked through forest. Every step I felt closer to Lily, until I saw the treeline breaking ahead. I signaled for the men to stop. Cautiously, I inched forward, the ruins coming into view. It was rubble; bricks and stones lay on the ground and in huge heaps where a castle once stood. One lonely tower stood strong against the elements, though it was covered in vines and the roof was all but nonexistent.

*"Ben?"* I mindlinked him.

*"Now?"*

*"Now."*

I crouched, waiting. Clara was suppose to lift the veil that hid the castle. A minute ticked by. Then another one. And another. I was losing patience when suddenly, the old scattered rubble and dilapidated tower in front of me became a beautiful stronghold, straight out of a book. The one tower was now accompanied by many, with lights glowing in the thin windows. The walls were high, solid brick and stone, lush vines crawling up and twisting together. Even the air changed; it cleared and held a noticeably different texture.

None of this held my attention though, because standing in front of the magnificent structure stood an immense gathering of wolves. Rogues. My eyes ran over them, thin, foaming from the mouth beasts. And landed on the man standing in front of them.

The resemblance to Lilys father was uncanny. It was truly hard to believe the weren't related by blood. The one big difference were his eyes. Cold, flat. Bloodthirsty.

"Bastian." I snarled viciously.

# CHAPTER 77

**DIMITRIS POV**

"Welcome to my home Alpha. Though I don't remember extending an invitation."

Ajax was going crazy in my head, begging to be let out so he could rip this mans head off. I was close too. My voice was icy and dangerous as I answered him.

"You extended the invitation the second you took my mate from me."

Bastian's eyebrows raised in disbelief. "Your mate?"

"Yes, *my* mate!" I growled. "Where is she?"

"Your mate... hmm..." He paced back in forth, finger on his chin as he pretended to think. The pretense was getting to me; Finally he halted and slow smile crept onto his face. "Ah. You mean Lily. I'm sorry to have to tell you this, but I don't think she views you that way anymore."

My spine rippled under my skin; My vision turned red. Distantly, I felt Ben and Luke's groups join me, the men behind me closing in around me. Preparing to fight. Bastian eyed us one by one, the ignorant smile never leaving. As if he found our attempt humorous. His eyes landed on Clara, raking up and down. Ben growled loudly, the sound echoing around us.

"You must be the witch. Mate to that wolf there." He jerked his chin in their direction.

"And you are the pyscho I've heard so much about." Clara deadpanned.

Bastian laughed heartily. "Is that what you think my dear? Well, at least I'm not boring. Tell me, are you happy where you are? Satisfied with the side you've chosen?"

This time, my growl joined Bens. I glanced down the line of wolves to see Clara giving Bastian an icy glare.

"More than happy in fact." She replied.

"Really? I was under the impression that you had qualms about your daughters safety, her future. Being raised amongst wolves instead of her *own* kind."

"You keep my daughter out of this!" Clara shouted.

"Just think about it dear Clara. You could free yourself from this mutt-" he gestured to Ben, "- And come join me. Your daughter would be raised amongst her own kind. Better, amongst the last of the Clan that was destroyed. I would teach her true magic, make her, and you, more powerful than you'd ever dreamed."

To my surprise, Clara laughed. Bastian's face fell slightly, a hint of confusion taking over.

"I would think..." She snickered. "That it would hard to teach anyone when your dead. And I don't foresee you living long enough to make that offer again."

"I never offer anything twice. But you seem to be forgetting that only one side here has a Mother Wolf. And it isn't *you*."

He snapped his fingers, again reminding me of Gideon. My attention was drawn to the heavy wooden doors behind him. They creaked inward slowly, revealing a small figure. My heart picked up double time. My breath stopped altogether. All I could see was the flame of red hair I loved so much, and the eyes that captivated me from the moment I set eyes on her.

"Lily." My voice was barely audible.

Bastian gestured to her, and the wolves behind him parted. She walked quickly down the steps, making her way to stand beside him. When she took his hand, smiling up at him like she did to me, my heart shattered in my chest.

"Lily." I took a step in her direction. "Lily, it's me."

She turned, but her face gave nothing away. No recognition. No smile. No love. What the fuck had he done to her?

"Is he the one?" She spoke to Bastian. Her voice was monotone, flat.

"Yes, that's him."

"What did you do? What did you tell her?!" I demanded.

"The truth. You are here to take her away from me, are you not?" He brushed her hair away from her face, and I almost shifted at the sight. "I told you he would come. He wants you for his own use. They even brought the witch, see?" He pointed to Clara.

"I do see." She gazed around emotionlessly.

"You know what you have to do."

"Yes."

"They are nothing compared to you."

"Yes."

Our eyes met. One second, Lily was a stranger. Cold, distant. The next, I saw the girl I loved. The girl I would do anything for. My chest just about cracked with relief and joy. A million questions danced in my head, but I pushed them aside for now. Her eyes pleaded with me; I kept whatever expression was on my face, ready for her signal. Lily stepped away from Bastian, her eyes only focused on me.

"It will be easy." She said. "Like... destroying a sand castle."

"NOW!" I shouted.

Men around me shifted on my command, running over the invisible line separating us. I gave control to Ajax, my clothes shredding into scraps around me. At the same time, Lily drew a sharp dagger from Goddess knows where, turning and aiming for Bastian's chest. He caught her wrist at the last second, his face going from confusion, to awe, and to then anger. I jumped at them as he threw her to the ground.

"How?!" He raged.

Lily smirked. "That's not part of the game, is it Bastian?"

"Bitch! I should have drained you of your blood the minute I had you in my grasp!"

"Yeah, you probably should have."

She sent a swift kick to his shin, causing him to stumble. Not missing my opportunity, I grabbed his shoulder with my teeth, tossing him a good ten feet into the fray of fighting wolves. Unfortunately, he recovered quickly, flicking his hand towards me. A stunning pain radiated through my body a second later; I yelped in surprise.

"You may be an Alpha, but you still don't outclass me." Bastian raised his hands again as I stood protectively in front of my mate. Before I could pounce, a bright green light shot out from the forest, hitting him in the stomach; He dropped to his knees, looking around wildly.

"Maybe he doesn't, but I do."

Gideon stepped from the thicket, a swarm of our warriors behind him. They immediately joined the battle, tearing into the rogues mercilessly.

A chunk of flesh landed in front of me, blood soaking into the ground. Bastian got to his feet, eyeing his opponent.

"I didn't think you'd come. Isn't hiding sort of your thing nowadays?"

"You've threatened my family long enough."

"Alright then *brother*. Let's see if you've learned anything while you were cowering in fear from me."

Bastian barely had his hands raised when Gideon sent another spell at him, this one making hitting his arm. Bastian screamed as the flesh started to melt, an intense burn scorching it.

"Because of you, I missed out on raising my daughter." Gideon hit him with another spell. "You've tortured my wife." "And another.

"You used her to kidnap our daughter." Bastian was sent flying backwards, slamming into an already mangled rogue. "Tonight, the last of your Clan will die."

The two started facing off, bolts of light flying from their fingertips. I spotted Luke taking on two rogues at once, with a third coming up from behind.

"Luke! Behind you!"

Lily's voice broke me out of my reverie. I looked at her with wide eyes, wondering why on Earth she hadn't shifted yet. She must have read the question in my eyes, because she answered my unspoken thoughts.

"I can't shift. Aya is protecting the pups."

I nodded once in response. That would explain why Ajax couldn't reach her earlier.

"Go help the others. I'm going to find my mom."

I shook my head violently. I didn't want her out of my sight. Lily reached up, taking my wolf face in her small hands. She kissed my nose, drawing a whine from me.

"I'll be fine. I promise. It's far safer in there- everyone is out here, fighting. They need you Dimitri."

I licked her face, nuzzling into her. She kissed my nose again before turning and running through the packed frenzy into the castle. I watched her until she disappeared, then turned my focus again on Bastian. He looked far worse in the few minutes I'd be distracted. Gideon seemed to be handling him well, but I wasn't risking anything. Taking off in their direction, I tore through countless rogues who attacked me. Three jumped at me at once, claws raking into my flank. Grabbing one by the throat, I dispatched him quickly before killing the other two. I was less than ten feet away now.

I watched as Gideon slammed Bastian against a nearby tree, falling limply to the ground. Together, we stalked toward him. Ben appeared at my side, Luke covering our backs. Bastian eyed the three of us, and for the first time, I saw fear in his eyes.

"No wait!" He gasped. "It's my right to choose how I die! That's the law of the Clans!"

"You don't get that right! You are an exile!" Gideon snapped.

I shifted back to my human form. The snarls and yelps behind me faded away as I glared down at my enemy.

"How would you choose to die?" I asked.

He met my gaze with wide eyes. I could see the gears turning in his head. "To the death. You and me."

Ben snorted behind me. Fast as lightening, I struck. Taking his head in my hands, I twisted with all my strength; I was left with a mangled corpse at my feet.

"I win." I turned to Gideon. "Burn the body."

He nodded, snapping his fingers. Flames erupted, hot and high. We turned away, facing the now still rogues before us.

# CHAPTER 78

**LILYS POV**

Why did this place have to be so *big*? I had no idea what was going on outside, but I knew it when Dimitri got hurt. My leg started to burn fiercely, but I knew it was his pain. I'd almost turned back, but I wasn't leaving my mom here.

"Mom! Mom, where are you?" I shouted. Nothing. Okay, next floor.

I raced up the stairway, throwing open the door at the top. A loud grunt left my lips when I collided with someone on the other side.

"Mom!"

"Not quite."

Shit! I should have counted on Bastian leaving someone to guard the castle. Instinct took over, and I swung my arm out, catching the rogue off guard. He stumbled backwards, holding his jaw. Using a trick Dimitri taught me, I quickly angled my left foot behind his right, placing my hand around neck and propelling him back. He went down, me landing on top of him. Not wanting to waste time in an all out brawl, I reached between his legs and grabbed his jewels tightly in my hand, twisting slightly when he bucked under me.

"Tell me where Rosalie is. Or you'll lose the only thing you're probably still proud of."

"Fuck you!"

I twisted harder, feeling something pop under his clothes. He shrieked loudly, tears forming at the corner of his eyes.

"Tell me!" I shouted.

"Okay, okay! She's in the last room on the right! Please, let go!"

I did, but not before twisting my hand all the way around. I left him on the floor, crying and holding himself while I ran to down the corridor. I'd barely come to a full stop before I pushed on the door. Which was locked. Of course.

"Mom! Are you in there?" I banged on the heavy wood.

"Lily?" Her voice came form the other side, small, but audible.

"Yes! Can you unlock the door?"

"I can't. It locks from the outside."

I looked at the guard again. He was still writhing on the ground, cursing the Goddess and somebody's mother. I jogged back, standing over him and cracking my knuckles. He peered up at me with a terrified expression.

"Keys. Now." I demanded.

"I-I don't have them! I swear! I was only put here to keep watch, I don't have them!" He gripped his package tighter, waiting for me to strike.

"Then break down the door!"

His face morphed into disbelief. "I can't even stand, how am I suppose to break down the fucking door?!"

Grabbing his collar, I lifted him so our eyes met.

"I'm running on limited time here. I can't access my wolf right now, so that leaves only one option- you. So either stand up and help me, or I swear I will rip off what's left of your dick!"

I hauled him to his feet and gave him a shove in the direction of my mothers room. His hand still cupped his injury but he slowly made his way, me trialing behind. He glanced back at me, raising an eyebrow.

"I'll help you on one condition." He said.

I scoffed. "I'm not in the mood to negotiate."

"I want you to take me with you."

*That* brought me up short. "Huh?"

"Bastian is going to lose-we all know it. Just nobody wanted to admit it. I don't want to stick around and be killed. I've lost too much already, my pack, my family... I want a new start."

My head was starting to hurt. I didn't have time for this.

"I can't make that promise."

"At least let me leave with you. I'll go my own way from there. Just get me off this island."

"Fine! Now open the door!"

"My name is Dante by the way."

"I don't care if your name is Mary fucking Poppins! Door!"

Finally, he turned away from me and got to work. Together, we kicked the door repeatedly until, with one final blow, it swung open with a resounding *bang*. I stepped in and looked around. The room was bare save for one small, filthy mattress, an even smaller but equally filthy blanket and a bucket in the corner. A thin window was placed well above eye level, letting in a single stream of moonlight. My eyes fell on my mother, arms hugging her torso standing against the wall.

"Mom." I opened my arms and she took a hesitant step towards me.

"Lily... what's going on? I heard fighting..."

"Dimitri is here. He's come for me, for us. We're going home."

"Home.." She breathed. She looked around the room, and for a second, I wondered if I would have to drag her out of here. How long had she been captive? Most of my life? I worried she would have some mental breakdown, refusing to leave. But to my relief, she simply nodded once and walked up to me. I allowed myself a brief moment of embracing her, this woman I didn't remember knowing but longed to have, before pulling away and taking her hand.

"Come on. We need to go."

"How are we getting home?"

"I'm not sure. But we *are* leaving."

"Bastian?"

"With any luck, he's already dead."

"Damn. Wish I could have done that myself."

I glanced back at her. Her eyes were filled with so much hatred and despise that I gulped. I think it was safe to say I got my temper from my mother. Over her shoulder, I saw the rogue, Dante, following us. We quickly made our way to the stairs, stopping at the top. I turned to him.

"You first. You want to leave with us, then you protect us first. Make sure it's clear."

"Fine with me."

I narrowed my eyes at him as he stepped passed me. His footsteps echoed off the stones as he descended, growing more and more distant. My mother and I waited at the top until his voice floated up to us.

"All good!"

"Come on." Taking her hand again, I led us down the stairs. Confirming there was no ambush waiting for us, I started to lead the way to the exit. Dante stepped in front of me, holding out his palms.

"Stop."

"What are you doing?"

He cocked his head slightly to the right. "It's quiet. I think... I think it's over."

My stomach started to churn uncomfortably. My hand pulled out of my mothers as I raced down the hall. Who had won? Was everyone okay? Was Dimitri okay? I still felt our bond. What about Clara? And Ben, and Luke? These worries ran through my head as fast as my feet carried me to the doors of the castle. I almost tripped over them as I saw a tall figure coming up the steps. My breath hitched and tears formed in my eyes. And then I was running again, launching myself into my mates arms. *Finally!*

I held him as tightly as held onto me, both of us holding back tears. I felt his fingers under my chin, lifting my face to his. His lips crashed down on mine with a passion so fierce, I swear my heart caught fire. Inside me, I felt Aya stir, acknowledging we were back with our mates. I kept my arms around him as he pulled back.

"I missed you so much." He sighed against my lips.

"I missed you too. How did you find me?"

"Clara."

"Remind me to thank her."

I peeked around him, stunned to see many rogues, now in human form, staring at us. I tapped Dimitri on the back, giving him a look. He sighed.

"They surrendered after I killed Bastian. They want to come back with us. I'm not up for it, honestly."

Mom and Dante joined us then. Dante walked past us into the crowd of waiting wolves, while Mom looked around anxiously.

"Rose."

I looked to where my Father was standing with Ben and Luke. He was gazing at my Mom with a mix of relief, hope, and fear. She took a small step in his direction, and then she was in his arms, him having transported himself in front of her. I watched my parents reunite, both of them crying, kissing, unwilling to let go of the other. Which reminded me that I had a message for them. Pulling Dimitri along with me, we walked over to the emotional scene. I cleared my throat loudly, getting Gideons attention.

"I have something for you two." I said. Mom turned to face me, her cheeks stained with tears. There was no way to say this without sounding completely crazy, so I just went for it. "Grandpa says he's sorry. And that's he's proud of you, Mom, for never giving up." I turned to Gideon. "He wanted me to tell you that even though you weren't his first pick for his daughter, you were undoubtedly the best. He's sorry, and hopes you can forgive him."

My parents looked at me like I was, indeed, crazy. Both of their eyes were wide as dinner plates, mouths hanging open. It was Dimitri who broke the shocked silence.

"How?" He asked me. I smiled up at him.

"I'll tell you everything. Later. Right now, I want to go home."

"Home sounds good." Mom said quietly.

"Agreed." Said Dimitri.

Together, we turned to face the rogues.

"Those who want to come with us, can. But know this; Until I can trust you, individually, you'll not be staying in my pack. There is land between my pack and another that you can make home on. In time, if I deem fit, you may join Blood Moon, or our neighbouring pack, or choose to go your own way."

I noticed Dante staring at me, and I gave him a nod. Dimitri tugged my hand, leading me down the steps and through the crowd. The smell of smoke registered in my nostrils, and I turned my head to a small fire burning under a tree.

"Is that...?"

"Yes." Dimitri answered without looking at me.

I looked back to the flames. "Good."

# CHAPTER 79

To my surprise, Killian joined us as we made our way through the portal Gideon had opened up. I hadn't even noticed him before. When we were safely back in Blood Moon, he wrapped me into a tight bear hug.

"I'm so happy your safe."

"Thanks. Can't.... breath.... Killian." I gasped.

He released me with a laugh. Dimitri was quick to claim me once more, pulling me into his side. We'd come out of the portal to the side of the pack house, which now had people running out of it. Mates reunited, children running into their fathers arms. The scene made me smile as I absentmindedly rubbed my stomach. Dimitris hand covered mine, gazing down at me with eyes full of love.

"Lily!"

Thara pushed through the crowd, and I let go of Dimitris hand to meet her halfway, crushing her in a hug.

"Thank the Goddess, I've been so worried about you!" She cried.

"I missed you too Thara. It's over now; He's dead."

"And thank the Goddess again! Come inside; Greta has food prepared, are you hungry?"

I laughed. "Starving!"

We made our way into the packhouse, stopping to thank the warriors who'd fought by our side. The rogues were left in Killian's charge, to take them to their new land. Temporary land, I thought. Perhaps some of them would join us, eventually. I took the time to look around as we walked; Blood Moon held a different perspective for me now. This was truly my home, and I was damn proud to be Luna. I bid goodnight to the last of the warriors who lingered, eager to have my mate to myself. Of course, it couldn't be that easy. The second the door closed behind our group, I was surrounded.

"Lily! I'm so glad your back!" Hazel pulled me in for a hug.

397

"You gave us all quite the scare child. Don't do that again." Greta chimed in.

Clint pulled Hazel away, kissing the top of her head. "I got to take down my fair share of rogues thanks to you." He grinned. Hazel and I rolled our eyes.

"Is the asshole dead?" Greta looked at Dimitri, who raised his eyebrows. I'm sure we all did; Greta rarely swore.

"Yes." Dimitri replied.

She nodded once. "Alright then. Come, sit. I have food and drinks coming." And she scurried off, leaving us with nothing to do but make our way to the cafeteria.

I sat at the first table I saw, exhausted. Dimitri sat beside me, Thara on the other. Ben and Clara took the seats opposite, Luke and Miguel beside them. Hazel and Clint sat farther down as Greta rolled out a trolley overflowing with food. My stomach growled at the sight; Goddess, I'd missed her cooking.

"Take what you like, there's more in the kitchen."

"You're the best Greta." I reached for one of her famous dinner rolls, filling my plate to the max. Gideon came to fill two plates for him and my Mother, who was sitting silently beside Thara, looking down at the table. I kept an eye on her as we ate.

"So.... just throwing this out there, but why didn't you shift? You know, back at the castle?" Clint asked me. He ripped off a piece of roll and dipped it in gravy before popping it into his mouth. Everyone looked at me expectantly.

"Uh.... I can't shift. Not right now anyways."

Instantly, every pair of eyes became worried.

"Why?"

"What did he do to you?"

"For how long?"

"Guys!" I held up my hands, making them stop. "It wasn't anything Bastian did. Well, okay, sort of. But it was my decision. I put Aya away, sort of in a dormant phase, to protect the pups."

"How?" Asked Hazel.

"Celeste."

"The Moon Goddess?" Clara asked.

"Yeah. So quick update time for those who don't know; I've been having random chats with her whenever she sees fit to pull me into her realm. Or my subconsciousness anyways."

Both my parents eyed me with bewilderment. I turned to them to explain.

"Bastian wanted me to forget everyone. Dimitri, you guys, Blood Moon. He forced me to drink some potion, but as soon as he did that, Celeste pulled me away. Only it wasn't her this time. It was your dad." I looked at my Mom. Her hand went to her mouth as I talked.

"You spoke with him, really?" She seemed on the verge of tears.

I nodded. "He said it was Celeste's version of a 'loop hole.'" I laughed to myself. "She can't interfere in our lives, our fates. So she gave him a choice. Whatever the potion was going to do to me, would do to him instead. I only had to act like it worked."

"And he agreed?" Gideon sounded a bit skeptical. Understandable though, given what my grandfather had done to them.

"Yes, he did. But not before he gave me the message for you two. He said it might be a blessing in disguise, to forget everything. Everything he did that hurt you."

"I'm not sure how to feel." Mom whispered. "On the one hand, I'm happy he realized and accepted his wrongdoings. On the other hand, when I meet him again, he won't remember me."

"I'm not sure about that, but I'm sure the Goddess has a plan in mind."

"I hope so."

Dimitri was tense and quiet beside me. I tried to meet his eyes, but he avoided it.

"Dimitri?" I placed my hand over his.

"You kissed him." He deadpanned.

I winced. I knew this would come up, but I was not going to deny it. I still felt guilty for the pain I know he must have felt.

"I'm sorry." I whispered.

"Did you... did you..." He didn't seem able to get the words out, but I knew what he was asking.

"You would have felt it, if I had."

He shook his head. "Clara took the pain away. So I didn't feel the pain of the betrayal."

I cringed at the word 'betrayal.' But I had. I couldn't deny it, even if I wanted to. But I could put his mind at ease some.

"It was one kiss, one time. He never took it further, and I never did either. I would have given up the charade in a second if he had. I didn't have a choice Dimitri..."

When he met my eyes, I saw a vulnerability I'd never seen before. I hadn't felt any pain, but I could only imagine what he had gone through. I vowed to make it up to him, anyway I could. Finally, he blew out a long breath.

"I know. I'm sorry. You did what you had to, to survive. I can't say I wouldn't have done the same, in your position. And you kept our children safe. Just the thought of him touching you makes me want to kill him all over again."

I gave him a weak smile. "I know. Thank you." The atmosphere became noticeably less tense at my words. I turned my attention to Clara.

"And thank you." I said.

She stared at me. "Me? For what?"

"For finding me. How did you find me anyways?"

"Locator spell." She shot a glare to my Father. Matter of fact, everyone did, except my Mother. Gideon fidgeted in his seat, avoiding everyone eyes. Now that I wasn't distracted, I noticed for the first time that he had two black eyes.

"What happened to your face?" I asked.

"Your mate punched me."

"What?" I rounded on Dimitri who shrugged nonchalantly.

"This idiot never thought to use a locator spell." Luke scowled.

"It wouldn't have worked." Rose said. Everyone stared at her. "Until Bastian had Lily, he used magic to hide our location. He wanted you to come Alpha, and you." She turned to her husband. "His plan was to kill all of you, and take over Blood Moon."

"Huh." Dimitri scratched his chin. "Well, then I guess I'm sorry I punched you."

"You *guess*?"

They started to bicker, and I couldn't help but laugh out loud. Ben started chuckling, and soon, we were all laughing. It felt so good to be home!

"So, how did the deal with your wolf come into play?" Luke asked me when we sobered.

"I guess that wasn't just my decision. We didn't know what was going to happen, or how long I'd have to keep fooling Bastian. So we agreed she would protect the pups until someone came for us."

"But your home now." Miguel pointed out.

"She knows that. I guess she'll come back when she's ready." I shrugged.

Dimitri wrapped his arm around my shoulder before letting out a yawn.

"I think we can continue this in the morning. I'm ready for bed."

Everyone agreed, and again, I was hugged by everyone. I stopped my Mother as everyone filed out the door.

"You're welcome to stay in the packhouse." I told her.

She looked at Gideon. "Where have you been staying?"

"Uhm... in the cells." He muttered. She looked at me, eyes wide.

"It's a long story Mom. Catch up with Ben, and tell him to find a room for you two."

"Okay. Thank you. And Lily..." She bit her lip. "I am sorry. For the part I played. I never meant to-"

"Stop." I stepped close to her, wrapping my arms around her waist. "I know. I'm not mad. I understand. You don't need to feel guilty, because I know you did it to protect the ones I love. And yourself. I could only be angry with you if you had sacrificed yourself instead. I never knew you, or I didn't remember until recently, but I want my Mom. I want us to know each other, and be a family again."

I felt her tears drip onto my shoulder as she hugged me back. "Thank you."

When I released her, I looked at my Father.

"I won't say I understand everything you did, but I understand better now. I also can't say I'm not still mad, because I am. But I'd like to work on our relationship too. I don't just want a Mom, I want my Dad too."

Tears shone in his eyes as he nodded. He opened his arms slowly, and I accepted his embrace. A little piece of me clicked inside, knowing I had the thing I wanted most my whole life; A family. I finally had my family back, and *nobody* was going to take that away from me.

# CHAPTER 80

**LILYS POV**

As soon as we were in our room, I tugged Dimitris face down to mine, kissing him lovingly. I don't remember how we ended up in bed, and I didn't care. I was making up for lost time with my mate. The sun was peeking over the horizon when I rolled over and gently caressed his face. Goddess, I loved this man.

A sharp movement in my torso had me shooting up the next minute. Instantly, Dimitri was awake, looking around the room.

"What is it?"

My hands were placed on my stomach, waiting. I held up a finger, telling him to wait. A few seconds later, I felt another kick.

"Oh my Goddess!" I squealed.

"What?!"

"Feel!"

I placed his hand on my stomach, right where I'd felt one of our babies. I watched his face as one of our pups kicked quickly three times into his palm. The smile that spread over his lips left me breathless. Slowly, Dimitri placed his face against my skin, over the bulge that appeared there.

"Hello, whichever one you are. I'm your daddy."

I was sure both pups heard him, because at his words I felt movement on either side on my stomach. I laughed joyfully, basking in the amazing sensation. A jolt spread down between my thighs with the next kick and I sighed in amusement.

"Now I have to pee." I laughed. Dimitri smiled and moved to let me up. When I came back, Dimitri was ready to place his hands on my skin again, eager to feel our children.

"I'm so happy the first time is here, with you." I said.

"Me too. This is amazing. You are amazing." He kissed my stomach tenderly.

Our moment of happiness was interrupted by a random thought. My random thought. But important nonetheless. I sat down on the edge of the bed, pulling the blanket around me before speaking it aloud.

"Dimitri... what happened to Jennine?" I looked at him.

His forehead creased. "Did she really leave the island then?"

"Huh?"

He explained about the phone call she'd made to him on the plane. Worry coursed through me, strongly.

"I-I didn't know she left." I whispered. My eyes wandered around the room as I thought. "She wasn't among the rogues? For sure?"

"No."

Worry quickly turned to fear as I cradled my baby bump now. Jennine was still out there. Out there, somewhere, and intent on revenge. And now she had magic on her side. Dimitri picked me up and placed me on his lap, taking my hands in his.

"I promise, no I *swear* to you, I will not let her come near you. I will not let her hurt you. You, or our children."

I searched his eyes; The sincerity and promise in them calmed my nerves. I kissed him fiercely, letting him know without words that I trusted him, heart and soul.

"I love you." I whispered.

"I love you too."

### *** TEN YEARS LATER ***

"Violet! Garret! It's time!" I called to my children.

They rushed over to me, followed by their friends. I smiled at the enthusiasm, the happiness on their faces. Who would have thought the twins tenth birthday would come so fast? It seemed like yesterday I was gazing into their tiny faces, all wrapped up and sleeping on my chest in the delivery room. All the while their Dad, big bad Alpha Dimitri Varlos, was sitting on a chair some feet away puking into a waste basket. I laughed quietly at the memory.

"Can we open presents now Mom?" Garret asked me.

"Not until you blow out the candles."

"I want cake first!" Violet declared.

"Don't you want to see what Isabelle got you?" Garret asked her. Violet thought about it for a minute before shaking her head, her black hair swinging around her face.

"Cake first!" She demanded.

I felt arms go around my waist as Dimitri laughed. "Patience you two. Your Mom went to a lot of trouble to plan this, so we go by her schedule."

"Yes Dad."

"Okay Daddy."

They gave him their most innocent smiles. Violets blue-green eyes shone like the clearest of oceans. Somehow, she ended up with a mix of mine and my moms eyes. They were exquisite, and only stood out more from the black hair she'd inherited from Dimitri. Garret on the other hand, got all of my red hair, and his Dads strong features. I was positive there would be a lot of broken hearts the day he found his mate.

Often I found myself watching my kids, wondering which of them had gotten Jennine's wolf. They were both strong individuals, and together, they schemed like nothing I'd ever seen. More sweets had disappeared from the kitchen since they'd come along then one would care to admit, with one always the diversion while the other did the thieving. Violet seemed to have inherited my sassiness, while Garret was a rather quiet boy, focused and attentive. Plus, he could negotiate better than his Dad. My parents had become official 'spoilers', unable to say no to him even when they wanted to. But they were still the best grandparents I could have ever asked for.

Yet, thinking about Nia only made me think about Jennine. Ten years, and nothing. No threats, no attempts. It was as if she'd fallen on the face of the Earth, but I knew she hadn't. Deep down, I knew she was out there, waiting for the opportune moment. Jennine was a threat that was distant, but never forgotten. Many times over the years, we'd get a lead here or there, and Dimitri always sent someone to follow it. And we were always just a little too late.

Mostly, I tried to focus on the happiness my children brought to my life. I never imagined I would feel more fulfilled than I did, being a mother. The feeling was indescribable, and everyday was a new adventure. Clara and I had become extremely close, especially after Ben and her got married. Finally! Isabelle and Violet were attached at the hip, and sometimes I wondered how I ended up with triplets instead of twins. Even Clara joked about it.

"You okay?" Dimitri whispered in my ear as the kids blew out the candles on the gigantic cake Greta had made. I clapped with everyone else, joining in a round of 'Happy Birthday'.

"Fine. Just thinking." I whispered back when the song ended.

"About?"

I watched my daughter took over distributing pieces of cake to the other kids. "Jennine."

Dimitri tensed behind me. "The pack is well guarded. Even better, with Killian's pack. Don't worry."

"I know."

Killian had maintained a permanent location outside Blood Moon. We were practically one pack, with them being only a thirty-minute run outside the border. Still, the nagging feeling in my gut wouldn't go away. I distracted myself by helping Luke, or Uncle Luke now, roll out the table with gifts for the twins. Cake abandoned, they seated themselves at the end of the table, huge grins of excitement adorning their faces.

We all gathered around to watch, laughing when Violet squealed upon opening Isabelle's gift; Her first make-up kit. Dimitri wasn't very impressed, but I shrugged it off. It's not like I'd let her leave the house made up like a prostitute. Garret received a couple new games for his PlayStation, and a couple new books from us. Mom and Dad got the kids tickets to some concert for a band they liked, which we would thankfully not have to go to. All in all, everyone was very happy.

"Mom! This one is for you!"

"Huh?"

I turned my attention to my son, who was pointing to a rather large box in front of him, wrapped with red paper. My Dad reached around him, flipping over the tag.

"He's right. It says, 'to Lily.'"

My eyebrows scrunched in confusion. Why would someone send *me* a gift on my kids' birthday? Unless it was from the twins; I could see them doing something like this. I walked over to the box, eyeing Violet and Garret.

"Did you two do this?" I asked.

"No." They shook their heads, their faces showing nothing but honesty.

Pulling the box towards me, I read the tag. I didn't recognize the handwriting, but the nagging feeling in my stomach had now turned into a pit of dread. Quickly, I tore of the bright red paper; I stared down at the plain white box, suddenly very nervous about opening it. My hands paused above the lid, and I glanced at Dimitri. He looked just as confused as everyone else. In my head, Aya whined quietly. Slowly, I lifted the lid and peered inside.

Every ounce of blood drained from my face; The lid of the box dropped from my hands and onto the floor. Memories invaded my mind and, unconsciously, I sent out a surge of power around the room. Everyone present gasped as they felt my emotions as if they were their own, and in turn, I was bombarded with a wave of their emotions. I grit my teeth, reigning in my emotions, and erasing the cloud of my powers over them. Dimitri was at my side, looking over my shoulder.

"Clara, Hazel, take the kids outside." He said in a hushed tone.

"Come on kids, let's go play in the bouncy castle hmm?" Hazel ushered the twins from their seats, motioning them towards the door.

"But I want to see what Mom got!"

"Me too!"

"Later. Come on, everyone outside!" Clara called.

The door swung closed, and Dimitri gently moved me to the side. My eyes hadn't moved from the object in the box once. Carefully, he picked it up and turned around. Gasps surrounded us.

"Isn't that-" Luke started.

"No fucking way." Ben finished.

"I'm going to inform the patrols." Killian stated. Thara left with him while I was still too stunned to speak or move. Nobody said anything as Dimitri set the metal claw on the table. Finally, I broke the silence.

"Why now?" I whispered.

"I don't know. But we knew she would send a message some time." Dimitri answered.

I stared at the claw, rusted and coated with old, dried blood. The exact tool used to kill Paige all those years ago. I closed my eyes, hoping it would disappear when I opened them, and I would be enjoying my children's birthday, just as I was ten minutes ago. Sadly, the gruesome thing was still there when I opened them. Fear engulfed me, strong and unavoidable.

"Get the twins back in here." I said. Dimitri looked at me in silence. "Now, Dimitri! I want them back in here, now!"

His eyes glazed over momentarily. I turned and ran out the door, down the hall. I reached the foyer just as Hazel and Clara were ushering the kids back inside. Grabbing my children, I wrapped them in my arms, Aya going crazy protective in my head.

"What's going on?"

"Are we being attacked?"

They looked up at me with worry, but I shook my head.

"No, nothing like that. I'm sorry guys, but I think the party needs to continue inside. Okay?"

"But what about the bouncy castle?" Violet pouted.

"And I wanted to go swimming." Garret said.

"I'm sorry. I'll make it up to you, okay? I promise. But I really, *really* need you guys to stay inside."

Neither of them looked happy, and I felt terrible. This wasn't how I wanted to celebrate their birthday. Thankfully, Hazel came to my rescue.

"How about a water gun tournament? Come on everyone!"

The kids cheered and I shot her a grateful look. Dimitri patted the twins' heads as they passed, before coming to my side.

"I want her found Dimitri. If I have to go myself-"

"You won't. We will take care of this. She will never touch them, Lily."

The worry in his eyes was distant, but I saw it. I looked at my Dad.

"Do a locator spell."

"Lily..."

"Don't argue with me Dad!"

Clara stepped forward, rubbing my arm in what was supposed to be a soothing gesture.

"Lily, it's not going to work. We've tried a dozen times." She said gently.

"Try again!"

A stray tear slipped from the corner of my eye as she hugged me. And just like that, the floodgates opened. Somewhere in the middle of Dimitri taking me back and helping me up the stairs, anger settled in.

*"We're going to find her. And when we do..."* I thought.

*"She'll wish she had never crossed us."* Aya finished.

# Don't miss out!

Visit the website below and you can sign up to receive emails whenever S.V. Smith publishes a new book. There's no charge and no obligation.

https://books2read.com/r/B-A-XCBY-OVFIC

**BOOKS 2 READ**

Connecting independent readers to independent writers.

Milton Keynes UK
Ingram Content Group UK Ltd.
UKHW010634040424
440620UK00001B/121